THE
SHADOW
OF WAR

THE
SHADOW
OF WAR

A NOVEL OF THE

CUBAN MISSILE CRISIS

JEFF SHAARA

ST. MARTIN'S PRESS
NEW YORK

First published in the United States by St. Martin's Press, an imprint of St. Martin's Publishing Group.

THE SHADOW OF WAR. Copyright © 2024 by Jeff Shaara. All rights reserved. Printed in the United States of America. For information, address St. Martin's Publishing Group, 120 Broadway, New York, NY 10271.

www.stmartins.com

Library of Congress Cataloging-in-Publication Data

Names: Shaara, Jeff, 1952– author.
Title: The shadow of war : a novel of the Cuban Missile Crisis / Jeff Shaara.
Description: First edition. | New York : St. Martin's Press, 2024.
Identifiers: LCCN 2023058063 | ISBN 9781250279965 (hardcover) |
    ISBN 9781250279972 (ebook)
Subjects: LCSH: Cuban Missile Crisis, 1962—Fiction. | LCGFT: Historical fiction. | Novels.
Classification: LCC PS3569.H18 S53 2024 | DDC 813/.54—dc23/eng/20231220
LC record available at https://lccn.loc.gov/2023058063

Our books may be purchased in bulk for promotional, educational, or business use. Please contact your local bookseller or the Macmillan Corporate and Premium Sales Department at 1-800-221-7945, extension 5442, or by email at MacmillanSpecialMarkets@macmillan.com.

First Edition: 2024

10 9 8 7 6 5 4 3 2 1

Dedicated to my sister,
Lila E. Shaara

TO THE READER

Those people of a certain age (including me), have some recollection of what transpired in October 1962. For a period of less than two weeks, there was genuine fear, if not outright terror that the two superpowers, the United States and the Soviet Union, were about to unleash a nuclear holocaust, an event the world had long feared but had not yet experienced.

This is that story. Told from both sides, from the White House to the Kremlin, from ships at sea to a family absorbing what they're hearing on the evening news, most of this story is told from the points of view of three principal characters.

Robert F. "Bobby" Kennedy is the abrasive and hard-nosed brother of the newly elected president, and in many ways, is the most trusted advisor his brother John has. Though officially, he is attorney general of the United States, he is directly involved in the discussions affecting this crisis, discussions heated and otherwise, that take place in the White House and elsewhere, decisions that affect history.

Nikita Khrushchev is officially the first secretary of the Communist Party, more commonly referred to as the chairman of the

Presidium, premier, absolute leader of the Soviet Union. It is his plan to plant nuclear missiles in Cuba, under the assumption that he can do it discreetly, and that once the installation is completed, the United States will not object. He is wildly mistaken on all counts.

Joseph Russo is a professor of English at Florida State University, lives with his wife and two children in Tallahassee, Florida. Politically, he supported Kennedy for president, in a community where Kennedy's opponent, Richard Nixon, had carried most of the vote. He begins to understand the different attitudes of the people around him toward a world where nuclear missiles are an everyday fact of life.

There are other characters as well, Russian and American, essential to the telling of this story, a story that spreads from Washington to Moscow, to Havana, Cuba, and beyond. It is a story based on the fear that much of the world experiences while the two sides wrestle through issues, claims, and promises, always with the threat that no one will survive.

As with every story I do, this story is told in a personal way, the dialogue and thoughts coming from the characters themselves. My research, always, calls on the words of those characters, their memoirs, diaries, etc., or those of the people around them, the people who were *there*. In this case, I had one advantage I've not experienced before. One of those witnesses was me.

Please indulge me, as I offer a profound thank you, in several directions. My longtime friend and now agent, Doug Grad, was responsible for introducing me to a new publisher, St. Martin's Press. There, I have now worked on two books with editor Keith Kahla and publisher Sally Richardson, and we've established an excellent working relationship. I offer them all a hearty *thank-you*.

And, once again I must thank my wife, Stephanie, who has aided me throughout this process, as she does every time. Amazingly, as I complete each chapter of the manuscript, she listens with perfect attention as I read aloud every word. That exercise is enormously helpful to me, but it requires stamina on her part. And, care.

If you did not live through the events in this story, I hope you will recognize, and perhaps appreciate just how dangerous a time this was. The threat of nuclear holocaust was very real, and the threats could not be hidden from the American (and Russian) public. If you are too young to have lived through this saga, I hope you'll find it enlightening. The story is true. And, of course, I hope you'll find this to be a good read.

Jeff Shaara

INTRODUCTION

In many ways this story begins in 1949, when the Soviet Union developed nuclear capabilities. Until that time, the United States had been the world's sole nuclear power and, as such, had very little to fear from other nations across the globe. With the Soviets now in possession of their own nuclear devices, a new balance of power was established, each side warily eyeing the other. As time passes, the governments involved begin to understand that the stark power to destroy humanity lies in opposing hands, in a way that guarantees *mutually assured destruction.* This realization tends to have a dampening effect on nuclear threats, since each side understands that any attack on the other would ensure the destruction of all. While this is reassuring to military heads, it is not so comforting to the average citizen, of any country.

Whereas the United States has a well-defined change of leadership through regularly scheduled elections, the Soviet Union has nothing of the kind. When Soviet leader Josef Stalin dies in 1953, a power struggle takes place, won, ultimately, by Nikita Khrushchev. Khrushchev has risen from peasant stock and is a crude and wily man who understands that power is useless unless you can hold on to it.

In the United States, the election of 1960 has produced a leader of many contrasts to Khrushchev. John F. Kennedy rises from aristocratic stock and is a man his powerful father has deemed destined to be president, a claim that proves true. Kennedy is careful, understands the extraordinary power of his office, immediately begins to rely on experts in every field, to help guide the way. Some of these experts dwell in the Central Intelligence Agency, and convince Kennedy that the time has come to eliminate Cuban dictator Fidel Castro. Kennedy, and his brother Bobby, despise Castro, see him as a standard bearer for the greatest threats to our country, leading a blatantly Communist government right on Florida's doorstep.

The Cuban government is backed and supported by Khrushchev and the Soviets, who see the Caribbean nation as a vital entryway into Latin America, where the Soviet Union's influence might expand. Though photographs show Khrushchev and Castro have a smiling friendship, in fact, Khrushchev is wary of Castro's tendency to talk too much. For his part, Castro embraces Soviet support as a way to expand his own power, no matter Moscow's cautions. But Castro has an almost paranoid fear that the United States will attempt to forcibly remove him from power. He thus relies on the Soviet Union to provide him with undeniable strength of his own. The Soviets, ever aware that America and her NATO allies have nuclear missiles spread across Europe, now believe they have a successful counter to such a strategy. Thus far, Soviet missiles of all kinds have been based only inside the borders of the Soviet Union, and with very few Intercontinental Ballistic Missiles, their armament is only a minor direct threat to the United States. Cuba offers Khrushchev a unique opportunity to move the needle, to balance Soviet missile strength with American. And Castro is only too willing to accept Soviet military aid.

Under Kennedy's predecessor, Dwight Eisenhower, plans had been laid by the CIA to sweep Castro from power. The agency is delighted that the new president enthusiastically embraces their plan to eliminate Castro with a full-on invasion force, consisting of some fourteen hundred Cuban émigrés, led by officers carefully trained by the CIA. In addition, to begin the operation, the CIA arranges for the Air Force to systematically eliminate Castro's air power in surgical air strikes, beginning days before the actual invasion. This will involve American planes and American pilots, causing concern in both the Pentagon and the White House, since it will be nearly impossible to disguise the obvious: that this is an American plan with American backing. To add to the concerns, the CIA's plan calls for American naval vessels, specifically destroyers, to lurk offshore, providing artillery fire as the troops on the beaches require it. Though the CIA goes to great lengths to convince Kennedy that no American fingerprint will be visible, Kennedy is concerned that he could be seen as a bully, trampling illegally across the borders of a sovereign country. That fear continues to fester as the mission begins. Even those at the CIA who delude themselves into believing the mission can be carried out as planned, begin to accept that the claims that the invasion is a Cuban operation, driven and led by Cubans, will be viewed around the world as nonsense. There are concerns as well throughout the American military community, which is not directly involved in the planning for the invasion. The CIA has been territorial with their details, secretive to a fault, not confiding in those in the U.S. military who could have offered advice and materiel. Though Kennedy shares the understandable nervousness about the plan, his drive to eliminate Castro wins out.

After fits and starts, changes and amendments to the plan, the location for the invasion is finally designated as an inlet southeast of Havana, on Cuba's southern coast. It is called the Bay of Pigs.

THE
SHADOW
OF WAR

PROLOGUE

Tuesday, April 18, 1961
Cuba, Bay of Pigs

The plane came in low, the sound of machine guns drifting over the men, the welcome flashes of light streaking toward the trees beyond. The bombs fell now, punching through the invisible wall of Cuban troops. Around Pepe, the men cheered, a brief show of triumph after two days that smelled of dismal failure.

"Yes! Get them! *Come around again.*" The voice came from beside him, Martinez, the radio man. He glanced at Pepe with a smile.

"I told you. They would not let us down."

Pepe was Jose Perez San Roman, and for another powerful moment, he felt the pride that came from commanding these men, from leading this mission onto the beaches. He slapped Martinez on the shoulder, his eyes still turned toward the rising smoke. "Yes. I knew they would come. But one plane is not what we need."

He eyed the radio, the strap heavy on Martinez' shoulder. No, he thought, I will wait. Surely there will be more planes. He searched the sky in the vain hope that more bombers would arrive. There had been other planes, but they were too few, nothing like what the invaders had been promised at the CIA's command center in Miami. After thirty-six hours on the beach, it was painfully clear that someone very high up, Washington perhaps, had called the air support away.

Pepe reached for the radio now, a quick glance at Martinez.

"Now is the time. We have to know."

Pepe raised the receiver, spoke firmly, a sharp edge to his voice.

"This is Pepe. Blue Beach. Where are the planes? We need support. Red Beach is wiped out. Supplies are low. We need the cargo ships to return. Can you give us covering fire, from the destroyers?"

Martinez stared at him, the receiver held tight against Pepe's ear, the crackling voice reaching him.

"Blue Beach. There is no more air support. Orders. Repeat . . . no support. The destroyers are too far . . ."

He gripped the receiver, a hard scowl on his face, his head dropping, the voice on the receiver fading away, Pepe lowering his head.

"Pepe out."

He handed the receiver to Martinez, said in a low voice, "They are not coming. Orders, they say. There is no more air support, beyond what we see. The destroyers are too far away. More orders." He paused. "We are on our own. I do not understand."

Martinez hoisted the radio aside, nothing to say, the two men watching the B-26 again, slow and painfully alone, Pepe begging silently that someone would do what was promised. He did as the men around him, searching the sky for the great mass of airpower they had been told to expect. He focused again on the single bomber, arcing circles over the Cuban positions, doing its job, strafing runs over the distant Cuban troops, a futile gesture of assault on the men who were now massed all back through the jungle, the troops blocking the main roads away from the beach.

A new sound came now, startling, a high scream, a streak of silver, the rattle of machine-gun fire, all eyes now on the smaller jet that rolled up behind the B-26.

Pepe stared, as they all did, and another man called out, "It's the Air Force. They've come. *Finally.*"

Martinez leaned closer to Pepe, his eyes on the sky, said in a low voice, "That's a Cuban plane. The markings . . ."

Pepe said nothing, could see the markings for himself.

He could see now, it was a T-33, only a trainer, but this one had guns, and they were effective, ripping through the helpless B-26. He kept his eyes on the jet, darting, swirling around the B-26, the larger plane now on fire, and then, a nosedive straight into the jungle.

The men were silent, huddled low, staring, and Pepe turned away, felt sick, the voices around him, one man crying, calling out in Spanish, "Castro. He has jets. Why? They were to be destroyed. What has happened?"

Pepe grabbed the man's shoulder, said, "No time for this. The enemy will come now, and we cannot stop them. Man your guns, and shoot carefully. We must preserve our ammunition. Watch those trees. They are preparing to come, I can feel it."

Pepe fingered his rifle, felt the weight of the magazines in his shirt, felt suddenly very weak. Martinez looked at him, said in a low voice, "They were supposed to eliminate Castro's air force, take them out completely. What happened?"

Pepe looked again toward the black smoke from the downed bomber.

"I am told . . . someone very high up . . . changed their minds."

Out front, along the trees, Pepe watched as a dozen men suddenly appeared out of the woods, a mad dash back toward their leader. Pepe said nothing, none of this a surprise now. Behind those men, the sound of engines, a rumble of tracks tearing along the dirt road, the tanks they had seen the day before, the great force that had helped shove these men back away from their objectives, back further, to their last stronghold on the beach. Firing began now, off to one side, one of the few anti-tank guns still working, the men seeking a target Pepe couldn't see. Rifles fired now, farther to the right, answered by machine-gun fire from the trees. More men emerged from the trees, Pepe's men, one of the groups cut off from the main force, a mad scamper away from the advancing Cubans. Men fell, cut down by the machine guns, but not all, some sliding into the shallow dunes, makeshift foxholes dug by Pepe's men. There was fire both ways now, and he kept his eyes on the trees. It was maddening, there was nothing to see, just the sounds of the guns, streaks of fire ripping through the men around him. Pepe called again for the radio, but he knew what he would hear, that there was no help at all now, no chance of success, the Cubans too strong, too many, with too much heavy armament. And the jets. Pepe grabbed the radio once more, spoke loudly in English, desperate, furious.

"This is Pepe. We are on Blue Beach, trying to hold on. Urgent request for support. Under attack from jets and heavy tanks. We cannot hold out. Red Beach already wiped out, repeat, wiped out. Send air support, *now*." Pepe listened again through the receiver, staring down into packed sand. "Please do not desert us. We need medical supplies urgently. We will fight to the end."

He waited, the response coming in crackling bursts through the receiver, the explanations, the excuses coming again. Still, there would be no help.

THE INVASION HAD a singular goal, to establish a firm base inland from the beach that could be strengthened and supplied, so that the force could direct its push directly on Castro himself. The purpose was simple and straightforward: remove Castro from power, and return Cuba to the Cubans. Part of that equation lay in the assumption that the Cubans did not support Castro, that there would be an enormous uprising of support for the invasion from Cuban citizens who were believed to despise their leader. So far, there had been no signs that anyone who met the invasion had any interest in joining it.

It had become clear since the first early morning landings the day before that something was wrong, that nothing they had expected had come to pass. The first landing craft had stumbled over heavy reefs of sharp coral that no one had anticipated. During the planning for the mission, the CIA reconnaissance planes had reported those bars were harmless seaweed, but for the fourteen hundred men landing in the pre-dawn, the coral meant a waist-deep trudge to the beach, the salt water fouling equipment and supplies. Once on the beach, opposition was limited, a small force of Castro's militia, and according to plan, the invaders pushed their way inland with very little difficulty. Along with the shore landing, a small force of paratroopers had made a drop farther inland, seizing key intersections, the goal being to prevent Castro's forces from reaching the landing zone. But problems sprung up from every quarter, much of that from a lack of communication. The radios of most of the outlying troops had become unworkable from their soaking in seawater. With little ability to coordinate their movements, many of the paratroopers were soon cut off, along with pockets of the infantry, now struggling to hold their advance beachheads. Castro's forces had responded far more quickly than expected, a well-armed mass of well-trained militia, accompanied by Castro himself, pushing rapidly from their bases near Havana. They came with tanks and artillery, and, of course, the aircraft that the fighters and light bombers were supposed to have destroyed.

The invasion force had some heavy equipment of their own, and the transport ships had successfully put ashore several tanks, along with anti-tank guns and recoilless rifles. The tanks had performed well at first, inflicting heavy casualties on the gathering Cubans. But with no air cover, the tanks were soon outclassed and outnumbered by Cuban anti-tank guns and bazookas, as well as by air assaults.

With the fighting unexpectedly fierce, and with so little coordination between the troops onshore and their supply ships lurking just out of artillery range, Pepe's forces soon ran low on ammunition, and many of the men, including the paratroopers, had lost, or never received, their rations, including drinking water. As the fighting grew more deadly, many of the surviving paratroopers made a quick dash back to the main body at Blue Beach. It was now obvious that the entire operation was in severe jeopardy.

As preparations for the invasion at the Bay of Pigs came to life, Pepe was heavily involved in most of the details and underwent training, as did most of the others, at makeshift bases in Guatemala. Secrecy was said to be paramount, but that secrecy was fragile; loud voices in Miami couldn't contain themselves. As if Castro himself couldn't read the American newspapers, the Miami papers broadcasted loud and clear the hope that a major military operation was inevitable and would topple Castro from power. If Castro required further confirmation, the Soviets had furnished him with intelligence from their own spies of a very specific gathering storm, a paramilitary operation that would soon be under way, pinpointing even when the operation would occur: April 1961. The only bit of information Castro did not have was precisely *where* the invasion would take place. On the morning of April 17, with the noisy landing of the invasion force at the Bay of Pigs on Cuba's southern coast, that question had been answered.

From the very beginning, and despite the CIA's best efforts, the invasion had suffered from the poor training of the volunteers, men whose passion for victory was overshadowed by their complete lack of experience as soldiers. Officers were trained by the CIA to manage that inexperience, but there had not been time to see the training take hold. Adding to that, the equipment the men had been given was mostly surplus, out-of-date weaponry. Worse, the men in charge, the CIA operatives who headed the planning held tightly to a complete misreading of their objectives and the challenges these men would confront. The CIA was not the military, and in fact, enormous efforts were made to keep the U.S. military, specifically the Joint Chiefs, completely in the dark, as though the CIA was zealously guarding its own territory. Without the input and organizational skills of the military, men who were well trained in invasion tactics and support, much of this mission became wrapped in a blanket of wishful thinking, hope that because the CIA wanted the plan to work, it certainly would. Even worse for the operation, the newly elected president, John Kennedy, who had inherited most of the planning from the Eisenhower administration, had given the go-ahead based on the assumption that it could not be directly connected to the United States, as though the entire mission would be handled and manned only by disgruntled Cubans seeking to re-take their country. It was as though the administration expected the rest of the world to fully accept that this military operation was solely the work of Cuban refugees, with no American involvement at all. From the beginning, from their various spies in Miami and Washington, the Soviets knew better. And they were happy to inform Castro.

With the invasion stalled, and worse, absorbing heavy casualties from Castro's massing forces, Kennedy's *plausible deniability* had crumbled, and so too had the president's stomach for the operation. Having cancelled the air strikes, and having ordered the warships far out away from the beaches, Kennedy had made his best effort to cover America's tracks. None of that was helpful to the men trapped on the beach at the Bay of Pigs.

With the assault now in complete collapse, more than a hundred men killed, and nearly twelve hundred men captured, the only remaining part of the operation was for the United States to accept some kind of responsibility.

PART ONE

CHAPTER ONE

RFK

Monday, May 1, 1961
The White House, Washington, DC

"There will not be, under any conditions, any intervention in Cuba by United States armed forces . . ."

Sorenson read from the text, stopped now, looked at the president, who said, "Yes, I said that. Every reporter in the country wrote it down."

Bobby stood in one corner, looked hard at his brother.

"Jack, you've put your foot in a few piles, but none like this. Jesus, you insisted on having that press conference a week before the operation? Why'd you have to mention anything about Cuba?"

Kennedy sat at his desk, arms in front of him.

"They ask, I answer. I'm not going to play games with the press. That's an enemy I don't need. If you recall, I also said there would be no Americans on the ground in Cuba at all, ever. I was told that was the truth. Apparently, I was wrong about that too."

Bobby looked down, knew he had been the source of that lie, that he had tried telling his brother no Americans had been in harm's way. Like so many of the others, Bobby had been a victim of his own wishful thinking. He looked now toward the fourth man in the room, General Maxwell Taylor, the president's primary military advisor. Taylor seemed grim, even more than the others.

"Mr. President, it is confirmed that we lost four pilots there. Shot down by Castro's jets. If they're prisoners, it will be especially embarrassing, in light of your . . . um . . . comments."

Bobby sniffed, folded his arms tightly crossed against his chest.

"I suppose we should hope that all four of them died." He regretted the words instantly, knew the president would have none of that kind of talk.

Sorenson seemed to struggle for words, as though seeking some way out of this for all of them.

"We could claim that the Americans who took part were renegades, that there was no knowledge among our people that they were even there."

The president looked at his brother, said, "Why did you try to tell me we had no Americans involved? I heard that from the CIA too. It was supposed to be Cubans, and only Cubans. How do you think this looks, like the great United States bullies its way into a neighboring country, without provocation."

Bobby let out a breath.

"I misspoke, obviously. There were a few Americans, mostly from the landing craft, who didn't make it out. One of the supply ships was destroyed by the Cuban jets, sank, presumably with loss of life."

Kennedy sat back, glared at his brother.

"*American* loss of life. I would assume the Cubans have the bodies. Next we'll hear that they're parading them all over Havana. What of this fellow, San Roman . . . Pepe?"

Taylor seemed to perk up at the name.

"He survived, sir. We picked him up, with a handful of others in a boat. Somehow they escaped off the beach, motored or paddled like hell to the middle of nowhere until one of the destroyers spotted them. He's being flown here, to be debriefed."

Kennedy shook his head.

"I'll talk to him myself. I want to hear it all, no matter how pissed off that man is. He has a right to be. He'll give it to me straight, which is probably more than anyone else has."

Bobby looked at Taylor, saw the same resignation they all felt. The general said, "There is blame enough to go around, sir. The CIA people, Bissell in particular, they're ready to admit they made some mistakes. This was Bissell's baby, and he knows there were screw-ups."

The president stared ahead, furious now, Bobby recognizing the signs. The others kept silent and Kennedy finally said, "*Mistakes*. Sounds pretty basic, doesn't it? Oh dear, someone made an error. Someone misrepresented this entire operation to the president of the United States. Whatever are we to do? Well, I'll tell you what we're going to do. The CIA just lost every bit of clout they ever had in this office. I don't know how they sold this plan to Ike, but that's not his problem anymore. The problem is they sold it to *me*, and I bought the whole package. I trusted the experts. Isn't that what a president is supposed to do? I'm new at this, I rely on the veterans, the professionals." He glanced at Bobby now. "I thought we needed to be rid of Castro, and they played on that. *Here, sir, a great idea, already planned out.* We can take out Castro and liberate Cuba in one swoop. No casualties, no one in the whole world will know we're behind it. Cubans for Cuba, that's what everyone will think. And the Cuban people, well, they'll just rise up in one great mass, a tidal wave of support for exactly what we want them to support. Just like that. And damn it all, I bought it. I wanted it, and the CIA, Dulles, Bissell, the rest, they put on their dog and pony show, and told me just what I wanted to hear." He paused, looked at Bobby, spit out the word again. "*Experts.*"

Bobby could see he was breathing heavily, his brother as angry as he had ever been. Sorenson said, "Sir, what now? We can't hide from the facts, not any longer."

Kennedy stood now, paced slowly before the windows of his office.

"I'm not allowed to be the new kid on the block, no one's excusing me for being wet behind the ears. People died, and I approved the plan. No blame can be fixed, no matter how tempting it is to hang those damn CIA people out to dry. They know they're through, especially Bissell. Dulles too, I suppose. The head man can't be immune. But that won't satisfy anyone else. It sure as hell won't satisfy me, or the American public. I'd like to go over to CIA, and smash their damned offices to splinters." He looked at Taylor now. "The damned Joint Chiefs, you sons of bitches who wear all that fruit salad on your shoulders, just sat there and accepted what the CIA told you. You treat me like I'm five years old, that you have to explain the simplest facts to me. But this time, when all of you should have been throwing cold water on the CIA, you sit back with your oh-so-superior smiles, and sign off on an operation none of you would have dared to approve on your own. You patronized your greenhorn president . . . and went along with what little the CIA told you, knowing none of this would fall on your heads. As pissed off as I am at all the counsel I received, I will not hide from it. No, gentlemen, this is my doing. It's my fault, and the blame rests right here in this office. The quicker I own up to that, the quicker we can move forward, put it behind us."

Sorenson said, "Own up to it publicly? A full statement to the press?"

"A full statement to everyone, the press, the public, the government, and even the damn Russians. If anyone is ever to take this administration seriously, they have to see full honesty, full accountability. The decisions were mine, and they were bad decisions. Mistakes were made, all the way up the chain of command, but the biggest mistake happened right here in this office. I gave the go-ahead."

Bobby held his pose, arms still folded tightly.

"You're right, Jack. It has to be done, to accept responsibility for all of it. But, Jesus, it's a hell of a way to start a presidency."

HE WALKED WITH his brother across the wet green lawn, a drizzle of soft rain. The president seemed to ignore that, and so Bobby did as well, knowing that Jack was still fuming. Bobby glanced at his shoes, black leather soaked now with the rain. After a long silence, he said, "You had to go along, Jack. Too much had been done, too many hours, too much training. Those Cubans in Miami wouldn't have let you call it off. It's all they live for."

Kennedy stopped, a glance upward.

"That shouldn't have mattered. The fact is, I want that son of a bitch out of Cuba too. So do you. I relied on my own hope that this would be the way, that he could be erased without any of us getting dirt on our hands. I learned something, Bobby. I'm new at this job, and I thought it was the wise thing to depend on the veterans, those who know how things work. But those people have failings too, have wishful thinking enough to go around. Just because a man's been in some high-up office for years doesn't mean he knows what the hell he's doing, and that goes for the CIA, the Joint Chiefs, and all the rest. That damned Bissell . . . he flat-out lied to me about the chance for this thing to succeed. I suppose they all did, in one way or another. They thought I needed . . . boosting. The new kid. A dose of confidence. Well, I've got confidence now. I've learned not to trust anyone just because he has a big office, or he wears a uniform. You might be it, little brother. From now on, I want you to be my ears, I want you to stick your nose into every dark corner. Figure out what's real and what's foolishness, or rather, what's dangerous. I've been thrown straight into the pot, and the water's boiling. Too many of my advisors are afraid to tell me things I might not like. I figured that one out pretty quickly. You won't hesitate to pound your boots up my ass plenty. Apparently, this job calls for that."

Bobby tried not to smile.

"If you insist. I've always had your behind, Jack. I learned that from Pop."

"I know. I need to go sit down with Sorenson, put some words on paper. If anyone will figure out the best way to tell the world I've been an idiot, it's my best speechwriter."

Bobby tugged on his coat, the drizzle increasing.

"Let's go inside. Listen, what do you want me to focus on first? I've got a truckload of work waiting for me over at Justice. If your attorney general is going to act as your troubleshooter too, I'll need to set some wheels in motion over there, get things to run without my hands-on every minute."

Kennedy stopped, seemed to notice the rain now.

"Do what you have to do. The Justice Department is your baby, and you'll run it however you want to. But beyond that, I want you to find some good people, the right people, to figure out how to get rid of that bastard Castro. He's a danger to this entire hemisphere."

"What do we do about the Soviets? Castro's already crawling into bed with them, and Khrushchev won't react well if someone plugs Castro with a sniper's rifle. There are Russian advisors in Cuba now, probably some troops. They've been sending in Russian equipment, including MiGs, and they're certainly training Cuban pilots to fly the things. They consider Castro their new best friend, and they're going to grease him up with every kind of weapon and training they can."

"So, if something happens to Castro, it has to come from inside Cuba. Figure out how to make that happen."

Bobby didn't respond, knew his brother had the same thoughts. Yeah, we tried that once before.

The president moved toward the White House portico, Bobby keeping up with quick wet steps. To one side, he saw the Secret Service guards, moving parallel, as miserable from the increasing rain as Bobby was now. They reached the cover of the main porch, climbed the steps, Bobby swiping the wetness off his shoulders.

"Jesus, Jack, I'll need a new suit. Let's take a walk when the weather's better."

Kennedy glanced out past his brother, the rain harder now.

"Just figure out a way to get rid of that son of a bitch. And don't tell me about it."

Bobby laughed.

"I just thought of Pop. His best advice. *Don't write anything down.*"

Jack glanced at him, unsmiling. They rarely spoke of Joe Kennedy these days, the great shadow of the man growing smaller now. All that the father had pushed for had come to pass already, one son the president, one the attorney general. There wasn't much else even the most ambitious father could ask for.

At the great doorway, the Marine guard saluted, the two men dripping their way inside. Bobby said, "So, you'll make your remarks to the nation, owning up to the Bay of Pigs. What do you think the Soviets will say?"

Kennedy stopped, an aide appearing with a pair of towels.

"I think they'll be surprised as hell that I'm not trying to cover anything up. That I'll admit we screwed up, and that, under this administration anyway, it won't happen again. That's not how they do things in Moscow."

Bobby wiped at his face with the welcome towel, ran it through the tussle of thick hair.

"They'll still find a way to accuse you of something sinister."

"Well, I suppose I'll find out. Already I surprised them about Vienna. They expected me to put off our scheduled summit, because of our . . . crisis. But I accepted the invitation anyway. I'll meet with Khrushchev June third. Jackie and mother will go with me. I thought it would be a good idea to put as much normalcy on this as I could."

"I'd love to sit down with Khrushchev, find out just what kind of balls he has."

Kennedy laughed.

"I have more important things to worry about, like whether or not he thinks he can blow up our half the world and get away with it. I intend to push hard for the nuclear test ban treaty. That's more important to me than his manhood."

FROM HIS EARLIEST days in Washington, Bobby Kennedy had built a reputation as a ruthless and aggressive advocate for whatever task he had been assigned. Some labeled him cold, unfeeling, dedicated to a fault, most often those critics who had been on the receiving end of his ambitious assaults. In the mid-1950s, he had served as counsel to the infamous Senator Joe McCarthy, who pursued alleged Communists that had supposedly infiltrated the U.S. government. But Kennedy had little of McCarthy's zeal for attacking the innocent, or elevating himself at the expense of the helpless or hapless who happened to stand in the way. When McCarthy's vicious campaign exhausted itself, crushed by outrage toward the senator's methods, the young Kennedy chased a new foe, organized crime, working as an attorney for the Justice Department. There, he pursued corruption springing from racketeering, targeting such figures as Teamsters Union president Jimmy Hoffa. But with the 1960 presidential election approaching, Bobby Kennedy's zeal turned closer to home, and he resigned his post at Justice to manage his brother Jack's campaign for the presidency. The brutal campaign pitched the handsome, rising star of the Senate against the vice president, Richard Nixon. Many assumed Nixon was the natural successor to the retiring Dwight Eisenhower, an assumption based partly on the uneasiness many voters had with Kennedy's Catholicism. But the Kennedy team made great use of Jack Kennedy's assets, a younger, vibrantly handsome family man, whose wife, Jackie, brought the kind of fashion and elegant charm to her position rarely seen in Washington. The margin was razor thin, but in the end, Kennedy prevailed, in no small part because of his younger brother's efforts. As the new administration settled into official Washington, one of the new president's earliest decisions raised eyebrows, and set off a furious contagion of tongue-wagging. Bobby Kennedy was chosen to be the new attorney general. At thirty-five, Bobby was the youngest ever appointed to the Cabinet. Though cries of nepotism echoed through Congress, fueled by Kennedy's Republican enemies, the Kennedys showed no hesitation in moving forward. Both men accepted that, in his younger brother, Jack had chosen a man who filled two great needs. He was absolutely qualified to do the job, and the president could trust him, absolutely.

As attorney general, Bobby Kennedy quickly erased concerns about his lack of expertise, or lack of ability to handle a position thought to be one of the toughest in Washington. His zeal for attacking organized crime had not waned, so much so that the nation's chief law enforcement officer, FBI head J. Edgar Hoover, began to see the young Kennedy as an annoying upstart, who didn't automatically bow down to Hoover's self-proclaimed superiority. It was a thorny relationship that, as time passed, grew thornier still.

As Bobby had done throughout his brother's public life, he quickly established himself as his brother's protector, willing to engage and confront any controversy that threatened the president's public stature, including both men's penchant for sexual affairs. Beyond the personal, Bobby continued to serve the new president in other ways, leading some to wonder if the younger Kennedy would be satisfied to keep to his office at the Justice Department. But neither man paid heed to that kind of criticism, and very quickly, Bobby Kennedy rose to become his brother's most sought-after and trusted advisor. If critics labeled Bobby as out of his depth with topics such as foreign policy, the president didn't seem to care. What meant more to both men was trust. Jack Kennedy knew he could trust his brother. It did not take long for official Washington to offer labels of their own. It was widely assumed that if the president ever required a hatchet man, someone to ram home an idea or suggestion, that man would be his younger brother.

He sat behind his desk, eyed the stuffed tiger beside his massive fireplace. He focused on the beast's claws, upraised, as though awaiting instructions to assault anyone the attorney general deemed worthy. Across from him sat John Siegenthaler, Bobby's newly appointed top advisor. Siegenthaler glanced at the tiger, smiled, said, "It's not enough that you've set tongues to wagging all over the city. Now you're giving some of the press people plenty of ammunition for calling you eccentric."

Bobby folded his hands behind his head, leaned back.

"Is that a problem? You know, Ernest Hemingway gave me that tiger. I don't much care who objects to it. I took it as a compliment, from a man whose compliments carry some weight."

"As you say, sir. I do admit, your appointment isn't raising quite as many eyebrows around here as it did a few weeks ago. I credit you for that. You've made it plain that you're up to the task."

Bobby laughed.

"You know, I wasn't Jack's first choice."

"What do you mean?"

"When Jack was elected, he went to Abe Ribicoff, governor of Connecticut, offered him the job."

Siegenthaler seemed surprised.

"Yes, I know of Governor Ribicoff. Fine man. Would have done a good job here I suspect. Not as good as you, of course."

Kennedy ignored the joke.

"He's a Jew. He turned down the offer, smart enough to realize that this job will be staring straight into a cannon barrel down south when it comes to Civil Rights issues. Abe didn't think that the first Catholic president ought to put a Jew in charge of confronting a bunch of racist white Anglo-Saxon Protestants. Sounds reasonable to me. I don't have those kinds of handicaps. They'll hate me for what I do, not just because my brother and I are Catholic."

"I'm curious, sir. You said you had never actually practiced law before. I know you served as counsel to the senator and all. Should we expect some difficulties from outside attorneys who still don't accept your qualifications?"

"Nah. I've worked hard at this. Like so many, I started as a young lawyer. I was ambitious, I studied, applied myself. I'd have gone far, too. But then, my brother was elected president of the United States. That sort of changed my priorities."

It was a rare joke, Bobby not cracking a smile.

"Well, then, yes, I can see how that qualified you for any number of jobs."

"I love saying that. But look, John. I've got good people here, dedicated people. I check on 'em, regularly, make my way through most of the offices, here and down the street. I'm surprised to hear that most of these folks have rarely ever shaken the hand of the attorney general, their boss, for God's sake. I changed that. They need to know who I am, and what we're doing here. If they have an issue, they come to see me. Tiger and all."

Tuesday, May 9, 1961
Washington, DC

"Excuse me, sir?"

Bobby looked up, annoyed at the interruption, saw the unsmiling face of Ed Guthman, one of his aides.

"What is it, Ed?"

"Sir, you know Frank Holeman, of the New York *Daily News*?"

"Maybe."

"Well, sir, he's friendly with a Russian, fellow by the name of Georgi Bolshakov. Bolshakov is a colonel in the Soviet military intel unit, the GRU. Nice enough chap, according to Holeman. Thinks it would be a good thing if he had access to the brother of the president."

"Good God, why?"

"This could be valuable, sir. A back-channel contact, someone who has the ear of Moscow, without gushing over it in the newspapers."

"But you said the *Daily News* . . ."

"Just a contact, sir. Colonel Bolshakov wants to meet you, maybe establish a relationship of sorts. Nothing official, nothing public. Would you be interested, sir?"

Bobby sat back, hands behind his head, his usual position.

"By God. Yes. Um . . . where?"

"They're holding him in a discreet place, sir. I assumed that if you were to meet with him, it should be out of doors, away from ears. I suggest, sir, downstairs, on the street corner."

"What if I had said no?"

"We'd have sent him on his way. And, forgive me for saying, sir, you would never have said no."

He was surprised. Bolshakov was nothing like he expected, a short round man, with what seemed to be a perpetual smile.

"You don't look anything like a spy."

The smile widened.

"Neither do you, Mr. Attorney General."

"Fair enough. I admit I read too much Ian Fleming. I expect every discreet meeting to take place with someone I presume resembles James Bond."

Bolshakov laughed.

"I've heard that before. No matter. Tell me, Mr. Attorney General, is this a social meeting, or is there more to your being here?"

"My name's Robert. Bobby, I suppose. I don't care for the name, but everybody on Earth insists on using it. You're Georgi, correct?"

"Quite so, sir."

"In that case, I want to know if you are interested in having the ear of the president of the United States. If so, I expect to meet occasionally with someone who has the ear of the Kremlin. Mutual benefit, as it were."

Bolshakov nodded, another chuckle.

"Good. To the point. I heard you were not a man for small talk, or mindless jabber. We should get along. I am curious about one thing. It is understood that my government values a pipeline, if you will, into the office of the president. Cuts out the complications, the jabber between governments, too often delayed in transmission. Your government has an annoying habit of relying on your newspapers for information, or even worse, for allowing those newspapers to print what they know. I'm hoping this relationship avoids such things. But I'm curious. What do you wish to gain from me?"

Bobby shifted his seat on the granite wall, waited while a pair of tourists walked past, one with a bouncing camera and the other wearing knee socks.

"Same thing. There is too much tension between our countries. We also do not wish to rely on the snail's pace of diplomatic channels when we can make our point directly, with no confusion. And one more thing. Any back-channel pipeline relies on truth. I must trust you, as you must trust me. There are no games to be played here. That's for diplomats. This is a dangerous world, and free speaking is essential for us to know just who we are, and what we mean to say."

"Your brother the president is sensitive to being perceived as weak, is he not? Your tragic Bay of Pigs event could paint a picture of him that he does not wish to paint, certainly not inside the Kremlin. It was an odd thing for us to hear him accept blame for his mistakes, or for the mistakes of others. That is unusual in our world. He must demonstrate that he is more than a suit full of apologies in order for the Kremlin to take him seriously."

"That's the gist of it. We are concerned that your people do not view the United States as a paper tiger. You must understand that we acknowledge our mistakes in Cuba, but it does not mean we are backing down from protecting our interests. It would be a mistake for your government to test us, to push against what you would see as weakness."

Bolshakov shrugged.

"I cannot tell Premier Khrushchev what to think. He will find out for himself what the president has for a spine when they meet in Vienna."

Bobby winced at the word, absorbed the subtle message that Bolshakov might open a pipeline but he had no real control over anything. Bobby glanced skyward.

"It's going to rain. There's a great deal of that here, especially when I choose to be outside. I ruin too many suits as it is. Let's walk."

Bolshakov slid his heavy frame off the wall, moved alongside Kennedy, seemed even shorter now. Halfway down the block, Bobby said, "If indeed you can pass my communications directly to Khrushchev, then we should do just fine. I assure you, I will do the same for my brother."

Bolshakov nodded, unsmiling now.

"We have many issues lying before us that are of great interest to my government. Cuba certainly, and more importantly, Berlin. No one among us should step into a powder keg tossing off sparks."

"Precisely."

"Then, Bobby, we shall certainly meet again."

CHAPTER TWO

Khrushchev

Thursday, June 1, 1961
Petsamo, Georgia, by the Black Sea

"For the life of me, I cannot grow carrots."

He looked up through the sunlight at his son, poked again at the dirt.

"Sergei, it is good I am a leader, because I would be a failure as a farmer."

Sergei laughed, stood tall above him, shielding the sun.

"Father, you are a marvelous success as a manager of agricultural programs. No one expects you to work the soil with your own hands. You command a nation and its programs, not its dirt."

Khrushchev sat back on the hard ground, said, "In that I am fortunate. My celery withers, my potatoes are like small rocks. I would imagine Chairman Stalin never dirtied his hands either. But if Stalin could see what kind of progress I am making in managing *his* precious nation, he would no doubt shoot me where I sit. As much as I worked beside him, I never gave much regard to seeking prosperity through the mass execution of our own citizens.

He stayed in power as long as he did because he executed anyone smart enough to defeat him. The generals, mostly. That was a problem when the Second World War began. The army had no one left who knew what he was doing. Stalin had purged them all." He fingered a small shovel, tossed it aside. "Russia is a land where strength allows survival, but with strength must also come guile. Wits. As long as I remained close to Stalin, I was feared. Through it all, I learned to make friends; powerful, useful friends. There was much chaos, confusion, *smoke* spread over this country when Stalin died. The smoke cleared, and here I sit. Well, not just *here*, mind you. This dirt is cold."

He knew Sergei had heard it all before, the son in his mid-twenties, accustomed to all the great tales his father delighted in recalling. The most prominent story of course was Khrushchev's rise to power, the careful manipulation of the entire Soviet system, so that one man could find his way to the top, and, with good fortune, remain there.

Khrushchev reached out a hand, and Sergei grasped it, helped Khrushchev to his feet, both men with a low grunt.

"I would prefer you be careful, Father. It is too easy to make enemies these days. The world has become complicated."

Khrushchev brushed dirt from the short stubs of his fingers.

"I am always careful, my son. It is another piece of the puzzle that is Russia. Someone always waits in the shadows. Weakness is never forgiven. Mistakes . . . well, one does not make mistakes. And, occasionally, there must be victories, great achievements that quiet the critics, when they dare to speak. If the people cheer you, the men in the shadows back away just a bit more. Of course, Stalin was a master at finding those people and putting a gun to their heads. I prefer to be more subtle. No matter. I would rather embrace our *successes*. Last month, we actually launched a rocket that carried a man into space. It's an achievement for all time, for all mankind. And it was *our* achievement. Even better than that, we finally shot down a U-2 . . . the Americans' infernal spy plane. They abused our sanctity by crisscrossing our country with cameras, too high for our guns to reach. But no more. Finally, another great victory for our people, for me." It was a point he rarely failed to mention: the year before, an American spy plane brought down by a ground-to-air missile, the pilot, Francis Gary Powers surviving, paraded across the world's media like a hunting trophy. "I have often wondered what we would have done if the Americans had shot down one of our planes, if we would have started a war. But the Americans are slow on the trigger. They ponder and analyze. Even Eisenhower, the great war hero, he did nothing to avenge the loss of their precious spy plane. The U-2 was shot down on his watch, and he showed embarrassment at their indiscretion, which is a weakness. In the great *cold war*, it was a battle I won decisively. There are no more spy planes flying over our territory."

"They will build better planes, Father."

"And we will build better missiles. And so, this *cold war* shall continue, until both sides exhaust themselves standing at attention. No, I am wrong. It will never end, unless one side loses patience, or makes a deadly mistake. In the meantime, both sides will push and shove, and play their games. And all the while, our scientists work in their laboratories, our generals remain ready, our newspapers and radios convince the people that all is well, that we are winning, that Russia must ultimately prevail."

"Must there always be missiles, Father?"

"So, you are worried about my young grandson? It is the shadow we all live under, Sergei. It is the natural order of things. Technology advances for good and for evil. The evil must be balanced for the good to survive. When you and I are gone, your son will have that responsibility."

"I'd rather not think of that, Father. He is an infant. I am more concerned for all the sons, all the children, and not just Russian. They know nothing of such things as guided missiles and nuclear bombs. Are they not entitled to grow up and live without the shadow of war?"

Khrushchev put his hands in his pockets, shook his head.

"I do not make the rules, Sergei. This is not a world I created. I have one task, one purpose in life, to ensure the survival and the prosperity of the people of the Soviet Union. And so, I must engage whenever I can to seek the advantage, to put our people in their best place." He paused. "And now I must go to Vienna and meet with this young fellow Kennedy. So far, I am not impressed. It was different with Eisenhower. That man had earned his reputation, and even though he could sometimes show weakness, he carried himself with a strong back. You knew you could push, but not far, and he was not afraid to show me his human side, away from all the bluster and official policy statements. Our trip to his Camp David, to his farm in Gettysburg . . . most delightful. We could converse as *grandfathers*, more interested in playing with our children than rattling sabers. This Kennedy . . . I don't know. He is too young, too untried. He has already made a catastrophic blunder in Cuba, and he grovels to the world with weak apologies."

"He is surely not a simpleton, Father. He will learn from his mistakes."

"Perhaps. But my task is to push him to make more. He will be cautious, he will hesitate. He must know that he has the upper hand when it comes to weapons, that we are working with a fever to catch up. He makes grand pronouncements in the newspapers how he will stand tall toward his adversaries, meaning, of course, *me*. He pretends to be arrogant, as though he will have the strong hand in any negotiation. But his caution will betray him. And so, we must take advantage. If the Soviet Union is to prosper, we must expand, and expand again. Cuba, Vietnam, Laos, and even Germany. As time passes, new opportunities will appear, new leaders will emerge in countries everywhere who will see value in our programs and the Soviet system. That is the great competition, that is the meaning of *cold war*. As our influence spreads, our strength will spread with it, to every corner of the world. I will not repeat Stalin's mistake. He first saw Russia as his target, and he spent too much energy pursuing enemies within his own backyard, while the rest of the world grew stronger. Unlike Stalin, I do not fear Russians."

"Just be cautious yourself, Father. Kennedy might be weak, but the Americans, their military, their economy are very strong. He could be replaced as well, with someone far more dangerous. It just takes their system a little longer than it might take here."

Khrushchev laughed, rubbed one dirty hand across his round belly.

"I will go to Vienna and find just how much of a spine he has. I will be civil, certainly. But there will be a hard edge, a razor's edge. He will have his hat in his hand, hoping for a benign friendship. Perhaps he will repeat his apologies for his Cuban debacle. I will shake his hand, give him a wide friendly smile. But I will hold the dagger hidden away."

Sunday, June 4, 1961
Vienna, Austria

He was exhausted. He moved down the long corridor, past the luxurious hotel rooms belonging to his staff, others in his party. His steps were deliberate, and he tried not to show just how tired he truly was, not to the men around him now, the security guards who must never see weakness. They reached his room, another waiting guard standing tall, one man with a key, the door opening.

The word had spread that the summit had ended, others emerging from their rooms, easing closer to his suite, hoping to hear the details. The meetings themselves had consisted of six men, Khrushchev and Kennedy, Russian foreign minister Andrei Gromyko, the two interpreters and the American secretary of state, Dean Rusk. But Rusk had played little role, the words coming almost exclusively from Kennedy, and even now, Khrushchev was wondering at the arrogance of that, if it was a mock show of strength.

He moved to the plush sofa, sat heavily, heard the tumult in the hallway, motioned to his staff to let them in. Gromyko was there first, seemed as exhausted as Khrushchev, waited for a signal to sit. The others gathered around now, diplomats and officials, his own assistants, so many sponges, waiting for the information Khrushchev chose to give them. To one side, a table, with a silver champagne bucket, iced and filled with a glorious bottle, a gracious offering from his Austrian hosts. He pointed.

"Open that."

An aide moved quickly, the sparkling gold filling a shallow glass. He took it gratefully, a glance at the bubbles, then downed it in a single swallow.

"Another."

He looked at Gromyko, a silent offer, Gromyko shaking his head no.

"Pity, Andre. More for me."

He downed the second glass, handed it again to the aide.

"Keep pouring."

The door to the enormous room closed and he glanced around, all faces expectant, staring dutifully, waiting for his briefing. He sipped more slowly at the third glass, then said, "The president is as I suspected. He is a charming man, well spoken, intelligent. He is well-versed on all the issues, and does not rely on a team of advisors to prompt him on what he should say. But beneath it all, he is tentative, fearful, possibly a weakling. He is not an Eisenhower, and he seems not to know his own strengths, the strengths of his country or its military. He refuses to understand our needs, our goals, preaches only of what is best for the United States. He drained me of energy, wishing to debate the merits of Western philosophy, trying to convince me that we must hold back on any thoughts of spreading our revolution. I listened, politely. And I have already forgotten most of what he said." He sat back, one hand on his stomach. He knew the men around him were waiting for more, and he gulped the champagne again. "We discussed so many topics, but my efforts to open his eyes to our way of thinking were clouded by his incessant need to debate, as though this entire summit was a contest, comparing our systems of government, our philosophies. I spoke of Berlin at great length. I told him of our need to settle that issue, why the presence of Western armies in the city posed a security threat to us. I told him of the objections of the Eastern German officials, who watch the flow of their citizens westward, along with their goods and their currency. I did not tell him, of course, that those same officials are pushing us hard to construct a barrier that will divide the city, the only way, apparently, to stop the flow of those goods and the refugees who carry them. For most of the afternoon, Kennedy seemed confused about Berlin, with no response other than to claim it is necessary for world peace to maintain a standoff there." He drank a fourth glass of champagne, ignored the growing effects, felt a belch rising, allowed it to escape noisily. "Request more bottles of this. It is quite good. No, I do not fear the Americans, and I do not fear their leader. The world will soon understand that by giving us the upper hand, Mr. Kennedy will indeed find his *world peace*. It will simply be on our terms."

CHAPTER THREE

RFK

Friday, June 9, 1961
The White House, Oval Office

He tread lightly, knew Jack was in a sour mood. The oval office was empty, just the two brothers, the president insisting that he needed time alone with the one man he could trust. Bobby knew to just let him talk.

"It was a goddamned disaster. Khrushchev wiped the floor with me. He played it perfectly smart, came in all smiles, heavy hand-shakes, that idiotic toothy grin of his. He has the fattest hands I've ever seen. I tried to make the points we needed to make. I thought that was the purpose, after all. He pretended to listen, then schooled me like a ten-year-old on the ways of the world. I truly thought if he could understand just why the United States does the things we do, he would appreciate our differences, and work together to make sure we got along. That sounded like a good strategy to me. Even Rusk thought so. So, Khrushchev listens politely, then tosses it all back in my face, expects me to understand his point of view as though it was the only thing worth considering."

Bobby kept to the far end of the room, arms crossed, one hand under his chin.

"Isn't that the way it works? Two points of view, maybe a little give and take, both sides learning that the other is not some maniacal beast ready to conquer the world."

The president slumped in his chair.

"Yep. And I did a piss-poor job of it. I gave speeches, for God's sake. I embarrassed myself so badly, I thought Rusk was going to crawl out the door. All I did was show the damn Soviets that I'm new at this game. They'll take that for weakness, I guarantee it. I made every effort to draw a line in the sand, great pronouncements of what we would not permit, blah blah blah. And I accomplished nothing. The Soviets are still adamant about Berlin, about everything else. I didn't change a damn thing."

Bobby eased closer to the desk.

"Did he mention anything about our domestic problems? I thought he might throw that in your face, the Civil Rights mess. I don't think the Soviets are beating the crap out of each other over sharing a lunch counter for a cup of coffee. That has to make us look pretty bad to the rest of the world."

Kennedy shook his head.

"No, he never mentioned Civil Rights. He showed a little bit of class, I thought. But it's one more symptom of how much work I still have to do in this office."

Bobby ached to change the subject, hated to see his brother suffering with self-doubt. After a silent moment, he said, "I assume you received all the details. The Freedom Riders got pretty beat up. All they wanted to do was make a point, that anybody should be able to ride a goddamn bus. A bunch of Alabama rednecks didn't see it that way. I sent Siegenthaler down there to manage things, and even he got whacked in the head. People could have died, Jack, a lot of people. We had nearly five hundred U.S. marshals down there to keep order, and they were outnumbered to beat hell. Even tear gas couldn't stop those mobs from wading right into our lines, swinging baseball bats and ax handles."

Kennedy sat back in his chair, slowly raised his feet up onto the desk, a wince of pain in his face.

"I know all this, Bobby. No matter how much energy I put into meeting with Khrushchev, I didn't forget what you were doing back here. How's Doctor King taking all this?"

"He knows we're trying to do the right thing, but it's a slow process, too slow for him. I get that. This has been going on since Reconstruction, and the Blacks are sick of it. My office will do all we can, but that's a slow process too. I'm leaning on the Interstate Commerce Commission to completely desegregate the bus lines, even the bus stations. There are still *white* and *colored* areas in nearly every station in the South. There's resistance to what we're trying to do, and not just in Mississippi and Georgia. Some of it's right here in Washington, a pretty good number of congressmen."

"Lean harder. On all of them."

Bobby nodded, rubbed a hand on his chin.

"You know I will. I don't mean to ignore this mess with the Soviets, but your domestic policies have to take center stage, especially if you want to do well in the midterm elections next year. Being popular overseas won't get us many votes at home." He paused. "It would be helpful if you take the bull by the horns, and talk to that jackass governor Barnett in Mississippi. He treats me like I'm in the way, like Mississippi is his private kingdom, and he'll treat the Negroes any way he damn well pleases. If there's a demonstration, and no one actually gets killed, he crows about it, like we should pat him on the damn back. Meanwhile, the KKK is burning crosses, and Negroes are being yanked out into the street and beaten to hell."

"Listen, Bobby, just make sure this stays front page news in the papers, *all* the papers. I need people in Oregon and Vermont and Michigan to see firsthand what's going on. We may have to make some dangerous decisions, like sending in troops to take charge down there. I want people to understand why."

The phone rang on the president's desk, and he picked up, listened, said, "Yeah, fine. Now's a good time."

He hung up the phone, looked at Bobby, said, "General Taylor is on his way here, asking that I debrief him on Khrushchev and the Soviets' Berlin position. The military is scared to hell they'll be the cause of World War Three by digging in their heels on this. They might be right. Khrushchev repeated over and over his point that the Russians will sign a treaty with the East Germans that will seal off Berlin, no matter what we say about it. It's so damn reasonable to just keep things the way they are, divide the city, keep Western troops in position. Standing face-to-face with your adversary is a damn good way to watch if the other guy blinks. It's the best way I know to be able to keep an eye on each other, staring across a wire fence. We're all looking for peace, so we keep saying. Germany was the spoils of war for all of us, the great prize. Just because the Soviets have staked their claim on the eastern half of that country is no reason we can't continue our occupation of Berlin. It's the capital, for God's sake, and it shouldn't matter that it happens to sit on the eastern side of the line. So, sure, the military is scared to hell that if they show too much muscle, Khrushchev will do the same, with more muscle, then more, and all of that nonsense. Now, Dean Acheson is shooting his mouth off, pushing us to stand firm, no matter what, no negotiation, no flexibility. That's all I need, Truman and Ike's people announcing to the world all that I'm doing wrong."

Bobby knew how much of a thorn Acheson had become. He had been the secretary of state under Harry Truman, but didn't settle quietly into retirement. Now, he spoke out noisily about the danger of doing business with the Soviets, and how Kennedy had to stand strong, no matter the potential cost.

Bobby saw the grimace on his brother's face, knew it had to be the chronic back pain. Kennedy reached into a desk drawer, retrieved a small bottle of pills, popped one into his mouth, said, "Truman and Ike handed me these messes, and now they bitch about the job I'm doing."

"Look, Jack. The Soviets aren't in a hurry to start World War Three, any more than we are. Let's focus on those things we can change, or address directly. We should worry about the Soviets when there's a good reason to."

CHAPTER FOUR

RFK

Thursday, July 27, 1961
Office of the Attorney General, Washington, DC

The tug of war over Berlin had begun shortly after World War Two, the Soviets liberating the city from the east, while British, French, and American troops had eventually secured the city from the west. But the territory around Berlin, now referred to as East Germany, was Soviet controlled, a full-on part of the new Soviet bloc of nations. That Western allies would continue to occupy their half of Berlin had become a serious sticking point to the Soviets, first under Stalin, and now, with Khrushchev. The issue, from Khrushchev's point of view was a simple one. There was no real reason he could see why Western troops should continue to occupy Berlin at all. It simply wasn't necessary.

Bobby sat alone in his office, read over a brief prepared by the State Department, yet another warning about Soviet intentions in Berlin. This is ridiculous, he thought. Eisenhower had the opportunity to solve this mess three years ago, and passed us the buck. Jack had a chance, I suppose, in Vienna, to address this in a way that could defuse it all, and Khrushchev wouldn't let him. At least, that's how Jack tells it. I'm sure Khrushchev has his own version, that the president is just being stubborn, that the poor harmless Soviets are just looking out for the peaceful people of East Germany. He looked at the intercom on his desk, punched the button, called out, "I need Siegenthaler. Right now."

He waited, drummed his fingers on the desk. The door opened, Siegenthaler, the one man who wasn't required to knock before entering.

"What's up? I was talking to your secretary. You sound annoyed."

"I'm always annoyed. This Berlin thing just keeps spinning forward, with no end in sight. All it does around here is ramp up the tension, that we're heading for a damned war. The Joint Chiefs are supposedly giddy about that, pushing their plans to wipe out the Soviets with *only* a loss of sixty million Americans. I'm getting damned tired of hearing about acceptable casualty rates. That doesn't play too well on the evening news. We don't need our citizens guessing if they'll be among the unfortunates. There is no way in hell I'm going to sit back and allow my brother to be the first president in history to slaughter millions of our own people. And, since no doubt Khrushchev feels the same way about *his* people, neither one of them is willing to concede any ground. There has to be something I can do. So, I'll try. Get me Bolshakov over here, for a meeting. At least I can get pissed off and nobody official has to hear about it."

Siegenthaler seemed to measure him, testing just how angry he was.

"I suppose there's no harm. But you know, you can't make any kind of deal. He'll know that too."

"I'm not looking for a deal. I just want to let the Soviets know . . .

well, maybe this one Soviet . . . that we need to settle this thing, and take it off the front page of the newspapers."

"I AM AT your service, Mr. Attorney General. To what do I owe the honor of your summons?"

Bobby led him across the street without speaking, away from the Justice Department, away from a steady stream of people moving past, some of whom seemed to recognize him. They reached a small park, the shade of the trees a welcome relief from the summer sun. He could see that Bolshakov was sweating, the short round man seeming to suffer inside the necessary formality of his suit. Bobby stopped now, eyed a bench, said, "Let's sit."

Bolshakov followed his lead, planted himself beside him, waited patiently for Bobby's chosen topic.

"We can't just pull out of Berlin. Our allies will follow our lead, except for this. If we withdraw our forces from Berlin, we'll leave the Brits and the French to handle things there alone. That will make them seriously unhappy. And, it won't do much for the morale of the citizens of West Berlin, who depend on us for security. If we withdraw, it will be a show of weakness to the whole world, that we're withdrawing from our commitment, a commitment we made after the war. No matter how much sense it might make to Khrushchev for us to leave, it simply doesn't work. How in hell do we make Khrushchev understand that? How do we make him understand that we simply cannot leave, no matter his threats?"

Bolshakov stared down, seemed to absorb Bobby's tirade.

"I cannot speak for Chairman Khrushchev. You know that."

"No, but you can reach him, through your superiors. You can at least push upon him my reasoning."

"That's an unfortunate choice of words, Mr. Attorney General.

No one will push anything upon Chairman Khrushchev. In Moscow, such things can be dangerous."

Bobby was feeling the heat of the day, adding to his impatience.

"Why so much formality? As I told you before, dammit, just call me Bobby."

"Sorry, of course. Bobby. I just never know what to expect, if you're going to be friendly, or lecture me."

"Look, I understand all of that. But we're at a place where Berlin is liable to become a spark, a very dangerous spark that neither of us want to see. This has gone on long enough. The tension level rises every time we talk about it, every time Khrushchev talks about it. We have tanks aiming their guns at your tanks, staring at each other every damned day. All it takes is one nervous tank commander, who thinks he sees a twitch he doesn't like . . ."

"I am aware, Bobby. I must mention to you that three years ago, Chairman Khrushchev made a pledge to you and your allies that if you withdrew from the city, it would become a free demilitarized city. You rejected his pledge, and so the chairman had no choice but to turn over management of the eastern portion of the city to the East German government. Since your government, and your allies would not comply, the chairman generously withdrew his pledge. He visited your President Eisenhower at his home in Gettysburg, hoping to discuss this in a friendly manner. The chairman tried to demonstrate to President Eisenhower that making Berlin a free city would have no detriment to the security of the United States. It was hoped by both sides that some kind of negotiation could be forthcoming to solve this problem."

Bobby rolled the thought through his mind, said, "Regardless of all that, you must understand that there is a strong wave of suspicion in the American government not to trust the pledges of Chairman

Khrushchev. It was difficult, if not impossible for Eisenhower to accept that all would happen exactly as Khrushchev said it would."

Bolshakov stared at him now, a change in the man's demeanor, the friendliness gone.

"You would speak of trust? No sooner had plans been made for both sides to make formal agreements to guarantee peace, our defense forces shot down your U-2 spy plane, capturing your pilot. I need not tell you what an outrage this was for us, that you would blatantly violate Soviet territorial airspace with your aircraft. That event changed attitudes in the Kremlin, to match the attitudes you speak of in Washington."

Bobby let out a long breath, shifted himself on the hard bench, loosened his tie.

"So, we are both guilty of protecting our interests. And since those interests seem to clash, to contradict each other . . ."

"Peace is not contradictory, Bobby. We just have differing paths to reach the same goal."

They sat silently for a long minute, then Bolshakov said, "It is very warm today. It has taken me a while to adjust to your climate. I imagine it is warm inside of those tanks in Berlin. You know, every day, citizens of the eastern part of the city, of East Germany, find their way into West Berlin. That alone produces tension, a need to stop such a flow of goods and citizens. Such a tide is costly, weakens the structure of the east. I have been told that measures are being considered that will stop such things."

Bobby looked at him, felt an itch.

"What kinds of thing? That could add considerably to tensions as they are now."

"I do not agree, Bobby. Dividing the city, with a clear boundary, could reduce tensions, especially among those tank gunners. I cannot speak for my government of course. I am not privy to everything that is happening. But I must believe that there is a means of solving our problems, allowing you to maintain your presence in West Berlin, while we can more effectively control the land in the east."

"You mean . . . control the people."

Bolshakov shrugged.

"I don't know what I mean. I serve only my superiors."

ON AUGUST 13, 1961, laboring quickly and with brutal efficiency, Soviet and East German construction workers completed a barrier, a wall that divided east and west Berlin, essentially into two cities. Where once German citizens could still move freely across the imaginary line, now that line was very real, and very deadly. The wall was concrete and wire, with guard towers and lookout posts that stretched across the city, denying anyone access to the other side. Khrushchev gambled that the rapid construction of the wall would calm tensions, and create a fait accompli in the city. He was right. Rather than continuing to rattle sabers, or make any kind of military effort to stop the wall, Kennedy and the Western allies in Britain and France accepted the wall as a solution, although an outrageous one. The diplomatic and public protests were long and loud, but in the end, neither side started shooting. As Kennedy phrased it, "*A wall is better than a war.*"

The Western military forces continued to occupy their positions in West Berlin, with only one significant confrontation. In October 1961, American general Lucius Clay decided to test the resolve of those on the eastern side of the wall, organizing forays to the eastern side, through the American gate known as Checkpoint Charlie. The aggressive forays, escorted by American tanks, finally produced a similar response from the other side, Soviet tanks lining the wall in a standoff barely one hundred yards apart. But cooler heads prevailed, orders coming to both General Clay and his Soviet counterpart to stand down. Though the Berlin crisis still simmered, for now, an uneasy sense of calm spread over the city.

As tense as the Berlin standoff had been, Kennedy realized that the wall had actually turned down the heat with the Russians. Unless Khrushchev made any effort to expand Russian influence into other lands, Kennedy could focus his attention more on the problems his administration faced at home, specifically, the building Civil Rights crisis, where blood, American blood, was being spilled from one end of the South to the other.

As attorney general, Bobby led the charge against the most extreme lawbreakers, pushing back into places where segregation had been absolute. Standing firm against the business-as-usual racist policies of men like Mississippi governor Ross Barnett, the Kennedys gradually won over the respect of the men in the trenches of the Civil Rights confrontations, men like Dr. Martin Luther King, Jr. While a national Civil Rights law was still to come, both Kennedys made it clear that the *old ways* were to change.

Whether or not the Soviets watched the unfolding of these crises with rapt interest, it was clear to Khrushchev that for now, Kennedy had his hands full with domestic issues. Foreign policy had taken a back seat, and no one in Washington had any reason to believe the Soviets intended to change that.

CHAPTER FIVE

Khrushchev

Wednesday, April 18, 1962
Petsamo, Georgia, by the Black Sea

He rarely had time anymore to visit his vacation home, but this week, he had made the exception. The struggles were ongoing in Moscow, the various programs supposed to better the lives of the Russian people rarely living up to his expectations. He kept that mostly to himself of course. It was, after all, his responsibility, supervising the noisy press releases filled with positive news and rosy predictions, mostly about agricultural production, his own specialty. His home was along the fringes of the great breadbasket of the Soviet Union, an area that had become another disappointment for its lack of fulfilling those lofty expectations. He knew the Americans had offered their own assistance, and during his visits to the United States, Khrushchev had befriended a successful Iowa farmer, Roswell Garst, a man eager to offer American know-how in the cultivation of various crops, especially corn. At first, Khrushchev welcomed the assistance, the better equipment, chemicals, farming techniques. The Russians embraced American breakthroughs in fertilizer, in rotating crops, all those things so utterly *American*. But it wasn't to be. Garst's corn seed proved not suitable to the cooler Russian climate, a problem made worse by resistance from those bureaucrats who supervised the agricultural collectives, who resisted changing their old ways. Khrushchev's own pride didn't help, and despite his affection for the plainspoken American farmer, in the end, Khrushchev had to put his energies behind Russian efforts, celebrating Russian accomplishments and Russian results, whether or not they compared favorably to their American counterparts. It was one more difficulty Khrushchev faced when dealing with uniquely Russian sensibilities, the need for homegrown solutions to vexing problems that never quite seemed to work. For the militants in the Kremlin, it was one more example of the Americans lording their supposed superiority, their superior systems which only inspired greater hostility, as though the Americans were constantly preaching just how grandly superior they were. It was infuriating, but Khrushchev felt a different frustration from many of those in his government. Somewhere, buried deeply in his conscience, he knew that when it came to agriculture, for increasing yields and a heartier brand of foodstuffs, the Americans were right. It was something he could never admit, even to himself.

The waters were calm, a chill in the air still, and he walked slowly along the hard-packed sand alongside his old friend, Rodion Malinovsky, Russia's defense minister. Malinovsky had a dacha of his own nearby, these morning walks something of a ritual when two busy men found time to take a breath. In a government where trust was a rare commodity, Khrushchev knew he could be completely open with his friend, the two with a long history, serving together in the Second World War, Malinovsky a genuine hero in holding off the German siege of Stalingrad. Then it was Stalin, who had suspicion enough for all, appointing Khrushchev to keep close to Malinovsky, testing his loyalty, even as Malinovsky was destroying German divisions. With

Stalin now long gone, Khrushchev was far more open to friendships, tested by years of working together to rescue the Soviet Union from Stalin's brutal abuses. To Khrushchev, it made much more sense to foster loyalty among those who served him in the government, encouraging loyalty through benevolence instead of terror, and inspiring a consensus of sorts as to policies, from agriculture to military. It wasn't always a simple matter. There were some in the Presidium who saw his actions in Berlin as somehow backing down to the Western allies, that the Soviets should have taken an even stronger stand to rid Berlin of Western military forces. Khrushchev mostly ignored the harping, knew that a compromise was always the smarter move, though he bristled at criticism of his wall. In his mind, he had won that battle, even if Western troops remained in Berlin.

Opinions on other policies still varied, but Khrushchev held a firm grip, and he understood that the loyalty of men like Malinovsky would only help to keep him in power.

Malinovsky was only a few years younger than Khrushchev, showed his age, gray hair and a square jaw, showed his experience through worn features, a grim face that rarely changed expression.

Khrushchev bent low, picked up a small round rock, spun it out into the soft waves.

"Nina is preparing a lunch. She said to invite you and your wife."

Malinovsky laughed, a rarity.

"Raisa is doing the same. I am to invite the two of *you*. Perhaps we may simply switch houses, and enjoy each other's repast. However, your wish is my command."

It was an unnecessary reminder of Khrushchev's absolute authority, Khrushchev wincing at his friend's constant awareness of who controlled who.

"We fool ourselves, Rodion, in believing that either of us are the authorities here. I for one have learned that when Nina summons me for anything, it is best just to obey."

Malinovsky stopped, stretched his back.

"A lesson well learned."

Malinovsky stared out across the open water, seemed lost in thought, and Khrushchev knew why. After a short moment, Malinovsky said, "They're watching us, even now. They have technicians by the dozen, plotting their courses, fine-tuning their aim on our targets. Every day it is worse. I have no doubt, there are those in high places in the American government who see this as their grand opportunity."

Khrushchev stared out as well, tried to lighten the man's mood.

"I doubt they can see us from so many miles away. And surely, the Americans understand that firing missiles at us, even from so close as Turkey, would just invite us to do the same to them. No one hopes for a great war, my friend. You and I have seen what wars can do. Not even the most passionate imperialist among the Americans is so blind."

Malinovsky looked at him now, still the grim expression.

"Are you so certain? Then explain to me why they must place their missiles so close to our borders, why they force us to stare down the barrels of their most dangerous weapons. And do not tell me we respond to them with the same strength. You and I both know they outpower us, outnumber us, their technology is better, their rocket engines are better, their warheads are more powerful . . ."

"Quiet, my friend. Even the surf has ears these days. The Americans might possess all these things, but they do not quite seem to understand just how superior they truly are. It is in our great interest to keep our inadequacies to ourselves. It is true they insist on preaching to us in the righteousness of their ways, as though they are so powerful they can dictate their will on all the world. But that only hides their insecurities. They have convinced themselves, at least to their public, that our weapons are just as numerous, and just as strong." He laughed. "I make sure I reinforce that notion in every speech. Our May Day celebration this year will be even more grandiose than ever, great parades of marching troops, escorting enormous missiles end to end, side by side."

"No matter if the warheads are filled with sawdust."

Khrushchev didn't want an argument, didn't want his friend's gloom to infect his joy at being in this place, his glorious seaside sanctuary.

"In time, Rodion. In time. Every day we are stronger, every day our scientists improve their thinking and their tools. And every day, I speak more loudly so the ears of the Americans will know it."

Malinovsky didn't move, still stared out across the open sea.

"Talk is all fine, Nikita. But there must be a more effective way to balance our concerns with theirs. There are too many among the military who believe the Americans are poised to make a first strike, that by having their missiles in Turkey, or Italy, they have an enormous advantage over us, no matter our bluster. Can we not do the same?"

"What do you mean?"

"We have a new ally, eager to become close to us, closer still."

"Castro?"

"He has enough bluster for all of us, claims to be the new light of Latin America, that under his leadership all of the Latins will one day be united against the brutal imperialism of the Americans."

Khrushchev laughed.

"Empty threats. He has a strong hold on his own country, and nothing else. Most of his neighbors fear him. Very few Latin countries seem ready to accept Communism, when their Big Brother America peers so closely over their shoulder. No, my friend, Fidel Castro is a master at the loud speech, passionate and verbose, furious emptiness. He has welcomed our friendship, and our financial assistance because he has nowhere else to turn. He fears the Americans far more than the glad-handed loyalty he offers us."

"But still . . . we have an opening, Nikita. Since the American disaster at the Bay of Pigs, there is constant talk that they will try again, that President Kennedy is intent on invading Cuba and removing Castro once and for all. Our spies are very clear on this. For his own reasons, Kennedy has a particular hatred for Castro, and will go to any extremes to eliminate such a threat of a Communist system so close to American shores."

Khrushchev was more serious now.

"Your spies tell you the truth, as confirmed by my own. Frankly, I am not too encouraged by Castro's great speeches of loyalty to us, when I know how quickly the Americans could simply wipe him away."

Malinovsky faced him now.

"We have sent military advisors, training experts, MiGs, other equipment to Cuba already. Castro keeps begging for more. Perhaps, Nikita, we should give him even more than he asks for. It is already proposed that we supply the Cubans with surface-to-air missiles, antiaircraft batteries, to help ward off an American invasion. Castro has insisted we send ground troops as well, to strengthen the Cuban army."

Khrushchev picked up another rock, launched it seaward.

"I have listened to his whining for some time. He does not seem to know how to ask politely for anything. He simply demands, and when that doesn't work, he resorts to begging. He believes that if Russian troops are on the ground, the Americans will hesitate to invade, knowing there would be Russian casualties. Forgive me, Rodion, but I believe him to be correct. Kennedy doesn't seem to be an American president who is carelessly pursuing a wider war."

"Nikita, it is a great game, a balancing act, if you will. There are American missiles across the Black Sea aimed at the heart of the

Soviet Union. We have virtually nothing in our arsenal to compare, few missiles that can easily find a target from thousands of miles away. It could be years before we can be confident of equality. But we do have a great number of medium- and short-range nuclear weapons. All we require is a launching pad as close to the American heartland as those missiles out there are to our own."

Khrushchev could feel Malinovsky's growing enthusiasm, contagious now.

"Cuba is that platform."

"Exactly. We should insist that Castro accept a curtain of nuclear missiles on his territory, as our gesture of security for his sovereignty. Call it our insurance policy. There is no possible way the Americans will invade Cuba if there is the real potential that we will launch a nuclear strike into their heartland. From Cuba, our missiles could reach most American cities, certainly in the eastern part of their country. Invading Cuba, only to risk losing New York or Washington?"

Khrushchev stroked his chin with a thick hand.

"Not even their most militant generals would consider such a trade. It is a brilliant idea, Rodion."

"Do you believe it will be difficult convincing Castro to accept such a plan?"

"He will accept and be grateful. The greatest challenge is secrecy, convincing him to keep his mouth shut until the missiles are in place."

"What do you mean?"

Khrushchev was surprised at the question.

"My friend, we cannot announce to the world that we intend to send a nuclear capability across a distant ocean to a foreign country, no matter how much an ally that country may be. The Americans would not simply stand by and watch. In fact, word of this plan would likely inspire them to launch their invasion more quickly, to preempt our gesture to Castro by eliminating Castro altogether. And, we would be excoriated by the United Nations, by every country in Latin America, not to mention America's allies in Western Europe. No, we must be careful, and apply the utmost discretion to every part of this plan."

"Yes, I understand. We must envelop every detail of this in an impenetrable fog."

Khrushchev felt energized, turned back toward his home.

"Let us enjoy a lunch, both houses if the wives insist. Then, we will return to Moscow, and begin discussions with those men whose job it will be to carry this out. The logistical planning must be absolute, and carefully thought out to the last detail. For now, Rodion, allow me to begin those discussions myself, with the Presidium. There will be doubts, of course, possibly even serious objections. I suppose it has to be that way. Men are allowed their opinions, until it is time for me to change them."

HE MOTIONED FOR Mikoyan to speak, the man now standing, obviously incensed.

"With all respect, Premier, this is madness. Do you expect the Americans will smile upon us, and welcome our intrusion, our violation of their precious Monroe Doctrine? It is one thing for a radical upstart like Castro to stake his claim on a small country, a country that is no real threat to the Americans. But sending our missiles across the Atlantic, anchoring them in a foreign land with no specific purpose other than to aim them at the cities of the United States . . . how can anyone assume the Americans will not react with outrage? *Military* outrage. Already there are American generals who see us as their primary threat and their primary target, who push their president to make the first strike, who advocate eliminating the Soviet Union *altogether*. Is this the course we would pursue, a duel of the great power of the atomic bombs, testing whether our scientists are correct, that a nuclear exchange will leave nothing behind, a world reduced to cinders? That is not the world I would leave for my grandchildren. Would you?"

The others kept silent, all eyes now on Khrushchev.

Anastas Mikoyan was his first deputy prime minister, a man Khrushchev admired as well as loved. Mikoyan's outburst was entirely expected; his focus seemed always on the most benign approach to any problem. But Khrushchev had not expected the passion in Mikoyan's words.

"Anastas, your concerns are noted. I am assured, and I assure you all that the military minds behind this plan have been most adamant that we can accomplish the placing of missiles on the island of Cuba in complete secrecy. Once the missiles are in place, the Americans will have to accept things as they are, or it is they who would start such a war. I do not believe Kennedy is such a man, and I believe the American people are as fearful of total destruction as our scientists. We are taking every precaution, ensuring utmost secrecy. Already, ships are being refitted to carry appropriate cargo, well disguised so that they resemble the same kinds of transports we have been using for some time. Along with the armaments, farm equipment and other essential hardware will continue to fill these ships, stirring no concern to any prying eyes, especially American eyes. Once our missiles are well established, once the bases are secure on Cuban soil, we shall announce to the world what we have done. Our reasons are simple and easily justified. Cuba is our ally. There is much talk that our ally is subject to yet another invasion from her greatest enemy, the Americans. We are only seeking bases there as a means of protection, of discouraging American aggression. I am confident, as you should all be, that by creating these missile bases on Cuban soil, the Cuban people will sleep far better knowing we are there to protect them. At the very least, that part of the world shall calm down, the threats that fly out of Miami and elsewhere will grow silent. We shall all benefit."

He scanned the room, most of the others already in line with his thinking. He focused now on Gromyko, his foreign minister. He knew Gromyko was very familiar with American behavior and attitudes, and he hoped that there would be little argument. Gromyko stirred in his seat, his eyes downward. After a silent moment, Khrushchev said, "You have something to say, Andrei?"

Gromyko looked at him now, spoke slowly.

"Castro has approved this plan? The last time I spoke with him, he was concerned that our friendship was a bit too one-sided, that we might demand more of him than he could provide. Now we are asking him to open up his countryside to our nuclear missiles."

Khrushchev knew he had to tread lightly, that Gromyko was among his most valuable allies in the Presidium.

"We have been negotiating . . . no, that is not the correct word. We have succeeded in *persuading* Castro that we are offering him the opportunity to demonstrate his own power to the rest of the world. He required little persuasion. After all, he will now achieve by our hand the one thing he crows about so loudly. He will be powerful. Perhaps, even invincible."

"Premier, I must add . . . I too am concerned with how the Americans will respond."

Around the room there were sniffs of disapproval, the more militant of his ministers with a show of disrespect for the caution of Mikoyan and Gromyko. To one side sat Marshal Dimitri Kochov, resplendent in his uniform, bedecked with medals and decorations he never failed to wear to the committee meetings. Kochov was an aggressive man, his long career in the army gaining him Khrushchev's respect, and occasionally, concerns that Kochov's ambitions might become too uncomfortable for Khrushchev to tolerate. Kochov announced himself with a loud clearing of his throat.

"The Americans have shown only weakness and indecisiveness. Their Bay of Pigs demonstrated to the world, and certainly to their own president, that they are not equipped to stand tall on the world stage. They are weak-willed. Once our missiles are in place, they will accept our move as an unfortunate necessity, an important move so that the threats to world peace are well balanced. That is, after all, what they preach about."

Mikoyan spoke again, not cowed by Kochov's scolding.

"And if we are wrong? If the Americans react with a military strike against our bases in Cuba? We will respond of course. And they will again. That is how wars begin, and this is not a war I would expect we would win. No one would win."

Khrushchev was wearying of the arguments.

"That is precisely why this will work to our advantage. Kennedy does not want to escalate a conflict into a war, a world war. He will accept our bases because he must. As we have accepted his bases in Turkey. Yes, it is a balance, and one we are entitled to achieve."

ON JUNE 10, 1962, Khrushchev gave the final order. With Russian and other leased ships preparing for the transatlantic crossing, blending in with the steady flow of supply ships already en route to Cuba, weaponry of all kinds, conventional and nuclear, were prepared for the trip. Along with the equipment for bases and launching sites, Russian troops were summoned, filling other transports with thousands of men who would either service or guard the missiles, or serve simply as ground troops, working alongside their Cuban allies in the event the Americans made good on their continuous threats to invade the island.

As the first flotilla of ships sailed through the Mediterranean

Sea, American observers flying overhead made their usual reconnaissance passes, noting only that the ships seemed likely to be carrying conventional military stores, along with other kinds of more humanitarian aid. It raised no unusual concern.

In Moscow, the operation took on a new name, *Anadyr*, named for a town on the eastern tip of Siberia. As though these ships were destined only to service Russian bases in that part of the world, the camouflage even included shipments of cold weather gear, down to fur hats and gloves. For the curious troops on board the ships, who had picked up hints that they were heading to warmer climates, the cargo seemed only to symbolize the ineptitude of Russian supply officers. No one among the troops could suppose just what Operation Anadyr truly involved, and what kind of cargo filled those ships where troops were not allowed.

CHAPTER SIX

RFK

Sunday, August 26, 1962
Hickory Hill, near McLean, Virginia

He bent low, his racket dangling from one hand. From the other side of the net, he heard her call out.

"You can't be that tired. I've only won two sets."

He forced himself upright, fought the heavy breathing, slapped the racket face against one hand.

"I'm letting you win. I feel generous today."

She laughed, both hands on her hips, one holding her racket.

"That nonsense again? Get back there and serve."

He reluctantly obeyed, backed to the end line, bounced a tennis ball on the hard surface, held it for a brief moment. He tossed it skyward, his racket making a perfect strike, the ball barely skimming the net, launched to her weak side. But she was there, the backhand perfect, the return sent whizzing past him, another point for her.

"I quit. You're on your game today. It's bad enough that you beat me every damn time, but a wipeout is unseemly. I am after all, a big wheel. What would the reporters say?"

She shrugged, laughed again.

"They'd say your wife is a better tennis player than her husband. Hardly breaking news."

He wouldn't give in, said to himself, they'd be right. But dammit all, I'll get her yet. He lofted a ball, a gentle slap with his racket, the tennis ball bouncing slowly toward the net. She still smiled, but it wasn't gloating. She'd never do that, rub it into his pride that Ethel Kennedy was a better athlete than her husband. It was the game they played, the exercise he craved, balanced against her better game, the score almost always lopsided. They walked together toward the edge of the court, and he said, "I need McNamara to show up. He's supposed to be here later, with his son. At least I can beat *him* once in a while."

She said nothing, focused her attention now on the calls of the children. There were a great many children, the estate a playground for their own seven, plus any of their friends or neighbors who happened by. It was tradition, that Hickory Hill was a place of laughter, joy, a sanctuary where Bobby could escape. The children only added to the fun, games galore, a movie theater, every kind of oversized toy imaginable. He relished the sounds, the squeals and sharp screams from the young girls, grand chases and games of tag, hide-and-seek, or any other adventures that came from the minds of so many children. There would be touch football as well, the adults usually easing their children aside, their competition taking over, just as it infected him in every tennis match. He had been grateful to find that the secretary of defense, Robert McNamara, enjoyed tennis as much as he did, their morning games a ritual both men seemed to require before charging off into their respective Washington offices. If McNamara wasn't available, Ethel took up the challenge, which usually resulted in a minor bruising of Bobby's ego. But still he enjoyed it, even the whippings. It was all a part of her life as the wife of an important man and the mother of his seven children.

Whether or not there would be more was quite clearly up to her, no one among their friends doubting that the Kennedys were destined for as many children as Ethel desired, that part of her life so separate from her husband's. All that would be required is an expansion to the grand home, plans already being drawn, Ethel's latest project, occupying her time while Bobby tended to the whirlwind of tensions around the Justice Department, and the president.

Jack would attend these festivities occasionally, as time allowed, though his wife, Jackie, was less inclined to be swallowed up by the frantic activity of so many children. She had two of her own, but had suffered through a miscarriage, and the birth of a stillborn infant, tragedies that seemed to yank much of the joy away from the president's marriage. Bobby was sensitive to that, would invite Jack to any gathering he thought his brother might enjoy, knowing full well the president had the most convenient excuse should he and his wife decide to keep to their own lives. He was, after all, one of the busiest men on the planet.

They walked together, Ethel focused more on the children now, separating from him, easing that way, welcoming other guests, parents just arriving, yet more children. Bobby looked toward the grand mansion, saw one of his aides at the door, no smile, knew there was some kind of issue he should attend to. It was all too common that, even on a Sunday, there was little time off, that no matter the festivities around his estate, the office was always there.

He moved closer, said to the young man, "Someone on the phone?"

"The president, sir. He chose not to wait, asked if you would be able to come to the White House at your earliest convenience."

"Did he say why?"

"No, sir."

Bobby took the notepad, glanced at the words, thought, my earliest convenience means *his* earliest convenience.

Bobby hadn't changed, still wore his tennis shorts and shoes, his dress ignored by his brother.

"Sorry to pull you away. I'm just getting so damn tired of hearing the harebrained plots by the CIA, not one of them resulting in anything useful, and every damn idea risks the chance that some damn reporter will catch wind and print the story, making us all look like complete morons."

Bobby stood, his usual posture.

"Which story is that?"

"Operation Mongoose."

"I thought that was mostly put to bed, that there was no real chance anything was going to work effectively."

"I've kept those people on the hook, Lansdale in particular, hoping somebody will figure out a way we can get Castro to disappear without bloodying our hands. Forgive me, poor choice of words."

Edward Lansdale had been recruited from the CIA to be the point man for Operation Mongoose, the all-out effort to remove Castro from power in Cuba by any means necessary. Lansdale carried the reputation of a spy's spy, a ruthless and efficient man who could manage any sized effort with the subtlety required. But the plans that emerged from his team had varied from the useless to the outright ridiculous, ranging from shore party raids on Cuban installations, to attempts to poison Castro with everything from lethal cigars to his favorite breakfast. The CIA's plots had begun back in the Eisenhower years, word passing on to Kennedy that the CIA had even recruited the Mafia, presuming them to have the more clever brand of hitmen, as the best way to get the job done. So far, none of the plans had offered any hint of success. Bobby agreed with his brother that clumsiness in any assassination attempt smelled too much like the Bay of Pigs fiasco and would only make the president seem, once again, utterly foolish.

"So, Lansdale coming up with more poison fountain pens? I especially liked the exploding seashell idea. All they had to do was get Castro to pick up the right one and hold it to his ear."

The president didn't smile, obviously in no mood for annoying memories.

"The CIA is following events in Cuba closely, mostly from their Miami base. They've got a few boots on the ground in Cuba and a radio link that stays pretty hot. We've known about Soviet ships unloading all manner of material there, tractors, trucks, that sort of thing. We also knew that military equipment was coming in, artillery, and those damn ground-to-air missiles. But that info is not very reliable. The reports the CIA is receiving are being offered by people with no real training in identifying weaponry. They tend to dramatize every sighting, and the CIA suspects that some of the reports are intended to alarm us so much, we'll go ahead and invade the island, which is of course, what those people want us to do. So far, most of what the CIA is picking up in Miami seems to fall into that trap. Best we can tell, it's mostly useless, since the U-2 flights have identified most of the obvious, artillery and the surface-to-air missiles. But to some Cuban working down there for the CIA, if he thinks he's got a scoop, he'll embellish it." He stood, moved slowly toward the window, obviously testing his back. "The Cubans are, whether we like it or not, Russian allies. The U-2 photos have indicated there are MiG fighters being delivered as well, so we assume the Russians are sending training personnel, pilots, and so forth. Castro has succeeded in buddying up to Khrushchev completely, and the Russians are only too happy to oblige him."

"I just can't help thinking there is more going on here. Why would the Russians send so much of their equipment so damn far away, out from their direct control. To what purpose?"

"Because they can. And, I'm pretty certain Castro has asked for the weapons, whether the Russians are still controlling them or not. Why wouldn't he? That's why I spoke again to Lansdale. Castro is well entrenched now, and he's starting to look beyond his own borders. It's a dangerous ambition, that he might think he can throw his weight around into other countries in Latin America. And, we can no longer assume the Cuban people are just waiting for any excuse to rise up and kick Castro off his island. That part of the planning from the CIA's point of view was hogwash. It's no different from the Bay of Pigs, when we assumed a million Cubans would welcome our invasion with open arms. Those *arms* are even less open now, since that whole damn place is about to be thorny with Russians. Those idiot congressmen are still shooting their mouths off, from Keating to Goldwater to Strom Thurmond, all calling for us to march down there with the 82nd Airborne Division and just take over. They're saying I'm weak for allowing the Russians to stockpile Cuba with antiaircraft guns and infantrymen. And that damn Keating . . . he says he has reliable information that the weapons being set up down there are for offense, aimed at attacking us. I'd love to know where the hell he's getting that kind of intel, unless he's listening to the CIA morons in Miami. He's using every opportunity to make me look weak, claiming I'm too hesitant to stop what the Russians are doing."

"I know, Jack. I've heard his bellowing. It's just politics."

"You and I know that. But how many voters are listening to him and thinking, gee, our president should be doing something about this. Well, just how the hell am I supposed to stop it? The answer is, I don't. And, if we try to invade now, we'll have a real war on our hands. Not even Ken Keating wants that. But Khrushchev isn't about to sit by peacefully if we start killing Russian soldiers down there, accidentally or not." Kennedy stretched, twisted his back, a show of obvious pain. "And, by the way, I've got the CIA and the Joint Chiefs both telling me that we had better protect Vietnam, that Khrushchev will likely do the same thing there, turning the place into an armed camp, just to piss us off. No, that's not right. They're doing it to spread Communism wherever they can. I'm told we need to send some people to Saigon, commit more troops than the advisors Ike already sent in there. You mark my words . . . I order that, and it will make all kinds of glorious headlines, the kind even Keating would approve of, how we're protecting the world from the Red Menace. Our troops will march in, the bands will play, the Vietnamese crowds will cheer, and then, in a week's time, they'll insist it's not enough, that we need to send in more. It's like taking a shot of booze. The effect wears off, and so you need another one." He paused, took a long breath. "And where after that? What kind of resources does Khrushchev have where he can insert his people into any place he feels like? We have no choice but to call his bluffs, or match his moves, like a damn chess game. Cuba's one pawn, North Vietnam's another. What's next, Egypt? Venezuela?"

Bobby crossed his arms, began to pace slowly.

"Is that it? You feel better?"

"You mean, did I pull you away from your pleasant barbecue to shoot off my mouth? Well, yeah, maybe." Kennedy scanned Bobby now, as though for the first time. "Why the hell didn't you change clothes?"

"Disguise. Any reporter sees me show up at the White House on a weekend in a suit, they'll ask questions. I'm just here to talk you into joining me for a tennis match."

"Very funny. My back hasn't let me play as much as marbles since my last operation. Reporters aren't that stupid. Let's change the subject." Kennedy sat again, easing slowly into the soft chair. "What do you hear from Martin Luther King?"

Bobby was grateful for the reprieve, knew he could at least offer his brother some news that might border on the positive.

"You mean the Meredith thing. Well, as you know, James Meredith has already applied twice to the University of Mississippi and been summarily turned down. The courts have had enough of that foolishness with a state-run college, so they've ordered him enrolled. Governor Barnett is standing firm, and is making it clear behind the scenes that the only way he'll allow a Black man into Ole Miss without bloodshed is if we show up down there with a thousand National Guardsmen and a hundred FBI agents with guns drawn, so he can save face by backing down at the point of a gun."

The president leaned back in his chair, a brief wince of pain.

"All because one Black man wants to go to college. Well, you may have to oblige that jackass Barnett by sending down troops. But Jesus, I sure as hell don't want an army of occupation anywhere in the South. This is so damn ridiculous. Why can't those people just accept that this is the way things are going to be. The courts have said it, I've said it, and most of the country agrees. We've had enough busted heads down there as it is. How many men have to die for this cause? Someone should remind those people that they lost the Civil War, for Chrissakes."

"Well, see how it goes next month. I'm preparing to send a good-sized force down there to protect Meredith. I'll say this. He's a brave son of a bitch."

Monday, September 3, 1962
Washington, DC

"He's waiting for you, down on the corner, sir."

Bobby pushed aside a sheaf of papers, said, "Right now? He says it's urgent?"

"He said *important*."

"Well, if a Russian spy has something important to say, I better hear it. Keep the fires burning."

Bobby moved out from behind the desk, past his aide, ran a hand quickly over the tiger's head. He hustled quickly through the offices, out into the corridor, down the stairways at a rapid jaunt, various staff moving aside, accustomed to seeing their boss in a hurry. He reached the ground floor, bright sunlight through tall windows, moved outside, focused. He saw Bolshakov, pacing slowly, the short round man seeming more agitated than usual. Bolshakov saw him now, stopped moving, seemed to force a smile.

"Ah, greetings. Sorry to interrupt your busy day. But *busy* is a word that applies to all of us these days, eh?"

Bobby moved close, a quick glance around, no one within earshot.

"Let's walk. Why the meeting?"

Bolshakov obeyed, the two men moving slowly away from the Justice Department building. After a dozen steps, Bolshakov said, "My superior wishes to meet with you directly, at a time convenient for you. Perhaps tomorrow morning."

"Which superior?"

"Ambassador Dobrynin, of course."

"At *my* convenience . . . as long as it's first thing in the morning?"

"Perceptive of you, sir. The ambassador has some issues he feels he should address with the man who is so close to the president. Important issues."

"Where?"

"He will be delighted to visit you in your office. There is no need for any discretion. The ambassador is a public figure, and he often is seen in public places. If that is acceptable to you, of course."

Bobby felt a twinge in his gut, could feel Bolshakov's tension, much more not being said.

"I am happy to invite Ambassador Dobrynin to my office. Tomorrow morning at nine."

"Most accommodating of you, sir. The ambassador will be delighted."

ANATOLY DOBRYNIN HAD become the Soviet ambassador only the January before, the second in the series of younger men sent West after the parade of sour grumps who had served under Stalin. Like his predecessor, Mikhail Menshikov, Dobrynin was a pleasant, smiling man, with an eager handshake. Unlike Menshikov though, Dobrynin was openly sociable, could more easily relate to Western culture and the Western ways of negotiation. If Khrushchev had seemed to President Kennedy to be forceful and aggressive, his ambassador was anything but, the perfect behavior of a key diplomat who straddled the line between two powers whose natural attitude toward each other was testy at best.

Dobrynin was only a few years older than Bobby, prematurely silver-haired in his early forties. Representing as he did a nation that seemed to prize secrecy above all else, Dobrynin gave the impression of surprising openness. From the time of his appointment eight months before, Dobrynin had been received warmly by both Kennedys with optimism that should any real crisis develop, Dobrynin would be an effective pipeline to the Soviet hierarchy, eager to defuse any serious argument.

Bobby stood, moved out from his desk, his hand extended. Dobrynin, always a smile, took his hand, a sturdy shake, then a slight bow.

"I am honored to be in your private office, Mr. Attorney General."

"You're always welcome here." He gestured toward the heavy leather chair. "Have a seat."

Dobrynin sat, appraised his surroundings, his eyes settling on the stuffed tiger.

"I have heard of this, yes. Magnificent. I have hunted the tiger in the east, the great wilderness near our border with China. They are too few in number anymore, unlike the glorious hunting expeditions of long ago. I understand this was a gift to you from Mr. Ernest Hemingway. How very fortunate for you."

Bobby absorbed the man's good cheer, thought, what else do you know about me?

"Yes, Mr. Hemingway was quite generous to my family."

There was silence now, Dobrynin feigning interest in every item on the walls. Bobby allowed him his moment, then said, "So, Mr. Ambassador, this meeting was at your request?"

Dobrynin focused on Bobby now, the smile fading.

"You have ambitious men in your Congress. Such a thing is not so well regarded in my country. In the Supreme Soviet, outspoken men are regarded with suspicion. Here, you seem to celebrate them."

"Who are we talking about?"

"Your Senator Keating for one. He has been most vocal about the dangerous threat you are perceiving from the intentions of the Cuban people, especially of course, Mr. Castro. Senator Keating is most belligerent toward us, as he is toward Mr. Castro. I'm not sure I understand why."

Bobby lowered his head, his chin resting on one hand.

"Allow me to be frank. Ken Keating is a gasbag. He is taking aim at the president's policies every chance he gets, since, as you know, we are facing midterm congressional elections this November. He preaches aggression because he believes the American people prefer strength, at any price. If he appears strong, his hopes are that the president will appear weak. Cuba is only Keating's latest pretext.

However . . ." He paused, saw Dobrynin lean forward an inch, no smile now, a clue to the real meaning of this meeting. "The president and the American people are becoming seriously concerned by the level of materiel you are supplying to the Cuban people."

Dobrynin smiled again, sat back.

"Precisely why I am here. Premier Khrushchev is deeply concerned about the volume of noise emerging from your government, particularly your Congress, about our alliance with the government of Cuba. I am here to assure you, on behalf of Premier Khrushchev, that this alliance is a peaceful one, mutually beneficial between our people and the Cubans. As an example, we are purchasing most of the Cuban sugar crop, a crop that once was purchased by you. You must admit, there has been considerable speculation, warranted, that your government has considered an invasion of the island nation. Such a move would be dangerous, and would violate the relationship that the Soviet people now have with the Cubans. We are in the process of supplying the Cubans with the means to better defend themselves, should such an attack occur. I do not believe President Kennedy wants a war, certainly not with the Soviet Union. To attack a sovereign country, on any pretext, is a violation of the United Nations Charter, and would invite serious condemnation from around the globe. It is in our interest to strengthen the defenses of Cuba, as our ally."

Bobby sat back, loosened his tie, didn't feel the need to be so formal with this man.

"Now that you mention it, Mr. Ambassador, Senator Keating seems to have information that the Soviet Union is planning on a great deal more than defensive weapons. We take such talk to be the stuff of aggressive campaigning. Nonetheless, the president does believe Senator Keating must have some grounds for his claims, that you are intending to locate offensive weapons, possibly ground-to-ground missiles in Cuba."

Dobrynin laughed now.

"You said it yourself. It is the talk of politics, mindless chatter to influence the most mindless of voters. I assure you once more, Mr. Attorney General, the only missile systems being installed in Cuba are ground-to-air, antiaircraft batteries. They are short-ranged, with no capacity to do harm to the United States. The MiG jets, which you certainly have noticed, are being offered to the Cuban air force to supplement their outdated planes. We will train their pilots, again, for defensive purposes. There are no offensive weapons being placed in Cuba, and the military supplies you have observed in transport are of no significance to you. Please convey that message to your president."

He tried to read Dobrynin, the smile again, an effective wall to whatever the man might truly be thinking. After a short moment, Bobby said, "I appreciate the tone and the substance of your message. I shall relate this to the president. And I assure you, if everything you say is true, neither of our governments has any reason to fear the other."

Tuesday, September 11, 1962
The White House, Cabinet Room

The talking was hushed, low conversations in small groups. The president appeared now, Bobby waiting to one side, away from the others. Jack sat in his usual chair at the center of the table, said, "All right. Opinions. The Soviets are going out of their way to assure us that we're under no threat, that everything going on in Cuba has to do with their new friendship with Castro, that they're just beefing up his military. I suppose that's an effective way for them to make friends."

Bobby moved slowly to one corner, behind some of the others, kept to his feet. Jack looked at him now, said, "So, do you trust Dobrynin?"

Bobby kept his arms crossed, said, "He's the Soviet ambassador to the United States. Aren't we supposed to trust him? If he's lying to us, he isn't much use as a go-between. Surely, he would know that as well."

In front of Bobby, Dean Rusk spoke up.

"I agree. I've dealt with him plenty, and he seems like a straight shooter. I would caution, however, that just because he's their ambassador, doesn't mean they're telling him everything they're doing. Sometimes, it's better to leave some of your own people in the dark. Fewer loose ends to worry about."

Kennedy said, "You wouldn't think they'd turn Dobrynin loose here and not keep him informed. If I was Dobrynin, I'd be pretty offended by that lack of trust."

McNamara sat beside Rusk, shuffled some papers in front of him, said, "Trust is not a common thread through the Soviet hierarchy. We can't assume that every communiqué we receive has the stamp of approval of every member of their Presidium, or their ambassadors in the field. This is Khrushchev's show, and he'll run it as he pleases. They don't do things like we do here."

There was low laughter at the joke, the president pretending to ignore McNamara's remark. He glanced at Bobby again, then around the table, said, "All we know of what the Soviets have done in Cuba is what we've been able to discern from the U-2 photographs. We know there is a pretty hefty ring of surface-to-air missiles, with support bases and personnel attached, and Khrushchev hasn't denied that. As Khrushchev has strained himself to convince us, those are no threat to us, unless we challenge them to a duel. I'm not inclined to do that. But Senator

Keating, and a few other loudmouths around here keep insisting that the danger is real, that the Russians are planning an offensive base in Cuba, something that I'm being told ought to scare the bejeezus out of us. I want to maintain a high level of reconnaissance over Cuba, keep those U-2s flying as often as possible. It's risky, since we don't know if the Soviets will attempt to shoot one down. I don't want to go through what Ike had to deal with, that whole Gary Powers mess."

Aides moved in and out, and now a new face entered, McGeorge Bundy, the president's national security advisor. There were brief greetings, Bundy handing the president a sealed envelope.

"Excuse me, Jack. You need to see this. We've been discussing this in my office, and there's consensus something needs to be done quickly."

Kennedy tore through the envelope, read briefly, said, "Holy mother of God."

He slid the paper toward McNamara, said, "Unbelievable. In case you all thought we could trust our allies to use brains, we've received word that the Communist Chinese have shot down a Taiwanese U-2 over the Chinese mainland."

Bobby looked at his brother, saw the rising fury, said, "I have to ask . . . whose idea was it to give the damned Taiwanese their own U-2s?"

Bundy spoke now, the room deathly silent.

"It was Ike's people, specifically Allen Dulles. The CIA thought it was a good idea to spread the wealth, so to speak. We trained their pilots to stay out of trouble, not anticipating that the Chinese could do what the damned Russians did, that they would have their own antiaircraft missiles, nor that they would know how to use them."

Kennedy read from the document, said, "No real details. We don't know how high the guy was flying, just what he was doing."

Bobby said, "Does it matter? This is another wonderful propaganda tool for the Chinese to use against us. It won't take Khrushchev long to jump on that train."

Kennedy sat with his hands folded, stared down at the paper.

"Where's McCone? This is on his watch."

John McCone was Allen Dulles's successor in charge of the CIA. Dulles had been the logical scapegoat after the Bay of Pigs fiasco and was long gone. McCone was an able successor, a man interested less in politics than his predecessor had been, and a man both Kennedys felt comfortable with in his role.

McNamara spoke now.

"McCone's away, Jack. You recall, he got married. He's on his honeymoon somewhere in France, won't be back until early October."

The president sat upright now, more fury.

"He's sixty damned years old. What the hell does he need with a honeymoon?"

Heads were bowed around the table, no one sure if that was in jest or not. Bundy said, "He's been sending in notes regularly. More or less. He's been pushing to make sure we're up to speed on the reconnaissance over Cuba. So, he's not completely, um . . . out of touch."

The president picked up the document.

"He sure as hell needs to know about this, and fast." He paused, and Bobby could see he was pondering his words. "We can't allow ourselves to be trapped by another idiotic provocation. If the Chinese can shoot down a U-2, you can bet the Soviets are aiming their SAMs as we speak. What artillery officer wouldn't want *that* feather in his cap. We can't let that happen." He looked at Bundy now. "What do you suggest about Cuba?"

Bundy sat, leaned both arms on the table.

"We can't afford to be clumsy about this. We can't give the Russians any reason to shoot down one of our planes over Cuba, just because they can. The Chinese are probably rubbing this in their faces, *Hey Comrade, look what we can do*. Khrushchev will try to one-up them, most likely, and we'll pay that price. Not to mention our loss of prestige worldwide, that we're far more vulnerable than we pretend to be."

Kennedy looked up at Bobby, then at the others.

"Right. Okay, I'm suspending all U-2 flights over Cuba until this blows over. Prestige is one thing, but we can't risk the loss of yet another plane, and those U-2s are the best recon tool we have."

Rusk spoke up now, seemed to weigh his words with his usual deliberate care.

"We can continue the flights, just not over Cuban airspace. How about we ring the island, just beyond the Cuban coast, keep the men flying so they can make their observations from an angle. Perhaps they can dip in and out as necessary, if there's a specific target we need to photograph. That should at least keep the Soviet missile fellows off guard."

Bobby was surprised, had little regard for Rusk beyond his perfunctory role as secretary of state. The president looked at Rusk, then at the others.

"So be it. Tell those pilots to do the best they can. Hopefully, they can still give us up-to-date information that will be worth something. If the damned Soviets are loading Cuba up with weapons we don't know about . . . well, this is a hell of a piece of bad timing for us."

Rusk said, "I suggest we keep in close touch with Dobrynin, try to discern any change in their official assurances. They have radar posts all over Cuba. Surely they'll figure out that we don't have the same eyes in the sky keeping watch on them."

Bobby looked at his brother, said, "I guess this means that, for now anyway, we'll have to believe everything the Russians tell us. I find no comfort in that."

CHAPTER SEVEN

Russo

Wednesday, September 12, 1962
Tallahassee, Florida

He had taught an early class, was home by three, in time to greet the school bus. The walk up his driveway was short, but he didn't mind escorting the two of them, the thirteen-year-old, Danny reacting with pure embarrassment that his father felt the need to lead him up the drive. His daughter, Becky, was a different story, bright blue eyes, always a smile, happy to see her daddy. For a second grader, she was unusually bright and gave her father the kind of pride he embraced with a combination of love and fear. The fear was there always, every day when they left the house, that today would be the horrible day, that something bad would happen to one of them. It was ridiculous and irrational, and he kept it to himself, knew his wife thought he was a lunatic for harboring such morbid fear for the safety of his children. But meeting the bus was a help, if only temporary, removing them from one kind of caretaker, the schools, to the more loving caretaker at home.

He glanced back toward the house, the driveway empty but

for his own car, his wife, Margaret, still at work. She was a social worker, a benign job description that hid the most urgent kind of duty, the need to help those whose lives were truly in need, the disabled, or those families on the outskirts of town whose jobs, if there were any, didn't provide. She wouldn't be home until after five, and again, he felt the fear. Her job took her out into the countryside, low hills and piney woods, to the rough shacks and clapboard houses where her clients lived. He feared for her safety every day, and she knew of his anxiety, laughed about it, tried to disarm him, convincing him that those people, no matter how poor or desperate for life's basic needs, weren't really a threat. He never quite believed her.

From the bus, Danny came out first, always, no chivalry in the thirteen-year-old, bounding down ahead of his sister. She made her way down carefully, a slow step at a time, the bus driver offering a short wave to Russo as he waited. What's that fellow really about, he thought. Bus drivers can't make all that much money. Maybe he just loves children. I just hope like hell he drives with some sanity.

"*Daddy.*"

She ran up to him, a brief hug, but the teenager kept his distance, rules of masculinity, aware of the eyes watching him from the bus.

"Hi, Pop."

"Okay, you two, into the house. Lots of homework?"

Becky held up her pink notebook, said, "Just one lesson."

He looked toward Danny, was surprised to see the boy looking away, toward the house.

"Hey, Pop. Do you have to have that thing on the car?"

Russo followed his look, saw the bumper sticker: *Kennedy for President.*

"Why? He won, you know."

"Yeah, well, I just don't like it."

This was something new, and Russo led them to the house, held the door, both children now inside.

"What's up, Dan-o?"

"I mean . . . people make fun, you know?"

"What kind of fun? What are you talking about?"

Danny stared down, obvious reluctance.

"A few of the boys . . . older guys. Some in my class. They say that anybody who voted for Kennedy is a . . . I can't say it. You told me never to use that word. They say you love the Negroes. Only they're a lot meaner about how they say it. They know that Mom's job . . . that she helps the Negroes with food and stuff. They talk about that too, like she should stay home, spend her time right here."

Russo let out a breath, watched as Becky disappeared into her room.

"Listen, Dan-o. You can't avoid stupid, and that's what you're hearing. Kennedy is a good man, and so far, I think he's a really good president. Negroes have had it rough for a long time, and he's doing something to straighten that out. No matter what anyone says to you, we're in the right. Just ignore it."

He knew it was dumb advice, that no thirteen-year-old could ignore anything tossed at him in school.

"I'm kinda worried about Halloween."

"Good lord, why?"

"Some of the boys say they might teach us a lesson, do something to the house. Unless you get rid of that bumper sticker."

He was angry now, tried to hold it down.

"Ignore that. I'll keep a sharp eye out on Halloween. That's a month away. They'll forget all about it in time. Just try not to pay attention to them. Maybe I should have a talk with some of the parents."

Danny seemed to flinch.

"Please don't do that, Pop."

Russo nodded, accepted a small defeat.

"No, that's where your friends are learning that stuff. I'd just make it worse."

"They say they don't like the Black people because they're Communists."

"*What?*"

"Martin Luther King . . . they say he's a Russian at heart. Trying to overthrow our country. The Communists are behind him."

"Oh, good God." He fought for the right words. "They're ignorant, Dan-o. That's all. They don't understand what this country is going through, so they blame everything on the Communists. It was the same when I was younger. People said the government was packed full of Communists, that we were fighting a red menace that was going to bring us down. It hasn't happened yet. All the Negroes want is to be able to enjoy the same basic things we take for granted, like sitting at a lunch counter or going to the movies. Why shouldn't a Black man drink out of the same water fountain as you and me or use the same door into the grocery store? It's pure silliness. No, that's not right. It's more than silly. It's dangerous. It's making those people angrier every day. Black people have the same rights we do. But there're just some people who live in the past, like they wish slavery was still here, keep the Negroes in their place, second-class citizens. It's awful, and stupid. Just try to ignore it."

The boy nodded, still not believing. A new thought seemed to jump in, and Danny said, "Did I tell you about my scout meeting? Monday, you know, Jimmy Hanks? He writes up the column that goes into the newspaper, all sorts of news what's going on with the scout troops around town. He wrote up something he got from the Black troops, and the scoutmaster told him to get rid of that. Said the paper wouldn't print it. That don't seem right to me, Pop."

"No. It's not. Jesus." He thought of the scoutmaster, an enormously fat man named Earle. *Idiot*. He searched himself for answers, something that the boy could take to heart. "Keep in mind, there're a lot of good people who don't believe what those ignorant boys are feeding you. Over at the college, good people, who know better. It's not just the junk you're hearing at school. Remember that. And no matter what anybody says, that Kennedy bumper sticker is staying put."

THE TV WAS turned off, and he stared at the blank screen, thought, Does CBS News ever have something good to say? At the far end of the table, Margaret said, "Well, what did you think?"

"About what?"

"The TV dinners. Honestly, where's your head?"

"Oh, they were okay. The Salisbury steak was pretty good."

To one side, Danny said, "I like the applesauce."

Margaret stood, moved around the table, scooping up the aluminum trays.

"See how easy? You just chuck all this in the trash. No dishes to wash. Makes my life a whole lot easier after working all day."

Danny spoke up again.

"Can we try the fried chicken next?"

"Tomorrow night. I bought a dozen. They're less than a dollar each, and you just toss 'em in the oven, and, in a few minutes, dinner is served."

Russo scanned the aluminum dish as she pulled it away, said, "Modern technology. Amazing."

Danny said, "Hey, Pop. Can I stay up to nine thirty? *The Beverly Hillbillies* is coming on tonight."

Russo braced himself for the inevitable argument. Across the table, Becky said, "Hey, what about me? I wanna stay up too."

Margaret came to the rescue.

"Nobody stays up tonight. School tomorrow. It's Wednesday, for Pete's sake."

The groans were entirely expected, and he smiled at her, then said to both, "Your mother rules the house. Besides, it's classroom night. My students will be here at eight."

Danny said, "Can I stay up for that? They just tell stories."

"It's called Creative Writing, and it's harder than it looks. They're reading stories they've written themselves. It's still school, even right here."

As she rose from her chair, Becky said, "Daddy, why do you have school at home?"

"Well, I could use a real classroom, but then I'd have to go back over to the college. The kids seem to like coming here. And besides, your mother serves them great snacks."

Another groan, and Margaret said, "Okay, one cookie for each of you. Then bed. But do your homework first. *The Beverly Hillbillies* can wait."

HE LAY IN bed beside her, stared at the ceiling. It had been another good class, twenty of the brightest and most creative students he had taught. Their stories had been all over the map, from the romantic to the bizarre, each story beginning with the phrase he had assigned them: *He came around the corner and saw three of them down by the river.* The students took it from there, and the results were as varied as the kids themselves.

"Thanks for being the good hostess."

She rolled toward him, said, "They appreciate it. It's fun. You'd think college students never get a treat or a decent cup of coffee."

He laughed. "They're privileged. Coming to the prof's home is a treat all by itself. It's like a night off from prison."

"I doubt that. College was never like a prison, for either one of us."

He was serious now.

"I'm not sure about that. Outside those gates, there's a town here with a lot of ugly. The students are insulated from it all, as long as they stay on campus. They call it *town versus gown*. Just listen to your son. He's being told Kennedy and the Negroes are Communists. I hear it myself. The Russians are everywhere, spies and infiltrators, mostly in the government. I know for certain we have neighbors, right across the street, who think we're teaching those college students nothing but Communist propaganda. It's a little scary. How do you fight raw ignorance? How do we protect Danny from being bullied about that stuff at school?"

She didn't respond, and he felt guilty now.

"Sorry. I preach too much. Let's go to sleep."

She faced him now.

"You won't sleep. You worry about too many things. Your children are doing just fine. They'll learn to think for themselves, to know what right from what's plain stupid. Have faith."

"It's hard to have faith, when you're surrounded by stupidity."

HE HAD SEEN the equipment, a tractor and backhoe, the noisy work ongoing behind the neighbor's house. He assumed it was a swimming pool, a welcome addition for the children in the neighborhood, that family's two children roughly the same age as his own. He walked down the sidewalk, the front-end loader belching black smoke as it dug at the widening abyss in the backyard. He saw the neighbor now, blue jeans and a blue flannel shirt, observing the work with hands on hips.

"Jerry! What's up? The kids say you're putting in a pool."

The man looked at him, no smile, never much cordiality between them.

"Hardly. I'm putting in a fallout shelter."

The words hung between them, and Russo fought through the surprise.

"Why?"

Jerry looked at him again, still no smile.

"I'm protecting my family. It's coming, you know. Matter of time. I'm intending to survive."

"A nuclear attack?"

"You better believe it, pal. I've been reading up on it. These shelters will hold a family safe, until the radiation clears away. We can live in there for weeks, if we have to, maybe longer."

Russo had read the same details, a concrete box buried in backyards, stocked with all manner of food and survival gear, water, radios and other supplies, keeping a family alive until, somehow, they learned it was safe to emerge. The concept seemed simple enough, though Russo had long pondered the questions asked by others. An entire family is to stay below ground in a small block box, sleeping, eating, living, for some length of time? And, then there was the question of sewage, other waste. The illogic seemed overwhelming and ridiculous, but people, including his own neighbors, were reacting with what seemed to be panic, constructing these concrete tombs as though it was their lifeline through World War Three.

"You really think this will work?"

The look on his neighbor's face said it all.

"Damn right, Professor. It's a fool who doesn't take the Commies seriously. I'll not be caught, and I'm protecting my family. Guns and ammo too. If the Russians come, I'm ready to hold 'em off, best I can. Others around here, we're talking about it." He paused, eyed Russo with narrowing eyes. "There's room for my family. That's it. I'll protect them against neighbors too, anybody gets an idea they can crowd in. You'd be good to put in your own. I'll not cotton to trespassers."

Russo put up both hands, took a step back.

"Wouldn't think of it. Good luck."

"I'm telling you, Professor. You'd be smart to build one yourself. The war's coming. You can be sure of that."

HE WAITED FOR them again, the school bus screeching to a halt, the door swinging open, Danny leading the way down. They repeated the routine, Danny keeping his discreet distance, a short greeting, Becky offering the hug. He led them again up the driveway, and Becky held his hand, said, "Daddy, what's an A-bomb?"

CHAPTER EIGHT

Khrushchev

Sunday, September 16, 1962
Moscow, the Kremlin

"Rockets Will Blast the United States If It Invades"

He stared at the words, the report handed him by Mikoyan.

"This is in their official newspaper?"

Mikoyan nodded.

"Havana, yes. The quote is said to be from Castro himself."

"Of course it is. The damn fool. I predicted this, I knew it would happen. Those people . . . hot-blooded Latins . . . too full of fire for their own good."

"There is perhaps no harm. He does not mention the key word . . . *nuclear.*"

Khrushchev tossed the dispatch onto his desk, let out a breath.

"Not yet. Give him time. He sent his friend or partner, whatever his title, Che Guevara. You were here when that strange man insisted we broadcast our agreement, tell the world that we were going to install those missiles even before the first shipments began. They are too eager, too reckless. This is a time for delicacy, and Mr. Castro does not know the word."

Mikoyan turned, stared out a tall window.

"Perhaps it will pass quietly. The Americans are accustomed to hearing bluster from the Cubans. It is only that."

"One can hope, Anastas. I have thought this through with great care. Once the missiles are in place, with warheads prepared and ready, I will send a private letter to President Kennedy. I will inform him of what we have done, with a soft warning that this should obviously prevent any invasion of Cuba. I will not be impatient, Anastas. The Americans are facing their election in November, and Kennedy is under a great deal of pressure to appear strong. If he knew of the missiles during the campaigns, he might react with violence, to quiet his critics. That would not benefit Castro, no matter how eager he is to announce Cuba's *invulnerability* to the world. I am doing Kennedy a favor by keeping our secrets. In November, he will have no choice but to accept the inevitable, once he learns our missiles are in place, and that we are prepared for the worst. There will be much shouting, their congressmen spouting off all manner of threats and curses, but in time, it will again grow quiet. It will be like Berlin, a stalemate. Their missiles in Turkey require a balance, to even the scale. No matter the rattling of sabers, both sides will understand that we will have achieved that balance. I am doing us *all* a favor. Send a message to Castro. Explain reality to him. It is in his best interests, after all, to maintain a happy relationship with us. There is an old saying: *If you raise your voice too much, the strain will soil your pants.* We must educate Castro on old sayings."

He walked slowly, careful to remain close beside her. It was one of his great joys, walking the beaches near his vacation home, his dacha, but only if she was nearby.

Since he had come to power nine years before, she had served dutifully as his first lady, a post rarely heard of in the Soviet Union. For the most part, the women behind the leaders stayed far behind, their role to provide a warm home and the comforts of marriage. Nina was not in fact his legal wife, but that mattered to no one. She had been his intimate for most of forty years, the official ceremony of a wedding seeming far less important than the partnership she offered him, a partnership that surprised only *his* friends, not hers. She was no quiet flower. Nina Kukharchuk spoke five languages, including English, had served with distinction in the Communist Party as far back as World War One. In a government where women seemed not to exist, she stood alongside him at state functions, was more comfortable with foreign dignitaries than he was, had easily charmed the Kennedys. His pride in her was enormous, especially since she had changed the way many Russians viewed the wives of the powerful. But her devotion to him was absolute, and if there was talk that she was too much the power behind the man, he silenced that. He knew, as did many others, that she was the essential piece of the machine that dealt with the smaller matters, that allowed Khrushchev to focus on the larger policies, the greater programs, without dealing with so much of the minutiae of government. It had never been this way before Khrushchev. Stalin's wife had died young, Stalin ruling the Soviet Union as a man who entertained mistresses, but never enjoyed the luxury of the loyalty of a strong woman.

Now, Nina walked beside him again, to listen, to advise, or just to feel the soft grip of his hand. He felt a soft breeze off the water, and after a long silence, said, "What do you think of this creature called Castro?"

She seemed to absorb the question, then said, "He seeks great advantages where they are slight. He believes respect is earned by the volume of his voice."

Khrushchev stopped walking, stared out across the great open expanse of choppy water.

"You are correct, of course. He is noisy. But he has impressed us with his zeal for Communism. It has to be that way, you know. One great lesson from Comrade Lenin I learned years ago. You cannot export our system to other lands, force it onto a people who will not embrace it. Castro embraced us almost immediately when he took control. That is rare. Too rare, I'm afraid."

She bent low, a small seashell in her hand. She studied it, tossed it to the shore, said, "You are correct, my darling. Stalin believed the entire continent would embrace us after the Second Great War, merely because we had defeated Hitler. It was a grave misjudgment."

It was a thorn to Khrushchev, knowing that he had agreed with Stalin. With most of Europe in shambles, the workers, the great mass of displaced peoples should certainly have risen up and accepted the Soviet way. He began to walk again, said, "We did not count on America. They offered their great wealth to the people all over Europe, fed them, clothed them, rebuilt their shattered cities. That gave those people a kind of hope and relief we could not provide. Their powerful bosses took control once more, and so, nothing changed. Arcane lessons on systems of government mean nothing to people whose bellies are full, and across western Europe, their bellies are full. So, Lenin was right. If we are to spread Communism to the world, it will have to be toward those who welcome us with open arms. That is why Castro's big mouth is a problem. The poorer countries of Latin America should embrace us, but his big talk only scares them, as though he intends to conquer, not to enlighten. I can only hope that in time, once we have established our strength in his backyard, he will listen more carefully. With strength comes a need for wisdom. It's up to us to teach him that."

Friday, September 21, 1962
Moscow, the Kremlin

Kochov stood before him, arms crossed, his usual posture of defiance.

"General Pliyev is disgruntled. He does not appreciate working in secret. Even his code name seems offensive to him."

Khrushchev was in no mood for griping, had used most of his energy beating back those in the Presidium who continued to express nervousness about placing the missiles in Cuba. Now, he had to endure another kind of critic, Marshal Dimitri Kochov, one of the few among the Central Committee who continued to believe that a first strike nuclear assault against the United States was not only possible, but essential to the survival of the Soviet Union.

To many, Kochov was a frightening man, though Khrushchev knew him to be first a soldier, that following orders was in his blood. His outspoken views represented the most radical militarism of the Soviet government, but so far, Khrushchev felt he had Kochov under control.

"General Kochov, we have appointed Marshal Pliyev to command of all of our forces in Cuba, a great honor to him. He must surely understand that until our bases are well established, secure, until our missiles are secure and in position, *care* must be exercised. I respect Marshal Pliyev. He has done great service to our nation and will do so again."

"I am not certain of this, Premier. I have my cautions. General Pliyev has no experience with missiles. He is a cavalryman. And, his impatience is showing. He is headstrong, and might be tempted to exercise more authority than you have given him."

"You are describing yourself, General. No matter. Pliyev has been given explicit orders that, once the missiles are in place, it will require a direct order from Moscow to fire them. On that I made myself clear, and General Pliyev accepted the order. We are not installing missiles in order to start a war, no matter how others, including you, might feel. I trust General Pliyev to follow orders. As I trust you."

"Must we disguise General Pliyev with such a demeaning title?"

"Title? You mean his code name? *Ivan Pavlov* is a simple Russian name that can easily be intercepted by eavesdropping Americans. There is no reason to reveal any more of our hand than we must. And, should they discover who General Pliyev is, and his position there, his lack of missile expertise will be an added disguise. He is, after all, only a cavalryman."

CHAPTER NINE

Pliyev

Monday, October 1, 1962
Near San Cristóbal, Cuba

He wiped at the sweat flooding his eyes, glanced upward at the blistering sun. He focused on his visitor now, the man's uniform standing out in a sea of civilian clothing. He'll learn, he thought. Starched collars don't do as well in this kind of heat. He saw the man run a finger along one side of his neck, pulling the fabric from his skin. Pliyev, enjoying the man's agony, spoke now.

"So, you see, General, all is proceeding as planned, though of course, we are experiencing some delays. It is due to the infernal weather and the conditions our men must labor under. In all our training, no one thought to advise the men that they would work without shirts or roast in the rock-hard dirt. Our bulldozers at this base are next to useless, with all the rocks in the soil."

His observer, General Gribkov, watched the workers with his hands behind his back, said nothing. It was infuriating to Pliyev that Moscow would send teams of brass to look over his shoulder, as though no one could lay concrete and build blockhouses without the highest supervision. It didn't help that the near-sixty-year-old Pliyev was being observed, if not judged, by a man twenty years his junior. After a long moment, Gribkov said, "It is always thus, General Pliyev. The old adage, *one soldier, one axe, one day, one stump* . . . seems to have taken root here. Is there no way you can speed up the progress? Moscow is working with a tight timetable for completion of these sites. The logistics are formidable."

Pliyev fought to hold his tongue, did not need to be told just how formidable the logistics truly were.

"General Gribkov, I am well aware that when this project is completed, forty-five thousand Soviet troops and support staff will be positioned here. I am aware that two entire antiaircraft divisions will be in place, manning seventy-two missile launchers to combat any possible invasion from the Americans. There is an entire regiment of helicopters en route, along with seventeen IL-28 bombers, six of which will be equipped to carry a nuclear payload. I assume that I need not detail all of the artillery pieces or armor. In addition to a great force of conventional weapons, we are thus far equipped with eight short-range Luna missiles, in the event the Americans unwisely attempt to overrun our infantry positions. The Lunas are capable of firing a tactical nuclear shell with a lighter yield sufficient as a battlefield weapon. Do you have any further questions, General Gribkov?"

He waited impatiently, knew he had strayed into insolence. Gribkov seemed to weigh his words, then said, "We do not question your ability to command these forces, General. We naturally expect you to know just what those forces are now and what they will be. We are merely concerned at the lack of progress. Where is your second-in-command, General Dankevich? Have you assigned him to other areas of the construction?"

It was already a sore point between Pliyev and his chief subordinate. Lieutenant General Pavel Dankevich had long commanded units of the Soviet rocket forces, and thus naturally considered himself the man most suited for the position handed to Pliyev. Dankevich chose to accept Pliyev's seniority largely by ignoring him, and worse, ignoring his own duties.

"General Dankevich is playing tennis. It seems that it is his passion."

Gribkov looked at him, and Pliyev ignored that, continued to stare at the ongoing labor.

"Tennis?"

"Quite. I understand he is quite good at it. He has made it plain that if he is to suffer through this interminable heat, he shall do it in his own way. Short of having him shot, I chose the more diplomatic approach. So, he plays tennis."

"It is your command, General. I just assumed you would make good use of whatever assets we had assigned you."

"I assure you, I have. Some men are more of an asset than others. I accept as my responsibility the right to determine which is which."

Gribkov stared at him, nodded slowly, pointed now.

"I must ask . . . why are all of your men, the ones still wearing their shirts . . . why are they all wearing the same checked shirt?"

Another sore point, Pliyev measuring his words.

"As you surely have noticed, we were ordered not to wear uniforms, as a part of our overall secrecy. Moscow provided these men with civilian shirts as a disguise. As you can see, every man is wearing the same exact shirt, and I assure you, you will not observe any Cuban wearing such a garment. Thus, you may properly describe those shirts as indicating . . . a uniform." He turned to Gribkov now. "I am following orders as best I can, General. We are constructing missile sites, such as this one, in appropriate places all over Cuba. The field commanders under me are the best we have, and they know their jobs. Operation Anadyr is a logistical officer's worst nightmare. You did not command in the Second Great War, is that correct?"

Gribkov took his time responding.

"I was too young for command."

"No fault of your own. I commanded division and corps, army and army groups. I did my duty defending Moscow and Stalingrad, to name but two campaigns. I am the only cavalry commander awarded two 'Hero of the Soviet Union' awards. Did you know that? I have received the Order of Lenin, and other awards I will not bore you with now. So, you see, General, when you come here to question whether or not I am doing my job, I must wonder if it is only because someone above you in Moscow is not doing *theirs*. Premier Khrushchev has placed great faith in my abilities to command a nearly impossible assignment, and I am serving my country as I did in the Second Great War." He paused, pushed away a hint of hesitation. "I am quite certain that when he has time to vacate the tennis court, General Dankevich grades my performance, hoping that Moscow will see the light of day and put him in my place. He is, after all, a man who knows missiles. But I know *command*, General. I understand logistics and supply, and I have accepted the need for utmost secrecy. What I have discovered above all else is that Moscow did not fully appreciate the challenges here in Cuba. I am meeting them the best way they can be met. That should be the report you take back to our superiors."

HE DRANK FROM the small coffee cup, the strong bitterness curling his nose.

"More sugar."

The aide obliged, a demitasse spoonful dumped into his cup, stirred briskly.

"Better. I'm not sure how these people tolerate this stuff. Is nothing ever served cold here?"

"The refrigerated units are not functioning, General. The power supply is too limited, and we require . . ."

"Yes, yes. I know. I suppose none of us requires luxury, when the men are baking under this sun." He looked at the young man now, a lieutenant, not more than twenty-five. "You have many questions, certainly. I cannot answer them. But I can tell you this. In the Second Great War, we moved enormous numbers of troops and equipment overland. None of us ever had to cross an ocean to establish a base. Here, we are more than seven thousand miles from the nearest Soviet port, and we are to manage only with what we can bring with us and what this place provides. We are entirely dependent on our navy and their ability to be discreet with the cargo they carry, with more discretion applied to that cargo when it is unloaded. We must guard against prying eyes, listening ears, careless talk. This is all a new adventure for me, and for these men. You could say that in future years, we will be described, you and I, as pioneers. Be proud."

"Yes, sir. Certainly, sir."

Pliyev laughed.

"You are too young and too gullible to recognize sarcasm. No matter. Bring me another of these coffees."

THE TRUCK BOUNCED its way slowly along the tall wire fence, scattered trees and brush beyond. It was one more inspection, another visit to another base, the constant need to push the work. He sat in the rear, a guard beside him, the driver and another guard in front, all in civilian clothes. They rounded a curve, caught a flash of a running man, vanishing into brush across the road, away from the fence. The driver said, "It is this way every day, General. The Cubans are curious. They hug the fences to see what we are doing."

Pliyev searched the brush for the man, long gone now.

"I don't blame them. Castro promised us a thousand laborers, men eager to please their new Russian friends. I reluctantly told him no, that we would handle the labor ourselves. Castro was mightily insulted, to be sure. I suppose these people have some right to know what we are doing in their country, what we are doing *to* their country. In time. But my orders are very explicit. No Cubans will be allowed near these bases until well after completion of the work. I don't want to have to shoot anyone, but I have notified the security teams that if they observe someone inside the wire, they are authorized to use force. I can only imagine what Castro will think of that."

They rounded another bend, came upon a slow-moving truck hauling an enormous cargo, shrouded with a canvas tarp.

"Should I pass them, sir?"

"No. We are close to the gate. Let those men do their job."

They halted, the large truck easing to the security gate, a dozen guards swarming around the truck, past it now, eyes on Pliyev's vehicle. Salutes were offered, and Pliyev winced, thought, Any Cuban watching that will surely figure out I'm brass. Old habits are hard to break.

The larger truck moved ahead now, Pliyev's truck following, more unwanted salutes as they passed through the wire. He couldn't help himself, scanned the land out to either side, the construction sites, great slabs of concrete nestled between all manner of low buildings, some still not completed. Out to both sides, the trees were scattered, so different from what he had been told to expect. The experts had assured him, as they had assured Moscow, that Cuba was rich with enormous thickets of palm trees, certain to hide either the labor or the bases themselves, that missiles standing tall would blend in perfectly with the towering trees. Instead, the ground here was mostly bare, trees in small clusters, pockets of thorny brush, little shade and little cover for anyone or any piece of equipment.

The workers were using hand implements, construction equipment sitting idly by, one more case where the ground was too difficult for anything but the shovel. We have rockets here that will strike a target a thousand miles away with precision, but we must dig holes like peasants. He thought of General Gribkov's adage, *one soldier, one axe, one day, one stump*. Indeed.

A formation of fuel trucks sat parked to one side, other smaller vehicles with them. There were great rolls of cable, and then, the first of the missile launchers, and far beyond, a row of heavy tarps, covering what he knew were missiles. He couldn't avoid butterflies in his stomach, the enormous secret, lying plainly in the open, the workers nearby toiling through the afternoon sun, carpenters and masons, rough laborers hauling heavy bags of concrete and mortar.

"Not very well hidden."

The words had come out before he caught himself, his own worst habit. In front of him, the driver said, "It's all right, sir. I'm told by the commander here that the Cubans can't see this far past the wire fences, that there is enough ground cover to disguise any of the structures, especially the launchers."

Pliyev looked skyward, knew that whenever the American U-2 spy planes were observed by radar, the orders were specific, that they were to be ignored. For a while now, the U-2s had seemed to stay out to sea, as though probing more carefully, afraid perhaps of the very missiles aimed their way. Pliyev understood that there was to be no provocation with the Americans, but Moscow had been so concerned about any possibility of an aggressive action from the Americans that they had even insisted that no radar be used to track the planes, as though every officer was to pretend they simply weren't there. It was maddening to him, and to the antiaircraft officers, the men whose ground-to-air missiles were the same as those that had brought down the U-2 over Russia two years before. Then, the American flyovers had been general, seemingly nonspecific, photographing the Russian countryside, searching for anything that wasn't supposed to be there, whatever the Americans believed that to be.

That was then, he thought.

The small truck crawled to a stop, the guards exiting, one man at his door, pulling it open. The driver said again,

"Truly, sir. The Cubans cannot observe any of this."

He stood out from the truck, still stared skyward.

"I'm not so worried about the Cubans."

CHAPTER TEN

RFK

John McCone had returned home from his honeymoon, and he had been in no mood to hear snide comments about his time away. Both Kennedys respected McCone, considered him a better fit for their version of the CIA than his predecessor, Allen Dulles. Dulles had been Eisenhower's man, and it showed, Dulles tending to regard the new president as strictly an amateur, that the CIA were the professionals, and as such, their view of the world held sway. That had all changed with the disaster at the Bay of Pigs, and Kennedy was far more careful about who he regarded as the *experts* whose counsel he should take seriously. That description seemed to fit McCone.

They sat in the conference room, Bobby in his usual spot, standing close to one corner, McCone and the defense secretary, Robert McNamara, across from Kennedy. To one side sat McGeorge Bundy, along with a scattering of high-ranking aides, those who knew when it was time to speak. From the mood of those present, this was not the time.

McCone scanned a short stack of papers, said to the president, "Excuse me, sir, but I'm damn tired of the reports we're getting from the Cubans. Our offices in Miami have been too eager to accept anything we hear at face value, and so far, those reports seem designed only to drag us into a war in Cuba. The operatives, as they call themselves, are far too concerned with their own political stance to help us with what we really want to know. I'm hearing too much of why we should invade first and ask questions later. My apologies for this, Mr. President. But I've learned that when a Cuban on the ground sees a truck carrying something covered in a tarp, he naturally assumes it to be the biggest baddest ICBM on the planet. Since we know the Soviets have very few of those, it's unlikely they're sending them to Cuba. Which means our info is at best juicy gossip, with a flair for the dramatic."

"But we have seen missiles."

"Everything I have seen points to Russian surface-to-air missiles, just as they continue to insist. I was surprised, sir, to find when I returned home that you have ordered the U-2 flights away from Cuban airspace. That only means that we're in the dark. With so much Soviet activity in Cuba, with so many freighters unloading so much materiel, it's not a comfortable place to be."

Bobby leaned closer to McCone, said, "What do you suggest? You've been briefed as to why we moved the flights. We just didn't want to risk another shoot-down."

McCone turned, looked at Bobby, then back at the president.

"The U-2 is the most effective reconnaissance tool we have. Would you prefer we rely on those Cuban operatives?"

Bobby knew it was unusual for a CIA man to dismiss his own observers, and he knew that if McCone was this discouraged by the reports coming into his own offices, it was a good idea to take him seriously.

McCone stared hard at Kennedy.

"Mr. President, it is essential that we resume the U-2 flights over Cuba, no matter the risk. The number of Soviet ships has increased, and it's folly that we don't attempt to monitor what their cargo could be. As you know, sir, I have had my doubts about Soviet claims that their intentions are strictly defensive. It just doesn't make sense that the Soviets would go to so much trouble just to construct a bunch of SAM missile sites. They must know that the SAMs alone would not deter us from invading Cuba, if that was our intention. Our first order of business would be to take them out, focus precision bombing strikes directly on the missile launchers. No, I believe the SAMs are there for something more important to the Soviets. I hesitate to say this again, sir, but you know my feelings. I am convinced the Soviets are planning to install offensive missile systems."

Bobby said, "Why? What's the point?"

McCone turned to face him.

"Cuba is the first piece of real estate that the Soviets have under their control that sits in direct proximity to the United States. How can we believe that Khrushchev wouldn't see this as an opportunity he cannot pass up? He doesn't have the capability to launch massive ICBM strikes out of Russia itself. Now, he doesn't have to. He can use his stock of short- and medium-range missiles, which we know he has in his arsenal, to do that same job."

Kennedy let out a deep breath, spoke now.

"Thus far, Khrushchev has shown no tendency to trust any of his allies to safeguard his nuclear missiles. There are no such missile sites in eastern Europe, for example. Everything is within the Soviet border. Isn't Khrushchev taking a huge chance having these missiles out from under his direct control?"

"But, sir, they are under his control. It's why the Cuban citizens are being kept away, why the only reports we receive come from scattered views of trucks from people who have not been allowed up close. The construction workers are Russians, the longshore-men, guards, their security, it's all Russian. I wouldn't trust Castro to manage something like this, and it's apparent, sir, that Khrush-chev doesn't either. One more point, sir. If Khrushchev provides the Cubans with offensive weapons, it will wake up Cuba's neigh-bors in Latin America. Who's the next head of state who might ask Khrushchev to offer him the same kind of power? Prestige goes a long way."

Kennedy stared down at the table in front of him, folded his hands.

"I can't argue against your concerns. I share them. We held back the U-2s as a cautionary move, so as not to provoke the So-viets into something rash. Things are tender enough down there with all of Castro's talk about how our invasion of Cuba is im-minent. It doesn't help that I've got senators bellyaching nonstop about how an invasion is exactly what we should do. The volume on that crap is louder now with the election a month away. But I know that anything we do that seems aggressive could be mag-nified to a point where Khrushchev feels he must respond. No one needs to be backed into a corner, certainly not the Soviets." He paused, glanced at Bobby, then McNamara. "All right, we'll resume the flights."

McCone seemed to jump at Kennedy's words.

"I suggest, sir, that we do flyovers of the entire island, with spe-cial emphasis on the western end. That seems to be the area where the most activity is taking place, closer to Havana. I would also focus on San Cristóbal."

Kennedy said, "Why? What's so special about that?"

McCone looked behind him now, at one of his subordinates in the room, Colonel Rufus Wright. McCone said, "Colonel Wright, now is the time."

Wright stood, held a paper in his hand.

"Mr. President, as you know, I work for the Defense Intelligence Agency, and I have been in contact with Director McCone's people regularly. One of my jobs has been to study the U-2 photographs in great detail and analyze just what we're seeing."

Kennedy said, "Go on. Is there something new?"

Wright shook his head, waving the paper.

"Not exactly, sir. It's just that . . . around San Cristóbal, the Soviets have positioned their SAM missiles in a geometric pattern I've seen before. These patterns have been used by the Soviets as antiaircraft protection for important installations throughout the Soviet Union."

"What kind of installations?"

"Their nuclear sites, primarily. They arrange their antiaircraft missiles for the greatest range of protection, as a matter of course. They set them up in a trapezoidal pattern, surrounding those important installations. That pattern is now repeated around San Cristóbal. I believe, sir, and I have suggested to my superiors at the DIA, that it would be prudent to focus a U-2 flyover in that area."

Kennedy sat back, wiped a hand over a tired brow.

"Then, gentlemen, that is what we'll do."

DELAYED FOR TWO days by heavy cloud cover, the U-2s finally went airborne over Cuba on Sunday, October 14. The pilots were Air Force men, Major Rudolf Anderson Jr. and Major Richard Heyser, specially trained to adapt to the U-2s they now flew. Previously, the pilots had been CIA trained, but with the newly perceived danger these men might face in the air over Cuba, the decision had been made to place veteran Air Force pilots in the cockpits. The CIA met this change with considerable protest, but the decision came from the top, bolstered by assurances from Defense Secretary McNamara that it was the wisest course. After rapid lessons in the quirks of the CIA's U-2s, the planes began their missions.

As ordered, the men photographed the length and breadth of Cuba, with special focus on the western third of the island. Surprisingly, they met with no opposition, no Cuban antiaircraft fire, though their film would show the Soviet surface-to-air missiles perched on their launchers.

Their mission complete, the pilots returned to their bases, where the film canisters were rapidly unloaded, and transported to the photo labs at the Defense Intelligence Agency. Here, trained experts did as they had done before, scanned the eight thousand feet of film frame by frame. Throughout a lengthy and tedious day, the men labored, making notes, charting the images that seemed to matter most. That evening, as official Washington began to enjoy a typical round of social gatherings and routine meetings, the experts continued their work, until finally, as darkness fell, the DIA's chief, General Joseph Carroll made the first phone call. General Carroll reached out to the most senior man he could locate, the deputy secretary of defense, Roswell Gilpatric. In a manner of a few hours, the official word was transmitted to others, including McGeorge Bundy. It was Bundy's decision not to inform the president, at least not yet. Kennedy had returned late from campaign stops, an exhausted, ailing man, and Bundy decided to allow him one more night's sleep. The meetings could begin in earnest the next morning.

On Tuesday, October 16, Bundy arrived early at the White house, made his way up to the presidential residence, where he found Kennedy reading a newspaper in his pajamas. Bundy's message to Kennedy was brief, and succinct.

"Mr. President, there is now hard photographic evidence, which you will see a little later, that the Russians have offensive missiles in Cuba."

PART TWO

CHAPTER ELEVEN

RFK

Tuesday, October 16, 1962
The White House, Cabinet Room

Bobby had gotten the call from his brother at nine that morning, the message terse and cryptic, that the country was facing a serious problem. Bobby wasted little time reaching the White House. There, others had been summoned, a lengthy list of those who, in official Washington, were the men Kennedy seemed most likely to trust. Included, naturally, were the secretaries of state, Dean Rusk, and defense, Robert McNamara. Undersecretaries were there as well, plus General Marshall Carter of the CIA, filling in for the absent John McCone. Kennedy's national security advisor, McGeorge Bundy, was there, as was chairman of the Joint Chiefs, General Maxwell Taylor, and the vice president, Lyndon Johnson. There were others, junior members of the most important offices that served the president, all men summoned because their advice and counsel could be trusted, whether or not the president agreed with what they might offer.

Kennedy had not been present at first, the reasons explained by the news that morning, a White House visit by astronaut

Walter Schirra, the latest hero in the brotherhood of men who had launched the United States into manned space flight. Schirra had completed his space mission only a few days before, was already proving to be as popular in a folksy sort of way as some of the others, including John Glenn and Alan Shepherd. Schirra brought his family, a perfect photo opportunity for both him and the president, Kennedy seeking any kind of positive attention that might take the heat off the morbid business of politics that plagued the upcoming election. Their glad-handing meeting had been necessarily brief, both men pleased, but quickly, Kennedy had pulled back into the interior of the White House, away from the cameras and inquiring reporters.

At one end of the Cabinet Room stood a pair of uniformed officers, unfamiliar faces, warily at attention as the room filled. They flanked a large easel, covered in white paper, drawing the curious stares of the others as they entered the room. The senior men, Rusk and McNamara, along with the vice president, took their usual chairs, the others, including General Taylor, filling in the other spaces. As always, Bobby assumed his position to one side, standing, a surprise to no one. He glanced at his watch. It was 11:45 a.m.

Kennedy entered now, trailed by his daughter, Caroline. Bobby chuckled at the playfulness of the little girl, but the rest of the room kept silent, surprised by the unexpected visitor. Kennedy whispered to her, then offered the child a playful pat as she exited. He looked around the room, acknowledged the men he knew well, then said, "You men have been chosen by me for this particular duty. I value your opinions, and right now, we need some serious counsel. Secrecy is essential, as will be made clear. We cannot afford leaks. There will be no leaks."

Men were nodding their heads, a reassuring gesture, no one

missing the point that this was not a usual strategy session. Bobby glanced at the faces, eyes still drifting toward the easel at the end of the room.

Kennedy spoke to General Carter now, said, "Tell us what's going on."

"Thank you, Mr. President. My men will now distribute copies of what I will show you here. These are photographs taken 14 October from our U-2 flights over the island of Cuba."

The cover came off the easel, the CIA men passing envelopes of photos to the men around the table. Bobby stepped closer to the easel, puzzled, and Carter seeming to read his audience, said, "Mr. President, gentlemen. What we are seeing here is a photograph of a Soviet missile-launching site near San Cristóbal, Cuba. The photo indicates missile launchers, and here . . . indications of the missiles themselves, covered in tarpaulins."

Bobby studied one of the photos, stared closely, shook his head.

"I'm sorry. Can you be more specific? This looks like a construction site perhaps. It could be a football field."

There were murmurs of agreement, something Carter seemed to expect.

"I assure you, what you are seeing here are works in progress, with construction of guided-missile launchpads. The trucks you see parked in formation are fuel-carrying vehicles, and there are a great many of them. Those elongated shapes you see clustered together are missiles, sheltered upon trailers. They are approximately eighty feet long. That is substantially larger than any of the surface-to-air missiles in the Soviet arsenal. There are additional missiles under cover, which appear to be somewhat shorter, likely short-range surface-to-surface missiles. There are motor pools, erector launches, and other vehicles used for transporting missiles, some of which have missiles on board. In this one complex, we have estimated there are sixteen to twenty-four missiles. This is one complex."

Kennedy studied a photograph in his hands, said, "Can we determine if these missiles have nuclear warheads?"

"Not from these photos, sir. However, the eighty-foot length of these missiles identifies them as medium-range ballistic missiles. It is apparent that there is very little point in creating a missile base for such a ballistic missile, if you weren't going to arm it with a warhead."

"Yes, of course."

"Since this site is still under construction, it is likely that nuclear warheads are being hidden . . . stored somewhere else, until the site is operational."

"Do we know how long that will take?"

Carter paused.

"Not long. I would point out, sir, that this photograph contrasts with a photo of the same area taken at the end of August. The Soviets are moving very quickly. I would guess . . . this base could become operational in as little as two weeks."

Kennedy, who held the photo in his hand still, said, "We will continue the U-2 flights, and focus on these bases, to monitor further progress. But I want daily flights. Every damn day. Your men have done exceptional work here, and I thank you, but we need to keep it up. Obviously, there is much for the rest of us to discuss. You are dismissed."

The CIA men acknowledged Kennedy with formal nods, exited the room in single file.

Bobby felt the temperature rising, his own, the rest of the room's. He stared at the easel still, tried to see what had been described, frustrated that he could only see a construction site. Kennedy said, "I have no doubt that what we've been told is accurate. These fellows are experts, the kind I trust to do their jobs."

Rusk said, "Mr. President, I believe we must set into motion a chain of events that will, in the end, eliminate the launch sites altogether. The question of course is how, whether we do it by an unannounced sudden strike or whether we push hard on the other side to remove the sites on their own."

General Taylor spoke now, his voice firm, unwavering.

"It is greatly important, Mr. President, that we strike with the benefit of surprise. Hit 'em without any warning whatsoever."

Kennedy held up his hand, silencing the others, said, "What would be the reason they'd plant these missiles? Seeking an advantage?"

Taylor responded, "They're certainly seeking the advantage of being able to launch their shorter-ranged missiles against the United States, as a supplement to their long-range ICBMs. We know they don't possess much of a force of the long-range missiles. This clearly evens the odds for them."

Rusk nodded, said, "I agree. However, the danger in taking immediate action is that it could provoke the Russians into making an aggressive move somewhere else. Berlin perhaps."

Other comments came now, a soft jumble, no one speaking out loud. Kennedy said, "It is clear we have three options. One, strike these missile bases without warning. Two, strike the missiles as well as a broader targeting, airfields, and so on. Three, launch a blockade, surrounding the island to prevent any more ships coming and going."

Bobby, stepping closer to the table, said, "Four. We can invade."

The conversations began to flow now, men seeming to line up behind the options of an immediate military strike against the missile bases, versus a wait-and-see attitude. As the meeting was adjourned, Kennedy made it very clear that the existence of this group, now to be referred to as the Executive Committee of the National Security Council, or *Excomm*, was to be held in absolute secret. They would continue to meet as soon as that afternoon, with Kennedy taking more of a backseat, allowing the men to freely discuss their own ideas without the heavy hand of the president's presence. Kennedy emphasized once more that no one, certainly no news reporter, was to have any inkling of the Excomm's existence. At least not yet.

BOBBY MOVED IN step with his brother through the residence hallway, neither man speaking. Kennedy, stopping outside his own bedroom, now said, "I have a meeting scheduled with the crown prince of Libya. I can't cancel. None of us can alter our set schedules, including you."

Bobby rubbed his chin, said, "It doesn't make sense, Jack. Why would Khrushchev do this? He knows we won't stand for it, that he's opening up a can of pretty nasty worms."

"I'm not sure about that, Bobby. He thinks he's tested me, that I won't react. We have an election coming up, and everybody around here is walking on tiptoe, afraid to do anything that could cost them votes."

"Then why all the secrecy, the speed of their construction?"

"That's the point. He couldn't announce that they were going to do this down the road, the whole world would scream at him. This way, if he completes their bases in secret, then announces it to the world as a done deal, the protests will be pretty hollow. Once the bases are established, up and running, all the bitching in the world won't move them. Castro will crow long and loud about it too, and you can bet he won't be intimidated into shutting them down. I can see the big day now, Castro and Khrushchev standing arm in arm, with a big god-damn missile in the background, announcing to the world how the Soviets are winning the arms race."

Bobby leaned against a wall to one side.

"It's possible that Khrushchev is just seeking leverage, that once he's got his missile bases, he'll use them to bargain with. He'll pull them out, if we get out of Berlin."

Kennedy shook his head.

"Doubt that. He's going to far too much trouble, and too much expense, just to use this as a bargaining chip. The CIA was pretty clear what those missiles can do. Those medium-range things can hit most of the U.S. It's why we have to figure this out in secret. It could panic the hell out of the American people if it gets out that missiles are aimed at downtown anywhere."

"I wish I knew the right move . . . your new committee won't agree on anything without a hell of a lot of debate. I think I know how Tojo felt when he planned Pearl Harbor. Little mistakes could become mighty big ones, mighty quick."

"We need the debate, Bobby, the meetings of the minds. This is too big to simply be left to a snap decision. And, there's more to this than a U.S.-Russia thing. The Latin countries look to us for leadership. If we allow the missiles to stay in Cuba, every damn member of the Organization of American States will question just how much their loyalty to us is worth. We preach all about our Monroe Doctrine, keeping foreigners out of our hemisphere. Well, like it or not, they're here. How much resolve do we have to change that? Clearly Khrushchev believes we're too timid to take any serious action. He wouldn't just openly risk nuclear war."

"Jesus, Jack. Are you sure? We don't know what kind of pressure he's under, what kind of hard-liners are in the Kremlin pushing him into making a first strike. They don't have the ICBMs to do the job, but with his shorter-range stuff right off Miami . . . hell, that changes everything."

Kennedy reached out a hand, put it on Bobby's shoulder.

"That's one thing we can agree on. The world has just changed. The question is . . . what do we do about it?"

CHAPTER TWELVE

RFK

Wednesday, October 17, 1962
The State Department, Washington, DC

The Excomm had met three times the day before, once without the president, the men appreciating the freedom to offer their own views without the weight of the president's judgment staring them in the face. The meetings had become forums for each man to flesh out his own ideas about just what the correct response should be to the presence of nuclear missiles in Cuba. Opinions seemed to change by the hour, some, like Dean Rusk, initially calling for a powerful military strike against the Soviet bases, then moderating his own view, as differing opinions were offered. By the second day of meetings, Wednesday, October 17, two distinct positions began to take shape.

Today, they met in a conference room on the seventh floor of the State Department building, a windowless tomb of a room, designed in an apparent attempt to avoid distractions from outside. John McCone had returned, cutting short a family emergency, and as he freely acknowledged, as director of the CIA, his place at the table was an absolute must. There was another new face as well, the ambassador to the United Nations, Adlai Stevenson. Stevenson had been a rival to Kennedy as the voice of the Democratic Party, had run unsuccessfully against Eisenhower in both 1952 and 1956. His post at the UN had been granted him by Kennedy as a plum, for his service to the party, yet few among the Excomm considered Stevenson important enough to influence anyone, believing him to be a man whose time had passed.

The president was absent again, this time off on another essential campaign stop, those kinds of scheduled events that no one wanted to change, offering the press or the public no hint that there was a greater crisis to deal with. In Kennedy's absence, the meeting was logically chaired by the secretary of state, Rusk, yet Bobby could immediately see that Rusk didn't feel up to the task. Even McNamara, equal in stature to Rusk in the Cabinet, seemed unwilling to take the lead in any discussion. At first, Bobby had been annoyed at the lack of a strong voice, but then, he reacted with his own instincts. If no one would run the show, it would be up to him.

GENERAL TAYLOR SPOKE, carrying the weight of the Joint Chiefs, whose own meetings had taken place late the day before.

"We are prepared to launch a surgical strike against the Soviet missiles and their installations, if that is the president's order. Such a strike can be made in a matter of a few days. Already, the armed forces are maneuvering people and equipment southward, under the guise of training, in the event these strikes call for an all-out invasion. However, I would offer a note of caution. A surgical strike, with limited targets, opens up enormous risk. There is consensus among the Chiefs that a massive assault is the wiser course. Consider the possibility that a surgical strike misses some of the targets. Then we would have tipped our hand, and the Soviets would be in a position to react with their remaining tactical weapons in Cuba or elsewhere. However, an all-out strike against the missiles, the airbases, MiG fighters, Soviet bombers, submarines, and patrol boats would demonstrate our absolute lack of tolerance for their presence. The message would be clear. And, should it then be seen as necessary for a ground invasion, the way would be open for our people to go in. I personally do not agree that a land invasion is called for, nor is it necessarily a wise move. Others among the Joint Chiefs disagree with me. Such an invasion could be put into motion within a couple of weeks."

The men around the room glanced at each other, and Bobby saw horror on some of the faces, nods of approval on others. He looked at McNamara, knew the defense secretary would have discussed this with Taylor already. McNamara caught his look, said, "There are issues to consider. An all-out invasion is a clear statement of war. Assaulting the Soviet installations and other facilities will kill Russians, possibly a great many Russians. I cannot believe that Khrushchev would accept those casualties without striking back, and, as General Taylor points out, there is no guarantee we will successfully eliminate every target. With such an assault under way, it is likely . . . no, it is probable, that a Soviet ground commander would launch his own still-functioning missiles at a target here. And then, gentlemen, we have nuclear war."

Bobby welcomed McNamara's more moderate tone, said, "What do you propose?"

"A blockade. Seal off the island from more shipping."

Others spoke up now, a sharp reaction to McNamara's backing

away from military action. Former secretary of state Dean Acheson, another new face, a longtime advocate of aggressive dealings with the Soviets, said, "A blockade will have no effect whatsoever on the missiles already in Cuba. If anything, it might hasten their being launched. At this moment, today, we have the least risk we will face. Every day of progress with their bases is a day closer to action on their part. We must strike now or not at all."

Douglas Dillon, the treasury secretary, spoke up now.

"A blockade would only heighten the confrontation directly with the Soviets. Soviet ships could be sunk, and we are fooling ourselves if we believe the Russians wouldn't react to *that*."

Bobby looked at McNamara, who stared downward, head shaking slowly. Bobby said, "Gentlemen, we have done an excellent job of fooling ourselves already. We did not believe the Soviets would ever put offensive weapons in Cuba, and here we are. But I cannot believe that it is the wisest move to invite all-out war."

To one side, Adlai Stevenson spoke now, a surprise to some, who had viewed his presence as ceremonial.

"Frankly, gentlemen, I would much prefer that we seek a peaceful solution to this problem. That is, after all, what the United Nations is for. Surely calmer heads will make the wisest decisions."

There were low murmurs, Bobby scanning the room for anyone who agreed. No one spoke. A phone rang on the table in front of him, Bobby picking up the receiver.

"Sir, there are CIA officers here, with information."

Bobby welcomed the break in the tension, the door opening, the same two CIA men from the day before entered. Envelopes were passed out, one man saying, "We have additional photographs. As well, we have continued to analyze the footage we have now." The officer didn't seem to know where to look, but Bobby said, "Tell us what you've got."

"We have confirmed the presence at San Cristóbal of twenty-eight launchpads for two types of ballistic missiles. The two ballistic missiles have capabilities as follows. The shorter-range missiles, which, in Soviet parlance are their medium-range missiles, have an effective range of approximately one thousand miles. The larger, intermediate-range missiles have an effective range of twenty-two hundred miles. These are immovable, fixed-position weapons, whose purpose is as a first-strike missile. In a counterattack, they are indefensible, and could easily be taken out. Their warheads could easily reach as far as Arizona, Wyoming, and Montana. We will continue to provide you with photographs as the film is developed, and further U-2 flights are undertaken."

Bobby scanned the photos, more of what he had seen before, some much clearer now.

"Thank you, gentlemen. That will be all. Fine work."

The men left the room, the meetings breaking down in orderliness now, busy men with busy agendas. But the core of the group stayed put, Acheson speaking out.

"It's very clear what must be done. Missiles so close to our shores are unacceptable and must be eliminated. This only shows just how much danger we are truly in."

McNamara said, "It is very little difference to the danger we face from Soviet ICBMs, should they be fired from within Russia. A few minutes time doesn't increase or decrease the danger. It is the hand on the trigger that matters. The most pressing question we face is how to get the missiles out of Cuba without starting a war."

THE DEBATES CONTINUED. Various plans were offered, including notifying Khrushchev of the discovery, suggesting in the strongest diplomatic terms that he voluntarily withdraw the missiles. This was widely rejected, no one expecting Khrushchev to simply admit he had made a mistake. Other diplomatic solutions seemed to fall on deaf ears, no one ignoring the logic that the Russians had placed the missiles in Cuba for a reason that mattered very much to them. It was highly unlikely they could simply be asked to pull them out with any success.

As the debates continued, the more military approaches still held traction, McNamara and Bundy pushing for various forms of blockade, while some of the others insisted still on a massive military strike. As the discussions continued, heating up, cooling down, Bobby felt himself pulled away from the military strike concept. The most logical reasoning for him was the argument that even an all-out military strike might miss some targets, which would lead to obvious consequences, and practically ensure the need for a full-on invasion of Cuba. This would guarantee enormous casualties for both sides, especially among the Cuban people, innocent bystanders to most of what was happening.

With Acheson, Dillon, and the others firm in their commitment to an immediate military strike, others, including Rusk, McNamara, Bundy, and Bobby, adjourned with the understanding that more discussion was to come, but that regardless of their disagreements or differences in philosophy, the ultimate decision would be made by the president.

BOBBY SAT WITH Ted Sorenson, Kennedy's primary speechwriter, huddled inside a black limo. Outside, the rain was relentless, but not so damaging as to prevent the president's plane from making its landing. Kennedy was returning from yet another campaign trip, the rain not keeping away well-wishers upon his landing, happy faces that seemed to greet Kennedy no matter the conditions, or where he might be. But the crowds gave way quickly, Kennedy moving directly toward the waiting car, the crowd not aware just who the passengers were. The president offered a final smile to the crowd, a lengthy wave, then slid quickly into the backseat, alongside the others, said, "Jesus, what a mess. Sorry if I'm dripping on you."

The smile was gone now, something Bobby had seen before, Kennedy playing the role the crowd hoped for, bright, optimistic, the energetic young man who was leading his country to greater heights. But in private, especially now, the happy talk and pleasant smiles gave way to the stark reality of what was happening around them.

Bobby handed his brother an envelope, a summary of the discussions from the latest Excomm meetings, Jack glancing at the contents, shaking his head.

"I didn't expect clear answers. But we're going to figure this out. We have to. Anything new?"

Bobby said, "Better photos from the U-2s. The interpreters are parsing out the details, just what we're looking at. Even if I can't identify everything they're seeing, I take their word for it. We have no choice, really."

"No, we don't. I always said that after the Bay of Pigs I wouldn't trust anything to the experts ever again. I was wrong. We have to accept that these are good people who know how to do their jobs. So, the boundary lines are being drawn? Acheson and Dillon want to bomb the hell out of everything, Stevenson wants to sit down and have a nice friendly talk. Everybody else is somewhere in between?"

Sorenson said, "That's pretty close. Some are just going along for the ride, playing wait and see, waiting for others to pave the way."

Jack looked at his brother now.

"You?"

Bobby looked down, wiped at the rivers of rainwater his brother had deposited on the car seat.

"I'm leaning toward a blockade. That's McNamara's position, primarily. There's danger there, of course, just like there's danger in all of this. But a full-on military strike . . . I don't see how daring the Soviets to bomb us is good policy. Killing Russians will do exactly that."

Kennedy wiped away the wetness on his face.

"Then how do we blockade Cuba without sinking Russian ships?"

There was a silent moment, Bobby looking at Sorenson, who shook his head. Sorenson said, "That's the problem in a nutshell. No matter what we decide to do, we're depending on Khrushchev not to react to us by launching missiles."

Thursday, October 18, 1962
Hickory Hill, near McLean, Virginia

McNamara had come to Bobby's home early that morning, a shared breakfast on the patio, a scattering of leaves drifting past as the trees gave way to winter. But today, there would be no tennis match.

They shared a pot of coffee, Ethel and the maid depositing a tray of muffins on the metal table, then disappearing into the house. It had always been that way, the understanding between Bobby and Ethel that his work was his alone, that whatever he was dealing with was not to be discussed. She seemed to prefer that, as much as he preferred not hearing every detail of life inside their home, every problem with the children. Now, that separation was more important than ever, the unspoken rule around his home that serious goings on were not discussed at all. Bobby assumed it was that way with every member of the Excomm, the president's strict rule that *secrecy* meant *secrecy* from anyone outside the meetings. Any kind of leak now could be catastrophic, even if it meant keeping wives in the dark.

McNamara toyed with one of the blueberry muffins, had always enjoyed whatever treat Ethel had provided.

"I miss the parties here. I could always count on you for something entertaining, including tossing some celebrity into your pool."

Bobby ignored the food, said, "Doesn't seem right, not now. Too many faces, too much talk. If we get through this without blowing ourselves up, I promise you, the parties will go on. Ethel wouldn't have it any other way."

McNamara chuckled.

"I doubt Ethel enjoys those gatherings as much as her husband. You just itch to embarrass some hotshot, bring them down a notch. Funny thing is, all those hotshots, whether government or Hollywood or anything else, they seem eager for your abuse. It's more important just to be here, to be a part of your world. Too bad Jack doesn't enjoy it more."

Bobby thought of his brother, the tragedy of Jackie's miscarriage, six years earlier, the incentive for Jack to sell this property to Bobby.

"He'll socialize, when he feels like it. But now, being president, I think he accepts that there are some limits to how he shows his face to the world."

McNamara took a bite from the muffin.

"You're right. It wouldn't do for the president of the United States to be dumped into the pool. The Secret Service might not approve." McNamara finished the muffin, wiped his hands together. "The meeting is at eleven this morning, right?"

Bobby pushed the coffee cup around in a slow circle, nervous energy.

"Yep. The State Department. We can ride together, one less limo. Jack's made it clear, we need to be discreet about the cars we use for these meetings. Any good reporter who sees a cluster of black limos outside any building in DC will smell something's up. We need to use the garages, do some walking."

McNamara made a slow swipe at a leaf drifting past.

"Right. Do you think the blockade is the right thing? Truly?"

Bobby expected this, knew that McNamara wasn't comfortable leading the way on any of these ideas.

"There're still questions, Bob. What exactly do you blockade? Offensive weapons only? Or, go the whole way, and stop every damn ship that comes toward Cuba?"

McNamara sipped from the coffee cup, popped a bite of muffin into his mouth.

"I've been thinking about that one a great deal. You can't just shut down all sea traffic into Cuba. There are humanitarian reasons. The Cuban people rely on all kinds of shipments, food, fuel, all of it. Stopping all of that could seriously wreck their economy."

"So, you focus only on weapons, military shipments?"

"I think so. Maybe oil too, but that could also cripple them. No, you have to spell it out plainly, no fogginess about what the blockade is for."

Bobby tossed the coffee from his half-filled cup out toward the grass, said, "The only way to separate what's allowed in and what's not, is to board ships. If the Russians say no . . ."

"If the Russians say no . . . it means I've misread Khrushchev. Maybe we all have. I think these missiles are just his way of evening the balance of power, maybe poking us in the eye for our missiles in Turkey. I cannot believe he is doing this just so we'll force him, or he'll force us, to start a damn war."

Bobby stood, walked a few steps out to the yard, looked up at the trees, a soft breeze rustling the limbs, a shower of leaves.

"This could be one of those things . . . where there is no right answer. Everything we do could be wrong. But you have to do it anyway."

CHAPTER THIRTEEN

Khrushchev

Sunday, October 14, 1962
Petsamo, Georgia, near the Black Sea

"Some more of this. It is exceptionally tasty today."

The servant moved quickly, Khrushchev's bowl filled again with the thick lumpy liquid. It was his favorite dish, one that he insisted be enjoyed by even his guests, whether or not they seemed to share his affection for *kulesh*.

Across from him, Malinovsky probed the stew with his fork, obvious hesitation, said, "Tell me again how you make this?"

Khrushchev happily obliged him.

"Pork fat and millet. Mixed together carefully so neither one takes over. Much like how I handle the government. Is it not to your liking?"

Malinovsky had been through this before, seemed always to err on the side of politeness.

"Alas, not today. My stomach is a bit foul."

Khrushchev didn't care if Malinovsky was making excuses.

"Then have a steak. We will prepare one for you immediately."

Khrushchev clapped his hands, the servant appearing. "Have the chef fix up a nice tenderloin for Comrade Malinovsky. He does not share my love for the simpler treats."

Malinovsky seemed to know when protest was futile. He smiled, said, "Yes, that would be fine. Thank you."

Khrushchev stuffed a forkful of the gooey liquid in his mouth, wiped clumsily with a cloth napkin, said, "What time is it?"

Malinovsky said, "Near two. Are you nervous?"

"Of course I'm nervous. We don't launch satellites every day, and we certainly do not launch ones with eyes. This will cancel out some of the advantages the Americans have with their U-2 planes."

The steak appeared, Malinovsky not objecting to the red juice filling the plate, the steak obviously too rare.

"Yes, this is fine, thank you. So, Nikita, they will call you when the launch is complete?"

"They know I am expecting to hear. I want to know we have success, and I want to know when the cameras begin to work. This is no longer *sport*, eh? The Americans believe they are superior to us in every way, especially technology. Now, we shall see about that."

THE MISSILE LIFTED off at a top-secret installation in Tyuratam, far out in a remote area of Kazakhstan. Officially, the missile was designated Kosmos X, and carried the Soviets' most advanced means of photographing ground installations. It had a low orbit, barely 120 miles above the surface, and was designed to skim over key areas of the North American continent, then return to Earth in a few days, where the film would be developed.

The launch and the flight were completely successful, and completely fruitful. With a flight path that carried the satellite over Florida, they were able to confirm the reports they had been hearing from spies on the ground. Among the many images from Kosmos X were convoys of troops, dark green trucks in long columns, carrying what could only be American military forces southward, presumably toward bases such as Tampa or Key West. Though Khrushchev would not let himself believe the Americans had any knowledge of the missiles now being planted in Cuba, the buildup seemed to indicate another problem, both for the Russians and Castro himself. The only purpose for such a mobilization, in Khrushchev's mind, was that the Americans were indeed preparing for an invasion of Cuba.

Thursday, October 18, 1962
Moscow, the Kremlin

The members of the Presidium all watched him, some of them learning only now about the latest spy satellite. Khrushchev adjusted his glasses, read from a notepad.

"I have studied the photographs. They confirm that the Americans are moving great numbers of men and equipment southward, to bases in Florida, and even into the Caribbean. The Americans have claimed that they have already made announcements, which we are to accept at face value, that this movement is for training exercises, primarily involving the United States Navy and Marines. According to our men on the ground, there are already paratroop drops taking place in the country of Honduras, designed to convince us, and the world, that this is little more than an exercise. Our satellite photographed a squadron of American jets on the ground at a base in Key West, a short flight time to Havana. It stretches the imagination that the Americans wish us to accept that all of this activity is strictly for fun. We have notified Castro what the Americans are doing, and what we believe may follow. I am astounded at the arrogance, that Kennedy would assume us so complacent we would not defend our ally. Even now, the Americans are strengthening their troop positions at a number of bases across the southern areas of their country. A considerable armada of their navy ships have been observed sailing southward, presumably to support whatever their plan might be. We are not yet prepared to counter the American gambit by announcing our placing of nuclear weapons in Cuba. I will not reveal our secrets to the Americans just yet. We are holding to our timetable, to announce the installation of the missiles, after the American election next month, once the bases become fully operational."

He paused, scanned the faces, saw approving nods, and unlike as so often happened, no one was distracted or dozing off. He was in no mood for politeness, pounded one fist on the rostrum.

"Comrades, we will not accept this provocative move by the Americans without a sharp acknowledgment of our own. I have ordered that an article appear in tomorrow's *Izvestia*, which will certainly reach the American newspapers within a few hours, that any attack on the island of Cuba by any foreign power, will prompt us to immediate and severe action. Simply put, it would mean war."

CHAPTER FOURTEEN

RFK

Thursday, October 18, 1962
The White House

He walked with his brother past the Rose Garden, where the president's aides and various stagehands were preparing a platform for a ceremony Kennedy was to preside over later that morning.

Bobby watched the labor, saw the faces eyeing them, said quietly, "What now?"

Kennedy ignored the work, had seen plenty of this before.

"Nine thirty. I present the Harmon International Award trophies. For excellence in flying. Well-deserved stuff. I don't mind this one. The recipients are good people, deserving."

Bobby glanced at his watch, after eight, a mental note of how long he might keep the president's attention. They walked out past the garden, across the wide lawn, Secret Service agents keeping a discreet distance. After a silent moment, the president said, "What time is the next meeting?"

Bobby watched his shoes sliding through the thick grass, said, "Eleven this morning. Another tonight, ten p.m."

"I'll probably make the late one. I want to hear some of this stuff firsthand." He looked at Bobby, a slight smile. "Not that I don't trust your version of events."

Bobby welcomed the touch of humor. He had carried around the weight of the meetings for two days. He glanced again at his watch, said, "We're not close to a decision, you know. Your decision, I mean. The military still wants to go in with guns blazing. The Republicans are out there spouting off the same thing. I heard Richard Nixon is campaigning somewhere in California, called you weak on everything. These idiots have no idea what they're talking about, but all that talk is pushing some pretty serious buttons around the country. People want to know you're strong on Cuba, but now, you can't tell them just how strong. Not yet anyway. How long are you gonna wait before you say something publicly?"

Kennedy stopped, looked around, seemed to check for listening ears.

"I can't say anything yet. Nothing. Not until we've reached a real decision on just what to do. If I announce we're going into Cuba, it might make the Republicans happy, but it will seriously piss off our allies, NATO, the OAS. We'll be seen as invading a sovereign country, missiles or not. We have to know exactly what we're going to say, and what the responses should be, before we say it. It's tough. I don't just want to scare hell out of the American people unless there's a good reason. By the way, I'm sending Acheson to Paris."

"Why?"

"Well, for one, he's a pain in the ass. But more importantly, I want our people in place alongside our allies, prepared to give them a heads-up as to our plans, just before I make any kind of public announcement. De Gaulle would expect to know something in advance, as would Prime Minister MacMillan. The British ambassador, Ormsby-Gore, will be our pipeline there. He's a good fellow, and he'll do what he can to calm nerves in London. We'll have to prepare our ambassadors in every country in Latin America. We make any announcement about Cuba, no matter what we decide, and those people will be directly affected."

Bobby glanced around, no one close, the agents keeping their distance.

"Jesus, Jack. I owe you an apology. I guess I forget just how many details you have to think about. I'm more concerned with the meetings, and who's saying what. It's all going to fall on you, before it's over. I guess I take that for granted."

"Don't. I'm relying on you all to come up with solutions that make sense and won't start World War Three. But nobody, not the Republicans, not the American people, is going to care what any committee says. You're right. It's on me. This might be the week I really earn my salary." He paused, started walking again, slow steps, Bobby following. He stopped again, said, "You read *Guns of August*?"

"Barbara Tuchman. Yeah, read it a couple months ago."

Kennedy thought a moment.

"She makes the point. World War One started because a bunch of idiotic heads of state kept escalating their threats, pushing each other into corners. Big talk became bigger action, until half the damn world was on fire. That's my fear, Bobby. You see *The New York Times* this morning? *Izvestia* printed another threat from Khrushchev, that if we set foot in Cuba, it will start a war, not with Cuba, but with the Soviets. They have plenty of eyes in this country, they have to know we're muscling up, and I'm hoping like hell they don't know why. If I was Khrushchev, and saw our exercises in the Caribbean, I'd assume it was a rehearsal for the invasion of Cuba. So, he reacts. Shoots his mouth off, maybe just to make Castro feel better."

"Um, Jack, that was one of the observations the CIA boys offered up. They said the Soviets have repositioned some missile-firing boats—Komar class, they're called. They moved them away from Havana and closer to Guantánamo. At first, it didn't make sense, that they'd move missiles farther away from our coastline. But if they think there's going to be an invasion, they're positioning their defensive people where they can do more good for them."

Kennedy rubbed a hand on his chin, then ran it through his hair.

"Or, it could mean they're gearing up for a direct attack on Guantánamo. Either way, it points to their uncertainty about just what we're up to. I suppose that's good. But uncertainty can be dangerous as hell, Bobby. That's what Tuchman says. Big talk without firm information, big threats that no one takes seriously. Backing people into corners. It's a recipe for catastrophe. And it scares the hell out of me." He looked hard at Bobby now. "That's why you need to keep meeting, debating, discussing, arguing. I need some confidence from you fellows, that whatever I'm doing isn't going to kill us all." He turned back toward the Rose Garden. "I'd better get ready. The crowds and the reporters will be here soon. Probably not good for us to be wandering around out here, sharing secrets. You know what the reporters will say."

"Wait, Jack. What about Gromyko?"

"You know about that, of course. Yep, I'm meeting with Gromyko this afternoon. That should be interesting."

Andrei Gromyko was the Soviet foreign minister, a direct connection to Khrushchev. Gromyko had been an effective member of the Soviet foreign service as far back as Stalin. Unlike the affable Dobrynin, Gromyko most often offered a portrait of stony silence, seemed devoid of personality, accepted the animosity between the two great superpowers almost personally, as though by his presence alone, he should be thought of as the real enemy the Americans should despise. And yet, he did his job, had requested to meet with President Kennedy this day, their meeting set for five that afternoon.

Bobby knew little of Gromyko, other than the odd contrast to the far friendlier Dobrynin.

"What do you think he wants, Jack?"

Kennedy shrugged.

"Either he's coming to tell me that we had better keep out of Cuba, that Khrushchev isn't fooling around with his threats . . . or he's going to tell me that the Soviets know what we know, that somehow, they found out what our U-2 flights have shown."

"Jesus. You think that?"

"Not really. He's just trying to put the lid a little tighter on the pot, keep the hard words from becoming hard actions. I have to believe that. I have to believe that the goddamn Soviets are as afraid of war as we are."

Bobby crossed his arms, the familiar stance.

"Maybe he's hoping you'll confess. Maybe they're wondering if you know anything you're not saying, and so, he'll be giving you an opportunity to let it out of the bag, chew him out about their missiles."

"Well, I suppose . . . we'll find out."

THE MEETING WITH Gromyko was a full-on state affair, the Oval Office the natural setting. Kennedy was flanked by Dean Rusk, McGeorge Bundy, Ted Sorenson, with pen and pad in hand, and the ambassador to Russia, Llewellyn Thompson. Gromyko was accompanied by the ever-smiling Dobrynin, and an interpreter, a man whose English was so perfect, it was often suggested he would have made an excellent spy. Gromyko was his usual taciturn self, seemed perpetually grumpy. Immediately, Kennedy's fears were relaxed, as Gromyko spent most of the time haranguing the Americans for acting the bully toward Cuba, claiming that helpless Cuba was deeply afraid of its massively dangerous neighbor to the north, that the Soviets were only there to quiet the possible storm. As if to emphasize that he was reflecting only the views from Moscow, Gromyko read aloud from previously prepared sheets of paper, offering the assurances that he was there to make clear that Soviet assistance to Cuba was for defensive purposes only, aid to an ally.

Kennedy's response was cordial and firm, with no mention of course of Soviet missiles. He simply stated that it was the goal of the United States to prevent any aggressive action by Cuba against any of America's allies in the Western Hemisphere. He further claimed that the United States had no intention of invading Cuba.

Whether or not Gromyko left the meeting feeling any better, Kennedy understood that what had just transpired was an exercise in meaninglessness. And, of course, Gromyko had lied.

THE EXCOMM MEETINGS went on, McNamara continuing to press his idea for a blockade, the other side still adamant that a blockade would only prolong the agony, possibly for months, more than enough time to allow the Soviets to have their missile bases already in Cuba fully operational. Again, the arguments flowed freely, the same as before, insistence that there was no guarantee that any military strike, no matter how *surgical*, would eliminate all the designated targets. For the first time, more attention was being paid to the impact such a move would have on America's allies, specifically the Latin countries, members of the Organization of American States, as well as the NATO countries in Europe. Attacking Cuba might be seen as a bully's move, the assault on a sovereign nation for a reason that might be difficult to justify, given the Soviets' denial that the missile bases were offensive. And then, there were Khrushchev's threats, no one certain if the Soviet leader was merely shooting fireworks, or if the Russians were fully prepared for an all-out nuclear confrontation.

It was pushing close to midnight, more debates, weary discussions from men who more than once had switched positions, rarely holding to the themes they had proposed from the beginning. Bobby was more surprised with McNamara, who seemed to be backing away from his blockade plan altogether. McNamara held the floor, aiming his words at Bobby as much as the president.

"The more I consider this, the more I realize it's a political problem. I just don't believe the Soviet missiles pose a military threat. They're seeking leverage, that's all, to counter the presence of our missiles in Turkey. If we push too hard, provoke them too much . . . it could lead to much more than we're supposing. And, we have to prepare the American people to accept that the missiles are there and might just have to stay there."

Rusk agreed, focusing on the impact any kind of aggressive action would have on America's allies, some of whom seemed to feel that the United States had a somewhat ridiculous obsession with Cuba. And yet, Rusk seemed to vacillate again, saying, "We should give the Soviets a deadline. If they don't stop construction of the missile sites by October 23, next week, we tell them we're going to hit them with air strikes. We should tell our allies about that in advance, give them time to react. And, Khrushchev should be notified almost at the same time of the strikes, warning him that if he takes any counteraction, it will mean war. If we don't do this . . . we go down with a whimper. I'd rather see us go down with a bang."

Bobby was shocked, pushed his voice through a sudden chorus of comments.

"Gentlemen, I don't want to see us go *down* at all."

The door opened, McCone suddenly appearing, as usual, a

sheaf of papers gripped in one hand. The president, mostly quiet up until now, pointed toward him, said, "What's up?"

McCone glanced around, nods of acknowledgment.

"We have just revised our estimates. It is now believed that the first medium-range missile installations will be ready for launch by the Soviets in less than twenty-four hours."

CHAPTER FIFTEEN

RFK

Early on Friday, October 19, the president had finally met directly with the Joint Chiefs, the men who had consistently urged immediate military action in Cuba. The most vocal had been the most predictable, Air Force general Curtis LeMay, a man with every right to claim the title American Hero. LeMay had engineered the bombing campaigns over Japan, which did much to bring about the end of World War Two, and he had been in charge of the Strategic Air Command, before assuming the role as Air Force chief of staff. Pugnacious to a fault, he had already made a number of indiscreet comments about the job Kennedy was doing, specifically the Bay of Pigs debacle. The president disliked LeMay, had learned to avoid the man when possible, but with the Joint Chiefs so closely involved in the debates over Cuba, that was no longer possible.

True to form, it was LeMay who suggested in the strongest terms that the United States cut to the chase and use nuclear bombs across Cuba, and possibly, engage the Soviet Union directly, since, in LeMay's view, the Soviets were just as likely to respond to any action on Kennedy's part with nuclear missiles of their own. At the very least, LeMay cautioned that the idea of a blockade was insanely dangerous and would only provoke the Soviets to nuclear war.

The meeting, exhausting in its own way, only delayed Kennedy's departure for another campaign trip. He was not swayed by LeMay's argument.

THE EXCOMM MEETINGS had gone throughout the day on Friday, the nineteenth, and as before, the two sides of the debate seemed to solidify their positions, though the concept of a blockade was gaining momentum. The president was absent throughout, the last of his essential campaign stops, this time the Midwest and Chicago. In his absence, McNamara and Bobby held firmly to their hopes for a blockade, while others, including, now, McGeorge Bundy, still pushed for a military strike.

It was becoming obvious that Kennedy himself was going to have to make the decision on just what was going to happen next. Bobby spoke to him several times throughout Friday, welcome interruptions to the president's mundane schedule of so many talking points in support of various Democratic candidates. By Saturday morning, the twentieth, Bobby had convinced the president to return home, to cut short the campaigning with the standby excuse that the president had caught a cold. Though the crowds were disappointed, no one begrudged Kennedy the right to take care of himself. By early afternoon on Saturday, he was back in Washington.

Saturday, October 20, 1962
The White House

Bobby sat beside the pool, watched as his brother swam slow laps, unraveling the persistent tightness in his back. After a long silence,

Jack said, "I never thought I'd use this thing. Indoor pools seemed a little stifling. But I give credit to FDR. He deserves the thanks of every president who follows him. This pool is a godsend. I can see why he would have used it often, with his crippled legs. My back's killing me, but at least I can walk. I think about FDR and I don't take that for granted. I need to figure out how to put a whirlpool on Air Force One."

Bobby, not sure if his brother was joking, said, "Take your time. The next meeting will start when you get there, close to three, so they've been told. It will be a larger group, as you requested. Not sure if the Joint Chiefs will come. They've been a little pissy about being left out of the Excomm group so far, since General Taylor briefs them secondhand."

"They're still pissy. They didn't appreciate me not jumping whole hog into their idea to blow up the world. One thing I've learned about the military. Those brass hats have one great advantage. If we listen to them, and do what they want us to do, none of us will be alive later to tell them they were wrong."

Bobby watched as Jack swam another slow lap, until Kennedy stopped, seeming winded, said, "Enough of this, I think. You've got me anxious to get started. One thing concerns me, and there isn't much we can do about it."

"What?"

"Reporters. There are some pretty smart cookies, like Scotty Reston, Walt Lippmann, they're sniffing pretty steadily around this whole affair. They know something's up, and they're pushing hard for a story. We can't give them anything yet, but I know how sharp some of those boys are. They're already figuring out this has to do with Cuba, and certainly the Russians. I can only go so far in telling them, or rather, begging them not to print any kind of story until we figure out what we're doing. For now, we've been feeding them word that these meetings all have to do with Berlin. It's working, to a point."

"Jack, they're already running stories, mostly based on the noise coming from the Republicans, doubts about our Cuba policy, our Berlin policy, our Civil Rights policy, hell they're bitching about what you had for breakfast. The Republicans are feeding Reston and those fellows anything they can."

"I know. But this is real news, not just political whining. We have to hold them off, every damn one of us. If there's a weak link, a single leak, it could really screw us with the Russians. And that's dangerous."

"Well, Jack, maybe it's best we make some hard decisions pretty quick, something we can tell the public. That's why I thought you should come back here now, cut through the chatter, the arguments. We're really not making any progress."

Kennedy climbed up out of the water, wrapped a towel around himself.

"Sorenson gave me the draft of a speech he's been working on, something to tell the public. It's not ready yet, because I'm not ready. He fed me a whole pile of documents too, notes from your meetings, notes from the CIA, so at least I'm up to speed. I have a pretty good idea what I want us to do, but I'm not cutting the floor out from under anyone, not yet. Let's go hear what they have to say."

Saturday, October 20, 1962
The White House, Cabinet Room

The room was bulging with men, a few standing against the walls, no place to sit.

The debates were spirited, but Kennedy's presence seemed to

tone down the rhetoric, particularly among those who seemed eager still to deploy the military.

McCone had begun the discussion by distributing the latest photos from the CIA's constant surveillance over Cuba.

"As you can see, the construction work is progressing at a rapid pace. A greater number of missiles will be operational within days, or at most, a couple of weeks."

McCone sat as the photos were examined by men who had just learned the details of what they were seeing. Kennedy kept silent, as usual, pointed to Rusk, who said, "I have prepared a lengthy note on this, my reasoning for a blockade." He read for a while, then said, "The essence is that a blockade is a place to start, the first rung on a ladder. It is not a perfect solution. It is not a safe and secure action. But it opens the door for further action if it is required."

McNamara spoke up now, said, "Both choices before us are risky, but I will say this. A blockade is the most likely way to encourage the Soviets to remove their missiles, without going to war. That is after all, the point. We have to allow Khrushchev to have a place to retreat to, to back down. Otherwise, how do we convince them to back down from their position without blowing up the world? A military strike opens the door to a complete breakdown, to retaliation that will result in greater retaliation after that. There is no good ending to that scenario."

The deputy secretary of defense, Roswell Gilpatric, said, "Essentially, Mr. President, we are faced with two options, limited action and unlimited action. Most of us think that it's better to start with limited action."

Kennedy sat looking down, Bobby scanning the room, looking for signs anyone else had something to say. The room was silent for a long moment, all eyes on the president, who finally said, "There is one argument that hasn't been made here. What are the principles of the United States, the principles we live and govern under? Go back to Teddy Roosevelt. *Walk softly and carry a big stick.* We have the stick. We are the most powerful nuclear nation on Earth, no matter what the Russians want everyone else to believe. But taking military action against a sovereign nation goes against the United Nations Charter, and it goes against the principles that are my responsibility to maintain. An air strike opens a door that cannot be closed. The potential for escalation is absolute, and certainly could result in an all-out invasion of Cuba. The air strike would cause Russian deaths. An invasion will cause deaths on all sides. That is not how we should begin. I agree that an air strike is an irreversible step. Our bombers, excellent weapons that they are, are not surgical instruments, but bludgeons. It may become necessary still to use those weapons, but it is not how we should start. I also prefer that we continue with troop and warship mobilization in the southeast, in the event our forces must act in short order. It cannot hurt our cause to show such a mobilization to both the Russians and Cubans, that we are serious in backing up our plans."

Rusk raised his hand, said, "Mr. President, I have been advised by one of my legal counsels, Mr. Meeker, that we forgo use of the word *blockade*, and instead refer to our action as a *quarantine.* The reasons make sense to me, that *blockade* is a far more militaristic term."

Bobby laughed, said, "Does it matter? Semantics won't change the way we'll be perceived, all over the world. Khrushchev won't care what we call it."

The president held up a hand.

"No, I don't agree. Semantics might mean a great deal. All right, for now, we refer to our action as a *quarantine* of Cuba, that we are preventing any more offensive weapons from entering the country. The quarantine specifically will put a halt to offensive weapons and weapon systems, but will not interfere in the legal transport of material goods, such as food and fuel for the Cuban people."

Bobby spoke up again, all heads turning his way.

"We should examine the legality here. By that I mean we should secure the approval of the OAS countries. I believe our charter calls for a two-thirds approval for any action. That means we would need at least fourteen of the twenty nations to approve what we're doing. Without that backing, we'll be out on a pretty big limb. And, we should immediately notify our allies in Europe, plus Canada and Australia, just what's going on. No one likes surprises, and this is a big one."

Kennedy nodded slowly, spoke in a low voice.

"Agreed. See to it. You all have your stations. Man them, with secrecy still, and efficiency. Wait for the final word from me. I still want to discuss the effectiveness of air strikes with our tactical bombing experts. But that is an option we must hold on to for now. I want all of you to understand that I have not ruled out a military strike. But I will not start with one. I hope you are all clear on that."

Bobby said, "What about your speech? Are you prepared to go forward with this publicly?"

"I had hoped tomorrow evening. But perhaps that's too soon for the work that must still be done. Let's schedule it for Monday night, October 22. I'll have the press people clear it with the networks. And I want it broadcast in Spanish as well, to reach as much of Latin America as possible, including, of course, Cuba."

The door opened, and Adlai Stevenson appeared, disheveled, moving with clumsy haste.

"Sorry. I couldn't get here sooner from New York. Mr. President, I have something to say."

Kennedy sat back, seemed to clamp down on his expression, said, "We have made great progress today, Adlai. But we will listen."

Bobby watched Stevenson, searching in vain for a chair. He doesn't care what's been decided, he thought. He just has to hear his own voice.

Stevenson, finally resigned to standing, said, "I propose, Mr.

President, that we summon the United Nations Security Council into session, to coincide with any public announcement of what we intend to do. I also believe we should inform the Soviets we are withdrawing from Guantánamo Naval Base, and that we will guarantee that we will demilitarize and neutralize the territorial integrity of Cuba. We should also announce that we will remove our missiles from Turkey as part of the arrangement whereby the Soviets will remove their missiles from Cuba. It's only fair, after all."

There was a hum of grumbling around the room, and Kennedy said, "We are already pursuing contacts with the OAS nations. I will not abandon Guantánamo, nor will I pull the missiles out of Turkey, merely as a sop to the Soviets. There are no secrets regarding our missiles in Turkey, but should we unilaterally decide to remove them, it could seriously weaken our NATO alliances. Missiles in Cuba serve no purpose other than to threaten us. Missiles in Turkey and Italy serve as a defensive deterrent against Soviet aggressive moves against NATO. Do you not see the difference? Besides, the Soviets have never threatened us with regard to those missiles. They have accepted their presence as a fait accompli. That is not the case with the missiles in Cuba, which, as things stand now, are still being installed in secret, presumably to be sprung on us later as a surprise. You seem to be suggesting that we are the provocateurs here, that we are threatening Cuba's integrity. We have done nothing of the sort, and for now, we do not intend to."

Others agreed, Bobby watching Stevenson's doughy face, the man clearly not expecting to have his suggestions refuted. Bobby looked to his brother now, saw exhausted aggravation, Kennedy gathering papers, preparation for ending the meeting. Bobby looked at his watch, 5:30, thought suddenly of Neville Chamberlain. Appeasement. That's what Adlai is suggesting. Give away the store, only so the Russians *might* oblige us by doing the same. That could be a catastrophic mistake. Assuming we offer all that Stevenson suggests, what if Khrushchev simply says no? We would be left with no alternative other than war. Well, perhaps we are left with that alternative regardless. But by God, I'm with Jack. It's essential that we have options. We can talk later about missiles in Turkey.

CHAPTER SIXTEEN

Russo

Sunday, October 21, 1962
Tallahassee, Florida

He hesitated at the stop sign, then sped through, made the sharp turn onto his street. He had taken a shortcut through side streets, since out on the main highway, the way was blocked by an enormous column of trucks, what seemed to be a never-ending parade. He reached his driveway, turned in, saw Danny, holding a football, the boy with a glance toward him, then staring out toward the highway.

"Hey, Pop! What's all that? Must be a million trucks. Eddie next door says it's all army, soldiers and stuff."

Russo was out of the car now, stood with his hands on his hips, saw neighbors doing the same, all eyes on the vast line of green vehicles. The sound was steady, a hard rumble, huge tires on pavement, engines belching black smoke. He could smell the exhaust now, said, "Yep. It's army. I heard the news, that there're some exercises down south, maybe toward the Keys. Seems like a lot of trouble for exercises. I guess our tax dollars are paying for it."

He looked down the street, saw his neighbor, Jerry, the man's fallout shelter nearly completed. Jerry saw him, moved closer, never a smile, said, "Well, Professor, what do you think? I'm bettin' we're going down to teach those Cuban Commies a lesson. I heard we're set to invade, toss Castro into the ocean. It's about damn time."

"Where'd you hear that?"

"Around. My oldest boy's maybe out there, one of those trucks. He's stationed at Fort Hood and wrote us that things were about to heat up. That's all he'd say. I guess they have to keep their mouths shut, so their mail doesn't get censored. He does a lot of secret stuff though. He's a damn fine soldier. We need a lot like him these days. I told you before, things are going to get nasty."

"If you say so. I heard it was all for drill, war games or something."

"Professor, for a smart fellow, you don't seem to pay much attention to things. I been listening to some of those fellows running for election. There's a lot of talk how Kennedy isn't doing the job, that he's letting Khrushchev walk all over him. Well, maybe Kennedy's decided to do something about it. I don't have much faith in that, but, well, there goes the army."

Russo didn't want to talk politics, ever, not with this man. He looked toward Jerry's house, said, "How's the fallout shelter coming?"

"Near done. Just put in the air pump yesterday. Ingenious. Hand cranks, brings in filtered air. Keeps out all the radioactivity."

"You sure about that?"

Jerry sniffed, as though talking to an imbecile.

"Read the brochure, Professor. It comes with a guarantee. I'm telling you, you'd be smart to invest in one of these things. But, the way things are looking right now, might not be time enough to install one. The world's getting hotter, if you know what I mean. All I gotta say is, my rifle's loaded."

HE PUSHED ASIDE the dinner plate, half his meat loaf still there.

"You didn't like it?"

He looked at her, tried to smile.

"No, it was fine. Just not all that hungry. I keep hearing those trucks. They're still coming. The third convoy today. They've got the main roads blocked off downtown, so those fellows can move through pretty quick. If they're still coming tomorrow, I'll have to take Duval Street to get to school."

"Hey Pop, you missed the end of the football game. Green Bay beat up on the 49ers. They're still undefeated."

He looked at his son, forced a smile.

"Yep, they'll probably win the championship, the way they're going. I'm more happy about FSU. They beat Georgia yesterday. That was a surprise."

He loved talking football with the boy, but his mind wouldn't focus, the sound of the trucks in the way.

"I think I'll go outside. It's not dark yet. Just for a minute."

He saw her look, concern, knew he couldn't hide how he was feeling. He pushed open the screen, went into the backyard, the sound of the trucks louder now. The glow of headlights came from the highway, the steady rumble. He stepped out farther, glanced skyward, Venus to one side, no other stars out yet. She was there now, moving up quietly beside him.

"This is really bothering you, isn't it?"

He let out a breath, said, "Yep. Not sure why. I want to believe what the news says, that this is all about training exercises down south. Then that idiot Jerry spouts out all his conspiracy nonsense, like he knows big secrets. There's too much talk. I can't believe the government is keeping so many secrets. But then, maybe it's best. Maybe we're not supposed to know what all's going on, so we're not scared to death. I just hope the people who are in charge know what the hell they're doing."

She hugged his arm, said nothing. Around them, lightning bugs began to appear, tiny flashes of light. He smiled, said, "When I was young, I used to catch those things, put them in a jar, watch them glow, even when they were captured. But I felt guilty about it, and let them go. I know Danny does that kind of stuff. I guess it's one of the rules about being a kid. Torture animals. I used to catch butterflies too. At least he doesn't do that."

Margaret laughed now.

"No, the only thing I've seen him torture is his ant farm. I finally threw that thing out, once he seemed to forget about it. A thousand dead ants. At least they didn't escape into the house." She paused, shared his attention on the lightning bugs. After a long moment, she said, "I have to go to Monticello tomorrow. They have some people out sick and need me to look in on some of their clients."

He thought of the euphemism, *clients*, the unfortunates who needed her help, the cartons she carried to them, surplus food, clothing provided by the government.

"Just be careful. The highway might be blocked off with more of these trucks."

"I know the back ways, Joe. I'll be okay."

"I know you will. I've been thinking about my classes tomorrow. They'll want to talk about this. They're sharp kids, and I know they'll ask all kinds of questions about what this all means. I'm sure the political science fellows will analyze this to death, but hell, I'm just an English teacher. I don't know any more of what's going on than my students do. I have no comforting words to offer anybody, not even my own family. I could be like Jerry, go buy a rifle, make like I'm John Wayne. Then maybe build us a concrete fortress in the backyard, pretend that will protect us from anything that goes wrong."

"You think something's wrong?"

He stared out through the growing darkness, flickers of head-lights from the highway.

"I think something's happening that we're not supposed to know. And that's scary as hell."

CHAPTER SEVENTEEN

RFK

Sunday, October 21, 1962
The White House

The press was swarming, seasoned reporters sniffing in every corner. They were experienced men who understood that routine meant calm, and among the president's closest advisors, the usual routines had seemed to vanish. Late night meetings had become normal, lights blazing in high offices, limousines gathered in unlikely places, standard meetings cancelled, the normalcy of state dinners and pleasant social interactions interrupted by *pressing matters.* Kennedy had made every effort to conduct business as usual, to throw the persistent reporters off the trail, but even he knew it was hopeless, that these men who had made Washington their news beat for so many years had an instinct for drama. In a futile gesture, as though making a good show, Kennedy attended worship services that morning alongside Jackie, a small unassuming Catholic church called St. Stephen the Martyr. As always, the press was waiting, recording his every move, which, on the surface seemed as mundane as any other Sunday. The service concluded,

Kennedy wasted no time with pleasantries and immediately returned to the White House.

The Excomm meeting was scheduled for later that afternoon, but Kennedy met now with a smaller group, men who insisted on a forum to discuss their own doubts. Along with Bobby sat McNamara, General Taylor, and Air Force general Walter Sweeney, as well as McCone and another CIA analyst, fresh with the latest intel from the U-2 flights. Bobby sat slightly apart from the others, as though appraising, measuring what he had heard so far, fighting the urge to raise holy hell.

McCone had the floor, examining the photos, now in each man's hands.

"We are certain, Mr. President, that as of right now, eight to twelve Soviet medium-range missiles are operational and can be fired with no more than a three- or four-hour advance notice. I urge you, sir, to reconsider your options."

Taylor spoke now, waving the photos like a small flag.

"I agree, sir. The Joint Chiefs and I are unanimous in our view that an air strike is called for, and quickly. We are firm in our belief that a blockade . . . excuse me, *quarantine*, will do nothing to eliminate the crisis we now face, and may in fact, make it worse."

McNamara said, "I am beginning to agree. I hadn't expected the Soviets to make such rapid progress with their deployments, their construction. The more I consider the quarantine, the less secure I am that the Soviets will respond the way we need them to. Khrushchev is a wild card, and we don't know what kind of pressure he is under at the Kremlin. Surely there are hard-liners, the same men who supported the installation of their missiles in the first place. It's doubtful they will simply change their minds."

Taylor said, "We know that there are at least forty missile

launchers in place. Even though there is no photograph which specifically shows nuclear warheads, there are indications of bunkers close to the launch sites, where the warheads likely are stored." He looked at Sweeney, who said, "Sir, I would suggest you authorize the bombing of those sites, as well as the airfields where the MiGs are now situated. We can commence that action within hours of your say-so."

Taylor leaned forward, his arms out on the table, as if to emphasize the importance of his words.

"Mr. President, an air strike will eliminate ninety percent of the known missile sites. If it becomes necessary to engage further, we can stage a full-on invasion within ten days. The preparations are being made even now, troop movements, Navy ships assembling within range. The carrier *Essex* is prepared to launch planes at a moment's notice."

Bobby could see the raw anger on the president's face. He held back, knew that Kennedy would have the final say, with no help from his brother.

"Gentlemen, your input is appreciated, but you are certainly aware, from our last meeting, that the decision has been made. We have weighed every piece of what you describe, and much more. We have made every effort to anticipate the Soviet response to any action we might take and have come to the conclusion that the quarantine is the first step. I'm surprised you would come to me now. Be advised that I will be announcing to the American people tomorrow evening that we are instituting a quarantine of Cuba. At this evening's executive meeting, we will examine every particle of that speech, and iron out every wrinkle." He paused, seemed to hesitate. "Look, it is important that you understand that I am not disregarding your counsel. You should continue with your preparations and be ready to launch an air strike on my command anytime. It's true, we cannot predict what Khrushchev will do. But assuming the worst is a mistake. That being said, I require you to *prepare* for the worst. That is, after all, the military's job. Right now, there are wheels in motion all over the world, our State Department people and others preparing to issue official notifications of our intentions to dozens of nations. I will not spread a smoke screen over anyone's eyes, only to spring some kind of surprise attack on Cuba. Every issue we discussed, every variable is still in play. But I will not start a war as a first step. Are we clear?"

There was a brief silence, Bobby staring at McNamara, eager to ask the obvious question, why did you change your mind yet again? He wondered now about the meeting to come later that day, if other members of Excomm were having second thoughts, if there was a growing consensus that an air strike might be the best decision after all. I suppose, he thought, we'll know soon enough.

THE TWO MEN were alone now, Kennedy's mood seeming more at ease. They had been visited by the British ambassador, David Ormsby-Gore, the man a close friend to both Kennedys. Ormsby-Gore had accepted news of the impending action against Cuba with the knowing smile of a man who had already figured out most of what was going on. It was little surprise that the British had quietly felt the pulse of the Soviets, as well as the goings-on in Washington, and with no real activity involving Berlin, by process of elimination, the British had assumed there was a crisis brewing in Cuba. Kennedy was completely frank about the Soviet missiles, Ormsby-Gore reacting as Kennedy would hope, pledging complete support for whatever action the Americans were to take. Ormsby-Gore would, of course, immediately report the news to his prime minister, Harold MacMillan, the first in a line of American allies to be briefed.

Dean Acheson, on his way to Paris, was scheduled to meet with

French president Charles de Gaulle. In Bonn, American ambassador Walter Dowling had arranged to confer with German chancellor Konrad Adenauer. The treasury secretary, Douglas Dillon, had flown to Mexico to meet with Mexican officials, an important link in the chain, since the Mexicans would wield considerable influence with other members of the OAS. Former U.S. ambassador Livingston Merchant had been tagged to sit down with Canadian prime minister John Diefenbaker. Diefenbaker was no friend to the Kennedys, and Merchant's job was to smooth over the prickly relationship between the Canadians and the American administration, to convince Diefenbaker that what Kennedy was planning was the only wise move. By meeting with Diefenbaker as a *special envoy*, it was hoped that Merchant could accomplish exactly that, to ensure Canadian cooperation.

With these aircraft in the skies, the president made specific phone calls himself, personal conversations with all three surviving U.S. presidents, Eisenhower, Truman, and Hoover. Though he didn't require their counsel, not at this late date, it was gratifying that, although they certainly had questions, none of the three objected to Kennedy's decision.

Sunday, October 21, 1962
Excomm meeting, the White House Cabinet Room

Rusk had the floor, and was standing, which was unusual, and addressed the room as much as he focused on the president.

"Mr. President, the State Department has prepared explanatory letters to the consulates of one hundred thirty-four countries. In addition, we have scheduled briefings here in Washington, for ninety-five foreign ambassadors. We have drafted a special text to be presented to the United Nations Security Council, and we have prepared detailed documents to be presented to an emergency meeting of the Organization of American States. The ambassadors from those countries will also be notified, of course. As we have discussed, the OAS is being asked to vote approval on our planned quarantine, as part of Article 51 of the United Nations Charter, which states that each member nation has the right to defend its own border. But more importantly, we are making the point that each member nation of the OAS is obliged to participate in collective measures in guarding the overall security of the Americas. We are hopeful that the majority of the Latin nations will understand that what the Soviets have done in Cuba is a threat to every sovereign nation in this hemisphere. Assuming we gain approval of at least fourteen of those nations, our actions will be deemed completely legal on the world stage."

Bobby stared at Rusk, and for the first time, he understood why his brother had been so adamant about Rusk being named secretary of state. Kennedy, who had absorbed Rusk's presentation without any expression, nodded slowly as Rusk sat down. Kennedy then motioned toward the chief of naval operations, Admiral George Anderson. Bobby liked Anderson, a tall, beefy man who looked the part of the firm-handed commander. The president said, "Admiral, you have received specific instructions regarding your role in the quarantine. Please fill in the committee as to those plans."

Anderson stood as well, consulted a legal pad.

"Mr. President, as per your orders, the quarantine line will be established at a point eight hundred miles from Cuban territorial waters, which places them out of range of the Soviet MiGs and their bombers that are now on Cuba. Each Soviet ship, or any ship in service to the Soviet Union, that approaches the line will be signaled to halt and commanded to prepare for boarding and inspection. If the ship does not respond, we will fire a shot across the bow. If the vessel continues to ignore the hail, one of our warships will fire a shot into the ship's rudder and cripple the ship. Unless we are directly fired upon, we will not take any action to sink the ship."

Bobby said, "Excuse me, Admiral, but can we do that effectively, with precision?"

He caught a brief smile on Anderson's face.

"Absolutely, Mr. Attorney General."

Kennedy kept his somber expression, his eyes still on the admiral.

"You realize, Admiral, how much we are depending on your people to carry this ball. The success of this entire operation depends on the actions of the Navy."

Anderson stiffened, said, "Mr. President, the Navy will not let you down."

Monday, October 22, 1962
Excomm meeting, the White House Cabinet Room

The meeting focused on Bundy, who still seemed to favor the military strike.

"The Republicans are going to raise hell, you know. They'll say that you knew about the missiles for weeks before doing anything, giving the Soviets plenty of time to complete their construction."

Kennedy seemed annoyed, said, "You know damn well that I only learned about these missiles a week ago, from the U-2 flights."

"But the Republicans will say they knew well before that. Keating, the others, they've been spouting off about this stuff since August. How the hell did they know?"

Bobby shared his brother's annoyance, said, "They didn't. They were being fed reports from the CIA people in Miami. That place leaks like a sponge. They took every report of any kind of missile and blew it up to something dramatic, reports from completely unreliable eyewitnesses that we had discounted as being useless." He looked at McCone now. "You confirmed that those reports were coming from utterly unreliable sources. Is that still the case?"

McCone shifted uncomfortably, but seemed to puff up against the obvious insinuation.

"What the Republicans believe they know has nothing to do with reality, with any hard information. They just happened to have guessed right. But they have no specifics, they know nothing about the position or quantity of MRBMs or IRBMs. They can claim anything they want. If they make too much noise, I wouldn't hesitate, Mr. President, to remind them that spreading this kind of information without confirmation puts them in a dicey legal position."

Kennedy seemed to be weary of any talk of politics.

"It won't come to that. I won't let it. Let them have their day in the sun. The greater problem is the issue we're dealing with, not who knew what at what time. You've been given drafts of the speech prepared by Sorenson. I've already nixed a few lines, a few points that don't belong."

Bobby said, "I think it's important to remember that there is nothing inherently illegal about the missiles being in Cuba. Instead, we should emphasize Khrushchev's lies, his complete duplicity about the offensive nature of the weapons."

McNamara said, "Mr. President, I would also refrain from offering details as to the number of missiles, their positions, etc. There is no need to show our hand when it comes to our intelligence capabilities. The Soviets know we're overhead taking pictures, but it isn't necessary to tell them just how good those pictures are."

Rusk said, "Your ultimatum, the whole purpose of the quarantine, should be aimed directly at Khrushchev, the Soviets, and not Cuba. We don't want to be seen as having a conflict with Cuba over this mess. That just makes us out to be a bully. This is a U.S. versus

Soviet problem. That should be emphasized. I also believe it would be wise to invite the United Nations inspectors to set up shop, to oversee the missile sites."

Kennedy shook his head.

"No. Bringing in the UN would take time, too much time. They would serve no real purpose, and frankly, I don't think the UN would view this with the same urgency we do."

Bobby stepped forward, leaned his hands on the table, the other eyes on him.

"We might not be able to completely predict Khrushchev's response, but we had best be prepared for anything that comes out of the Kremlin."

Kennedy held up a hand, said, "I think it's pretty obvious that we can expect the Soviets to increase the speed of their construction, and they might be prompted to do something aggressive toward Berlin, some kind of tit-for-tat. You can be damned sure that Khrushchev will bellow out a new warning about any invasion of Cuba. That's his one strength, protecting the sovereignty of Cuba, and now that we know about the missiles, he'll up the ante with his threats. I fully expect he'll tell us, if you invade Cuba, we'll fire the missiles."

Bobby was impressed, had wondered just how far ahead his brother was thinking. But the words stirred up his gut, the faces in the room sharing the same uneasiness. The room was silent for a long moment, and Bobby said, "If he makes that threat, do you think he'll mean it? You think he's willing to start a nuclear war?"

Kennedy scanned the room, looked down now, his hands clasped on the table.

"That's the question, isn't it?"

WITH THE SPEECH scheduled for Monday night, all doubts about the nature of this crisis had been swept away from the eyes of the news reporters. Kennedy accepted the inevitable, that if the major news outlets printed the story detailing offensive missiles in Cuba prior to his speech, any hope of surprising Khrushchev would be gone. Kennedy reacted proactively, contacting directly the key players at *The Washington Post*, *The New York Times*, and the *New York Herald-Tribune*. Kennedy confirmed what they all had suspected, openly admitting the coming action, with the hoped-for stipulation that the newspapers would hold off on running the complete story until Kennedy had notified the public himself. They agreed to comply. But still, the stories were spreading, and even if many of the news outlets didn't know exact details, the sense of alarm was being communicated. The *San Francisco Examiner* blared in its Monday morning headline, "A Day of Mystery in D.C.!" Though *The New York Times* had agreed not to publish specifics until after Kennedy's scheduled speech, the *Times* still offered an opening line to tease its readers: "There was an air of crisis in the capital tonight . . ."

Monday, October 22, 1962

Throughout the day, the Excomm continued to wrestle with the speech Kennedy was now set to give at seven that night. The television networks had been notified, a request for airtime, all of them complying without question. Arrangements had been made, at Kennedy's request, for a Spanish language broadcast that would reach into Cuba, and much farther, into most of Latin America's capitals.

In Washington, the Joint Chiefs issued their orders to the naval force, already deployed throughout the Caribbean. One hundred eighty warships had assembled off the coast of Florida and Cuba, with the quarantine line to be comprised of destroyers, backed up by a force of cruisers. With the Air Force now ordered into readiness, one-eighth of the Strategic Air Command's B-52 bombers would remain airborne at all times, armed with nuclear bombs. The remaining flight crews would be on alert, prepared to become airborne in fifteen minutes. The Air Force's missile crews, manning silos spread across the nation, were ordered into maximum alert.

With Excomm now firmly committed to Kennedy's speech, with the specific points settled under full agreement, Kennedy scheduled one last meeting. For weeks now, he had endured the criticism coming from Congress, including from members of his own party. Two hours before he went on the air, he met with twenty congressional leaders from both parties. With the assistance of McCone, Rusk, and McNamara, the entire scenario was laid before the astonished congressmen, but their responses were not what Kennedy had hoped to hear. To Kennedy's enormous annoyance, the congressmen seemed too eager to jump into the fray, dismissing the quarantine idea, opting instead for a full-on invasion of Cuba, starting of course with a massive bombing campaign to eliminate the Soviet missiles. Democratic Senators Russell of Georgia and Fulbright of Arkansas, along with several Republicans, suggested in the strongest terms that the invasion option was the proper way to go. Egos came to the fore as well, the Republican leader of the House, Indiana congressman Charles Halleck, among others, insisting that the record show that the congressmen were merely being *informed*, and not *consulted*. Kennedy blunted as much of the criticism as possible by pointing out that the quarantine was only a first step, that military options were still on the table. After all, the complete bulk of the nation's military power had been activated or placed on alert. After so much criticism, Kennedy's patience had worn thin, especially since he had not believed that key members of his own party would stand up in opposition to the quarantine plan. After more than an hour, the meeting ended abruptly, a furious Kennedy making every effort to hold on to his temper. His final comment to Bobby summed up his mood. *"I should have let them read about it in the paper."*

There was one final detail that required prompt attention. With one hour to go before the president's broadcast, Secretary of State Rusk met with Soviet ambassador Dobrynin. By six o'clock, there was no longer any need for subterfuge. Dobrynin was given a full copy of Kennedy's speech. Shortly after in Moscow, Ambassador Foy Kohler did the same, offering the text to the office of the Soviet premier.

CHAPTER EIGHTEEN

Russo

Monday, October 22, 1962
Tallahassee, Florida

He pulled into the driveway, avoided the ever-present football, eased the car to a stop. He expected a greeting, but the yard was empty, assumed both children were inside. Margaret's car was already there, unusual, and he climbed out of the Ford, thought, a short day for her. That's good. She'll be in a good mood.

He picked up the football, wondered about Danny, knew the boy would never miss the chance for a catch. It was the boy's dream, to play football, at any level that would have him. The boy had a surprising talent, amazing hands, could catch anything thrown his way. Already, coaches at the middle school were asking him to come out for the team, though Russo was nervous about that. The boy was undersized, and Russo imagined every parent's nightmare, to sit in some grandstands, while your child ended up being carried off the field. Danny took it well, though Russo knew the boy was hanging around the practice field at school, the coach teaching him how to run pass patterns, both of them no doubt wondering if the time would come when Danny would finally be allowed to play.

He tossed the ball into the grass, thought again of the controversy at the middle school, so many of the parents on both sides of the issue making the big fuss about finally allowing Black students to attend the school. Incredibly, there were only to be two students, a bizarre example of tokenism, as though baby steps were the only way such a move could be accepted by most of the white parents. The boy was named Leroy Powell, and it didn't escape Russo that he actually knew the boy's name, along with everyone else in town. It was no coincidence that Leroy was an exceptional athlete, so naturally, a way was found to bring the boy into the all-white school. There had been a girl too, her name obscure, Danny talking about Julia something, Danny accepting her presence as just another day at school. But Russo wondered about her, the sheer terror of walking into a school where you're *the only one*. God help her, he thought. Hopefully, someone will have the brains to allow more of the Black kids to come over from the Black school, or maybe, one day, there won't even be a *Black* school, just . . . school.

Maybe I should run for the school board.

He moved toward the front door, no sounds from the house, opened the door, and caught the fantastic smell.

"Hello? My God, what is that?"

He heard her call out, "I'm in the kitchen. Wipe your feet, and get ready for dinner. It will be ready in a minute. Sorry to be so early, but I've never really done this before. It took less time than I thought."

"Whatever it is, I approve."

He saw both children now, drawn as he was to the smells from the kitchen. Danny said, "What's Mom making?"

"I guess we'll find out soon enough."

SHE HAD PREPARED fried chicken for dinner. It wasn't the usual TV-dinner variety, but fresh, the kitchen now a mess of spattered grease and the heavy odor of frying. It was a rare treat, only happening when Margaret had the extra time to give, home early, finally making use of a recipe offered her by one of her clients, an old couple out east of town who did everything the Southern way. They had even supplied her with a package of field peas, another treat she could never find in the grocery store.

He sat back in the chair, rubbed his stomach, ran his tongue through the last coating of grease in his mouth, knew it would be a long while before she sacrificed the cleanliness of her kitchen to do this again. Beside him, Danny said, "Mom, that was great. How come we don't have fried chicken more often?"

Margaret stood, moved away from the table, plates in hand, said, "Because this house will smell like this for three days, and I'll be wiping grease off the stove for an hour. So, I hope you enjoyed it. That elderly couple, the Johnsons, they've been offering me all sorts of recipes to try, and they grew those peas in their garden. They don't think I'm feeding you well enough, that it's important to have a good helping of lard every now and then. Well, there you go. Tomorrow night, it's salad."

Russo wasn't sure if she was kidding or not, tossed the last piece of crispy chicken skin into his mouth, saw happy smiles on the faces of both children. Becky said, "Daddy, there's pie."

Margaret set the plates in the sink, said, "Yes, there's pie. Peach, to be exact. Another gift from Mrs. Johnson. That woman is determined that I not fit into my clothes. Give me one minute, and I'll dish it out."

Russo loved pie, and it didn't matter what kind.

"You should go visit the Johnsons more often. I could get used to this. But I'll enjoy the salad too." He glanced at his watch, not quite seven. "Save my pie for later. I think I'll catch the news, see what bad tidings Walter Cronkite has for us today."

He carried his plate to the sink, a quick kiss on the cheek for Margaret, then moved to the living room. He sat heavily on the soft sofa, felt the weight in his stomach once more. Good thing she doesn't cook like that every day, he thought. I'd weigh a ton. He bent forward, reached out, turned the knob on the TV set, leaned back, glanced toward the kitchen, the sound of dishes in the sink. I should help her, he thought. But right now, I feel like a whale.

"We interrupt this nightly news report, for a special bulletin. The president of the United States."

Russo stared at the TV, felt a twist in his gut, always the reaction to a special news bulletin. What's Kennedy want, he thought.

"Hey, Margaret. The president's on TV."

She came in, dish towel in one hand, the children trailing behind. They sat, as the figure of the president appeared, seated at a desk, flags behind him.

"Good evening my fellow citizens. This government, as promised, has maintained the closest surveillance of the Soviet military buildup on the island of Cuba. Within the past week, unmistakable evidence has established the fact that a series of offensive missile sites is now in preparation on that imprisoned island. The purpose of these bases can be none other than to provide a nuclear strike capability against the Western Hemisphere.

"Upon receiving the first preliminary hard information of this nature last Tuesday morning at nine a.m., I directed that our surveillance be stepped up. And having now confirmed and completed our evaluation of the evidence and our decision on a course of action, this government feels obliged to report this new crisis to you in fullest detail.

"The characteristics of these new missile sites indicate two distinct types of installations. Several of them include medium-range ballistic missiles capable of carrying a nuclear warhead for a distance of more than one thousand nautical miles. Each of these missiles, in short, is capable of striking Washington, D.C., the Panama Canal, Cape Canaveral, Mexico City, or any other city in the southeastern part of the United States, in Central America, or in the Caribbean area.

"Additional sites not yet completed appear to be designed for intermediate-range ballistic missiles—capable of traveling more than twice as far—and thus capable of striking most of the major cities in the Western Hemisphere, ranging as far north as Hudson Bay, Canada, and as far south as Lima, Peru. In addition, jet bombers, capable of carrying nuclear weapons, are now being uncrated and assembled in Cuba, while the necessary air bases are being prepared.

"This urgent transformation of Cuba into an important strategic base—by the presence of these large, long-range, and clearly offensive weapons of sudden mass destruction—constitutes an explicit threat to the peace and security of all the Americas, in flagrant and deliberate defiance of the Rio Pact of 1947, the traditions of this nation and hemisphere, the joint resolution of the 87th Congress, the Charter of the United Nations, and my own public warnings to the Soviets on September 4 and 13. This action also contradicts the repeated assurances of Soviet spokesmen, both publicly and privately delivered, that the arms buildup in Cuba would retain its original defensive character, and that the Soviet Union had no need or desire to station strategic missiles on the territory of any other nation.

"The size of this undertaking makes clear that it has been planned for some months. Yet only last month, after I had made clear the distinction between any introduction of ground-to-ground missiles and the existence of defensive antiaircraft missiles, the Soviet government publicly stated on September 11, and I quote, 'the armaments and military equipment sent to Cuba are designed exclusively for defensive purposes,' that, and I quote the Soviet government, 'there is no need for the Soviet government to shift its weapons . . . for a retaliatory blow to any other country, for instance Cuba,' and that, and I quote their government, 'the Soviet Union has so many powerful rockets to carry these nuclear warheads that there is no need to search for sites for them beyond the boundaries of the Soviet Union.' That statement was false.

"Only last Thursday, as evidence of this rapid offensive buildup was already in my hand, Soviet foreign minister Gromyko told me in my office that he was instructed to make it clear once again, as he said his government had already done, that Soviet assistance to Cuba, and I quote, 'pursued solely the purpose of contributing to the defense capabilities of Cuba,' that, and I quote him, 'training by Soviet specialists of Cuban nationals in handling defensive armaments was by no means offensive, and if it were otherwise,' Mr. Gromyko went on, 'the Soviet government would never become involved in rendering such assistance.' That statement also was false.

"Neither the United States of America nor the world community of nations can tolerate deliberate deception and offensive threats on the part of any nation, large or small. We no longer live in a world where only the actual firing of weapons represents a sufficient challenge to a nation's security to constitute maximum peril. Nuclear weapons are so destructive and ballistic missiles are so swift, that any substantially increased possibility of their use or any sudden change in their deployment may well be regarded as a definite threat to peace.

"For many years both the Soviet Union and the United States, recognizing this fact, have deployed strategic nuclear weapons with great care, never upsetting the precarious status quo which ensured that these weapons would not be used in the absence of some vital challenge. Our own strategic missiles have never been transferred to the territory of any other nation under a cloak of secrecy and deception; and our history—unlike that of the Soviets since the end of World War II—demonstrates that we have no desire to dominate or conquer any other nation or impose our system upon its people. Nevertheless, American citizens have become adjusted to living daily on the bull's-eye of Soviet missiles located inside the U.S.S.R. or in submarines.

"In that sense, missiles in Cuba add to an already clear and present danger—although it should be noted the nations of Latin America have never previously been subjected to a potential nuclear threat.

"But this secret, swift, and extraordinary buildup of Communist missiles—in an area well known to have a special and historical relationship to the United States and the nations of the Western Hemisphere, in violation of Soviet assurances, and in defiance of American and hemispheric policy—this sudden, clandestine decision to station strategic weapons for the first time outside of Soviet soil—is a deliberately provocative and unjustified change in the status quo which cannot be accepted by this country, if our courage and our commitments are ever to be trusted again by either friend or foe.

"The 1930s taught us a clear lesson: aggressive conduct, if allowed to go unchecked and unchallenged ultimately leads to war. This nation is opposed to war. We are also true to our word. Our unswerving objective, therefore, must be to prevent the use of these missiles against this or any other country and to secure their withdrawal or elimination from the Western Hemisphere.

"Our policy has been one of patience and restraint, as befits a peaceful and powerful nation, which leads a worldwide alliance. We have been determined not to be diverted from our central concerns by mere irritants and fanatics. But now further action is required—and it is under way; and these actions may only be the beginning. We will not prematurely or unnecessarily risk the costs of worldwide nuclear war in which even the fruits of victory would be ashes in our mouth—but neither will we shrink from that risk at any time it must be faced.

"Acting, therefore, in the defense of our own security and of the entire Western Hemisphere, and under the authority entrusted to me by the Constitution as endorsed by the resolution of the Congress, I have directed that the following initial steps be taken immediately:

"First: To halt this offensive buildup, a strict quarantine on all offensive military equipment under shipment to Cuba is being initiated. All ships of any kind bound for Cuba from whatever nation or port will, if found to contain cargoes of offensive weapons, be turned back. This quarantine will be extended, if needed, to other types of cargo and carriers. We are not at this time, however, denying the necessities of life as the Soviets attempted to do in their Berlin blockade of 1948.

"Second: I have directed the continued and increased close surveillance of Cuba and its military buildup. The foreign ministers of the OAS, in their communiqué of October 6, rejected secrecy in such matters in this hemisphere. Should these offensive military preparations continue, thus increasing the threat to the hemisphere, further action will be justified. I have directed the armed forces to prepare for any eventualities; and I trust that in the interest of both the Cuban people and the Soviet technicians at the sites, the hazards to all concerned in continuing this threat will be recognized.

"Third: It shall be the policy of this nation to regard any nuclear missile launched from Cuba against any nation in the Western

Hemisphere as an attack by the Soviet Union on the United States, requiring a full retaliatory response upon the Soviet Union.

"Fourth: As a necessary military precaution, I have reinforced our base at Guantánamo, evacuated today the dependents of our personnel there, and ordered additional military units to be on a standby alert basis.

"Fifth: We are calling tonight for an immediate meeting of the Organ of Consultation under the Organization of American States, to consider this threat to hemispheric security and to invoke Articles 6 and 8 of the Rio Treaty in support of all necessary action. The United Nations Charter allows for regional security arrangements—and the nations of this hemisphere decided long ago against the military presence of outside powers. Our other allies around the world have also been alerted.

"Sixth: Under the Charter of the United Nations, we are asking tonight that an emergency meeting of the Security Council be convoked without delay to take action against this latest Soviet threat to world peace. Our resolution will call for the prompt dismantling and withdrawal of all offensive weapons in Cuba, under the supervision of UN observers, before the quarantine can be lifted.

"Seventh and finally: I call upon Chairman Khrushchev to halt and eliminate this clandestine, reckless, and provocative threat to world peace and to stabilize relations between our two nations. I call upon him further to abandon this course of world domination, and to join in an historic effort to end the perilous arms race and to transform the history of man. He has an opportunity now to move the world back from the abyss of destruction—by returning to his government's own words that it had no need to station missiles outside its own territory, and withdrawing these weapons from Cuba—by refraining from any action which will widen or deepen the present crisis—and then by participating in a search for peaceful and permanent solutions.

"This nation is prepared to present its case against the Soviet threat to peace, and our own proposals for a peaceful world, at any time and in any forum—in the OAS, in the United Nations, or in any other meeting that could be useful—without limiting our freedom of action. We have in the past made strenuous efforts to limit the spread of nuclear weapons. We have proposed the elimination of all arms and military bases in a fair and effective disarmament treaty. We are prepared to discuss new proposals for the removal of tensions on both sides—including the possibility of a genuinely independent Cuba, free to determine its own destiny. We have no wish to war with the Soviet Union—for we are a peaceful people who desire to live in peace with all other peoples.

"But it is difficult to settle or even discuss these problems in an atmosphere of intimidation. That is why this latest Soviet threat—or any other threat which is made either independently or in response to our actions this week—must and will be met with determination. Any hostile move anywhere in the world against the safety and freedom of peoples to whom we are committed—including in particular the brave people of West Berlin—will be met by whatever action is needed.

"Finally, I want to say a few words to the captive people of Cuba, to whom this speech is being directly carried by special radio facilities. I speak to you as a friend, as one who knows of your deep attachment to your fatherland, as one who shares your aspirations for liberty and justice for all. And I have watched and the American people have watched with deep sorrow how your nationalist revolution was betrayed—and how your fatherland fell under foreign domination. Now your leaders are no longer Cuban leaders inspired by Cuban ideals. They are puppets and agents of an international conspiracy which has turned Cuba against your friends and neighbors in the Americas—and turned it into the first Latin American country to become a target for nuclear war—the first Latin American country to have these weapons on its soil.

"These new weapons are not in your interest. They contribute nothing to your peace and well-being. They can only undermine it. But this country has no wish to cause you to suffer or to impose any system upon you. We know that your lives and land are being used as pawns by those who deny your freedom.

"Many times in the past, the Cuban people have risen to throw out tyrants who destroyed their liberty. And I have no doubt that most Cubans today look forward to the time when they will be truly free—free from foreign domination, free to choose their own leaders, free to select their own system, free to own their own land, free to speak and write and worship without fear or degradation. And then shall Cuba be welcomed back to the society of free nations and to the associations of this hemisphere.

"My fellow citizens: let no one doubt that this is a difficult and dangerous effort on which we have set out. No one can see precisely what course it will take or what costs or casualties will be incurred. Many months of sacrifice and self-discipline lie ahead—months in which our patience and our will will be tested—months in which many threats and denunciations will keep us aware of our dangers. But the greatest danger of all would be to do nothing.

"The path we have chosen for the present is full of hazards, as all paths are—but it is the one most consistent with our character and courage as a nation and our commitments around the world. The cost of freedom is always high—and Americans have always paid it. And one path we shall never choose, and that is the path of surrender or submission.

"Our goal is not the victory of might, but the vindication of right—not peace at the expense of freedom, but both peace and freedom, here in this hemisphere, and, we hope, around the world. God willing, that goal will be achieved.

"Thank you and good night."

"*This was a special bulletin from CBS News . . .*"

Russo sat back, stared at the TV, ignored the news program now beginning. After a long moment, he leaned forward, turned the set off, said, "Good God."

Margaret sat beside him now, said, "What does it mean? Are we going to war?"

Becky said, "What's happening, Daddy? It sounds scary."

"I don't know. He doesn't want a war, but there may be no choice. The damn Russians have put missiles in Cuba. What the hell?"

Danny was bouncing on the couch with nervous energy, said, "We gonna bomb the Russians? We gonna bomb Cuba?"

Russo tried to organize his thoughts, to respond. But his mind was swirling with images, missiles, bombs, all those trucks that passed through town, on their way to . . .

"I don't know, Dan-o. Maybe Kennedy doesn't know. He's told the Russians to get out of Cuba, and maybe they will. And maybe they won't. If they don't . . . this could be pretty serious."

Margaret said, "Joe, how serious?"

He hesitated, couldn't just say the words . . . *nuclear war*. After a silent moment, he said, "Maybe we should have built our own fallout shelter."

CHAPTER NINETEEN

Khrushchev

Tuesday, October 23, 1962
Moscow, the Kremlin

Throughout the day on Monday, Khrushchev had felt an odd itch, that something was happening in Washington that no one around him could truly explain. Vague reports still flowed from various sources in the American capital, those whose job it was to keep their ears to the ground, picking up any tidbits of information that could tell Khrushchev just what might be going on in the hearts and minds of the American leaders. This Monday had been particularly intriguing, word coming from Dobrynin's office, as well as the far more low-key source, the spy Bolshakov, reporting a heightened sense of agitation in the capital. It had become clear that great efforts were being made to display a business-as-usual attitude, yet nothing about the behavior of several key American officials was *usual* at all. Most obvious was the absence of men like Rusk and McNamara from their usual haunts, social and diplomatic gatherings; if they were present at all, it was for short minutes. Gone seemed to be the social chatter that usually surrounded Kennedy and his staff, and in Moscow, it was seen as most strange that Kennedy himself seemed to cut short his efforts at campaigning for the midterm elections. But Khrushchev knew not to trust rumor, even from those he otherwise trusted completely, though the heightened presence of American troops and ships near Cuba was no rumor at all. Khrushchev still couldn't believe that Kennedy would be reckless enough to invade Cuba, not with so many warnings passing from Moscow to Washington. Kosygin had been no help at all defusing the mystery, his meeting with Kennedy as bland as both men tried to portray. As usual, there had been the perfunctory warnings passed back and forth about Berlin and Cuba, and if Kennedy had anything of substance to say, he didn't say it to Kosygin. Dobrynin seemed more interested in playing the role of the genial diplomat, enjoying the various state dinners, all the while trying to feel the pulse of official Washington. But Dobrynin had nothing useful to offer, and Khrushchev had begun to wonder if Dobrynin was enjoying himself a bit too much in Washington. At any rate, Khrushchev had long since avoided passing on highly sensitive information to his ambassador. If Dobrynin didn't have secrets to reveal, he couldn't reveal them.

He looked at his watch, after midnight, stretched his back, felt the weariness of another day of haphazard news and unreliable reporting. But finally, word had come from Dobrynin that Kennedy was to speak to the American people via television, which seemed to be Kennedy's favorite venue. Khrushchev received that news with a sense of relief, that surely, Kennedy wouldn't waste his time speaking to his public unless he had something significant to say. With so many mysteries about, perhaps Kennedy would clear them up.

Kennedy's speech had prompted him to summon the Presidium into a rare nighttime session, preparing, as always, to react to any kind of important news. He knew the rumors were flying, something he couldn't prevent, the members of the Presidium each with their own fears and doubts about just what the Americans were about. He remained in his office, for now, his son, Sergei, keeping him company, didn't need anyone outside of his own family observing that he was as anxious as the members of the Presidium.

Sergei sat in a thick leather chair to one side, scanned through a small book, a gift from a friend, supposed to be for his children.

"This is infantile. I would not inflict this on my son, whether he understood it or not."

Khrushchev had drifted away, pulled himself back to the moment.

"What? The book?"

"Did you fall asleep, Father?"

Khrushchev shook his head, laid his hands flat on the desk.

"No time for sleep."

There was a sharp knock, Khrushchev pushing himself to stand. Sergei moved that way quickly, pulled the door open, and Khrushchev was surprised to see Malinovsky.

"Excuse me. We have more news from Ambassador Dobrynin. He has wired us the text of Kennedy's speech. I have just completed reading it. You should know the details immediately."

"That is excellent. Dobrynin is doing his job for once. I don't need Kennedy's pleasantries. Just give me the short points."

Malinovsky stepped inside, Sergei closing the door behind him. Malinovsky took a long breath, glanced at a notepad in his hand.

"They have discovered the missiles. They are responding by implementing a blockade around Cuba. Kennedy insists that we remove the missiles and their launchers from Cuba."

Khrushchev felt a stab of ice.

"I knew they would discover them. *I knew it.* Could we not have hidden the damned things with more care? Who is to blame?

Pliyev? No, perhaps it is Castro, leaking information like wine from a broken bottle, telling anyone who will listen about his precious nuclear missiles."

His voice had risen, and Malinovsky glanced at Sergei, then said, "Kennedy's message appears to be one of restraint. He did not bellow demands. And, he claims there will be no invasion of Cuba. On that, we should believe him, since it is unlikely he would make such a speech, only to change his mind a few days later. It would make him look irrational to the rest of the world, and certainly damage his credibility."

Khrushchev rose from his chair, plodded heavily across the room, then back again.

"I trust you are correct. But if he knows of our missiles, then he must know they are vulnerable to attack. Since he is not sending his bombers, we must believe that he is seeking some sort of negotiation."

"Or, Nikita, it is a pre-election trick, something aimed only at his opponents in their Congress. Big pronouncements, to get votes, and nothing more."

He knew Malinovsky was offering him a bone, trying to boost his spirits.

The election, he thought. All this to gain votes?

"No, my friend, the Americans have beaten us to the punch. We underestimated the power of their U-2s, their skill at identifying our missiles from grainy photographs. We have been sloppy, and now, we will pay the price. We are now forced to repeat to the world what we have been saying all along, that the missiles are there for defensive purposes. We must continue to emphasize that we are only defending our ally from the aggressive posture of the United States. After all, we are doing nothing to the United States that they have not already done to us. They find it *uncomfortable* to have nuclear missiles on their doorstep. That is the reality we have lived under for years. I will not be ordered about by Kennedy, or anyone else."

"I agree, Nikita. But the immediate question is how we respond to their blockade."

Khrushchev pondered the word, clenched his fist.

"It is simply an outrage. It will not be supported by the rest of the world, not even the Latin nations. Heavy-handed stupidity."

"But, as you say, it is not an attack. Not yet. Only a threat. He refers to the blockade as a *quarantine*. There is a reason for such a euphemism. He does not wish to appear too warlike."

Khrushchev stopped beside his enormous desk, pounded a fist down hard. "A blockade is a *blockade*. It is unlawful, piracy on the high seas. He has no right to enforce such a thing. I will not recall our ships. They have every right to continue their journeys, to deliver their goods to Cuba. We will order submarines to be stationed near their blockade line, prepared to sink any American ship that sinks one of our own." His voice rose again. "This is an outrage that shall not stand."

"Nikita, you must prepare a public response."

"Oh, I will respond. I will also raise the alert level of all our military installations, and I will instruct General Pliyev to heighten his attention to the possibility of an invasion that may yet come. I will not be fooled."

Sergei said, "Father, can you trust General Pliyev not to engage his nuclear warheads? If the Americans are truly showing restraint, shouldn't we? There is no call yet for us to go to war."

His son's voice calmed him.

"Perhaps . . . if Kennedy is using restraint, then we shall as well. I will instruct General Pliyev that he is to respond, along with the Cuban army, to any kind of invasion, any aggressive action by the Americans with the full military assets he has at his disposal. But he is not to fire any nuclear missiles or nuclear artillery without my permission. It is annoying that I must give such an order. I would hope he would know not to start a nuclear war on his own."

Malinovsky said, "That is the correct action."

Khrushchev sat heavily in the chair, slumped toward his desk.

"We have made mistakes, Rodion. We should have shipped all the missiles to Cuba in a short period of time, instead of dragging out the shipments. I should have made sure Pliyev used his brains in how the missiles were arranged and situated. But dammit, *a blockade* . . . it's an act of war. Kennedy knows that. We cannot just accept being denied access to our ally."

"It is a blockade of weapons only. Supplies will not be stopped."

"So he says. We must rely on the wisdom of some American navy captain far out to sea, who does not feel the itch in his trigger finger, seeking a feather in his cap by sinking a Soviet ship. I will not sit here and pretend that will not start a war. Action must be met with action. There is no other way. We cannot allow any of our ships to be turned away or boarded. Illegal piracy. That's all it is."

Malinovsky said, "The Presidium is being seated. Perhaps we should join them? There is much to discuss."

"Yes. They must be informed of Kennedy's words. But we must maintain our decorum from prying eyes. I want the Presidium members to sleep in their offices here tonight, so the Americans will not see us scrambling through the night like frightened mice."

Sergei said, "What of the people? What will you tell them?"

Khrushchev was surprised by the question.

"The people? We will tell them none of this. I will order *Izvestia* to print nothing of Kennedy's speech, no mention of nuclear missiles. We need not have such anxiety in the streets of Moscow. Now, leave me for a moment. Before I attend the Presidium, I must begin to prepare my official response to Kennedy's words."

———

"I SHOULD SAY *frankly that measures outlined in your statement represent serious threats to peace and security ... We confirm that the armaments now in Cuba, regardless of the classification to which they belong, are destined exclusively for defensive purposes, in order to secure the Cuban Republic from attack ... I hope that the United States government will display wisdom and renounce the actions pursued by you, which may lead to catastrophic consequences for world peace."*

CHAPTER TWENTY

RFK

Tuesday morning, October 23, 1962
Washington, DC

Bobby had slept in a small anteroom near his office, knew that after Jack's speech the night before, Ethel wouldn't ask for an explanation. The cot had been added for nights just like this one. But as Bobby struggled to make himself comfortable, he knew there had never been another night like this one.

He woke early, before seven, was drawn toward the window, the dawn creeping over Washington. It suddenly occurred to him what he was seeing: a city at rest, the first stirrings of a new day, perhaps a normal day. No, he thought, there is nothing normal these days. Perhaps we've changed the world, awakened a vicious giant, brought the threat of nuclear war front and center. It wasn't just us, of course. We had to respond. There is one good thing, for certain. The city is still here. I'm still here. At least Khrushchev didn't react like a madman, and launch his missiles. That's a hopeful sign, that he knows we caught him with his pants down, and now he has to be a man about it, and accept what we're telling him to do.

Or, is that wishful thinking? Is it possible for a man in his position to back down, or will it cost him his power, maybe his life? How many madmen might there be in the Kremlin who are pushing him hard *not* to back down? And how many have their fingers poised on those buttons that launch Russian missiles who might not care for negotiation at all?

KENNEDY HAD ORDERED that the Excomm now meet daily at ten each morning, and Bobby was surprised to see the number of smiles around the room.

Kennedy led off, seemed full of energy.

"We have heard from all of our allies. There is complete support for what we're doing. Right now, Rusk is speaking to the OAS, seeking their official approval. Fingers crossed on that one. I'm optimistic, since none of those countries have seemed to cozy up to Castro to any great extent. I suspect few will want to see him gain such a leg up over all of Latin America by having Soviet missiles in his front yard."

Bobby knew that Jack's optimism was overstated, that there was no predicting what the leaders of the Latin countries would do. And, as usual, Bobby had little faith in Rusk's abilities as an effective diplomat, certainly not one to sway an opposing opinion.

To one side, Rusk's undersecretary, George Ball said, "I would offer, Mr. President, a hopeful note from the secretary of state. He greeted me this morning with a smile, stating that we had already won a great victory. After all, we're all still alive." There was low laughter, and Ball continued, "We are hearing reports, particularly from the British, that there are already protests springing up. One British paper, the *Daily Mail*, headlined that what we're doing is an act of war. There are similar protests from some of the other papers. And, there are protestors gathering outside our embassy in London."

Bobby said, "We've always known that the British, the Germans, all the rest, have never taken our feelings about Castro seriously. They have to understand our feelings about having nuclear missiles on our doorstep."

Bundy spoke now, setting aside a cup of coffee.

"There is one problem with that. Germany sits with Soviet missiles on her own doorstep. Western Europe isn't that far from dozens of launch sites within Russia. I expected there would be some grousing about the severity of our reaction, since this is a shadow they've been living under for years. Some of their academics, their media people are going to blame us for overreacting."

Kennedy said, "I've heard what I needed to hear from our allies. We can't help that there are protesters. Nobody wants to hear that a nuclear holocaust is a possibility. But it's naïve for anyone to think that if we had said nothing about Soviet missiles, the world would go merrily on its peaceful way." He looked at Ball. "Rusk is speaking to the OAS right now?"

"Yes, sir."

"Hopefully, they'll vote their approval as quickly as possible. Surely, they'll recognize the importance. I won't sign the declaration that officially launches the quarantine until I give them the opportunity to respond. Stevenson is speaking to the UN this afternoon, and I imagine that will be a testy affair. Based on Khrushchev's response, I'm certain Ambassador Zorin will protest vehemently, and I'm sure the Cubans will have something to say. What's the Cuban ambassador's name?"

Ball said, "García Incháustequi."

Kennedy stared at Ball for a long second. "You think Castro chose him just to annoy the rest of us trying to pronounce his name?"

More laughter now, and Bobby felt cautious, knew that good humor was contagious, but it certainly meant the men were hiding just how anxious they truly were.

McNamara spoke up now. "Mr. President, might I read the restrictions in the quarantine document, just so we're all in agreement?"

Kennedy said, "Yes, by all means."

"This is the list of those items that will be halted by our ships, and not allowed to pass. Surface-to-air missiles, bomber aircraft, bombs, air-to-surface rockets and guided missiles, warheads for any of the above weapons, mechanical or electronic equipment to support or operate the above items, and any other class of material hereafter designated by the secretary of defense. As you can see, we have purposely not included petroleum or petroleum products."

Kennedy said, "Yes, that's correct, I will reserve the right to add petroleum to the quarantine list should we feel it is necessary. I've been thinking about another potential problem. We are maintaining a substantial number of U-2 flights over Cuba still. We know they have the ground-to-air missiles, and so far, they've shown restraint in not targeting the U-2s. But now, that could change. How should we respond if one of our planes is shot down?"

McNamara said, "Take out the missile's launch site. Bomb it immediately. Be very specific about it."

The others nodded in agreement, and Bobby said, "Be *very* specific. We don't want our response to trigger a wider attack, either from them, or from us. I'm concerned things could escalate and get out of hand pretty quick."

McNamara said, "That isn't too much of a concern, unless the Soviets start firing off missiles all over the island. Actually, I think they'd respect our restraint, and they might actually expect us to react against their launch site. By the way, we've received word from the U-2 flights that the Soviets are suddenly scrambling to camouflage their missile launchers."

Bobby fought the urge to laugh, said, "Now?"

McNamara shrugged.

"Now."

The door opened, McCone slipping in. He didn't sit, waited for a break in the talk, said, "Mr. President, we have learned that there are a number of Soviet submarines making their way toward the quarantine zone. We must assume that the Soviets intend to protect their shipping against any kind of aggressive action on our part. In addition, there are an enormous number of encoded messages being transmitted to their ships at sea. We don't know the substance of those messages, unfortunately."

It was one more piece of the puzzle, just what the Russians were planning to do next. The room was silent for a long moment, then Bobby said, "Khrushchev's response last night did indicate that he would order his ships to push straight through the quarantine. I thought that was bluster, but this could mean he's serious."

Kennedy said, "How far away are the nearest Soviet ships to our line?"

McNamara said, "The first ship should reach the line tomorrow. There are approximately twenty-five Soviet and Soviet supporting ships en route."

The mood had changed completely now, the smiles gone. Ball said, "Sir, until you actually sign the proclamation for the quarantine, there really is no official line for us to observe."

Kennedy said, "I know. But I won't act until we receive something from the OAS."

By three that afternoon, the ministers of the Organization of American States had avoided their usual lengthy speeches and responded directly to Rusk's plea. Rusk's remarks had been firm and direct, and those who sat in attendance seemed to fully grasp the importance of just what they were being asked to do. To Rusk's amazement, of the twenty nations represented, nineteen voted to support the actions of the United States. There was one abstention, Uruguay, only because their ambassador could not reach his superiors in his capital.

At the United Nations, Adlai Stevenson displayed a rarely seen energy, detailing the justifications and causes for the actions by his government. As a capstone to his remarks, Stevenson offered the Security Council a resolution, calling for *the immediate dismantling and withdrawal of all offensive weapons* from Cuba.

As expected, the Cubans reacted with passionate vitriol, their ambassador accusing the United States of plotting to overthrow the Cuban government, among other charges. The Soviet ambassador, Valerian Zorin spoke next, making much the same charge, claiming still that the American suggestion that the Soviets had placed offensive missiles in Cuba was simply *a lie*. Tellingly though, Zorin did not issue specific threats. If there was any hidden meaning to his restraint, it might have been the suggestion that Khrushchev had left the door open, ever so slightly, to some kind of negotiation. But negotiation seemed far away, both Kennedys understanding that Khrushchev was no doubt dealing with both hard-liners and soft peddlers in his own government. Bobby had been surprised by the hard line taken by the American military chiefs, and he had to assume that the Soviet military might be pressuring Khrushchev even more to respond to the quarantine by launching an immediate nuclear strike.

The men had gathered, some from the Excomm, a number of reporters, a semicircle in front of the president's desk. The photographers were already snapping their pictures, no different from a hundred such gatherings, where the president signed into law some new bill or some kind of presidential decree.

Bobby stood back, on the far side of the gathering, watched as Jack's secretary, Evelyn Lincoln, carried in a tray of pens. It was customary that Kennedy sign his name one letter and one pen at a time, providing souvenirs for those who watched. Kennedy looked at the tray, shook his head.

"No, not this time. Souvenirs aren't appropriate right now." He retrieved a pen from his own pocket, scanned the document, then placed his signature at the bottom. The pen returned to his breast pocket, and Kennedy said, "Forgive me, but this one, I'm going to keep."

Bobby felt a strange rush, a nervous chill, watched as the cameramen snapped their prized photos. He knew what Jack knew, that there was no backing away. It was official. The quarantine would go into effect Wednesday morning, October 24, at 10 a.m.

Tuesday night, October 23, 1962
The White House, Cabinet Room

It was after supper, all the men present feeling the effects of a very long day. But McNamara had insisted, McCone as well, the Excomm now in their second meeting of the day.

Rusk seemed as exhausted as any of the others, too tired to crow about his enormous success at the OAS. But the OAS meeting was only part of his responsibilities.

"Sir, I've been on the line with our ambassadors in Senegal and Guinea. We have received assurances that those government do not wish to participate in any way in the conflict between the United States and the Soviet Union. Thus, they are declining to welcome any military flights from either country onto their territory."

Kennedy was smiling, Bobby not sure why. Kennedy said, "In other words, no plane may land there, say, for example, to refuel."

"That is correct, sir."

McNamara slapped the table, said, "Outstanding. It was a real concern."

Bobby said, "I'm not sure . . ."

McNamara interrupted.

"It had been suggested that the Soviets might attempt to import into Cuba additional nuclear warheads. Since they would not want to risk them being discovered on a ship, it was assumed by our people that they might attempt to fly warheads into Cuba on one of their big Ilyushins. Obviously, our quarantine does not extend into the skies. But to reach Cuba, they would need a refueling stop, presumably at either Dakar or Conakry."

Rusk was beaming through tired eyes, a satisfied smile.

"And that is now unlikely. As I said, both governments have refused to allow their airports to be used for any kind of military flight."

Bobby understood now, wondered why this had not been thought of sooner.

"So, whatever warheads the Soviets have now in Cuba are all they're going to have. Somehow, I don't take comfort in that thought."

Kennedy said, "Neither do I. But we've started the ball rolling, and the next step will be for the Soviets to understand that we're completely serious. They can respond by dismantling their missile launchers, or they can test us to see what we'll do next."

Bobby glanced around the room, saw the seriousness of the expressions.

"Or they can decide to solve their problems another way and obliterate New York. Or Washington."

There was no response, each man inside himself, most with thoughts of family, all of them terrified of a world gone completely mad.

As the Excomm meeting wound down, the buoyant mood from that morning was gone, replaced by the reality that no one could predict just what Khrushchev was going to do next. With increasing urgency, Kennedy, rather than waiting for some official response from Moscow, chose to confront the issue directly, or at least, as directly as could be done in Washington. He sent Bobby to meet face-to-face with the Soviet ambassador, Anatoly Dobrynin.

Tuesday night, October 23, 1962
Soviet Embassy, Washington, DC

He was shocked by Dobrynin's expression, none of the glad-handing cheerfulness from times before. The man seemed beaten down, dark eyes, lines on his face, no smile at all. He met Bobby with an extended hand, seemed almost apologetic, as though a meeting like this should never have been requested. They sat, facing each other, brief pleasantries, Dobrynin's aide offering Bobby something to drink. His mind begged for a stiff Scotch, but this was no time for fog.

"No, thank you. I'm fine as is."

Dobrynin signaled to the aide, and another man lurking behind, *leave.* They obeyed reluctantly, and it was clear to Bobby that Dobrynin was rarely alone in any meeting inside his own embassy.

But they were alone now, and he focused on Dobrynin, still expected the customary smile. It didn't come. All right, he thought. Get to it.

"You are no doubt aware why I am here, Ambassador. For the past several weeks, we have been told that there are no offensive missiles in Cuba. One week ago we obtained incontrovertible evidence to the contrary. You told me directly that your country had placed no long-distance missiles in Cuba, and further, that you had no intention of doing so in the future." He hesitated, did not want to call this man a liar to his face.

Dobrynin said, "You are correct. I told you precisely those things. I believe, in fact, that I gave you my word."

Bobby was relieved, thought, no argument. Thank God.

"You must understand, Ambassador, that the president has taken a much less belligerent attitude toward the Soviet Union's actions than others close to him would have preferred. But the president is aware that he has been deceived by you, which is a dangerous state of affairs for peace, especially between two countries who have the capability of annihilating the human race."

"I must attempt to defend myself, Mr. Attorney General. It is important you understand ... for our future relationship, that I only repeated to you what I was told by my premier. Even now, in the light of all that has happened, in the light of what you now have come to discover, I have not been told anything different by my government. Frankly speaking, I do not know about missiles in Cuba even at this moment. That is not a denial. I just want you to know the facts as they are told to me."

Bobby weighed Dobrynin's words, thought, is it possible they would keep their ambassador in the dark? But somehow ... I believe him. It shows in his face.

Dobrynin cleared his throat, said, "I must ask you . . . why, when you had this information, did President Kennedy not reveal that fact to Foreign Minister Gromyko, in their meeting last Thursday?"

Bobby wondered if this would come up.

"I believe you that you were not informed about the missiles. I do not believe we can say the same for Gromyko. He had the same opportunity to be forthcoming, and instead, he chose to sing the same old song, protesting any claim that your arms in Cuba were anything but defensive. During the past week, the president has been deeply involved in meetings with a select group in our government, including the military, and when he met with Gromyko, there had not yet been a conclusion made as to what action we would take. It would have been premature to reveal what we knew at that time. However, the president was shocked that Gromyko continued to tell the same lies."

Dobrynin looked down, seemed wounded by the comment.

"I understand."

"Ambassador, we are following the progress of some two dozen Soviet ships en route to Cuba, certain to intersect our quarantine line. I must ask you if you know the intentions of those ships. Will they turn back, or is it Mr. Khrushchev's intention to purposely cause a potentially violent confrontation?"

Dobrynin's eyes grew wider, and he seemed to fight for words.

"I only know . . . the ship captains have been told nothing that would alter their course."

"Then, sir, tomorrow should be an interesting day."

CHAPTER TWENTY-ONE

Khrushchev

Wednesday, October 24, 1962
Moscow, the Kremlin

"If the United Sates government carries out the program of piratical actions outlined by it, we shall have to resort to means of defense against the aggressor to defend our rights."

It was yet another necessary response to the Kennedy blockade order, a copy of which had been sent to Khrushchev through Dobrynin.

He hadn't slept, paced now in his long narrow office, his breathing hard and short. I am too old for crises, he thought. He moved to a window, a heavy cloth curtain covering, and he pulled it aside, saw a grim gray day, a storm of sleet. He thought of the American, William Knox, an invitation Khrushchev had sent, requesting a brief conversation. I have inconvenienced the man, no doubt. He would rather sit comfortably in his hotel room and perhaps drink our vodka. But unless he is a complete fool, Mr. Knox will be useful.

He let go of the curtain, the room suffering from dim light against pale walls. He paced again, thought, so much is happening, so quickly. We are treading heavily toward a doomsday scenario. Kennedy surely doesn't want this, surely he will not begin firing his missiles. It is all so foolish. I am caught in a tight squeeze, between those in the military, like Marshal Kochov, who would push the nuclear button with little provocation, sitting across from those who pray for the health of their children. There is no place in the middle of that, and yet, here I am.

He moved toward the office door, pulled it open, surprising his office staff.

"Is Mr. Knox here yet?"

"I will check, sir. Allow me one moment."

The aide moved quickly away, the outer door closing, Khrushchev looking at the others, his interpreter sitting to one side, summoned just an hour before. Khrushchev motioned to him.

"Viktor, inside, now. Be certain of your English. This could be an important day, and I want no mistakes."

"I assure you, Premier, I will make no mistakes. Who are we speaking to?"

It was an unusual question asked by someone who rarely had questions at all. But Khrushchev knew that these were extraordinary times, for all of them. The man would be allowed his fears.

"His name is William Knox. He, presumably, is the president of the Westinghouse International Corporation, but I also assume him to be a spy. He has been here allegedly to offer advice on patents to our new state trading organization. But corporate giants who lurk within our borders are rarely here for reasons that benefit us."

The door opened again, his aide there.

"He is here, sir. Shall I send him in?"

"Wait. Then send him into my office."

Khrushchev knew protocol, would let the man come to him. He slipped quickly back into his office, the interpreter pulling the door closed. After a short minute, the aide knocked, opened the door, Khrushchev sitting at his desk, as though he had been there all the while.

"Premier, Mr. Knox has accepted your invitation. He is here, sir."

Knox was in the doorway now, a hesitant smile, his eyes darting around the room, absorbing every detail. That's what a spy does, Khrushchev thought. He is older than I expected. Not as old as me. No one is as old as me.

Khrushchev studied the man in return, Knox seeming to expect that, standing patiently. Khrushchev stood now, extended a hand, Knox coming forward, a genial shake. Khrushchev said, "Let us sit at my conference table. I have much to discuss with you."

Knox made a short bow, moved to a chair at the table, waited for Khrushchev to sit, then followed suit.

"Your invitation was a surprise, Premier. I will do all I can to answer whatever questions you have. Though, I admit, I'm not sure exactly what information I can provide."

Khrushchev folded his hands in front of him, a glance at the interpreter, who completed Knox's words. He stared hard at Knox, said, "I require a go-between for myself and President Kennedy. Not directly or publicly of course. That's why we have ambassadors. I require someone to transmit a private message to your president. I am concerned that events are spiraling, with too many uncertainties. I want Kennedy to know exactly what I am thinking."

Knox was clearly surprised, said, "I don't know the president personally. But I am sure I can get a message through to the State Department. I have a close contact there."

"Yes, I'm certain you do. I wish you to tell Mr. Kennedy the following." He glanced at his interpreter again, who sat on the far side of the table, a pad of paper in hand. "I am loathe to think that the president's speech that occurred on October 22 was only for electoral reasons. It sounded to me to stem from hysteria, and I have tried to address that. The president is a very young man. I am finding it difficult to relate to such a man. I do not understand how he thinks."

He stopped, poured a glass of water from a pitcher to one side. Knox had paper of his own now, had come prepared. He scribbled furiously, then looked up. Khrushchev said, "Except in time of war, a *blockade* is illegal, no matter what name you call it. If the U.S. stops and searches Soviet ships, this would be piracy. I must emphasize that the ships now en route to Cuba are unarmed. And your president must know this. If the United States Navy was to sink a Soviet ship, we will return the favor with our submarines. And that will escalate to the third world war. Should the president seek still to invade and occupy Cuba, that would not be possible. We possess considerable defensive forces there now, and alongside our Cuban allies, I can assure you, it would be a bloody affair."

Khrushchev paused, and Knox said, "Premier, I understand that the president is most angry that you have placed offensive missiles in Cuba, all the while denying their existence. Lies can be a common commodity in the corporate world. But between superpowers, it can lead to the most serious consequences of all."

"Do not lecture me on offensive versus defensive. Tell me about your missiles in Turkey. They are alleged to be defensive, and yet, what is their range? How far into the Soviet Union can they reach? Tell me, sir, if I point a pistol at you, in order to attack you, it is an offensive weapon, yes? But if I aim to keep you from shooting me, it is defensive, is it not? But I am tired of so many accusations and lies, threats and counterthreats. There is no longer any need for subterfuge. You will tell the president, and be perfectly clear, that the Soviet Union admits to having placed ballistic missiles in Cuba, with nuclear warheads. I do not necessarily trust the Cubans to manage such weapons, and so, be advised that the weapons are in the hands of Russians and will be fired, if necessary, by Russians. But I say now, they will not be fired except in defense of Cuba. If the U.S. does not believe this, they should attack Cuba, and learn the answer. I assure you, Guantánamo would disappear from the Earth in the first hour."

Khrushchev gave Knox time to make his notes, felt himself sweating, flexed his fingers, tried to calm his breathing. Knox finished writing, looked at Khrushchev with wide eyes. Khrushchev forced a smile, said, "This should get you an audience at your State Department. Allow me to conclude this meeting with a story. A farmer learned to get along with a goat, to accept the goat in his barnyard, even though the goat smelled and was not very nice. The Soviet Union has its smelly, disagreeable goats in Italy, Greece, Turkey, et cetera. We have accepted them, learned to live with them. You may tell your president that the U.S. now has its own goat, in Cuba."

Wednesday evening, October 24, 1962
Moscow, the Kremlin

It had been another difficult, very long day. He sat at his desk, shuffled through messages from his various departments, messages from Cuba, from various embassies around the world. As if there wasn't enough for him to grow anxious about, he had a report from the agricultural ministry, indicating that this year's corn harvest had been considerably below expectations.

"Corn. I hate corn. I hate everything to do with it, and yet, we must grow it, to feed our animals. How can it be so difficult?"

He realized he had been talking out loud, knew they could hear him in the outer office. No, he thought, I am not crazy, not yet. I am just . . . very tired.

There was a brief knock, Khrushchev answering, "Yes, what is it?"

The door opened; his aide, Vasily.

"Premier, we have received an urgent message from the Secretary General of the United Nations, Mr. U Thant."

He held up a paper, and Khrushchev waved him forward.

"Well, what might he want? Is he afraid we're going to blow up the world on his watch?"

He took the paper, read.

"This says an identical letter has been sent to Kennedy."

"I have been asked by the permanent representatives of a large number of member governments, to address an urgent appeal to you in the present critical situation."

He spoke to himself, ignored his aide.

"Yes, yes, they are concerned for world peace."

". . . the voluntary suspension of all arms shipments to Cuba, and also the voluntary suspension of the quarantine . . . I believe such voluntary suspension for two or three weeks will greatly ease the situation . . ."

He put down the paper, struggled to see the words.

"I am very tired, Vasily. Perhaps it is a good thing, if U Thant wishes to broker a meeting, a summit between me and Kennedy. But Kennedy is like a child, compared to so many of those in his own government, and certainly to those in my own. How do you negotiate with a man who speaks in such absolutes, who stirs up a pot with his citizens, causing them to fear global war? How does he find the way to back down? And if he does not . . . what happens then?"

CHAPTER TWENTY-TWO

RFK

Wednesday, October 24, 1962
The White House, Oval Office

The two men sat quietly for a long moment, the president reading a document, yet another official posting from the Navy regarding positioning of ships.

"I've moved the quarantine line forward from eight hundred, to five hundred miles out from Cuba. I got some good advice from Ormsby-Gore, that it might give us some more flexibility, allow us to tighten the quarantine line, plus give us some time before we have to confront the Soviet ships. I agreed with his thinking, and I gave the order early this morning. The Navy went along, thought it was the correct decision. Admiral Anderson is confident we're still keeping out of range of whatever Soviet planes might try to interfere."

Bobby could see the stress on his brother's face, said, "I guess every decision now is a big one, regardless. Nobody wants to make a mistake."

Kennedy laughed.

"You can make all the mistakes you want. Just don't bring them to me. I'm the one who has to be perfect."

"Frankly, Jack, I think every decision that has come out of this office has been pretty damn perfect."

"Yeah, maybe. You see the message we got this morning from U Thant?"

"No. What's the UN want?"

"He's begging us to back down, to suspend the quarantine for a couple of weeks, as long as the Soviets will back down on their arms shipments. I've already gotten word that Khrushchev is going along with it, but I haven't heard that directly from the Kremlin."

"They want us to back down, disband the quarantine. Just like that?"

"Just like that. I talked to Stevenson. He says there are more than forty nonaligned countries signing on to this, mostly Africa and Asia, who have no horse in this race. I suppose they don't want the world to blow up any more than we do, but, dammit all, just because they're *nonaligned* doesn't mean they understand our position." He slid papers aside, picked up one, held it out toward Bobby. "Here. My response to U Thant. He'll get it by this afternoon."

"*I deeply appreciate the spirit which prompted your message . . . As we made clear in the Security Council, the existing threat was created by the secret introduction of offensive weapons into Cuba, and the answer lies in the removal of such weapons . . .*"

Bobby returned the paper.

"Did he tell the Russians they have to pull their missiles out?"

Kennedy shook his head.

"No. That's the point. Stopping more ships from going to

Cuba . . . hell, we're doing that right now. His efforts sound good on the surface, telling us both to take a breath, but I guarantee you those construction workers in Cuba aren't taking a breath. Our photos show the work is ongoing at all those missile sites, and according to McCone, it looks as though they've picked up the pace. Until Khrushchev agrees to pull his missiles out of there, we won't . . . we can't change a thing. The Navy's in position, and we're monitoring the Soviet ships that are closing in on the new quarantine line. With respect to U Thant, I will not order our people to just twiddle their thumbs for a couple of weeks while the Russians are working like hell to complete their construction."

Bobby looked at his watch.

"The meeting will start in a few minutes."

"Yeah. Head on over to the Cabinet Room, I'll be there in a minute."

Bobby stood, hesitated, a concerned look at his brother's face.

"This is tough stuff, Jack. How are you holding up?"

Kennedy sat back, twisted his back, a sharp grimace, something Bobby was used to seeing. He seemed to ponder Bobby's question, said, "I don't know if any of this is right. Or wise. It's dangerous, I know that. But, dammit all, there was no other choice. If the Russians can get this mean in our hemisphere, and we don't call them on it, what's to stop them anywhere else?"

Bobby moved closer to the door, stopped, said, "You know damn well, if you hadn't acted the way you did, you'd have been impeached. The Republicans wouldn't have let you alone knowing there are missiles in Cuba. And, I'd have agreed with them."

Kennedy leaned his chin into one hand.

"Impeached. Yep. It may come to that yet. We're in this pretty deep, and there's no changing our minds."

Wednesday, October 24

The White House, Cabinet Room

There was no laughter to kick off this morning's meeting, none of the joviality that had marked past meetings. The talk was subdued, Kennedy bringing them to order, McNamara opening the way.

"The Strategic Air Command has raised their alert level to DEFCON 2. They sent out the message in the clear, obviously intending the Soviets to receive it, giving them one more reason to respect our intentions. As you all know, DEFCON 1 is a state of war. We can all pray to God we never see that."

Rusk said, "Mr. President, the Soviets have refused to acknowledge the rules of contact we sent them regarding our quarantine. They're continuing to refer to the quarantine as an act of piracy."

Kennedy stared at Rusk, said, "I suppose . . . it was too much to hope they'd simply go along."

McCone spoke up now, shuffling paper as he spoke.

"Mr. President, it seems obvious that the Soviets have accelerated work at their missile sites to an even greater extent than we observed yesterday. I recommend we increase our recon flights to include low-level observation."

McNamara said, "I've discussed this with the Air Force. The P8U jets are perfect for that. They can fly in and out just above treetop level, up to maybe eight hundred feet, far too low and too quick for antiaircraft batteries to draw a bead. I can order that to begin immediately."

Kennedy nodded.

"Do it. They can be equipped with cameras, like the U-2s?"

"Some already are. Different technology, since they're so much closer to what they're targeting."

"Excellent. Tell those pilots to be damned careful."

There was a knock at the door, unusual. Bobby was closest to the door, waited for a cue from the president, then opened the door. He was surprised to see Mrs. Lincoln, the president's secretary, who said, "Forgive me, but a message has come for the secretary of defense. They said it was urgent."

Bobby took the envelope, nodded to her with a brief smile, closed the door. He handed the envelope to McNamara, who broke the seal, opened, read. The room stayed silent, eyes on McNamara, his expression turning grim.

"Mr. President, it seems that two Soviet ships . . . the *Gagarin* and the *Kimovsk* are approaching the quarantine line. They appear to be escorted by a submarine."

Kennedy put a hand across his mouth, stared at McNamara, then said, "God, I don't want to have to confront a submarine. It's one thing to show muscle to an unarmed freighter, but a sub captain's got his orders, and most likely, it's to protect those ships. And if that happens, we've got *another* real problem."

McNamara said, "Sir, it doesn't have to come down to shooting. The Navy has assured me already that they can confront subs with practice depth charges, with a bang that's little more than a firecracker. It's a signal that we know they're there, and they had better surface, before we use the real thing. I want to believe the Soviet captain won't respond by firing torpedoes."

The room stirred with low talk, the anxiety level growing again. Kennedy quieted them, said, "If we sink a Soviet ship trying to run the blockade, we will have backed Khrushchev into a corner. He will have to retaliate. We know there are at least six Soviet subs in the vicinity of the quarantine line."

Bobby said, "And every one of those captains is waiting for orders to do something. But we can't forget . . . I'm still concerned about Berlin. If we take a strong action, like sinking a ship, won't Khrushchev be just as likely to blockade Berlin? That's the one place where he has the upper hand, and in some ways, it's a logical response, a logical way for him to retaliate."

Kennedy responded in a low voice, slow words.

"That's the danger here. It always has been. A blockade of Berlin forces us to use aircraft there, which the Soviets no doubt will shoot down. And of course, we must respond to that."

McNamara said, "We cannot predict what Khrushchev will do, and we cannot yet know what kind of pressure he is under in the Kremlin. It's the wild card. But so far, none of his letters and claims have even touched on Berlin."

Another knock on the door, Bobby opening, a CIA officer with yet another envelope. Bobby took the paper, saw the name on the envelope, handed it to McCone.

They waited again, Kennedy's fingers drumming the table, a few low comments. McCone said, "My God. I have a report here that six Soviet ships have altered course, away from the quarantine line. Reconnaissance had shown us that these freighters all had extra-large hatches, which makes them ideal for transporting missiles. It is possible the Soviets don't wish us to stumble onto a shipload of offensive weapons, right off the bat."

There was a surge of talk now.

McNamara, looking as though he had swallowed something awful, said, "It's also possible the ships are turning around to re-group, possibly seeking a submarine escort, and together they'll hit the quarantine line in one push. The Navy needs to keep an eye on them."

Beside him, Rusk said in a low voice, "I don't know. It feels to me that we're eyeball to eyeball, and the other guy just blinked."

BY NOON ON the twenty-fourth, the White House authorized release of a vast trove of photographs taken by the U-2 flights over

Cuba. There had been pressure to do so, insistence from America's allies that even though the governments of most major powers had agreed with Kennedy, many of their citizens did not. Evidenced by the surge of support in the UN for U Thant's plea for both sides to take a two- or three-week pause, Kennedy understood that Adlai Stevenson had a difficult lobbying job in front of him at the UN. It would be up to Stevenson to provide substantial and incontrovertible evidence to the nonaligned nations that the Americans were justified in their actions. Surprisingly, many governments and their media outlets had openly rejected the claim that there were ballistic missiles in Cuba. Kennedy knew that by providing these photographs to these same outlets, minds might be changed. If he was wrong, at least he could maintain that the United States was being fully transparent.

Wednesday afternoon, October 24, 1962
The White House, Oval Office

"It was passed along to us through Alex Johnson at the State Department, a letter from William Knox in Moscow. He's the head of Westinghouse, and apparently, Khrushchev decided to bend his ear. It seems like Khrushchev's looking for another opening, another way to make himself heard."

Bobby finished reading the letter.

"Goats? He talks about smelly goats?"

"He's trying to be folksy. Or maybe he *is* folksy. But there's more."

Kennedy held up another piece of paper.

"I wanted to believe he had ordered his ships to turn around as a serious gesture, a way to defuse this. Now, he says this. *'Just imagine, Mr. President that we had presented you with the conditions of* an ultimatum which you have presented to us by your action. How would you have reacted to this? I think you would have been indignant. You, Mr. President, are not declaring a quarantine, but rather are setting forth an ultimatum and threatening that if we do not give in to your demands, you will use force. If you coolly weigh the situation which has developed, not giving way to passions, then you will understand that the Soviet Union cannot fail to reject the arbitrary demands of the U.S.A. I cannot possibly order my seamen to obey American orders, and we shall defend our ships as necessary. If the United States insists on war, then we shall meet in hell.'"

Bobby stared at his brother, slowly shook his head.

"Nothing has changed. He admitted to this fellow Knox that they have put their missiles in Cuba, but says nothing about fixing the problem. McCone was right. They turned those ships around only because they were carrying cargo they didn't want us to see. Meanwhile, they go merrily on their way in Cuba getting their missiles ready to fire at us."

Kennedy picked up another paper.

"I have to respond to Khrushchev. Sorenson and I worked on a text. See if this sounds all right. 'I regret very much that you still do not appear to understand what it is that has moved us in this matter. You gave us solemn assurances that you would place no offensive ballistic missiles in Cuba. However, the facts as we both know them, required the responses I have announced. I hope your government will take the necessary action to permit a restoration of the earlier situation.'"

"The earlier situation being that they weren't threatening to blow up the world."

Kennedy put the paper down, and Bobby could see exhaustion.

"Bobby, there are still too many questions. I have a call in tonight to Prime Minister MacMillan, to see what the British position will be if I have to give the order."

"Which order?"

"To go into Cuba. Take them out."

"I thought . . ."

"I know. I had hoped . . . maybe it was too much wishful thinking, that the quarantine would send enough of a message, that the Soviets would figure they had no choice but to take down their missiles. And maybe I'm too impatient. But this is not a game anyone is going to win, there is no victory here. How do we avoid a nuclear war? Khrushchev is still rattling his sabers long and loud, and he expects us to just accept things as they are right now. I won't do that. The country won't stand for it, knowing we're facing potential obliteration in a matter of minutes. From the beginning of this, I've rejected the idea that we have to invade Cuba as our only course. But if the Soviets don't do anything to remove the missiles they have in Cuba right now, what else can I do? We know a surgical bombing strike won't be sufficient to solve the problem. It might be the only decision left to us."

"Jesus, Jack. It might be the last decision you ever have to make."

CHAPTER TWENTY-THREE

Russo

Thursday, October 25, 1962
Tallahassee, Florida

He waited again for the school bus, admitted to himself that seeing his children come home safely had become more of a priority than ever before. The bus was there now, a squeal of brakes, the two children descending the steps. He waited for Becky's boisterous greeting, but it didn't come, the girl moving up to him quickly, taking his hand.

"Can we go inside, Daddy? It's safer in there."

He didn't understand that, led them inside without speaking, Danny as subdued as his sister. They slipped past the front door, moved into the living room, and Russo said, "What's up, you two? How was your day?"

Becky said, "I got a gold star on my spelling test. The teacher said I was the highest score in class. But then the principal made an announcement. We had to stop everything."

"What announcement?"

"The principal told us to crawl down and get under our desks.

Put our hands over our heads. We had to stay like that for a few minutes, and the teacher closed the blinds in our room. I was scared."

Russo didn't know what to say, looked at Danny, who said, "Yeah, we did it too. They called it *duck and cover*. The teacher said it was the best way for us to live through a nuclear attack, that we had to be prepared. She asked us if our parents had built fallout shelters. I didn't say anything. Some of the kids said yeah."

Russo moved to his easy chair, sat.

"*Duck and cover*? You protect yourself from nuclear bombs by hiding under a desk?"

Becky moved close to him, sat on the floor.

"The principal said it would protect us. But it was scary, thinking about big bombs."

Russo was speechless, didn't want to say anything that would scare his daughter more than she already seemed to be. Danny moved to the sofa, sat, said, "The coach still wants me to play football, wants to talk to you about it. He said he thinks the duck and cover stuff is nonsense. He says if there's a nuclear attack, we'll all be turned to dust anyway. Is he right?"

Russo looked down at Becky, saw the fear, said, "Okay, Dan-o, no more talk like that. Just, you do what the teachers tell you to do. But I'm certain there won't be a nuclear attack. Kennedy's doing what he has to do to protect us. The Russians know how powerful we are. They're not going to start a war. It would be just as bad for them as it would be for us."

Both children were silent now, and Russo ached to say the right words, wondered how many parents were hearing these same fears. Well, he thought, there's Jerry, with his damned fallout shelter. He thinks he's safe. I guess there isn't much difference between a concrete box in your backyard and hiding under a desk. Tell yourself whatever lies you have to, just to feel safe. Maybe, just like me . . .

tell lies to my children so they'll feel better. I wonder how many lies Kennedy is telling us, for the same reason? No, you can't think like that. You have to trust that those people have things under control, are making the right decisions, that Khrushchev isn't some kind of wild animal.

I wonder how many lies the Russians are telling *their* children?

HE SAT ALONE in the bedroom, his small desk in one corner, scanning papers that were due to be graded by the next day. From the living room, he heard the television, Danny allowed to watch until his mother came home. But the boy was in the bedroom doorway now, his voice loud.

"Hey Pop! *American Bandstand*'s not on! What a gyp! Some news thing."

Russo turned, saw the irritation on the boy's face, said, "What news thing? Oh, hell, another bulletin?"

He was up quickly, into the living room, the television focused on a gathering of men, official, a huge table, each man seated. One man in particular was familiar.

"That's Adlai Stevenson. This is the UN. What's going on?"

The boy was gone, uninterested, and Russo sat on the sofa, turned up the volume, a narrator describing what was happening.

"*The speaker now is the Soviet ambassador, Mr. Zorin.*"

"*I challenge you, sir, to produce evidence that the Soviet Union has installed long-range ballistic missiles in Cuba.*"

Russo called out, "Dan-o, you really ought to be watching this. Our UN Ambassador, Adlai Stevenson, is about to speak about the missiles."

"*Well, let me say something to you, Mr. Ambassador. We do have the evidence. We have it and it is clear and incontrovertible. And let me say something else. Those weapons must be taken out of Cuba.*"

You, the Soviet Union, have sent these weapons to Cuba. You, the Soviet Union, have created this new danger—not the United States. Finally, Mr. Zorin, I remind you that you did not deny the existence of these weapons. But today, again, if I heard you correctly, you now say that they do not exist or that we haven't proved they exist. All right, sir, let me ask you one simple question. Do you, Ambassador Zorin, deny that the USSR has placed and is placing medium- and intermediate-range missiles and sites in Cuba? Yes or no? Don't wait for the translation. Yes or no?"

Russo felt Danny sitting beside him, said quietly, as though not to interrupt the television,

"That's Zorin, the Russian. He's going to answer."

"I am not in an American courtroom, sir, and therefore I do not wish to answer a question that is put to me in the fashion in which a prosecutor puts questions. In due course, sir, you will have your answer."

"You are in the courtroom of world opinion right now, and you can answer yes or no. You have denied that they exist and I want to know whether I have understood you correctly."

"You will have your answer in due course."

"Ambassador Zorin, I am prepared to wait for my answer until hell freezes over, if that's your decision. And I am also prepared to present the evidence in this room."

Russo's mouth was open, and he leaned closer, watched as Stevenson turned to a row of easels, unveiling each one, enormous photographs.

"Good God. It's pictures of the missiles."

For the next minute, Russo watched as Stevenson explained the details of the photographs. It was clear that the Security Council was watching in rapt attention.

Zorin attempted to have the last word.

"The Soviet Union has no need to station missiles in Cuba."

"We know the facts, and so do you, sir, and we are ready to talk about them. Our job here is not to score debating points. Our job, Mr. Zorin, is to save the peace. And if you are ready to try, we are."

"What's it mean, Pop?"

"It means we just showed the whole world proof of the missiles the Russians have put in Cuba. It means all of this . . . is real." He kept the rest to himself, thought, it means, Dan-o, I'm as scared of this stuff as you are.

Thursday night, October 25, 1962

He had barely touched the TV dinner, no appetite for whatever it was that filled the compartments of his aluminum foil plate. He had left the table, moved into the living room, stared at the television, a show he enjoyed, *Perry Mason*. The plot had slipped by him though, his mind wandering. He glanced toward the children's bedrooms, no sound, both certainly asleep by now. He heard Margaret, tinkering in the bathroom, struggled with what he could say to her, as though he had to comfort them both. Your whole life is words, he thought. Find some good ones now. She emerged now, a smear of white cream on her face, and he wanted to laugh, to tease her about it, as he had so often. But the gibes would not come.

"Hey, Margie, come, sit down, when you can."

"Just give me a minute. I need a fresh towel."

She vanished back into the bedroom, more tinkering, but she returned quickly, and he felt guilty, knew he had pulled her away from her routine.

"I'm sorry. I just wanted you to . . . sit."

She moved close beside him, sat on the sofa, odd fragrances filling him.

"I know. Becky told me about hiding under her desk. I suppose the school thinks they're doing some good."

He surprised himself with his anger, said, "The school is just lying to the kids. Pretending this is all so harmless, that all we have to do is close the curtains and it will all go away. But it's not just the schools. I was told today that the college has a half-dozen buildings designated as civil defense shelters, places I'm supposed to run to if the bombs fall. I guess it's just like Jerry's fallout shelter, only bigger. No one explained to me just how long we're supposed to stay inside the damn things, and how I'm supposed to find my family."

"I've thought about it, Joe. There's one advantage to me being out in the country, away from town. If there's a bomb, I'll probably be safe. Maybe I can get to the kids."

"Small comfort if I have no idea how to reach you. Or the kids. Good Christ, this is madness. Why would Tallahassee even be a target? I would think they'd be more interested in taking out the air bases in Tampa, Jacksonville, maybe Panama City. Atlanta's probably a target, all the big cities. I guess that's why the Russians brought missiles to Cuba. But we've caught them red-handed, and Kennedy is forcing them . . . well, he's trying to force them to pull them out of there. Both sides are being stubborn about this, and the whole world is watching. Meanwhile, they're telling us to go to the physics building, where we'll be safe. How long before there's a full-blown panic about this?"

"It's already starting. I saw Doris, Jerry's wife, at the Winn-Dixie this afternoon. She had a cart full of canned goods, baked beans, everything else. Other people were doing the same thing, cleaning off the shelves of anything they could carry. I hate to say it felt like panic . . . but I guess it did. Doris made it sound like we were going to starve if I didn't do the same thing. She told me they're sleeping now in their fallout shelter . . . just in case."

He sniffed.

"Just in case. Just in case they wake up and humanity is obliterated. *Surprise.* Welcome to Armageddon. Make sure you go easy on those baked beans. They might have to last for a thousand years."

He stood abruptly, paced.

"What are we supposed to think? How do we act? Are the Russians evil? Is that all there is to it? Or do they think America's evil? Maybe that's the problem. We're so busy calling each other names that neither side can back up and say, wait a minute, maybe we don't need to destroy mankind just to prove how right we are. You live over there, and we'll live right here, and . . . we'll leave each other be. Is that so damned hard?"

He realized he had been shouting, saw Danny standing in the hallway.

"Come in here, Dan-o. I'm sorry. I'm just upset."

Danny moved with hesitancy, sat on the far end of the sofa.

Russo looked at him, said, "That coach of yours never should have told you what he did about nuclear war. But he told you the truth. That duck and cover nonsense is just that . . . nonsense. We have to believe that President Kennedy is doing the right thing, that Khrushchev isn't a madman, that both of them realize that there are millions of young people like you, who want a future, who trust the grown-ups not to screw it all up."

"What made the problem, Pop? What started it all? My friends in school say it's all the Commies, trying to take over the world."

The words flashed through his mind, but he kept it to himself. *Your friends are idiots.*

"It's too easy to paint a picture of someone as the enemy, the bad guy. Maybe those other people are just like us. But the governments get in the way. I have no idea why Khrushchev wanted to put missiles into Cuba, but I understand why Kennedy wants them removed. If I was Russian, I might think it's perfectly fine to have missiles in Cuba, and what's all the fuss about?" He paused, fought still for the right words. "I have faith in the president. I have faith that the people in charge of this whole mess, on both sides, won't get too angry about it, won't react by . . . well, by starting a war. I have to believe that President Kennedy, somewhere inside his head, somewhere in the midst of all the arguments and challenges and negotiations . . . that he'll remember there are a whole lot of people counting on him to do the right thing. People just like *us*."

CHAPTER TWENTY-FOUR

RFK

Friday, October 26, 1962

The White House

The brothers sat together, breakfast between them. Bobby had slept at his office again, knew that with the Excomm meeting set once more for 10 a.m., there wasn't much point in taking a chance with Washington's morning traffic. A short walk to the White House at least meant he could enjoy a real breakfast.

He finished eating, said to Jack, "Your cook is first-rate. Best eggs Benedict I've had in a while. Ethel doesn't even make the attempt anymore. The kids like it simple. They're ecstatic over pancakes."

Kennedy laughed, stuffed a final bite into his mouth.

"A piece of advice. Don't call Chef Verdon a *cook*. Those people are a little touchy about that sort of thing. Jackie was fortunate enough to find him, and we use him for just about everything, not just state dinners. Most of my meals used to be prepared by Navy stewards, but after one too many servings of white beans, Jackie put a stop to that."

Bobby sat back, hoisted his coffee cup.

"Salutes to Jackie."

Jack leaned back now, reached for a newspaper scattered on the floor behind him.

"I assume you saw Walt Lippmann's column in the *Post*."

The smile was gone now, and Bobby shook his head.

"No. Haven't seen a paper at all yet."

"Here. Read this."

"There are three ways to get rid of the missiles already in Cuba. One is to invade and occupy Cuba. The second way is to institute a total blockade, particularly of oil shipments, which would in a few months ruin the Cuban economy. The third way is to try . . . to negotiate a face-saving agreement . . . The only place that is truly comparable with Cuba is Turkey . . . The Soviet military base in Cuba is defenseless and the base in Turkey is all but obsolete. The two bases could be dismantled without altering the world balance of power."

Bobby lowered the paper, said, "I don't suppose we needed him talking publicly about Turkey. But he makes sense. This is an idea that's been lurking in the background with the Excomm for a while."

Kennedy slid his plate aside.

"Yeah, fine. He makes sense. Too much sense right now. I don't need reporters, even sage old farts like Lippmann telling me what I ought to do. It's too damned easy for someone with opinions to broadcast their *logical* points of view without any repercussions. I'm sure Khrushchev will have his hands on a copy of the *Post* before long, and read the same damn thing."

"What's the harm? Lippmann used the right term . . . face-saving. Isn't that what we've been trying to figure out with Khrushchev? You said yourself, we have to give him room to maneuver. We still don't know what he's having to deal with in the Kremlin. I can't believe there's any way he simply surrenders and hauls those missiles back to Russia. We have to give him something he can claim some kind of victory over, some kind of plum."

Kennedy stood now, paced across the room.

"Lippmann is a smart man. There are a lot of smart men in this town. But being smart means you don't throw away your ace in the hole. Right now, if we tell Khrushchev we'll pull our missiles out of Turkey, it's all we've got to give. Do you trust Khrushchev to do what he says he'll do? The one thing we've determined without any doubt is that the Russians are capable of lying through their teeth. We offer to pull our missiles out of Turkey, and Khrushchev reneges on removing his missiles from Cuba, and all we've done is give away the store. There are no more bargaining chips. And what about the Turks, the government there, or the rest of our NATO allies? If we're in a hurry to pull missiles out of Turkey, those people will entirely be in their rights to say we sold out our allies, just to make our own borders safer. It could weaken the entire NATO alliance, especially with countries like Greece and Italy, as well as Turkey. Some of those people aren't all that friendly to us even now, and if they feel like we've pulled the rug out, they might start looking for another kind of alliance. Maybe with the Soviets. I'm sure Khrushchev would promise Turkey the world if he thought he could split those people away from NATO. So, you see? Lippmann's logic sounds wonderful. But there's more to think about than just a simple tit-for-tat trade."

"Jesus, Jack. That's why you're the boss. I guess . . . we just keep the idea in the back of our heads. We still don't know what Khrushchev's planning with his shipping. You're right. It's too soon to toss Khrushchev a bone like Turkey, especially with his submarines scurrying all over the place near our quarantine line."

"The ship was the *Bucharest*, and we determined to our satisfaction that it was an oil tanker, with no capability of housing offensive weapons. It was allowed to cross the quarantine line earlier."

Kennedy nodded toward McNamara, said, "So, it is apparent that Khrushchev hasn't told all of his ships to turn around and go home."

McNamara seemed surprised at Kennedy's remark.

"Actually, Mr. President, we're not sure any of the Soviet vessels have headed for home. Just that some have changed course away from the quarantine line. Others are sitting dead in the water, so of course, we're not sure what their captains are being ordered to do. There's a lot of wait-and-see."

Behind McNamara, Bobby said, "So, we allowed the *Bucharest* to pass unsearched?"

McNamara glanced back at Bobby, then said, "Yes. She was not searched. I realize there were some among you who insisted we halt the ship and board her. I also realize that the intention was to send a strong message to Khrushchev of our resolve and the seriousness of the quarantine. But this did not appear to be an appropriate target for that kind of aggressive statement. She was hailed, and responded appropriately, indicating her cargo only to be petroleum." He paused, read from a piece of paper. "In addition, there was an East German passenger ship, the *Volkerfreund*, said to be carrying some fifteen hundred civilians, plus a number of soldiers. In both cases, the ships were granted time to respond to our hails, presumably to allow their captains to seek instructions from Moscow. The *Volkerfreund* was also allowed to pass, unsearched. There were no incidents."

Bobby said, "Well, that's something to be thankful for."

Kennedy pointed a finger at McNamara.

"You make damned sure the Navy understands that there will be *no incidents*, without my authority. No gunfire, no shooting off rudders, unless the order comes from here. I don't want to have a sunken ship tossed into the mix with everything else we're dancing around. And I sure as hell don't want us to kill a bunch of Russian sailors."

McNamara responded, "Certainly. I've made that clear to Admiral Anderson and stressed that he should do the same to his senior commanders. There will be no loose cannons out there."

Bobby looked around the room, most of the men in agreement, said, "Are we certain the Soviets have turned away any ship that might be suitable for inspection? Can we assume they have blunted the sword of the quarantine by keeping their freighters well back?"

McNamara said, "Unfortunately, no. We are monitoring several ships that are drawing closer to the quarantine line. We have no way to predict what will happen, but I will make sure we're doing everything we can to avoid surprises."

Kennedy thought for a moment, said, "We have to board a ship. We have to give the message to the entire world that we're serious here. If the Soviets keep pushing . . . well, they're testing us, seeing what kind of resolve we have. We've gone well out on a pretty dangerous limb with this quarantine, but we can't play around, allow every damn ship that challenges us to pass through. What the hell's the point of that?"

McNamara nodded.

"I agree. They're definitely going to test us at some point. If it's not with a freighter carrying missiles, it will be something more innocuous."

Bobby said, "I can't believe they'd send a ship into the line loaded with missiles. It's just asking for escalation, and it will confirm all our claims. No, I agree, they'll send a ship through that might or might not seem fairly harmless, just to see what we'll do, whether or not we'll stop it."

Kennedy looked at McNamara.

"Make sure everybody down there is prepared for that. And make sure everybody's got their orders straight, that the orders have to come from here. Are we clear on that?"

"Perfectly, sir."

McCone spoke up, said, "Excuse me, Secretary McNamara, but I need to bring up a different topic. Our low-level flyovers over Cuba are taking place daily. Those jets are hanging as low to the deck as they can, and taking some good photos of the missile sites and airfields. It has been determined that the Soviets are uncrating a number of medium bombers, their IL-28s. Clearly, they aren't trying to hide any of that, and sure as hell, they're not making any effort to pack anything up for a trip home."

Bundy laughed, said, "I would imagine having those jets scream past over the treetops scares the hell out of anybody on the ground. That has to be driving Castro nuts."

McCone said, "With all due respect, sir, it's not a laughing matter. We're hearing that Castro is ordering his antiaircraft batteries to take down our jets anytime there's an opportunity. The Soviet SAMs are worthless against low-flying jets, but Castro has a substantial number of conventional antiaircraft batteries. We need to stay lucky."

Rusk spoke now, scanned a piece of paper.

"Mr. President, if I may, U Thant continues to press us on the issue of pausing the quarantine. From what we can tell, Khrushchev is kissing up to U Thant by responding positively to his entreaties, however, neither the UN nor the Soviets have addressed the issue of the removal of the missiles from Cuba. The only proposal U Thant is sticking to is that everybody just pauses. However, despite

Khrushchev's apparent willingness to do just that, the work is continuing on the bases in Cuba."

Kennedy said, "Well, with all due respect to U Thant, unless the Soviets agree to begin dismantling their missile launchers and pack up their missiles, the idea that we should all step back and take a breath is an issue that's going nowhere."

Rusk said, "Agreed, sir."

Kennedy scanned the room, said, "I want to comment on Adlai's performance at the UN. It is no secret that he and I are not the best of friends and that I have had some difficulties with his input to this group. However, I admit to being very pleased and very surprised by the strength of his remarks to Ambassador Zorin. It certainly made for good television. I have telephoned him and offered him sincere compliments. However, one thing I did not mention to him was that, although his dramatics went down well to the American people, his insistence that we wait until *hell freezes over* for a Soviet response is not what I would have intended. I am hopeful that we receive substantial responses and action of a positive nature well before there are icicles in Cuba."

CHAPTER TWENTY-FIVE

Grayson

Friday, October 26, 1962
USS *Joseph P. Kennedy Jr.* DD850, at sea

He stayed close to the bridge, binoculars in hand, could see the ship off the port bow. Behind the freighter, another shape, more familiar, a destroyer, and he said, "Skipper, the *Pierce* is alongside her."

The ship's captain, Commander Mikhalevsky, had binoculars of his own, said, "That's where she's supposed to be. They're doing the same thing we are, waiting for orders. Where the hell is that radioman? We should have heard something by now."

Grayson saw the young man scrambling up the ladder, paper in hand.

"Sir, the decoded message from Admiral Ward. It passed through the *Elokomin*, Captain Spears. Not sure why, sir."

Mikhalevsky took the message, said, "It's called chain of command, son. These orders are coming all the way from Washington, and you can damn well bet the chief of Naval Operations is doing things by the book. I wouldn't be surprised if these orders are coming all the way from the top. The president. Let's do him proud." He scanned the text, let out a deep breath, glanced at Grayson. "Well, we have our orders. That freighter's the *Marucla*, and we're to board her. Check her out for contraband, weapons, et cetera." He folded the paper, slipped it into his shirt pocket, looked at the faces around the bridge. "You boys wanted to see some action. Well, you're about to. If that ship's got something dangerous on board, we just might start World War Three."

Grayson could feel the skipper's anxiety, felt it himself. For days now, there had been no real activity along this part of the quarantine line, nothing to suggest there was a crisis at all. Now, that had suddenly changed.

Mikhalevsky looked at Grayson now.

"Signal the *Pierce*. Tell her to motor her exec over here, in his full-dress whites."

Grayson moved to the signal station, wrote out the instructions, the seaman reading with wide eyes. He flashed the lights now, a series of Morse-coded words. A long minute passed, Grayson watching the *Pierce*, then a signal of her own, responding. Grayson tried to decode the signal himself, knew the signalman would do a better job, the young man scribbling furiously on paper.

"Here, sir."

Grayson slipped back into the bridge, said, "Skipper, he's on his way."

"You get his name?"

"No, sir. They probably thought it best not to broadcast that with a potential enemy ship paying attention."

"And they're right."

Mikhalevsky spoke into the intercom now.

"Commander Reynolds, to the bridge."

In a short minute, Reynolds, the executive officer was there.

"Sir. We boarding that ship out there?"

Mikhalevsky gazed again through his binoculars, and Grayson could see the tension in his face, could hear it in his words.

"Casey, we've been ordered to board and search her. You will lead the boarding party. The exec from *Pierce* is on his way over . . . yep, there he is."

Grayson scanned the open water, saw the motor launch heading their way, a single passenger in white.

Mikhalevsky continued, "That fellow will join you."

In a few minutes, Grayson saw an officer in white, a quick jog up the ladder, out of breath, adjusting his jacket. He hesitated, a nodding glance at Grayson, then he looked toward the other officers, said, "Commander Dwight Osborne, sir. Permission to be on your bridge."

"Permission granted. You're the exec on the *Pierce*?"

"I am, sir."

"Well, you're now part of the boarding party."

"That's what I was told, sir. Excuse me, but do we know what's so special about the *Marucla*?"

Mikhalevsky pulled the written order from his pocket, said, "Admiral Ward is passing on to us the information coming down from the CNO that *Marucla* is an old U.S.-built Liberty ship, now under a Lebanese flag, commanded by a Greek skipper, under charter to the Russians. She is en route to Cuba, and our orders are to inspect her cargo, apparently whether she likes it or not. Once the boarding party is prepared, and that means dress whites, we'll pull up alongside. I'll signal her to stop, and I would have to imagine that with two destroyers flanking her, she'll pay attention."

———

LIEUTENANT PAUL GRAYSON had served on the *Kennedy* for most of two years, had come to the Navy from a family of sailors that dated back to the 1800s. His father had seen action at Pearl Harbor, and well after, throughout World War II, serving on destroyers like this one. But Grayson knew his father wouldn't have recognized the kinds of technology he worked with now, from the antisubmarine rocket-launcher to the computerized fire control system. Enjoying a recent refit, the destroyer now had its own submarine-spotting helicopter, and besides her twin five-inch guns, carried thirty-two torpedoes. She had a top speed of more than thirty-five knots, and should the need arise, could launch nuclear depth charges, a source of pride that no one really wanted to experience.

There was another source of pride: the destroyer's name. She had been christened to honor the president's older brother, who had been killed during World War II. That Joseph P. Kennedy's brother was now the president only added to the prestige the crew felt serving on his family's namesake. For Grayson, there was pride enough in wearing the uniform, a junior officer hoping to climb the Navy's ladder. Thus far, the primary claim to fame for the *Kennedy* had been in service to the space launches out of Cape Canaveral, the ship serving as one part of the Mercury Seven astronaut program as a potential rescue vessel. The orders to join the quarantine had been a stark surprise, inspiring a rapid scramble to reach the designated quarantine line, as part of Commander Task Group 136.3. Immediately, the reconnaissance helicopter had been sent airborne, with constant radio contact with other members of the task force, one fleet oiler, the USS *Elokomin*, and several destroyers. So far, contacts with potential target ships had been fairly minimal, most of the cargo vessels they were to monitor staying out of range.

For the crew, the duty was both an adventure and a serious dose of nervousness, many of the younger crewmen experiencing a sea-borne journey for the first time. Gone were the drills, the mundane duties that seemed designed solely to give the crew something to do. Now, when the radio operators relayed messages, everyone seemed to freeze, wondering if, this time, they might be called to battle stations. And with all the men knew of what was happening around Cuba, no one expected it to be a drill.

With the first light, the ship had been ordered to general quarters, the guns manned, fire stations monitored. As torpedo officer, Grayson also manned the bridge lookout, and from first light, he had kept his position peering out to port, and even now, the sun was not yet fully above the horizon. They had shadowed the *Marucla* throughout the night, keeping constant contact with the destroyer *John Pierce*, and with first light, *Pierce* had drawn much closer to the *Marucla*, though the *Marucla* had not yet slowed her speed. He could feel the heightened attention of everyone around him, eyes mostly focusing on the skipper.

Mikhalevsky spoke to the helmsman, said, "Slide up alongside her. Keep your distance. No traffic accidents." After a long pause, he said, "Signal station, raise signal flags *Oscar November*."

Grayson thought, that's a clear message. *Stop.* The flags went up, the order for the freighter to halt dead in the water. The surge of speed from *Kennedy*'s engines drew her much closer to the freighter, and Grayson stared through binoculars, saw activity on the *Marucla*'s deck, the ship not seeming to slow. Mikhalevsky seemed to read his mind, said, "Give her a few minutes. Maybe they haven't had their coffee yet. They're a little slow on the uptake."

They waited five more minutes, all eyes on the *Marucla*, still plowing forward, and beyond, the *Pierce* keeping pace.

The radioman was there again, the young man out of breath, his nervousness obvious.

"Sir, a message from Captain Spears, on *Elokomin*."

"What the hell's he want? Jesus." He took the message, read, looked out away from *Marucla*, toward the horizon. There was a silent minute on the bridge, no one speaking. Mikhalevsky turned to Osborne, *Pierce's* executive officer, said, "There's a Russian sub, Foxtrot class, fifteen miles east. Seems to be heading this way. She's on the surface, so there are no secrets, not yet anyway." He focused his binoculars on the *Marucla* now. "What the hell's wrong with those people? All right, no more flags. Signalman, on my command, flash '*Request you stop. I intend to board you. Request you advise when your sea ladder is ready.*'"

Another long minute, Grayson glancing out east, wondering if he would actually see a submarine. And worse, would she try to interfere?

"Sir, she's slowing."

There were small cheers, silenced now, the exec officer, Reynolds appearing, now in his whites, a quick handshake to Osborne.

"How do we do this, sir? I assume we have orders for everything?"

Mikhalevsky said, "Casey, today, I'm not going to the head without orders. Now, Lieutenant Grayson, go get dressed, like it's your mama's birthday. Where's that translator, Seaman Mass? Get him into his whites too. Radioman, you're going with them. Get dressed." He looked around, pointed to a CPO. "Chief, you'll join 'em." The chief put a hand on his holster, the .45 secure. "No. No weapons. No mistakes. This isn't the wild west. Remember, we're under orders that go all the way up to heaven. Every detail."

THE *MARUCLA* HAD finally obeyed, gave the signal that her ladder had been lowered. The launch pulled away from the *Kennedy*, the six men bobbing about in the low swells like an out-of-place wedding party. The journey took short minutes, the destroyer now alongside the *Marucla*. The *Kennedy's* executive officer, Casey Reynolds, commanded the boarding party, the man holding tight to a legal pad, notes written out, but no one was quite certain what to expect or what kind of reception they would receive. Grayson felt the butterflies, looked back at the destroyer, comforted by the guns, the gunners' mates visible, lookouts with sharp eyes in all directions, the nagging thought of an approaching submarine.

They reached the flank of the *Marucla*, the Jacob's ladder dangling, crewmen steadying it as much as possible. The men stepped clear of the launch, climbed slowly, Grayson grateful there were six of them.

He climbed, then swung his legs over to the deck now, joined the others, an awkward silence, the crewmen of the *Marucla* with mostly smiles. One man emerged now, a ragged uniform, his hand extended.

"I am Georgio Condorrigos. I am the captain. Welcome aboard my ship."

THE COFFEE WAS painfully strong, Commander Reynolds leading the way by accepting the Greek's hospitality. All six men struggled through the coffee, the captain enjoying himself at their expense.

"We have breakfast for you, if you wish. Nothing like what your American ships can offer, but my men do not starve."

Reynolds said, "We appreciate your kind reception to our request, Captain. But we have official duties here. We must determine if your cargo is acceptable to pass the quarantine. Surely you understand our purpose here."

The captain stood, still smiling, and Grayson thought, he is either an expert at lying, or he knows he's out of danger. I guess we have to find out which.

Condorrigos produced a thick sheaf of papers.

"Here is my manifest, and my bills of lading. Please notice my cargo. You have already seen that I have trucks parked along my upper deck. I have rolls of paper below, along with barrels of sulfur, truck parts, and some petroleum and electronics."

Reynolds took the manifest, handed it to Grayson, said in a low voice, "Look it over."

Reynolds said to the captain, "I should like to examine your hold, sir. If you do not mind."

Condorrigos still smiled, pointed the way. He led them down two flights of ladders, a hatchway, then pointed to a locked door. Reynolds said, "Open, please."

A crewman stood nearby, unsmiling, the captain barking a sharp order, the man obeying. The hold was dark, piled high with boxes, and Reynolds said to no one in particular,

"The writing on those boxes is Russian. Interpreter."

Behind Grayson, the man stepped forward, said, "Electronics, sir. It says *precision instruments*."

The captain kept his smile, said, "Well, yes, of course. It is electronic gear, intended for Russian use. My ship is under charter to the Russians, as I am sure you know. Shall I open the rest of the cargo holds? I assure you, it is more of the same. Mostly truck and tractor parts."

Reynolds seemed to ponder his options, a glance back toward Grayson, the others.

"No, that will not be necessary. You have shown us what we came to see. Your ship will remain in this position until we return to our ship. Orders will follow."

The captain seemed to lose his smile, said, "I have done nothing to alarm you, sir. I am aware of the contraband you seek, and there is nothing of that here. Please allow us to be on our way."

"When we return to our ship, we shall issue you the order. It has to be this way. I am under orders of my own."

Condorrigos lowered his head, seemed to accept his fate.

"Then I shall escort you to the ladder."

THEY RETURNED TO *Kennedy*, Reynolds reporting the details of the ship's cargo that he had seen and catalogued. Commander Mikhalevsky radioed the results to his superiors, those details traveling quickly up the line, as he had expected, from his own task force command, to the fleet command, the chief of Naval Operations, all the way to the White House. As Captain Condorrigos had insisted, the ship's cargo bore no resemblance to the kinds of weaponry or materials the quarantine line had been created to stop. With no further reason to hold the *Marucla*, she was given the order releasing her to resume her voyage to Cuba.

The submarine that had been observed only minutes before the rendezvous made no effort to intrude and soon disappeared.

CHAPTER TWENTY-SIX

RFK

Friday, October 26, 1962
The White House, Cabinet Room

"The ship *Marucla* was stopped, boarded, and a search was made of her cargo. No contraband was discovered, and according to the captain of the *Joseph P. Kennedy*, Commander Mikhalevsky, there was no indication that a more thorough search would have resulted in any other kind of problem. Acting under instructions from the chief of Naval Operations, and of course, myself and you, Mr. President, the *Marucla* was allowed to go on her way."

McNamara lowered the paper, and Bobby looked at his brother, said, "Did you order that particular destroyer to make the search?"

Kennedy smiled back at him, shook his head.

"Pure chance, I assure you. But at least we can say the family name's staying front and center."

There was laughter throughout the room, a light moment in an otherwise dreary day. McNamara shifted papers on the table in front of him, said, "If I may, sir, I have some figures as provided me by the Joint Chiefs. The Marines are now in force at Guantánamo, and there are twenty-five thousand additional Marines on board a number of ships stationed within a short distance of Cuban territorial waters. Besides the *Essex*, two additional aircraft carriers are rapidly approaching those same waters, the *Independence* and the *Enterprise*. A number of light and heavy cruisers are moving into position where their fire can be most effective against the Cuban coastline. Throughout bases in Florida, some one hundred thousand soldiers are now positioned, and can be mobilized in a matter of hours. The Air Force has shifted a number of fighter and bomber squadrons to air bases in Florida, from Key West up to Jacksonville. There are approximately four hundred forty-eight fighters and attack planes available on a moment's notice. In short, preparations have been completed in the event you order the full-on invasion of Cuba." McNamara stopped, seemed to struggle for words. "I must add . . . this gives me great pause, as I have mentioned before. Even the most optimistic estimates coming from the Pentagon predict substantial casualties in such an operation."

McCone said, "I would also suggest caution, Mr. President. The Cubans now have a hell of a lot of equipment, and, as we learned in Korea, it will be damned tough to shoot them out of the hills. We also must be aware that the Soviets have brought in their Luna artillery shells. These are low-yield nuclear artillery, which can be fired at targets less than thirty miles away. I only remind you, sir, that, as the secretary has said, any invasion of Cuba will most certainly result in substantial casualties."

Kennedy kept his eyes on McNamara, said, "I am aware of that. This has always been, and is now, a last step. We are only discussing this because I am extremely frustrated that our quarantine has produced no real results, no real progress in solving this crisis. It was always the problem, that stopping any flow of goods to Cuba did nothing at all to remove the missiles that are already there. U Thant continues to push us, as, apparently Khrushchev is pushing him, to halt our efforts along the quarantine line, in return for the Soviets recalling their ships, the ships we would intend to stop anyway. Around the world, intelligent and reasonable heads of state are suggesting that this will solve all our problems. It is frustrating in the extreme that no one seems concerned that the Soviets are rapidly preparing their missiles for launch inside Cuba. As you all know, there are signs that the preparation of their launch sites continues at a rapid pace, and yet we are supposed to applaud their willingness to turn their ships around, so that they do not add more weapons, more armament, and indeed, more missiles to what they already have in place."

Rusk said, "There is still the option of adding items to the quarantine list, including all petroleum products. It would serve to strangle the Cubans a bit harder, and thus, give us a little more leverage."

Bobby felt his anger rising, said, "And how long would that take? How much longer can we afford to wait before the Soviets have their missile sites, *all* of their missile sites, up and running, with warheads aimed at Washington, New York, and any other city they see fit? What happens then? Assuming it is not their intention to launch a first strike, then what? Blackmail? We would be at their mercy, with regard to issues of trade, of exports, and we certainly would be at their mercy when it came to Berlin. From now on, we would dare not antagonize them. It's as though we'd be petting a dangerous dog. One wrong move, and the teeth come out, and those teeth are ninety miles from our border."

Kennedy said, "One thing we haven't really addressed yet. Let us look ahead. I am concerned that, for now, we are dealing with one man, Khrushchev, who seems, at least on the surface, to be a somewhat reasonable man. But we know how things work in Russia. Who will follow Khrushchev? Whoever it might be, whether a friend or someone who is outright dangerous, he will have missiles aimed at our hearts. This is simply unacceptable, and although our close allies understand this, I cannot seem to get that point across to U Thant and the rest of the world. That is why we must consider the very real possibility that the only way to remove those missiles from Cuba might be to remove them ourselves." He looked at McNamara now. "I understand casualty counts. But you and I both know that pinpoint bombing raids will almost certainly be ineffective."

McNamara said, "Should it come to that . . . if you make that decision . . . the Air Force is prepared to launch on your order, at least three raids per day, as many as two thousand sorties. But . . . yes, we have to assume that those raids cannot be one hundred percent successful, and so, what will remain are missiles, however few, pointed at the United States. We must also assume that in the event of such action on our part that those missiles will be fired."

Kennedy stared down at the table, his hands coming together.

"And that . . . is war."

Friday, October 26, 1962
White House Residence

Kennedy spoke with a full mouth.

"Decent sandwich. You sure you don't want one?"

Bobby felt a painful twinge in his stomach, shook his head.

"No appetite. One of my aides asked me if I wanted a Cuban sandwich. Jokers, every damn one of them."

They sat at the table, alone but for an aide who came and went, bits and pieces of the president's day. Bobby watched Jack eat, no urge to do the same, and he saw Bundy now, the familiar sense of urgency. Bundy didn't hesitate, approached the pair, said, "Sorry to interrupt, Mr. President. Just received a somewhat urgent note from the speaker of the House. In essence, he's wondering if it isn't time for the whole of Congress to vacate the premises, and head for West Virginia. That's a question only for you, sir."

Kennedy stopped eating, wiped the cloth napkin across his mouth.

"Never thought I'd see John McCormick panic."

"Oh, I don't think it's panic, sir. He's just expressing concern that, since we have that facility available, and since things seem to be heating up, that Congress might be better off relocating, at least for the time being."

It was one of the government's best-kept secrets, that beneath the posh Greenbrier Hotel in White Sulphur Springs, West Virginia, a massive bunker had been constructed, starting four years before, completed only recently. The bunker was in effect an enormous fallout shelter, designed to house all of Congress, including a good many aides, to preserve some semblance of an organized legislative government that might survive a nuclear holocaust.

Bobby could see Bundy was deadly serious, no irony in the man's tone. Bobby said, "Does the speaker actually believe that all of Congress can just shuffle quietly away, and no one will ask questions? I thought that bunker was to be used in the event of an atomic war, not just *in case one might happen.*"

Kennedy seemed to ponder the question, said, "Ike approved that project. It seemed to make sense to his people. Certainly it would make sense to any member of Congress who feels like his butt's in the fire. But I know McCormick better than to believe he's ready to leave a sinking ship. Somebody's lighting that fuse near him, maybe his own staff."

Bobby said, "Congress doesn't all know about that place, do they? I thought it was a pretty tight secret."

Bundy shook his head, said, "No, it's still a secret. The speaker and the president pro tempore, and sure, maybe some of their staffers, but that's it. Of course, nothing's perfect, and there are some folks on Capitol Hill who've probably heard rumors, especially now. So, what do you think, sir?"

Kennedy couldn't hide a look of mild disgust.

"I think McCormick should tell his buddies that they should think more about what's good for this country than what's good for their own asses. I've never really thought it was a good idea to assume our precious Congress would go right on functioning, while the rest of the nation was on fire. If it's coming to that, a bunch of safe and secure congressmen aren't going to do anybody much good."

Bundy seemed to search for words, said, "Listen, Jack. We're also thinking of you. Raven Rock . . . Site R . . . is all prepared in the event you need to take shelter of your own."

"I know. I've been briefed by the Joint Chiefs on all their contingency plans. There are bunkers set up all over the country for the military brass. It makes me think of turning the light on in your basement, and a dozen mice go scattering. If there's a war, there's going to be a hell of a lot of scattering."

"Site R is the best alternative for you, sir. There's a working staff there now, and preparations are being made for a rapid evacuation. Once DEFCON 1 is announced, there's no turning back. The Army and Air Force have fleets of helicopters prepared to whisk you and your staff out of here, and relocate you to Site R. My office has suggested . . . that perhaps we should not wait for DEFCON 1."

It was one more secret, that plans had been made to protect the president, should there be a nuclear attack. Site R, located at Raven Rock Mountain, lay close to the presidential retreat known as Camp David, near the Maryland-Pennsylvania border. The site was fully functional as an operations and communications center, both for the president and the military chiefs. As far back as the Truman administration, plans had been in place to remove the president and his staff to the vastly secure underground facility in the event of a catastrophic emergency.

Bobby could see the concern on Jack's face, said, "Jesus, Jack. How the hell is this going to work? Like you said, scattering mice. I can see helicopters filled with Washington VIPs, crashing into each other trying to get the hell out of town. And, forgive me for asking, but what about our families? Gathering them up in a parade of helicopters, from spots all over hell and gone, seems a little clumsy."

Kennedy said, "I sent Jackie and the kids out to one of our vacation homes in Glen Ora, Virginia. Maybe it's selfish, but I thought I should at least put them out of range of a goddamn mushroom cloud over DC."

Bobby said, "Christ, Jack, you're allowed to be selfish. You sit in the big chair."

Kennedy shook his head.

"Maybe. Doesn't matter. I'm not leaving here no matter what happens. Jackie will come back here in a few days, and if this thing gets a hell of a lot nastier, we'll be together. I'm not going to separate myself from my family, especially to go hide out in some mountain in Maryland, knowing the rest of the country might get blown to hell. How about you?"

Bobby glanced up at Bundy, said, "Ethel and I have already talked about it. She's staying put, and I guess I will too. If it gets really bad, I'd rather be with my kids. The idea that any of us can be safe, or protected, or that we'll just carry on like normal after the fires go out . . . that's insane. I've been hearing a lot about this lately, like there's some kind of national panic, people doing what they think they have to do to keep safe, to survive. It used to be that the military, and official Washington could rely on some kind of contingency plan, knowing it took so many hours for Soviet bombers to reach our cities. With missiles in Cuba, there's not going to be enough time to spit."

Kennedy pushed his half-eaten sandwich away, said, "Thanks. Now *my* appetite is shot to hell. But you've made the point, the one thing we have to pursue above all else. Get those damned missiles out of Cuba."

CHAPTER TWENTY-SEVEN

Pliyev

October 26, 1962
Cuba, outside Havana

He was growing angrier by the day. He had no real complaint with the men in the field, the soldiers who had served more as workers, since there were still no Cubans allowed near the missile sites. But he had lost patience with the officers, those who seemed to drag behind their men. For weeks now, he had stewed about their poor performance, that even with his strict orders that they supervise their men personally, too often the officers behaved as though Cuba was their prime vacation home.

He stood in the shadow of the largest launcher, the officers gathered nearby, waiting, as usual, for his harangue.

"How long will it require for you to make this missile ready for launch? Keeping in mind, of course, that it should have been ready weeks ago."

One man stepped forward, unwisely defiant.

"Sir, conditions here do not allow us to prepare the missiles as we would have back home. These launchers are prepared to fire, but we do not yet have the nuclear warheads affixed, and, as you certainly know, sir, it requires most of a full day to fuel the missiles for launch."

Pliyev forced himself to ignore the man's insolence, knew he was right about the miserable conditions. For weeks now, a steady stream of men had drifted into the medical facilities, most struck down by the never-ending heat. He had accepted that as a fact of life here, that most of these men were Russian, were accustomed to Russian Octobers, where, already, snow was blanketing the military bases where these men had once been stationed.

He stared up at the missile, perched in the wide open, thought of the American observation planes, the invisible U-2s, and the jets screaming through the treetops nearly every hour. All they see is missiles, he thought. They don't know how toothless these weapons are, mere statues to Soviet strength. If they come, and by God, they will come, these launchers are helpless, will never stand up to a bombing attack. Why will they not allow me to bring the warheads close, position them at each launch site? At least then, we can be prepared, strike back at the Americans with genuine power. If they insist on starting a world war, we can oblige them.

He ignored the officers, moved back to his truck, his driver pulling open the door. He looked back at the colonel, said, "I will secure permission to relocate some of the warheads, bring them closer. You will respond accordingly, treat this operation with the seriousness it deserves. You command enormous power here. Behave like you understand that. Perhaps fewer hours lying on the beach."

HE FINISHED A hasty lunch, had grown used to some of the more tropical foods, sampling some of what the Cubans around his headquarters seemed to believe were delicacies. The fruit was unusual enough, oranges and limes, eaten whole, or blended into a variety of alcoholic drinks, usually with rum. He had made that mistake early on, a hefty tumbler of some particularly satisfying liquid, fruity and sweet, only to find that within a half hour, he couldn't feel his legs. Now, he kept his beverages more conservative, rarely strayed from his private stock of vodka, though he knew the men around his headquarters still enjoyed a good party.

He pushed the plate away, tugged at the napkin stuffed into the top of his shirt, said, "This was exceptional, thank you."

Pliyev wasn't sure if his Cuban servant understood Russian at all, but the old man was always smiling, removed his empty plates with a cheerful nod. I wonder if he's a spy, he thought. Castro probably has a dozen of them scattered around my headquarters, assumes we're keeping secrets from him on a regular basis. Well, maybe we are. I have my orders, after all.

He stood, moved to the open window, a soft breeze keeping away the heat. I must go out to San Cristóbal, push those people yet again to complete their work. It is certainly more important now. It was an odd feeling, the strange sense that the entire American military was staring at him, waiting for . . . what? Are they coming? Castro thinks so. If Castro had a genuine navy, he'd be attacking Miami right now. Damned fool. Just let us do our work, whether the Americans are watching or not. And for whatever reason, the Americans haven't tried to stop us. That's the most important thing, at least right now. They found our missiles, they set up their blockade, they send their recon jets over every couple of hours, but they haven't done anything to stop our progress. Castro wants to shoot them down, every jet. Good luck, sir. American pilots are superior to Cuban gunners.

Since Kennedy's speech, broadcast throughout Cuba, Pliyev had kept his men on high alert, but just what they were alert for didn't seem to matter, at least not yet. For all the activity surrounding Cuba, the American navy setting up into position for . . . something, Pliyev could only do his job. There were officers out in the field, the men whose armament included the Luna artillery and the cruise missiles, who seemed almost eager for the Americans to come. He had wondered about American intelligence. It is one thing to photograph a missile launcher, but what do you know about our troops on the ground, the weapons they carry? Surely, if you come, if you try to sweep us away, it will be you who is swept away. Would I even need the nuclear Lunas? I might never find out.

It was a source of frustration for him that Moscow had emphasized repeatedly that even though he should heighten the alert for his forces, he was not to engage the nuclear artillery, or any nuclear warheads at all, without express orders from Moscow. That was a change from his original orders, when Khrushchev had granted him the power to deploy the nuclear artillery, especially since any assault from the Americans would likely sever his lines of communication with Moscow. Things have gotten much hotter, he thought, and so, they've clamped down on me. I'm not sure how that's supposed to work. If the Americans come, they will come hard and fast, they will strike our vulnerable missile launchers, and there will be no time to reach out halfway across the world, for *permission* to use my strongest weapons.

He moved to his desk, sat, no breeze here, the office stifling. His orders were in thick folders, separated by category, the nuclear options the most important. But there were other orders as well, some of them uselessly redundant, some simply annoying. He scanned a paper now, shook his head. It was a directive that, in the event of an American invasion, his field officers and soldiers were to work closely alongside the Cubans, to coordinate their defenses. The Cubans, after all, would be defending their own country. Moscow seemed to believe that the Cubans would fight as ferociously as the Soviet forces under Pliyev's command. Castro would certainly believe that. Pliyev did not.

He heard footsteps on the wooden floor, turned, was surprised to see Colonel Beloborodov. Beloborodov commanded the nuclear stockpiles, including the missiles, most stored at the main depot at Bejucal.

"Colonel, come in. I did not expect to see you. Did you have lunch? I can arrange a plate for you."

"No, sir. I mean, yes, I had lunch. Forgive the intrusion. I just needed to see you . . . to confirm once more my orders, if there are any changes. As you know, I command the storage of all the nuclear warheads on the island. I am receiving questions from some of the battlefield commanders, when we will distribute these warheads into the field. There is great concern that with so much tension, with the Americans preparing to invade, a rapid deployment might be called for."

"Your orders have not changed, Colonel. But, refresh my memory. What exactly do you now have in your arsenal?"

"At Bejucal, sir, we have nuclear warheads for thirty-six R-12 missiles, forty short-range cruise missiles, and twelve Luna artillery rockets. I am also safeguarding forty additional warheads, plus six atomic bombs to be fitted to the Ilyushin bombers. These are parked right now at Santa Clara."

Pliyev's first thought rolled through his mind. Then, what the hell are *you* doing *here*?

"Colonel, as you know, there can be no firing of any nuclear missiles under my command without orders from Moscow. That order has been emphasized to me yet again. However, I agree that tensions have reached a point where we must prepare for the worst. I have it on some authority, Cuban authority, that the Americans will invade here as early as tomorrow. They will certainly begin with an overwhelming bombing campaign, for which we can do little. But maintaining a stockpile of our warheads mostly in one location is unwise. I do not believe it would cause problems in Moscow if I authorize you to relocate some of the mobile technical support bases nearer to the rocket launchers where they could be used. This you will do after dark and as discreetly as possible. Neither the Americans nor the Cubans need to be informed just what you are doing."

Beloborodov smiled, obviously pleased.

"It shall be done, General. This should put minds at ease at many of the launch sites. Though the work is progressing rapidly, there is still much to do, and knowing their warheads are nearby will add incentive to the officers to complete their work."

"I wish they did not require additional incentive. Never mind. You may begin distributing the warheads to the depot areas to which they have been assigned. Now, Colonel, if there is nothing else, I must travel out to San Cristóbal."

"Nothing else, sir. Thank you."

Beloborodov left quickly, and Pliyev thought, that's all it takes, I suppose. Give them something important to do, and they snap to.

October 26, 1962
San Cristóbal, Cuba

Pliyev was surprised to see the truck, plastered with the insignia of the Cuban army. He climbed from his own truck, saw their uniforms now, the only ones in sight, sagged slightly under the smiling gaze of General Ramos.

"Ah, General Pliyev, a fine coincidence. I was sent here by Fidel, to check on the progress of the launch sites. Things are coming along nicely, eh?"

Ramos's Russian language skills were about halfway understandable, and he made up for a lack of comprehension by backslapping good cheer, which Pliyev had never trusted.

Pliyev spoke slowly, tried to enunciate carefully.

"Very nice to see you again, General."

"Yes. To the point. Fidel is suggesting your men now wear their uniforms. With invasion certain any day now, it will help morale."

Pliyev glanced toward his own men, the ridiculous checked shirts, some men with no shirts at all, a lapse of discipline Pliyev had ignored.

"General Ramos, my men require no additional morale. They know the dangers we face here, and they will respond. Unless, of course, you mean that the Cuban soldiers require a boost in morale."

Ramos digested his words, frowned.

"Certainly not. The Cuban army is prepared to annihilate the Americans on our beaches. If your men wish to accompany us, we shall share the glory. How many men can you now provide?"

Pliyev felt caution, but he knew it would be no secret in Havana, that Castro was well aware how many Russians were on his island.

"I command forty thousand men here, General. And, yes, we would gladly share your glory."

Ramos seemed satisfied, offered a crisp salute, didn't wait for a response, climbed into his truck. The engine turned over, a cloud of black smoke, and the Cubans were quickly gone.

Pliyev breathed through the choking exhaust, moved away, now saw the man he sought, Colonel Ivanov, who approached him with a salute, and Ivanov said, "Thank you for your timely arrival. That man . . . he asks so many questions. He says he speaks for Fidel, reports directly to him, all of that. But our orders are to keep such talk to ourselves . . ."

"Yes, I know your orders. They have not changed. But, we must tolerate the questions. Despite all of their boasting, Havana is full of fear right now. Castro understands that his days might be numbered, and he continues to insist that we prepare the nuclear warheads for immediate launch. We are in a dangerous situation as it is, Colonel, we don't need to be pushed from behind by the

Cubans. I will report to Moscow that the Cubans want to know every detail."

Ivanov seemed to hesitate, said, "Sir, my officers are greatly concerned. The Cubans we've dealt with insist that the Americans have a great naval force offshore, and they are preparing to bomb us." He looked toward the missile launchers now. "We are not yet prepared for a full response to such an assault. It will require eighteen hours to fuel the missiles, and additional time to place the warheads. I am concerned, sir, that we will be caught unprepared. What else can be done?"

Pliyev hated the question.

"You are asking me if we will respond with nuclear force to any action by the Americans. I cannot answer that. The trigger to such weapons lies in Moscow. But I would caution you, Colonel. Do not be in such a rush to destroy the world."

CHAPTER TWENTY-EIGHT

Khrushchev

October 26, 1962
Moscow, the Kremlin

He paced through the office, slow plodding steps. His hands were clamped behind him, his stare toward the blank yellow wall. I hate diplomats, he thought. U Thant most of all. He begs me for some comfort, for relief, a way to end this crisis, and then he pledges nothing in return. I go along, I try to soften the blows between us, find a way to communicate intelligently with this young fellow Kennedy, and U Thant is no help at all. He cannot break through the American . . . what? Blood lust? Is that what it is? They are drunk with their own power? They know they have more missiles, they can destroy us with a single order to do so. Surely they understand we will respond in kind. A nuclear war is no one's solution. And yet, Kennedy digs in his heels, ignores U Thant, perhaps he is ignoring his own peacemakers. Their military follows his lead, their bases in Florida and everywhere else swelling with weapons and men eager for war. Their politicians push Kennedy, accuse him of weakness so that he must stand up strong. But how foolish is a show of strength? No one needs to be convinced how powerful the other side is.

He changed his stride, moved to the closed office door, pulled it open, saw the faces of his aide, his secretary.

"Where is Marshal Malinovsky? Find him."

He didn't wait for a response, knew that as minister of defense, Malinovsky was monitoring events as closely as he was, would surely be nearby.

He backed into his office, closed the door, moved slowly to his desk, was surprised by a sharp knock at the door.

"Yes, enter."

Malinovsky seemed out of breath, no smile, a brief nod.

"Nikita, things are not progressing well."

"What has happened now?"

Malinovsky glanced toward a chair, and Khrushchev pointed toward it, said, "Please, sit. I will do the same."

Malinovsky pulled a paper from his jacket pocket, said, "I have emphasized once more to General Pliyev that no nuclear missile or artillery is to be used in Cuba without direct orders from here. General Pliyev seems to think that some of his commanders, some renegade perhaps, might consider his orders to be . . . *optional*. I respect Pliyev for verifying his status." He let out a breath, stared briefly at the piece of paper. "Then, of course, there is Mr. Castro."

"What now?"

Malinovsky shook his head.

"I do not know if he actually believes the Americans are intending to invade Cuba. Regardless of what he *truly* believes, he wants *us* to believe it. I have never, in many years, found a man to be so eager to start a war. He has gone so far as to suggest that, once our missiles are prepared for use, that we fire them into the United States. A first strike."

Khrushchev felt a cold twinge in his chest, said, "He would send us all over the brink . . . why?"

Malinovsky shrugged.

"Perhaps he believes the missiles would only fly across the oceans, destroying the U.S. and the Soviet Union alone, that his part of the world would be immune from destruction. Perhaps he believes that he alone would survive such a catastrophe, that he could then start his own world order as he sees fit."

"That's delusional. Or insane."

Malinovsky shook his head.

"Or he is simply too fond of his own pronouncements. We have known that for some time, that he enjoys bellicose speeches."

Khrushchev slapped one hand on the desk, was angry now.

"This is no time for bellicose speeches, for waving our hands over the nuclear triggers as a threat."

"There is no further advance on the diplomatic efforts?"

Khrushchev gripped his hands together, felt a sudden sadness.

"We will not prevail in this, Rodion. We have been clumsy and stupid. It was my plan to install those missiles completely, before we grandly announced to the world, and to Mr. Kennedy, what we had done. But we took too much time, and we underestimated how effective the American reconnaissance would be. It is the first time we attempted to create bases far beyond our own borders and we did not understand the difficulties of logistics."

Malinovsky seemed concerned now, said, "Why are you speaking this way? We are under no pressure to remove the missiles from Cuba, any more than we are under pressure from Castro. We still have the upper hand here."

Khrushchev shook his head slowly.

"No, my friend. The Americans have succeeded in turning the entire world against us. If we had ever believed that offering such power to the Cubans would have encouraged other nations to invite us in . . . that has become a folly. What we have accomplished instead is that we have frightened people."

"You have already made a decision. I know you too well, Nikita."

"I have already sent a wire, to one of our agents in the embassy in Washington, Alexander Fomin. He has contacts deep within the American news media and has proven useful on many occasions. It is an avenue we have not yet traveled this time, a way of testing the temperature of the American government from an unlikely source. I have ordered Mr. Fomin to seek out his most reliable contact and offer possibilities of solutions to this crisis."

"What kinds of solutions?"

"I am trusting Mr. Fomin to reach out to someone in the American media who has strong and private contacts within their State Department, to test whether they would accept terms . . ." He pulled a paper from his desk, read. "The missile sites would be dismantled and shipped back to the Soviet Union under United Nations supervision. Fidel Castro would pledge himself to accept no offensive weapons in the future. The United States would pledge itself not to invade Cuba."

Malinovsky stared at him, his mouth slightly open. After a long silent moment, he said, "Have you communicated this to anyone among the Presidium? No, you have not."

"No, I have not. Mikoyan knows. He accepts my judgment."

"What of Marshal Kochov? He will not accept this lightly."

"Kochov wishes us to throw missiles in every direction, as though nuclear war is merely some sort of May Day festivity. I will handle Kochov, as I have handled him before. Allow him to bellow and bitch, make his red-faced pronouncements, and when he has run out of steam, tell him to sit down."

Malinovsky didn't seem convinced.

"Tread carefully, Nikita. The Presidium will not accept shame without seeking answers. There will be blame."

"There is already blame. Please understand, Rodion, I have no idea how the Americans will respond to this backdoor proposal. Kennedy has been adamant, too adamant in his pledges to see this through the way he wishes. We have already ordered most of our ships to turn about, to avoid the American blockade. Kennedy knows we have purposely avoided a dangerous confrontation at sea. But he has his *Kochovs* too, his powerful military men who see the world only through the eyes of a soldier. We must not delude ourselves. After all, we lit this fuse."

"When will you know if this Fomin fellow has done his job?"

"I'm not leaving anything to chance. Right now, Mikoyan and Gromyko are preparing the skeleton of a lengthy letter which will be sent to Kennedy as quickly as it can be delivered. I will write the text."

Malinovsky seemed annoyed now.

"Are you offering your surrender?"

"Be careful, my friend. I will do what we must do to avoid a war none of us want. Whether or not I am successful is not, after all, up to me, or to any of us here. We must hope . . . yes, that is a good word . . . hope. We must hope the Americans are as fond of peace."

CHAPTER TWENTY-NINE

RFK

Friday afternoon, October 26, 1962
The White House, Oval Office

The meeting was called in a rush, Secretary of State Rusk all but demanding that the president drop what he was doing, insisting that this particular bit of news could not wait.

Bobby joined his brother in the Oval Office, both men preparing for yet another Excomm meeting later that night. Kennedy sat behind his desk, leaning back in a stretch, his frequent attempt to unload the kinks in his back. Bobby stood to one side, his usual place, and was already wondering if Rusk had pushed some sort of foolish panic button. After a long silent moment, he said, "I would expect something like this from McNamara, maybe McCone. Rusk . . . not sure."

Kennedy leaned over his desk now, the pains still in his face.

"We'll find out in a minute."

The door opened, the guard announcing with no fanfare, "Sir, the secretary of state."

Rusk hurried in past the guard, an unusual entrance for a man not given to excitement. But in his tow came another man, familiar, wide eyes scanning the surroundings. Rusk seemed out of breath, said, "Mr. President, I believe you are acquainted with John Scali, ABC News?"

Scali was near Kennedy's age, balding, with a poor attempt at hiding a bald head. Bobby scanned him, thought, he looks like a history professor, not a television reporter. But Bobby respected the man for his job, an able, efficient newshound who seemed to find himself at the center of stories others were merely chasing. That seemed to be the case right now.

Rusk turned to Scali, said, "Go ahead."

Scali seemed to stand at attention, cleared his throat, said, "Mr. President, at lunchtime today, I was contacted by one of my Soviet sources, Mr. Alexander Fomin, of the Soviet embassy. Mr. Fomin expressed the urgent need for a meeting face-to-face. I obliged him." Scali paused, seemed to swallow hard. "Sir, I am accustomed to seeking out the news, not becoming part of the story. Mr. Fomin insisted I convey a message to my contacts in the State Department, in the hopes that his message would reach . . . higher authorities."

All eyes were on Scali now, and Kennedy seemed impatient, said, "What message?"

"Mr. Fomin inquired if the United Sates government might be interested in a way to settle the Cuban crisis. He suggested three specific proposals. One, the UN would supervise the dismantling of the missiles in Cuba and return them to the Soviet Union. Two, Castro would pledge in certain terms that he would never again accept offensive weapons. In return, three, the United States . . . you, sir, would pledge that in the future, there would be no invasion of Cuba."

"Did he expect you to give him an answer?"

"Mr. President, I told him that I do not speak for my government, that I could only be a conduit to higher sources."

Bobby stood with his arms tightly crossed, said, "My God. This sounds awfully simple."

Rusk said, "I agree. But how can we not take this seriously?"

Bobby said, "What do we know of this Fomin fellow?"

Rusk said, "He's pretty clearly a KGB operative, masquerading as what they label a *counselor* within their embassy. I doubt seriously he is some loose cannon just mouthing off. This sort of contact is ordered from high up the chain. Mr. President, I wrote out a response to be given Mr. Fomin, for your approval."

Rusk handed Kennedy a slip of paper, and Kennedy read aloud.

"*I have reason to believe that the U.S. Government sees real possibilities in this and supposes that representatives of the two governments could work this matter out with U Thant and with each other. It would seem, however, that time is very urgent.*"

Kennedy nodded slowly, said to Scali, "Take the secretary's note to Mr. Fomin, with all haste. But, do not use my name. For now, the Soviets don't need to know I'm open to anything they're suggesting."

Scali seemed to wait for a final word, and Rusk said, "We will keep you informed, Mr. President."

The two men moved out quickly, and Bobby moved to a chair, sat.

"What do you make of that, Jack?"

Kennedy shook his head.

"I don't make anything of it yet. That's hardly a negotiation from a position of strength. It's hard to believe that the Soviets would just throw in the towel, without a serious action on our side."

Bobby leaned one arm out on the president's desk.

"I suppose there isn't anything we can do but wait. If this Fomin fellow speaks for the Kremlin, he'll surely have more to say. If he's just some loudmouth KGB spy who likes to stir the pot on his own . . . well, I guess we'll find that out too. This has to be a huge feather in Scali's cap, though."

Kennedy thought a moment, said, "This isn't about anyone collecting feathers. I trust him to keep his mouth shut, and if I hear this broadcast on tomorrow's ABC news, I'll hang Scali by his privates."

"I trust him, Jack. This is too important, and Scali has to be impressed as hell that some KGB agent reached out to him directly. He might end up a hero for this."

"That can come later. For now, he's just another newsman who has the ear of a Soviet spy. Nothing more."

Friday night, October 26, 1962
The White House, Oval Office

"I'm not sure what we're expecting to hear."

Kennedy looked at his brother, then at Rusk.

"I hate being patient. But there's a shoe that has to drop. Scali should have communicated his note to that Fomin fellow, and I would assume Fomin will produce some kind of response pretty quickly."

Rusk fingered a cup of coffee, said, "I hate to say it, but this could take a while. We don't know what kind of linkup Fomin has with the Kremlin. There could be a half dozen layers of bureaucracy he has to sift through."

Kennedy shook his head.

"Doubt that. Unless Fomin's just some spy shooting his mouth off, he's getting orders straight out of Moscow. They're waiting on their end, just like we are here."

The phone buzzed on Kennedy's desk, and Bobby felt his stomach jump. Kennedy picked up the receiver, said, "Yes?"

He listened for a long moment, then said, "We'll be there in twenty minutes. The secretary of state is with me here. Get word to Secretary McNamara and the rest of the Excomm. We'll meet over there."

Kennedy hung up the receiver, and Bobby could feel the weight of the silent seconds. Kennedy stared ahead, and Rusk said, "Scali?"

Kennedy looked at him now, then at Bobby.

"Forget Scali. We're going to the State Department. They just received a lengthy correspondence directly from Khrushchev."

Friday night, October 26, 1962
The State Department Conference Room

The text was wordy and rambling, much like Khrushchev himself, one great clue that the letter did in fact come directly from the Soviet leader. The letter was both bullying and conciliatory, defensive and pleading, Khrushchev seeming to accept that the danger of the current crisis far outweighed any benefit the Soviets would receive by having missiles in Cuba. For long typewritten pages, the translation offered lengthy rants about Khrushchev's own experiences in war, the deadly consequences of thoughtless aggression, some of that sounding more apologetic than threatening. Unlike the diplomatic claims from days before, Khrushchev's letter freely acknowledged that the Soviet Union had placed missiles in Cuba, designed to counter the perceived threat offered by the United States, not only of a new invasion of the island, but that some kind of continuation was taking place from the Bay of Pigs operation, as though the United States had unfinished business there. As Scali's contact had emphasized, should the United States pledge not to invade Cuba, the existence of the missiles on Cuban soil would become meaningless, since, in Soviet terms, they had been positioned there only to defend Cuba in the first place. Strangely, Khrushchev acknowledged acceptance of the American blockade by claiming that it had come too late to be effective, since the very weapons the Americans were seeking to halt had already been installed in Cuba.

"If assurances were given that the president of the United States would not participate in an attack on Cuba, and the blockade lifted, then the question of the removal or the destruction of the missile sites in Cuba would then be an entirely different question. Armaments only bring disasters. Consequently, only a madman can believe that armaments are the principal means in the life of society. If people do not show wisdom, then in the final analysis they will come to a clash, like blind moles, and then reciprocal extermination will begin.

"Mr. President, I appeal to you to weigh well what the aggressive, piratical actions . . . would lead to. If you did this as the first step towards the unleashing of war, well then it is evident that nothing else is left to us but to accept this challenge of yours. If, however, you have not lost your self-control, and sensibly conceive what this might lead to, then, Mr. President, we and you ought not now pull on the ends of the rope in which you have tied the knot of war, because the more the two of us pull, the tighter that knot will be tied. And a moment may come when the knot will be tied so tight that even he who tied it will not have the strength to untie it, and then it will be necessary to cut that knot; and what that would mean is not for me to explain it to you, because you yourself understand perfectly well of what terrible forces our countries dispose. Consequently, if there is no intention to . . . doom the world to the catastrophe of thermonuclear war, then let us not only relax the forces pulling on the ends of the rope. Let us take measures to untie the knot. We are ready for this."

They passed the papers around, reading and rereading the voluminous letter. The mood was nearly buoyant, as though the crisis had suddenly been deflated, but not all members of the Excomm, including the president, saw this as the final solution.

Kennedy still read through another fragment of the letter, cut through the chatter around him.

"Listen, dammit. Nowhere in this tome does Khrushchev say what he is going to do. It insists that Castro offer a pledge, that the United States offers a pledge, and, just like that, there will no longer be any need for Soviet technicians to be housed in Cuba. *Technicians?* What about the damn missiles? He's asking us to pledge not to invade Cuba, but he doesn't pledge anything in return. He simply insists that the crisis will go away on its own . . . depending on what we do. What *I* do."

The room grew quiet, and Rusk said, "Sir, weigh this together with the approach to Scali. Fomin's proposal said that the missiles will be removed under UN supervision, if we agree not to invade."

"Then why doesn't Khrushchev repeat that here? He freely acknowledges that they've succeeded in placing their weapons throughout Cuba, as they had first intended, but now, because we caught them at it, we should calm down and accept their statement that the missiles are no longer necessary. There's a big gap between removing technicians and removing missiles."

Rusk said nothing, others in the room still poring through the pages. To one side, Bobby said, "He still doesn't use the word *offensive* to describe their weapons. Maybe he just can't admit that. We have to consider that he has his own people reading this at the same time we are, and it's a good bet that some of the hard-liners in Moscow aren't taking this too well."

McNamara said, "One encouraging note. We're all still alive. If the true hard-liners in the Kremlin had taken control, we wouldn't have gotten this far."

McCone sat across from Kennedy, said, "Our people in Miami are hearing plenty of chatter out of Cuba that Castro is pushing the Soviets to launch the damn missiles as soon as they're ready to go. Since we know some of those sites are in fact up and running, it has to be encouraging to us that Castro's not in command of the situation. The finger on the trigger is Russian, not Cuban."

Bobby said, "Castro is just talking. He has to know damn well that if a single one of those missiles is fired, one of our first responses will be to obliterate Havana."

Kennedy held up his hand.

"Eyes on the prize, gentlemen. Dean, I want your experts here to go over this letter word for word, if it takes all night. This was first received at our embassy in Moscow, so make sure the translation is accurate in every detail. I want to believe this is a breakthrough, but we can't pretend everything's just peachy. For now, let's go home, and try to get a good night's sleep. We'll meet tomorrow morning."

IT WAS AFTER midnight, Bobby's mind drifting as the car slipped easily through nearly deserted streets. He was used to spending most of these nights near his office, the convenience of being close to any summons from the president. But tonight there was a difference, a different need, to be closer to his family, to see the faces of his children. His fear had been mounting, that the turmoil around this crisis was even more dangerous than the meetings revealed it to be, that beyond the discussions and debates, there was the very real chance that the Russians were preparing for something truly awful, that their negotiating was in fact only to delay until more of their missiles were ready to fire. Even now, the letter from Khrushchev weighed on him, frightening doubts. He thought of the Excomm members, some of them labeling Khrushchev as unstable, the letter filled with non sequiturs, scattered logic, odd displays of emotion unlike anything they would expect. Is he unstable, after all? So much of the letter was personal, from a man who isn't supposed to be personal, ever. It's all about image and for years we've viewed

Khrushchev as tough, inflexible, the *enemy*. How much of that is accurate, how much is what we've been trained to believe? For over a week now, we've spent every day tossing around bad news, frightening possibilities, making decisions that could be deadly mistakes. What has Khrushchev been doing? He has enemies within his own system to be sure. Not just political enemies like we have, so many Republicans with big mouths. His enemies are more dangerous, would remove him from power, erase him . . . kill him? I have to believe him when he says he fears war. Only a madman seeks war as an answer to anything. Some of the Excomm seem to believe that Khrushchev's letter is an unqualified olive branch, an easy way out, as though he stepped too far forward, and now he's simply backing away. I don't see anything in this letter that sounds like an apology, and I know Jack agrees with me. As much as we want to believe that Khrushchev has blinked, that he's caving in, he hasn't actually done anything but suggest this is all a big damned shame, something to feel sorry for. And yet . . . they still have those missiles. And they're still pointed right at our families.

He turned onto the bridge, the route so familiar, crossed over into Virginia. The streetlights were gone now, the night very dark, the headlights showing the way. He thought of Ethel, the children. *They are terrified, no matter how much comfort I try to give them that everything will be just fine. I wish I could believe that myself. I never expected . . . hell, I'm just the attorney general, for Chrissakes. I don't solve the world's problems, and none of us ever expected this. Jack never expected that by becoming president, he would find himself risking the destruction of the entire world.*

He thought again of the Excomm members, some of them reliable bureaucrats, some just carefully chosen politicians, suddenly finding themselves with an awesome responsibility to weigh decisions that could . . . what? *Kill us all?* So, what's the alternative decision? Convince ourselves that missiles in Cuba aren't such a bad thing after all? If nothing else, it would ensure that Jack is a one-term president. The Republicans would roast him for being weak against Commies, one of their favorite mantras. And then what? Do we really want to see people like Goldwater or Keating stepping forward to confront this situation down the road? Half the Republicans in Congress think we should be launching a first strike. Probably just as many Soviet generals feel the same way. God help us.

He was frustrated now, knew Jack would offer some jewels of wisdom, something to calm him down. No, don't lather yourself into a panic. We're handling this as well as it can be handled. The American people are depending on us to work our way through this, to end the crisis without blowing up the world. Khrushchev started this mess, and now, he's fumbling his way through a solution as well. But I have to believe we're making progress, that there's a light at the end of this that will satisfy both sides. The fact that Khrushchev is even writing this kind of letter shows he feels the same way.

He turned onto the narrower road, fought to see his own driveway in the darkness. He slowed the car, made the tight turn, saw lights on in the house, wondered how many of his children were still awake. Thank God for them, he thought. If we ever need to know why we are doing all of this, just pay attention to that. Maybe tomorrow, Jack will come up with the right kind of answer to send Khrushchev, and we'll be that much closer to ending this thing. Meanwhile, our families . . . every family is hoping like hell we can tiptoe through the minefield.

CHAPTER THIRTY

RFK

Saturday morning, October 27, 1962
Office of the Attorney General, Washington, DC

The Excomm meeting had been set for the usual time, 10 a.m. Bobby had stopped first by his office, his typical routine, making sure the business of the attorney general was functioning smoothly. He did not expect to find J. Edgar Hoover waiting for him.

He despised the aging FBI boss, and the feeling had always been mutual. Hoover saw himself very much as the nation's primary law enforcement officer, which usually meant that he was operating by his own rules. To Hoover, Bobby was an upstart child, daring to tell the seasoned expert how to behave.

Hoover was seated in front of Bobby's desk, a coffee cup in his hand. He barely acknowledged Bobby's entrance, said, "Your secretaries make a good pot of coffee. Careful, I'll hire them away from you. So, big goings-on this morning? I was told you'd come by here first, make sure the Justice Department remembers who you are. You always work on weekends?"

Bobby moved around the desk, sat, was not in the mood for a jousting match with the FBI.

"I'm where I have to be. To what do I owe the pleasure of your visit?"

Hoover made a grand gesture out of removing a paper from his jacket pocket, as though imparting a treasured secret.

"You might want to know what's been happening outside of Washington over the past couple of days. Here is my memorandum. Read it at your leisure. Carry it perhaps to your *top secret* meeting. I'll be on my way."

Hoover was up and gone quickly, his half-empty coffee cup still on Bobby's desk. Bobby ignored that, tried to shake off the uneasiness he always felt when Hoover was present, scanned the memorandum, now read slowly.

"Holy Jesus."

Saturday morning, October 27, 1962
The White House, Cabinet Room

McCone had opened the meeting as usual, with his intel briefing. There was little that was new, the Soviets continuing with their construction on the missile sites in Cuba, confirmation that six of the sites were operational, prepared to fire. Bobby had entered just prior to the president, took his place to one side, waited for McCone to complete his report. He waited for a break in the chatter, said aloud, "Excuse me. I have some news."

The faces turned toward him, and Kennedy nodded his way. Bobby said, "The FBI has confirmed that within the Soviet consulate in New York, the staffs are burning documents. The FBI doesn't have complete confirmation just what it is they're burning, other than to observe that the documents are of a sensitive nature. The interpretation of this can be made . . ."

General Taylor said, "The interpretation is clear. They're preparing for war. That's what embassies do when the fighting is about to start. They have to assume they won't be able to keep their walls secure, so they clean out their files. This is certain?"

Bobby nodded toward Taylor.

"The FBI regularly monitors activity within foreign embassies, as much as can be done discreetly. It's hard to hide a burning trash pile in the middle of a city, even if it's behind walls. I'm not sure just what else we need to say about this, and we will continue to monitor the situation closely. The FBI is on that."

Kennedy sat with both hands on the table in front of him.

"Why in hell . . . ? No, we can't read too much into this, not yet. We still have Khrushchev's letter, and there's nothing there that hints that Khrushchev is expecting a war to break out."

Rusk waited for more of the members to seat themselves, then said, "Sir, the interpreters spent most of the night parsing Khrushchev's letter, and the translations we had yesterday are sound, no major changes."

To one side, George Ball, Rusk's assistant secretary of state, seemed flustered, late to the meeting. Ball said, "I'm not sure we can count on that. Mr. President, we have received a second letter, ostensibly from Khrushchev. Some translation is still ongoing, but what we have so far is right here."

Ball slid a handful of papers across the table to Kennedy, unwrapped more paper from his briefcase, began distributing them around the room.

Kennedy said, "What the hell do you mean, another letter? How was it transmitted?"

Ball said, "They're broadcasting it over Moscow radio. I assume they're trying to avoid any delays in written correspondence and are trying to make the translation a simpler matter."

"Broadcasting . . . to the whole world? I thought Khrushchev's letter yesterday was issued as top secret."

Rusk said, "It was."

Kennedy scanned the papers now, the room falling silent, the papers shuffled from each member, the letter absorbed. After a long moment, Kennedy said, "What's he done? He's negated the entire letter from yesterday. He's upped the ante, increased his demands."

Ball said, "Quite so. If this letter does in fact come from Khrushchev, he is now demanding that in order to remove the missiles from Cuba, we must do the same from Turkey. He goes so far as to suggest . . .

"*You are disturbed over Cuba . . . ninety miles by sea from the coast of the United States. You have placed destructive rocket weapons which you call offensive, in Turkey, literally right next to us. Do you believe that you have the right to demand security for your country, and the removal of such weapons as you qualify as offensive, while not recognizing this right for us?*

"*I therefore make this proposal. We are willing to remove from Cuba the means which you regard as offensive . . . the United States will remove its analogous means from Turkey.*

"*We will make a statement within the framework of the Security Council to the effect that the Soviet government gives a solemn promise to respect the inviolability of the borders and sovereignty of Turkey . . . the United States government will make a similar statement within the framework of the Security Council regarding Cuba.*"

McNamara said, "He has suddenly tossed an invasion of Turkey onto the table. This is completely different from his letter yesterday. What the hell is going on?"

McCone said, "There is something strange about this, and I

268

don't just mean the subject matter. The whole tone is different, too matter-of-fact. There are no flourishes, there's no emotion."

Kennedy sat back, and Bobby could see the anger on his face.

"I don't believe this. We were on the right path . . . the settlement was right in our hands."

McNamara said, "You don't suppose Khrushchev's been overthrown? Yesterday, his letter seemed ready to settle this, with an admission that the Soviets were in the wrong, that they would take the steps necessary to end this mess. Now, suddenly . . ."

Bobby said, "It sounds like somebody's put a gun to his head. I know this sounds a little Hollywood . . . but it's as though he's writing this for broadcast with a handful of generals standing in front of him, pointing at him with a machine gun. The timing is too odd. He sends a plaintive letter yesterday, and within, what? Twelve hours? He voids it and offers much tougher terms. Somebody in the Kremlin got pissed off at his first letter."

Kennedy held up his hands, still a hard scowl.

"We don't know anything of the sort. What we know is that the game has changed. We were concerned about delaying tactics before, allowing them to get more of their missile launchers up and running. Well, that's what this is. There is no way I will jerk our Jupiter missiles out of Turkey without a careful negotiation with our allies there. How the hell do we tell most of NATO that we're going to yank their defenses away, just so we can become more comfortable here at home? Those people live under the shadow of Soviet nuclear missiles every day, and even if those Jupiters are obsolete, pulling them out of Turkey is a hugely symbolic gesture that will have an impact all the way across NATO. And by the way, I thought we had begun making arrangements to remove those things months ago, and replace them with far superior Polaris subs."

Bundy said, "Yes, sir. You had ordered us to begin the process of removing the Jupiters last August. It was taking longer than expected.

As you note, sir, negotiating with the Turks has been problematic. They rather like having a backyard full of our missiles."

Bobby saw the anxiety on his brother's face.

"If this second letter comes from Khrushchev, truly, it appears obvious that someone convinced him he didn't have to give away the store by pulling his missiles out of Cuba. There had to be something on our side, something far costlier to us than a guarantee we wouldn't invade. There might not be a gun to his head, just a fresh analysis of our offensive weapons that are sitting on his doorstep. But this deal is a nonstarter, and surely, he has to know that."

Bobby said, "And so, is this about delay? Stalling this process so they can get more work done in Cuba?"

The phone rang, Kennedy picking up the receiver, a quick hand off to McNamara, who answered, "Yes?"

There was silence for a long minute, McNamara seeming to droop.

"When? Do we know of the pilot?" More silence, then McNamara hung up the phone.

"I have just received word . . . God almighty. A U-2 recon plane has been shot down over Cuba. Apparently three SAM missiles were fired, one found its mark. The pilot was Major Rudolph Anderson, from South Carolina. He did not survive."

There were low groans, mumbles, and Kennedy said, "Good Christ. Get word to his family. Do it right." He paused. "So, now it's a shooting war. Yesterday, Khrushchev moaned about escalation, how we had to avoid that at all costs. Today, he escalates. How the hell do I order more U-2 flights down there if they're so damned vulnerable? It's come to this. We can't allow the SAM sites to continue operating. Do you understand what this means?" Kennedy looked at McNamara now. "How quickly can we launch a full-on air strike against the missile sites?"

McNamara hesitated, said, "Forty-eight hours. Thirty hours if you push."

"And the invasion? Following the air strikes by how long?"

"Four to six days."

Kennedy folded his hands together, stared down, the room silent.

"Someone in here, maybe it was me, said that we couldn't afford to back Khrushchev into a corner. Well, that corner is right here, and we're in it. More than a corner . . . this feels like a noose."

CHAPTER THIRTY-ONE

Khrushchev

Saturday night, October 27, 1962
Moscow, the Kremlin

"The pilot is dead?"

Malinovsky looked up from the paper, said, "Yes. It is confirmed."

Khrushchev let out a long breath, leaned back in his chair, scanned the three men in front of him, Malinovsky to one side, Marshal Kochov front and center. Khrushchev took the report from Malinovsky's hand, read slowly, then said, "So, you spend all last night demanding I withdraw my letter to Kennedy, demanding that I make a stronger statement, that I not demonstrate such a willingness to negotiate. I would submit to you that killing an American pilot is a *stronger statement* we did not need. Perhaps, Marshal Kochov, you would have preferred that I keep all of my words to myself, and allow our SAM missiles to do all the talking."

Kochov grunted, and Khrushchev looked up at him, saw a scowl of arrogance.

"Premier, must I point out to you that this is no great tragedy.

Simply put, an American soldier has died, fighting for his country. This is not so rare in a time of war. That pilot knew he was flying in a war zone, that his enemies were observing him, that his life was in danger every minute he was over Cuba. I have not understood why you insisted that General Pliyev avoid shooting every one of the American spy planes out of the sky. Well, wonder no longer. Now the message has been sent. Violate our air space, and you will pay the price."

Khrushchev felt a boiling fury, wanted to strangle away the smugness on Kochov's face. He clamped it down, said in a hiss, "That will be all, Marshal Kochov. Have you not other duties to attend to?"

Kochov didn't take the bait, the arrogance continuing.

"Premier, it is my opinion that if the Americans have a back-bone, they will react, and with force. If there were doubts before as to whether they would send their army into Cuba, those doubts are wiped away. I would counsel you, Premier, as per my position and that of Marshal Malinovsky, that we prepare our forces there for an immediate attack, and prepare the Cubans to expect the same. The time for hesitation, for prevarication has concluded. Now we shall find out who is the better prepared for war."

Khrushchev had had enough.

"That will be all, Marshal Kochov. You are dismissed. Your *counsel* will be taken under advisement. Please return to your office, and . . . monitor activity from Cuba. If the Americans are indeed mounting an invasion, I should seek your *counsel* again."

Kochov slapped his heels together, a crisp salute, said no more. As he left, he pulled the door sharply closed. Khrushchev felt the room deflating, said, "He would have us in a third world war."

Malinovsky said, "There are some in the Presidium who support that position. There is much talk still that you have been too timid."

"Did I not respond to that kind of talk? Did I not issue a further demand on the Americans?"

Malinovsky looked at Vodyev, nodded.

"Yes. But I must mention . . . I cautioned you. I suggested that your first letter was unwise. You should have consulted the Presidium before offering to withdraw from Cuba."

"I am no fool, Rodion. If I made a mistake, I corrected it. I may have been too emotional, I may have expressed strong feelings that we do not sink into the abyss Marshal Kochov prefers. Perhaps I am not a strong businessman, not like the capitalists. My powers of bargaining are weak. But I have corrected that. By broadcasting the second message over Moscow radio, I have notified the entire world what our demands must be. That has given us an enormous advantage, since the Americans can no longer deny or ignore what we are asking for. Now everyone can see that our demands are reasonable, a fair trade. We have again reclaimed the stronger position."

To one side, Vodyev, one of Khrushchev's favorite Presidium members, spoke up.

"I would suggest, Premier, that whatever *strong position* you sought has been swept away by the loss of the American spy plane. The Americans are not likely to treat such a loss as a bargaining chip. They will respond emotionally."

Khrushchev looked again at Malinovsky.

"I will read this report in detail. I want to know what exactly happened down there."

Khrushchev shuffled through several sheets of paper, but he had no patience for the minutiae of this kind of report. Malinovsky seemed to understand, said, "Premier, if I may cut through the details. Once the American plane was shot down, General Grechko immediately made his report to General Pliyev. Grechko commands all of our air defenses on Cuba. It seems that Castro had ordered his own antiaircraft batteries to attempt to shoot down any American plane. Naturally, the Cubans do not possess weapons capable of reaching the spy plane, which flies at an altitude of some seventy thousand feet. It seems that the Cubans were discharging their antiaircraft weapons freely, giving the impression to our own troops that a great struggle was beginning, that the Americans were arriving in force. Our SAM operators, under the command of General Grechko, were placed on extremely high alert. General Grechko had previously requested authorization to aid the Cubans by all available antiaircraft means in the event of American attacks on our installations. General Pliyev was apparently not available to respond to Grechko's request, thus, when his missiles had locked onto a target, General Grechko felt he had no choice, and he gave the order to fire. General Grechko claims that he believed there was a general engagement starting, that possibly the American invasion was under way, and without clarification of that fact, he erred on the side of aggression."

Khrushchev stared at Malinovsky, tried to read the man's true feelings about what had happened. Malinovsky offered no clue. Khrushchev said, "What do you suggest be done with General Grechko?"

Malinovsky seemed surprised by the question.

"On my authority as minister of defense, I responded to his report already. I agree that he was too hasty in shooting down the American plane. But given the circumstances, it was a reasonable response."

Khrushchev felt the fury returning.

"That's it? It was *reasonable*? We allow Castro with his hot head to drag us into an unfortunate confrontation, while at the same time, I am seeking the peaceful means to end this crisis? On that count Vodyev is right. The Americans will respond emotionally, as perhaps I would. Remember, gentlemen, the Americans have their own Kochovs, men who will push Kennedy to escalate, to seek revenge for our bloody act. How much voice will they have? How much sway will they hold over such a young and inexperienced leader? Kennedy has already been humiliated by his bumbling into the Bay of Pigs fiasco. If he fails to respond to our act of aggression, it could be a mistake fatal to him politically. Certainly he knows this."

Vodyev said, "Premier, is not the greater mistake ignoring the opportunity to defuse this crisis? Kennedy must be made to understand that this was merely an error on our part, that we are not escalating the danger here."

Khrushchev looked down at his hands, spread now on the desk.

"Unfortunately, I do not know what Kennedy understands. I suppose we should await his reaction to our second letter. Certainly, that holds the key to diffusing this crisis. Again, what are we to do about General Grechko?"

Malinovsky said, "Premier, General Grechko and his officers responded appropriately to the situation as they saw it. They should not be punished."

Khrushchev knew he should bow to Malinovsky's judgment. After all, as defense minister, this decision should rest with the man who understands the facts. Khrushchev stood slowly now, hobbled on stiff knees, walked around the office, the others watching him silently.

"This is about Castro. It would not surprise me if somehow Castro tricked General Grechko into believing there was an invasion. If we are to avoid mistakes in the future, gentlemen, let that be a lesson worth learning. This nation must make our alliances with those we can rely upon, who might have our best interests at heart, as well as their own. If there is a single reason above all others that we should remove our missiles from Cuba, it is that we have formed an unreliable alliance. Meanwhile, I must wonder if young Mr. Kennedy is about to go to war."

CHAPTER THIRTY-TWO

RFK

Saturday afternoon, October 27, 1962
The White House, Cabinet Room

"Your own words, Mr. President. Your own words. *First option.* The Joint Chiefs and myself went along with the idea of a quarantine as a *first option*, that it was the first attempt to encourage the Soviets to remove the missiles. It's apparent, both by their actions, and by Khrushchev's response, that the quarantine hasn't worked."

All eyes were on General Taylor, the man's temper on a knife's edge. It had been this way throughout the meeting, those who had always been the more militant now recognizing their opportunity to speak up.

Taylor continued, "With the loss of the U-2, the Soviets have made it clear that they are not inclined to support our position, and with Khrushchev's new letter, it is obvious that they are in no hurry to remove their missiles at all. Mr. President, we have no choice but to expand our operations to the next step. The Joint Chiefs have reinforced their position that an air strike of all the SAM positions in Cuba can be made by tomorrow morning."

There were mumbles around the room, many of the Excomm members seeming to welcome Taylor's aggressiveness.

Kennedy had kept his calm, Bobby impressed with that, since he had been under steady pressure by some of the others. Kennedy looked at Taylor now, said, "I am not so worried about the *next step*. We all can expect that our *next step* shall lead to a *next step* by the Soviets. In that event, it is the fourth and fifth steps that we should be concerned about, because by that time, none of us will be around." He looked at McNamara. "Are we absolutely certain the U-2 was shot down and didn't suffer some kind of mechanical malfunction?"

McNamara said, "Unfortunately, yes. We have evidence that three Soviet SAM missiles were fired. Two missed, one did not. Sir, the military plan is now clear. We must move past a limited strike. We must have the reconnaissance aircraft at our disposal without worrying just how many of them will be shot down. So, the military plan must take priority, a full-on invasion following the air strike on all Soviet missile batteries. If we do not invade, we will have to assume the Soviets or their Cuban allies will respond to our air strike by firing missiles, perhaps a great many missiles, with targets around the country. With the invasion, they will have their hands full closer to home. Once our troops are on the ground across Cuba, we can remove the balance of the Soviet missile sites that might be missed by the air strike."

McNamara had been shouting, seemed out of breath, and Bobby stared at him with an open mouth. The word rolled through Bobby's head, *calm*. My God, he's lost his composure. None of us can afford that, not now.

Kennedy seemed to feel the same way, said slowly, "Bob, I believe there is another step we can take that does not involve going to war. It has always been an option to strengthen the quarantine by stopping the flow of petroleum goods to Cuba. This emphasizes our seriousness since this will have a deadly effect on the Cuban economy. Surely . . ."

Taylor stood now.

"Surely nothing, Mr. President. With all due respect, if you want to *emphasize our seriousness*, you take out those SAM sites, as well as the ballistic missile sites that are already up and running. The invasion, if so ordered, can begin as soon as four days later. How many more U-2 flights can we order, knowing the Soviets are now willing to target them?"

Kennedy held up his hands, a clear signal: *quiet*. Taylor sat again, angry, seemed to fight for control. Bobby couldn't ignore a bellyful of butterflies, thought, we're talking about war, about a real shooting war. He stared at his brother, grateful for Kennedy's demeanor, said, "If we go to war in Cuba, we must understand that it will not be confined to Cuba. Turkey will be vulnerable, and so, if the Soviets hit Turkey, do we respond by firing our missiles there? It's the same question they must be asking about their missiles in Cuba. What of Berlin? Do they blockade there, squeezing us in yet another way? What role do our NATO allies play in making these decisions? We might be condemning our allies to death by the decisions we make here, and they have no say in the matter."

Kennedy nodded, his hands still raised, as though trying to defuse tempers.

"There are implications in every step we might take, far beyond this room, and far beyond Cuba. I wonder if our NATO allies truly understand the danger we could be placing them in. Any decision made right here, could create a life and death situation for a dozen or more nations around the world."

Bobby said, "It's not a dozen, Jack. It's all of mankind."

More mumbling followed, no one willing to speak out loud. Bobby watched McNamara, who seemed to be embarrassed for his outburst. Kennedy stared down at the table in front of him, and after a long minute, said, "We won't attack tomorrow. There will be no air strikes, not yet. We'll try again to respond to Khrushchev. I have to believe that Khrushchev is not in a hurry to see this explode out of control. For all we know, he feels that shooting down the U-2 was a deadly mistake, some field commander's blunder. We have to give him time to act on that."

Rusk said, "Mr. President, my people at State have been working on the draft of a response letter, which thus far, addresses each of the points in the second Khrushchev letter, explanations why we cannot agree with his demands."

More arguments exploded now, Taylor and others worn down by a long day's tensions, voices insisting that Khrushchev's letter be treated with every response from disdain to ridicule. After a long minute, and a jumble of arguments, Bobby said, "This won't work, Jack. We have to respond to Khrushchev, but I don't agree with what the State Department is trying to say. I think we should completely ignore the second letter and focus solely on the first. In that letter, Khrushchev made no demands on us that we could not accept, and his points were reinforced by the message given to Scali. Let's respond to that, and for now, ignore any talk of Turkey."

Kennedy pointed at Bobby.

"Fine. You don't like the State Department letter, go write your own. Take Sorenson with you. Put a draft together as quick as you can. I'll try to hold down the tempers here."

Dear Mr. Chairman,

I have read your letter of October 26 with great care and welcomed the statement of your desire to seek a prompt solution to the problem. The first thing that needs to be done, however, is for work to cease on offensive missile bases in Cuba, and for all weapons systems in Cuba capable of offensive use to be rendered inoperable, under effective United Nations arrangements. Assuming this is done promptly, I have given my representatives in New York instructions that will permit them to work out this weekend . . . an arrangement for a permanent solution to the Cuban problem, along the lines suggested in your letter of October 26. The key elements of your proposals—which seem generally acceptable as I understand them—are as follows:

1. *You would agree to remove these weapons systems from Cuba under appropriate United Nations observation and supervision, and undertake, with suitable safeguards, to halt the further introduction of such weapons systems into Cuba.*
2. *We, on our part, would agree a) to remove promptly the quarantine measures now in effect and b) to give assurances against an invasion of Cuba.*

   There is no reason why we should not be able to complete these arrangements and announce them to the world within a couple of days. The effect of such a settlement on easing world tensions would enable us to work toward a more general arrangement regarding "other armaments" as proposed in your second letter, which you made public. I would like to say again that the United States is very much interested in reducing tensions and halting the arms race; and if your letter signifies that you are prepared to discuss a détente affecting NATO and the Warsaw Pact, we are quite prepared to consider with our allies any useful proposals.

   But the first ingredient, let me emphasize, is the cessation of work on missile sites in Cuba, and measures to render such weapons inoperable, under effective international guarantees. The continuation of this threat, or a prolonging of this discussion concerning Cuba by linking these problems to the broader questions of European and world security, would surely lead to an intensification of the Cuban crisis and a grave risk to the peace of the world . . .

John F. Kennedy

Saturday, late afternoon, October 27
White House, Kennedy's private office

"Nicely done, Bobby."

"It's Sorenson. He has the golden tongue. I just argue about it."

"I'm tired of arguments. But regardless, I've ordered another meeting tonight at nine. There's too much happening all at once to ignore that. I wish I could keep the hotheads quiet, convince those people we have to err on the side of caution, instead of reacting with an all-out blitz."

"Jack, you have to let everyone have their say. Otherwise, what's the point? You didn't go into this thing convinced exactly what you were going to do, and I'm not sure you're convinced now. You have to hear all sides. And if the Joint Chiefs are all gung-ho for a war, isn't it better to hear them out, so you can address their points?"

"There's a lot of tension, a lot of stress, and I guess it needs to be released. And the Joint Chiefs. They opt for the simplest answers. They know how to do one thing really well, so that's all they want to do. They deal in things like *acceptable casualties*, weighing the cost on a balance scale. I keep thinking about the U-2 pilot, Major Anderson, the man's family. Despite what Taylor says, Anderson didn't go to work each day expecting to be shot down. It used to be that a U-2 was invulnerable, that it flew too high for ground weapons."

"The weapons caught up. That's the way it works."

"And, I suppose miscalculations are a part of it too. It goes back to that book, *The Guns of August*, the start of World War One. In 1914, the worst weapon you had to contend with was the cannon, maybe mustard gas. Now, a miscalculation destroys mankind. Yeah, the weapons have caught up. I can't believe that the Soviets want to fight a war any more than we do. But we're on that path. That's why the letter matters, why we have to keep trying to find a way to end this. Sure, I guess both sides have to save face. No one can accept being humiliated. So, you back off the big demands, the deal killers. Surely Khrushchev understands that too. But damn it all, it doesn't change the fact that unless Khrushchev pulls those missiles out of Cuba, we'll have to go get them."

"That's your decision, Jack. I understand why it might be necessary. But I can't help thinking about the kids. Not just my own, but kids everywhere. They have no say in any of this, and when it comes to a war, they serve one role: they're casualties. For us to make that kind of decision, to control the lives of so many who have no control over what we decide to do . . . Jesus, Jack."

A voice at the door. "Sir, the secretary of state."

Rusk was there now, held out a paper.

"Here it is, all typed up, ready to go. Several copies." He paused. "It's a good letter, Bobby. I have to believe this will work. Mr. President, I have a thought. I believe it might be a good idea to present a copy of this directly to Ambassador Dobrynin. For one thing, Bobby can add a more personal, private message to Khrushchev that goes beyond the letter. Am I right that you're intending to make the letter public?"

Kennedy looked at Bobby, said, "Yes. Khrushchev started that, so there's no reason to hide anything, not anymore."

Rusk seemed troubled, sat now.

"Jack, if Khrushchev keeps on leaning on the Turkey deal, it could be that's a corner he's backed into at home. I guarantee there are Russians generals fuming about those missiles staring at them across their border, and Khrushchev keeping them powerless to change that. We've been hearing about public demonstrations, damned near riots, near our embassy in Moscow, and at other government buildings there. Not to mention demonstrations in London, Paris, and so forth. But the Russian demonstrations are worrisome, since very little happens there that isn't orchestrated. Those demonstrations, bordering on violence, might be for Khrushchev's benefit, not just ours. It might be a way that certain powers in Moscow are telling Khrushchev to get those damn missiles out of Turkey, or face consequences. It explains why Khrushchev went public with his demands in the second letter. I know we're going to try to ignore that demand for now, but we can't ignore it for long. It's Khrushchev's ace in the hole." Rusk paused. "Jack, if this entire deal hinges on us pulling our missiles out of Turkey, wouldn't you be willing to do that to avoid a war?"

Kennedy seemed annoyed.

"We've been over this. The Turks will have a fit, and it could wreck the NATO alliance."

Bobby weighed Rusk's words, then looked at his brother, said, "Jack, it might take some time, but surely we can convince the Turks that there is a better alternative to those obsolete Jupiters. Positioning a Polaris sub off their coast would surely make the difference."

Kennedy rubbed a hand on his face.

"They haven't wanted to accept that those Jupiters are obsolete. It might be nothing more than Turkish generals who like their photographs taken in front of missile launchers. It's hard to do that with a submarine."

Bobby said, "In this afternoon's meeting, McCone said that Khrushchev has made a great show of claiming that thus far, he has saved Cuba, that he has stopped an invasion. I agree with that, and I still think Khrushchev is more concerned about what we do to Cuba than he is old missiles in Turkey, even if he's getting pressured by his generals."

Kennedy shook his head.

"But that's not what his second letter says."

"Jack, we're addressing his first letter, basically ignoring the second one."

"Publicly. But I want you to take this deal to Dobrynin. Convince him that our proposal in the letter is the best way to stop this escalation, but that, quietly, we might offer more down the road." He looked at Rusk. "Dean, what do you think?"

"Agreed. Let the letter explain our position publicly. But Bobby can offer Dobrynin a bit more."

Kennedy looked at Bobby now.

"Dobrynin seems to like you. What do you think?"

Bobby took the typewritten letter from Rusk, scanned it, said, "I think I'll phone him right now and invite him to come over to Justice. Hopefully he doesn't have important dinner plans."

Saturday night, October 27
Department of Justice, Office of the Attorney General

Dobrynin stood in front of the stuffed tiger, said, "I cannot quite become accustomed to your beast. I find I must touch it, though I suspect he no longer minds."

Bobby watched Dobrynin's hand on the tiger's head, slow movements, no telltale signs of nervousness. Of course not, he thought. He is, above all else, cool.

"If I may get to the point, Mr. Ambassador. Please sit down. You are aware that Premier Khrushchev has offered communications to President Kennedy, as a means of settling this unfortunate disagreement."

Dobrynin continued to play with the tiger's fur.

"Yes, certainly. It would be so much better for us all if this matter was put behind us."

"I will be direct, sir. There is no need at this late hour for me to waste your time, or for you to waste mine. We are aware that work is continuing on the missile bases in Cuba, and in the past few days, it has been expedited. You must certainly know that this morning, one of our U-2 reconnaissance planes was shot down by your SAM missiles, with the loss of life of the pilot. That is, for us, a most serious turn of events."

Dobrynin left the tiger alone, tried not to appear too eager to hear more of what Bobby had to say.

"Loss of life is most unfortunate."

"Mr. Ambassador, the president does not want a military confrontation. We have done everything possible to avoid escalating this matter into an armed confrontation, but the downing of our plane has forced our hand."

Dobrynin moved to the chair, sat slowly.

"I must point out, Mr. Attorney General, that the Cubans welcome our air defenses, and they feel as though the United States is continually violating the sanctity of their air space."

"Mr. Ambassador, if Mr. Khrushchev had not deceived us as to the construction of your missile sites all over Cuba, there would have been no need for reconnaissance flights in the first place. It has been confirmed that you have offered us descriptions of various sites throughout Cuba which are not accurate. Thus, we must continue to photograph these sites, to protect ourselves. You must understand that if the Cubans, or the Soviets, continue to shoot at our reconnaissance planes, we will have to shoot back. This will inevitably lead to further incidents, and to escalation of the conflict, with very grave implications for us all. Mr. Ambassador, the Soviet Union has secretly established missile bases in Cuba, while proclaiming both publicly and privately that this would never be done. I must request in the strongest terms that you offer us a commitment by tomorrow that those bases will be removed. Please understand that this is not an ultimatum, but a question of fact. Please understand that if you do not pledge to remove those bases, we shall remove them ourselves. President Kennedy has great respect for the people of the Soviet Union, and we understand that your country might feel it necessary to take retaliatory action. Before that is over, there will be not only dead Americans, but dead Russians as well."

"Mr. Attorney General, are you making a specific offer to my government?"

Dobrynin's voice was quivering just enough to tell Bobby that he had struck a chord.

"I have a letter for Premier Khrushchev, a copy for you. A copy has already been transmitted to the premier."

Dobrynin took the letter, read slowly, reached the end, seemed surprised there was no more. He finished reading, and Bobby said, "I must emphasize to you, sir, that should there not be a positive response to these entreaties, the president has ordered the military to launch extensive bombing attacks throughout Cuba, to remove the missile launch sites ourselves. This possibility has been mentioned before, and the president feels that the gravity of such a response has not been taken seriously by you. I assure you, Ambassador. The president is serious. This is not a decision taken lightly, but in the president's view, it is essential to the security of the United States."

Dobrynin folded the letter slowly, slipped it into his coat pocket. He stared down at the desk, seemed deep in thought, and after a silent moment, said, "I understand. In that event, I must ask you . . . what about the removal of your missiles from Turkey?"

Bobby hesitated, formed his words carefully.

"There can be no arrangement made under pressure or threat. The decision of missiles in Turkey is one that must be made by NATO. However, the president has been anxious to remove those missiles for a long period of time. He had ordered a discussion regarding their removal some time ago, and it is our judgment that, within a short time after this crisis is over, those missiles will in fact be gone."

Dobrynin seemed to flinch, made a slow nod.

"A short time. How much time?"

"The president estimates four to five months. And I can assure you . . . those sites and their missiles will be closed down and removed in that time period . . . but there is one important . . . essential condition."

"Yes?"

"The Soviet Union must respect this promise to you as a secret, never to be linked with the Cuban missile agreement." He paused, gave Dobrynin time to absorb the full meaning.

"Mr. Attorney General, this is important information. I am grateful to receive it."

"President Kennedy wishes to resolve the problems that confront us in Europe and Southeast Asia. He wishes to move forward on the control of nuclear weapons. However, we can make progress on those matters only when this crisis in Cuba is behind us. Sir, time is running out. We have only a few more hours before the vital decision will be made to remove the missiles sites from Cuba by force. We must have your answer by tomorrow. You may wonder if there are generals among us, who are prepared, who are itching for a fight. Surely you have such men in Moscow. Those passions are very real, and frankly, sir, we must both consider them terrifying."

Dobrynin looked down, and Bobby could see the acknowledgment on his face, though he knew Dobrynin would never admit it. After a silent moment, Dobrynin said, "I should like to contact Moscow."

Bobby's mind rolled with the words . . . *do it now*. But protocol had to be maintained. Dobrynin recognized the meeting had concluded, and he stood.

"Mr. Attorney General, allow me to take your leave."

He turned, moved back through the office, one hand reaching out, a slow stroke of the tiger's head.

CHAPTER THIRTY-THREE

Russo

Saturday night, October 27, 1962
Tallahassee, Florida

The TV was his tonight, the hour he commanded for himself, watching *The Jackie Gleason Show*. It bothered him not at all that Margaret didn't care for Gleason, the rotund comedian who presented a larger-than-life image as a man about town, all the while making great fun of the stuffed shirts he portrayed. She was occupied with a joy of her own, playing Candyland with Becky on the kitchen table. The Saturday night was typical for Danny as well, the boy sequestered in his room, engaged in something only a boy understands.

Russo sat back on the sofa, coffee cup to one side, the opening credits appearing, the familiar theme music, and now, an abrupt change.

"We interrupt this program for a special bulletin from CBS News."

"Oh, good God," he said aloud. "What now?"

"We now join a press conference by the United States secretary of defense, Robert McNamara."

He felt Margaret come in from the kitchen, a quick glance in her direction, worry on her face. She stood beside him, and he wrapped one arm around her legs, an instinct he had become used to. She said, "What is it?"

"Don't know. There's McNamara."

"My fellow Americans. I bring you an unfortunate piece of news. Earlier today, over the island nation of Cuba, an American reconnaissance plane was targeted and shot down by a Soviet surface-to-air missile. It is with great regret that I announce that the pilot did not survive . . ."

His arm squeezed her tighter, the words from the television flowing over both of them, fear for the future, for what might happen next, reassuring words from McNamara that weren't all that reassuring. Just as quickly as the bulletin had begun, it was over, the screen suddenly filled with the image of Jackie Gleason. He felt her hand on his shoulder, her voice barely audible.

"What does it mean?"

He stood, moved to the television, switched it off.

"The Russians shot down one of our planes. He didn't say what kind, but I guess it doesn't matter. They shot it down with a missile."

Margaret sat now, pulled him down closer. "I guess that proves what Kennedy's been saying all along, that they have missiles down there."

"Two different things. An antiaircraft missile, surface to air, that's not the nuclear kind. But I believe Kennedy, that there are still the more dangerous kind aimed this way. Dammit, Margie, this is . . . I'm really scared about this. We're sending planes over Cuba to keep an eye on them, and they don't like it. So, they shoot them down. If it wasn't for our planes, we might never have spotted their missiles, so I guess we have to keep doing that. But now . . . I don't know what the hell the Russians think they're accomplishing, other than to scare hell out of Americans. Earlier today, the news talked about a letter from Khrushchev, that if he's to pull out of Cuba, he's demanding we remove our own missiles from Turkey. Hell, I didn't even know we had missiles in Turkey."

"Is that all there is to it? Why doesn't Kennedy just say yes and agree to that? Why do we need missiles way over there anyway?"

Russo sat back, tried to feel comfortable on the soft couch.

"I don't know. I guess . . . we're not supposed to know."

"Do you think Kennedy will do what's right?"

"Jesus, Margie, no one wants a war. At least, I don't think so. We have to trust the president that he's handling this the best way it can be handled."

"Maybe we should have put in a fallout shelter after all."

"Oh, hell. I'm not going to panic like Jerry and assume that if there's a war, my family will be just fine as long as I have my rifle."

She leaned her head against his shoulder, said, "No, I know. It's just terrifying. I hate that the children are living under this kind of shadow."

Russo glanced toward Danny's room, said, "It's the world they're inheriting, the world we're giving them. Years from now, I guess this will be a normal thing, unless we blow ourselves up. Just so they don't depend on all that duck and cover nonsense. That's even more stupid than Jerry's fallout shelter."

There was a clatter of noise from the back of the house, Danny appearing now, a quizzical glance at the television.

"How come no Jackie Gleason, Pop?"

"I wasn't in the mood, Dan-o. What's up?"

"You know that new game you bought me, Tactics II? I've been playing it for a couple weeks now. Pretty much got it figured out. I think I can make my own game boards too, different countries and borders and all of that. You should play it, Pop. Two armies, the Russians are red and the Americans are blue, and you've got all their infantry and armor divisions, paratroopers, the whole works. They got mountain troops to go through the mountains, amphibious troops to hit the beaches. It's great, Pop. I wish you'd play it with me. I bet I can beat you."

Russo held Margaret's hand, a tight squeeze, said to her, "When it comes down to it, maybe that's what will become normal to them. What seems so terrifying to us, to him . . . it's just a board game."

CHAPTER THIRTY-FOUR

Arkhipov

Saturday afternoon, October 27, 1962
Submarine B-59, at sea, off Cuba

It was hot, the crewmen around him sweating, what had passed
for normal in most of the Soviet subs. It meant more to Arkhipov,
and he glanced around, couldn't escape the nervousness of just
what the heat might mean. To this crew, the sweat and grime was
part of a day's duty, the sub keeping below the surface throughout
daylight hours, surfacing only in the darkness. It was unavoidable
that within the confines of the submerged vessel, the temperature
rose and the air grew more stale with each hour they stayed under.
But Arkhipov had a different experience, the year before, a different craft, nuclear submarine K-19. It had been near Greenland, a
routine training mission, the cooling system for the nuclear power
plant breaking down, a significant leak. The tension had been high
as the men struggled to solve the problem, most of the crew, including Arkhipov, exposed to far more deadly radiation than was
acceptable. But eventually, the cooling system had been repaired,
a lesson carried by that entire crew that this new technology, the

precious nuclear submarines, could be more deadly than the old reliable diesel.

The B-59 was diesel, noisy, dirty, but Arkhipov welcomed his assignment, escaping the various unknowns that seemed to haunt the nuclear-powered subs. For now, his official position was commodore, a key officer who served in partial command of the four-sub fleet, all of them cruising now near Cuba. To the captain of the B-59, Valentin Savitsky, such a grand title didn't seem to carry much weight. Out here, so far from any land base, the B-59 belonged to Savitsky, a fact made clear to Arkhipov the first day they had released the lines. Arkhipov had no reason to look for an argument, and so far, the mission had been reasonably routine. They had one job to do: monitor the Americans enforcing their blockade line around Cuba. If any Soviet vessel required aid, no matter what kind of aid, the B-59 and the other three subs were there to provide it. What that might mean was anybody's guess.

Arkhipov kept to his position, near the navigator, one eye on the man's charts. Behind him, the captain called out, his usual request.

"Depth?"

"Sixty meters, sir."

"Sixty meters. Heading?"

"One eight zero, sir. Eight knots."

"Enemy position."

"Two American destroyers to starboard, range eight kilometers and at least twelve kilometers."

The captain cursed, said to no one in particular, "Our orders insist we must stay submerged. But no one says we can't take a closer look. Helm, change course to two five zero, maintain speed."

Arkhipov shook his head, kept his thoughts to himself. Our orders do not tell us to play a chess game with American warships.

Certainly they know we're here, or they'll detect us when we get closer. This is foolishness.

The bulkheads around him groaned with the course change, the telltale sign of the aging sub, and the primary reason they could rarely sail close to a destroyer undetected. The batteries are getting low, and it's getting hotter in here, he thought. The air will begin to foul soon. We should lie low until dark, save our energy until we can surface. But here I am only the second-in-command. It's Savitsky's boat.

From the sonar station, a hushed voice.

"Sir, the American destroyer has changed course, to intercept us. She is closing rapidly."

Arkhipov looked at Savitsky, hoped to see some contrition, that he would accept that playing tag might be a poor idea. The captain seemed annoyed, wiped his brow with a dirty white handkerchief.

"Change course, give him room. Return to one eight zero."

"Aye, sir."

Arkhipov waited and heard the groans again, the sub leaning to port as it made the turn. Long minutes passed, no one speaking, Arkhipov pulling his shirt away from his skin, the sweat soaking through. From his command chair, Savitsky said, "Where is he?"

The sonar man responded with a useless whisper.

"Sir, he's caught us. He's . . . less than a kilometer to starboard, closing."

The captain slapped the arm of his chair.

"What in the devil does he want with us? Or is he playing his little cat and mouse game too?"

Arkhipov obeyed his instincts, looked upward, as though he might actually see the destroyer passing over. Others did the same, eyes upward, and Savitsky said, "Submerge to eighty meters. Maintain heading."

The rattling thunder came now, a short burst, then another,

more following. Arkhipov steadied himself against a railing, the navigator beside him, very young, suddenly very afraid.

"Depth charges. They're hunting us!"

Arkhipov put a hand on the young man's shoulder.

"They know where we are. They're just letting us know. Those are signal charges, low yield."

Savitsky said aloud, "They're telling us we're captured. It's their order for us to surface. Damn them to hell. They will have to do more than spit at us."

Arkhipov looked at the captain, said, "They're probably checking up on us, just to make sure we're aware of the blockade line. It might be a good idea to obey them. Chances are, once they identify us, they'll move on past."

Savitsky looked at him with a hard sneer.

"Commodore Arkhipov, command has made you soft. I have been expecting this. It is my greatest fear, and yet I welcome it. It is quite clear that the war has begun. They're seeking a prize. I won't give them one."

"*War?*"

"Yes, Commodore. You are aware that we have been unable to raise our home base, or any base, for several days. My guess is that they have far more to contend with than one lonely submarine. Simply put, Commodore, we're on our own out here."

Arkhipov looked toward the radioman, said, "Have you tried contacting base today?"

The young man glanced at the captain, then said, "No, sir. Last night. But there was interference. I had to charge the batteries before I could try again, but today, we've been submerged."

"What about right now?"

"No, sir, we're too deep."

The depth charges came again, thumps and rattles to one side of the sub. Arkhipov said, "Captain, that's definitely a signal. They are demanding that we surface."

Savitsky rose from his seat, moved toward him, motioned with his hand.

"Commodore, in my quarters, now, if you please." He scanned the con, said, "Find that political officer and have him report to my quarters immediately."

One of the crewmen left quickly, and Savitsky motioned toward Arkhipov. "Now."

Arkhipov followed the captain through the narrow corridor, saw the political officer, Maslennikov, moving toward them. Maslennikov wore the same uniform, but was no navy man, had been assigned to duty on the submarine seemingly to test loyalties, to catch someone at any sort of indiscretion that would reflect badly on him in Moscow. As such, he was extremely unpopular, though Arkhipov had yet to see any sign that the man cared what any one of the crew thought about him. Maslennikov said with a smile, "Yes, Captain. Something you need?"

Savitsky opened the hatch to his quarters, said, "Inside, both of you."

The captain remained standing, pointed to a small chair and the edge of his bed. The other two sat, and Savitsky stood with his arms crossed, said, "It is my belief that we are at war with the United States. It has been expected for some time, and we have made preparations in that event. For the past few days, our guard has been down, and so, the American destroyer caught us easily. That is my fault. He could have destroyed us an hour ago, but instead he is seeking our capture. I do not have to tell either one of you, this is unacceptable."

The hull rattled again, more small blasts peppering the sub.

"The American navy will bring reinforcements, to aid in the

capture. No doubt, other ships are steaming our way. It is what I would do. Should they be unsuccessful in calling us to the surface, their patience will run out. Then they will kill us."

Maslennikov seemed to absorb what the captain was saying, the smile gone, a strong nod.

"That sounds correct, Captain. But why do you believe we are at war?"

"It was inevitable. It is not widely known, but I am aware that we have constructed nuclear missile launchers in Cuba and have prepared them for offensive use. There is only one reason to position your greatest weapons so close to the enemy. You intend to use them. Clearly, the Americans discovered what we have done, thus, they have positioned this blockade, to prevent additional arms from entering Cuba. Until now, there has been no effort to interfere with our submarine traffic, since it is expected that we would observe and protect our own ships. But obviously, that has changed. And, if you consider we have not been able to contact any land base . . . I believe that is the result of a deadly engagement. It is quite likely that our cities, and the cities of the Americans exist as smoldering ruins. And in that, we have one great advantage. We are very far away, and so, when war erupts, when so much destruction spreads over so much of our lands, our cities, our people . . . we survive."

Arkhipov felt cold in his gut.

"But you have no proof of this. What are you suggesting?"

"I rely on intuition, Commodore. And I say this with no enthusiasm, with no joy. But the time has come to fight for our country. We have a very limited window of time before the American destroyers finally destroy us. I intend to employ our *Special Weapon*. We will arm our torpedoes with the nuclear warheads, and we will eliminate the threat from the American ships."

Maslennikov stood, a show of excitement.

"This is grand, Captain. This will strike a blow that will be heard all the way to Moscow."

Arkhipov said, "Captain, please. If such a *blow* is heard in Russia, it will be because there are people alive to hear it. I have no evidence that there is a war, however should you do this, you will risk starting one. I am not convinced that the American destroyers are doing any more than signaling to us to surface, so that they might identify us and our intentions. This is their blockade, after all."

Savitsky kept his arms crossed, stared at Arkhipov with disgust.

"Yes, you have grown soft. This war, my friend, has been going on since World War Two. For seventeen years, we have been positioning ourselves for the great blow. Why else would we put missiles in Cuba? Why else would we have been sent to this blockade, except to destroy it? Commodore, it is my belief that this war that scares you so has already begun. You have children, yes?"

"I have a daughter."

"I hope she survives. But if we do not fight, here and now, and instead we pretend there is no war . . . we return home to what? A charred and desolate land? You will find nothing of your family, so how will you feel? You could have done something, made a decisive move, inflicted great damage on the enemy, and instead you chose to *wait and see*."

Maslennikov looked at him now, said, "I truly believe he is correct, Commodore. Our opportunity could be brief. I do not wish to become just one more casualty, when we can strike hard at the enemy with a weapon they cannot withstand. I know very little of glory in battle, but I know opportunity. This is opportunity."

There was a faint knock on the captain's hatch, and Savitsky moved that way, pulled it open, a terse "Yes?"

"Sir, two more American destroyers are approaching. And, we are picking up the sound of aircraft."

"Good. Back to your station." He turned to Arkhipov now. "You see? As I predicted. They are moving in for the kill. It is time to act, Commodore. I will not die a coward's death, when I could have taken down the enemy. I will launch the nuclear torpedo, and eliminate at least one, or perhaps two American ships. And they can do nothing in response."

Arkhipov was feeling a panicky helplessness, said, "You are wrong, Captain. If we start this war, there shall be response aplenty. We don't know why there are missiles in Cuba. That is not for us to know. We have no orders to fire our nuclear weapons, in any event. I would surface, allow the Americans to do what they intend to do, and when they allow us to move on our way, we contact land base, while we're on the surface."

Savitsky stared at him, shook his head.

"Have you heard nothing I've said? If we surface, we will be offering the Americans our surrender. We will hand them our ship and our crew without any struggle. As long as this is my submarine, gentlemen, I will decide its fate. You both know my orders, that I am required to accede to both of you before using our *Special Weapon*. I believe I know where you stand, Comrade Maslennikov. Now tell me, Commodore. Will you stand with Russia, with your navy, with your honor?"

Arkhipov stood now.

"When Russia calls upon me to fight a nuclear war, I will do so. But I will not accept that such a war exists without direct evidence, without proof, and without orders. I will not approve your use of our *Special Weapon*, and you cannot employ that weapon without my approval. Captain, I will not allow you to start such a war."

Savitsky stared at him, red-faced, seemed ready to burst. He looked at Maslennikov now, said, "I have no choice but to accede to his decision. My orders are specific on this point. This decision must be unanimous." He looked at Arkhipov now. "Be wary, Commodore. I will not allow this kind of treachery to occur again. I will surface, as the Americans demand. But know this. You have doomed us to an inglorious surrender."

THEY BROKE THE surface near one of the destroyers, the hatch opening quickly. It was nearly dark, Savitsky climbing up out the hatch of the conning tower, Arkhipov close behind. He had seen the captain strap on his sidearm, a show of defiance that seemed faintly ridiculous under the five-inch gun and antiaircraft batteries of the destroyer. Above came the roar of an aircraft, and the officers looked that way, a searchlight suddenly glaring down, blinding light. Arkhipov lowered his head, blinked, stared into the dark hatch, and now a new sound, the plane's machine guns coming to life.

Savitsky shouted, "They're firing on us! Get below, prepare to dive!"

Arkhipov looked up again, the searchlight passing by, machine-gun fire spraying the surface of the water, clear out past one side of the sub. Now another flyover, but no machine guns, the planes circling, coming back around.

Arkhipov said, "No! They're just getting our attention. Look, Captain. A boat."

From one side of the nearest destroyer, a boat was lowered into the water, a handful of officers on board. The boat began to approach, and Arkhipov saw Savitsky's sidearm come up. He put a hand on Savitsky's arm, said, "No, Captain. If there was a war, we'd already be dead."

"I don't trust them."

Arkhipov watched the small boat drawing closer, saw officers without sidearms. He saw one man, obviously in command, the man smiling, a saluting wave. Arkhipov slowly raised his hand in response, thought, one day there could be a war. But it is not today.

AFTER ENGAGING WITH the Americans in a tense yet amicable standoff, the destroyers moved off, allowing B-59 to go on its way. To Captain Savitsky's credit, his first order while still on the surface was to attempt to contact a land base once again. This time they were successful, and confirmation was received that, in fact, no war had yet begun. B-59 received one additional order: The sub was to leave the waters near Cuba and return to her base in the Soviet Union. Her mission to monitor the American blockade line was concluded.

CHAPTER THIRTY-FIVE

Khrushchev

Sunday, October 28, 1962, early morning
Khrushchev's dacha, outside Moscow

He had slept well, but woke with a jolt, the events of the past few days driving him quickly out of bed. He slipped quietly into his robe, his slippers, shuffled softly from the bedroom, would not wake his wife, no reason to inflict upon her the inescapable anxieties that infected him every day.

His son, Sergei, was upstairs in the guest room, Sergei's wife, Galina, insisting that Khrushchev's grandson, Nikita, visit as often as Khrushchev would allow. The poorly kept secret was that Khrushchev preferred the company of his family to anyone who occupied a position in the Presidium, with the possible exception of his friend Malinovsky. But Malinovsky was too focused now on the business at hand, and any conversation between them involved the most pressing anxieties of the day. Once in a while, Khrushchev could still ease his own tension by making silly faces at his two-year-old grandson.

He crept into the kitchen, slippers on the stone floor, was relieved to see no sign of the housemaid, the overly efficient woman not yet at work. He stared briefly through the tall kitchen window, a thin blanket of snow covering the grounds. But the day was dawning clear and blue, a tease for what surely would come once winter settled upon Moscow.

He glanced at the cabinet that held the vodka, shook his head, no. I might be tempted, but not yet. I will need a clear head today. There is much to do, decisions that must be made.

He heard commotion out by the front entrance, voices, the door closing. Visitors, he thought, this early? He regretted the robe, thought of slipping back into his room, but it was not to be. An aide appeared, fully dressed, the young man efficient as always.

"Good morning, Premier. A messenger has just delivered this parcel. He was accompanied by armed guards, so I assume the contents of this are for your eyes only."

Khrushchev recognized the pouch, knew it had come from the Kremlin, and if it was this time of day, he knew it could not wait. He looked out again at the snow, let out a breath, thought, so much for the peaceful time. He took the pouch, opened it slowly, slid a small handful of papers out, could see immediately it was a translation of a message from the president of the United States. He tossed the empty pouch on his kitchen table, said, "In Washington it is what time?"

"It is six here, so ten last evening in Washington. It is eight hours difference, Premier."

"Yes, of course. This seems to be a response to my letters to President Kennedy. Obviously, someone in the Kremlin felt it could not wait. They're probably right."

"Yes, sir. We also received a call from Ambassador Dobrynin."

"Yes, Dimitri, I know. I spoke with him earlier. I believe I already know what this letter will say." He fingered the paper, still couldn't avoid the nervousness. "I am wondering if I should summon the Presidium to meet with me here."

"I can issue the summons, on your command, sir."

"Dimitri, you are too efficient for your own good. Let them sleep a moment longer. Allow me to find some breakfast. I will grant myself the luxury of a brief time with my grandson. You are excused. Go back to your room. Enjoy a moment's rest."

"Of course, Premier. My apologies."

The young man slid away, and Khrushchev sat at his round wooden breakfast table, read Kennedy's response slowly. He felt a churning in his stomach, thought, he doesn't mention Turkey. He does that only through his brother, to Dobrynin. Careful move. And clever. He avoids the most contentious of my points, those issues pushed upon me by the Presidium, by Kochov and the mindless militants. Clever again.

He reread the letter, thought of the Presidium. They will be expecting to hear something. I cannot keep them in the dark. Dimitri is correct, they can be summoned to meet with me here. At least there might be one more day before I must sleep again in my office.

He heard footsteps on the stairs, glanced up, a muffled whisper.

"Good morning, Father."

His son padded into the room, and Khrushchev welcomed the interruption, responded with a whisper of his own.

"So, my grandson still sleeps?"

Sergei laughed.

"It is a precious time, these few minutes of quiet. He will command this house soon enough."

Khrushchev tried to return the good humor, but there was no laughter, no smile. Sergei read him well, said, "Is it not going well, Father?"

Khrushchev laid the papers on the table.

"No, Sergei, it is not going well. Kennedy has responded to my last communication, and he is proving to be more of a rock than I would have thought. Of course, it could be those men behind him, who push hard keeping him upright. But the Americans are holding firm to their demands, and it is placing me in a position I have not yet experienced." He paused. "I have never felt this way before, never truly felt the weight of this office, a weight others take for granted. I have within my hands the power to inflict the most deadly catastrophe that this world has ever endured. And I am face-to-face with another man who has exactly the same power. Some would say we are engaged in a negotiation, but you do not negotiate the end of the world. One of us must admit a mistake and back away before we come to the edge of the abyss. I believe I understand this young man Kennedy. What I do not know is how much pressure he is under from behind, pushed by those who seem not to care if they destroy the world, just so they can prove their point."

"Father, why did you put missiles in Cuba? Was it not to prove a point?"

Khrushchev thought a moment.

"I suppose . . . of course. We must support our allies. We must create equal footing in the nuclear age by matching power for power. *Mutually assured destruction*, so some American general once said. It has to be that way. It is after all, what the Americans are doing with their manufacture of so many bombs. We sought merely to equal the balance, to stand up toe-to-toe and support a position that is in the best interests of the Soviet Union."

"Father, you are speaking as though I am a reporter from *Izvestia*. Perhaps the balance is not meant to be equal. Perhaps the equity, the peace comes not from so many bombs, but from good relations, a clear understanding and respect for the other side. Father, do you know if Mr. Kennedy has children?"

Khrushchev was surprised by the question.

"Two. They're young."

"Do you believe Mr. Kennedy wishes to see his children grow older?"

It was a new thought, and he weighed the words, the concept. He was distracted by motion behind Sergei, his daughter-in-law, Galina, carrying a large squirming bundle. Khrushchev wanted to smile, to take the boy, but something stopped him, a strange paralysis. She handed the boy off to Sergei, who said, "Now the men have assembled properly. Perhaps some breakfast, Galina?"

She laughed, said, "Perhaps. The cook is stirring. I suspect she is not accustomed to the men of this house rising so early. But she should teach you how to cook for yourselves. Excuse me, I must get dressed."

She disappeared up the stairs, and Khrushchev stared at his grandson, saw wide eyes, and a sleepy smile.

"I hope, Sergei, that you do not come to regret naming your son after me. *Nikita* might not be a name respected for much longer. I have decisions to make which might push me out of favor in the Kremlin. Such is the nature of the uncertainty we must live under."

Sergei sat at the table, the young boy coming fully awake, a beaming smile toward his grandfather.

"Nonsense, Father. He will respect you always, no matter anyone else. Besides, he will make a path for himself."

Words stuck in Khrushchev's throat. *If that path still exists.* He stood abruptly, said, "Forgive me. I must withdraw to my office here. I have some things I must work on. It can't be helped. I must carefully examine Mr. Kennedy's letter. And I must prepare a different letter, to Fidel Castro. I must convince him to stop shooting at American airplanes."

Sergei knew his father well, did not object. Khrushchev rose, secured his robe, padded his way through the house, to his private study. He closed the door behind him, moved to his desk, sat, the response from Kennedy still in his hand. He read it again, thought, yes, a very clever man. No matter how much we believe we have the upper hand, he remains on top. He is trusting that I do not want a war, and it is a wise wager. And yet that is the decision facing me. It has been so through this entire crisis, where either one of us could have said, all right, that's all. No more talk, no more threats and bluster. That's where I am right now. My generals, Kochov for one, would push me to tilt the table in our favor, fire off one or more of those missiles as a stark warning to the United States that we are not merely fooling around. Perhaps we would eliminate a small city, just to prove our resolve. And so, Kennedy would do the same, perhaps eliminate two of our cities . . . and there we have it. No one could stop that word . . . *escalation*. And so, history would record the two of us as mass murderers, responsible for the destruction of humanity. No, don't be silly. There would be no history. It would simply end.

He stood, moved away from the desk, had to see the snow once more. We both understand with perfect clarity, he thought, that no matter the generals and their weapons, no matter how much we might strive to save face, no matter the agreements we make with foolish allies, in the end we must ask ourselves just what we value the most. Just how much do we love our children?

CHAPTER THIRTY-SIX

RFK

Sunday, October 28, 1962, early morning
Hickory Hill, near McLean, Virginia

"Daddy, are we still going? You promised."

"Get your sister up and dressed. There's a car waiting for us."

His oldest child bounded away, and he smiled, thought, God, she loves horses. I thought having them here would satisfy her craving, but clearly it's not enough. Now her sister's right there with her. You'd think those two had dreams of competing in the Olympics. Well, maybe so.

It was a promise he had made weeks before, well before Excomm meetings and so many threats of disaster. The International Horse Show had been founded a few years before, as though aimed squarely at Kathleen, Bobby's oldest daughter. The girl had long insisted that her father drop anything of lesser importance, such as his activities as attorney general, to attend the festivities at the Washington Armory. At eleven years old, Kathleen was prime age to pursue horseback riding on her own, and he and Ethel had obliged her with a horse of her own, shared often with her siblings. Bobby was concerned that his daughter Courtney, now only six, might push too hard for her own opportunities to ride. Ethel had already made it clear to all concerned, that the younger girl was not quite ready for that kind of risk, though, at Hickory Hill, when it came to playing with the variety of livestock, there were few rules.

The two girls emerged from their bedrooms, full of squeals, followed him now to the waiting car. He spent the drive watching them, chatter and excitement, then focused his gaze out beyond the car, showers of falling leaves. He thought of Jack, no, he won't be attending any horse show. He's probably sitting at his desk, staring at the telephone, wondering how long it will be before he hears something new. Bobby tried to avoid the guilt of that, knew that many of the Excomm members were doing the same thing, huddled with various deputies in quiet offices, all of them debating what Khrushchev was going to do next. Hell no, he thought. I can't ignore my own life. This is far more important, at least right now. Until there is some real news, the Excomm can wait.

The armory came into view now, the excitement from the girls increasing. He tried to share the moment, saw the hordes pushing through the entrances, an enormous percentage of young girls in the crowd. What is it with girls and horses, he thought. At least my boys have cheaper hobbies, usually involving a ball of some sort.

They bailed from the car, Bobby with a quick thank-you to the driver, a brief word as to where the car could be found later. The girls knew to stay close to him, and he led them into the crowd, no one paying attention to his presence, the attorney general not nearly as important as those fortunate few inside the armory who even now were putting their horses through their paces. The girls surged forward, found vantage points along a rail fence, the horses beyond, jumping barricades, fully capturing their attention. Bobby watched from behind, shook his head. They'll want more horses when this is through. I'll need Ethel for that, a firm foot saying no. But Ethel almost never says no.

He stood in the crowd for a long half hour, let the girls have their way, their excitement never waning. He caught glances from some of the crowd around him, recognition, the occasional smile, brief nods from strangers. He tried to ignore that, but couldn't help feeling gratified that so many people offered him a positive gesture. These were, after all, voters.

He felt a tap on his shoulder, turned, was surprised to see his driver and another man.

"Sir, important call for you. This fellow sought me out at the car. There's a phone behind that table. If you'd like, sir, I'll stay with the girls."

Bobby felt a jolt of nervousness, a quick glance at his two daughters, said, "Yes. Stay close to them. I'll be right back."

He was led through the crowd by the other man, saw a handful of people move aside at the ticket table.

"You have a phone call for me?"

"Yes, sir. Here."

He saw the receiver, picked it up, stared at it for a short moment, his mind racing in every direction.

"Hello? This is the attorney general."

He welcomed the familiar voice on the other end of the line. It was Dean Rusk.

"*Bobby. You should come to the White House right now, if you can.*"

"What's going on?"

"*We've received word from the Russians. They're agreeing to withdraw their missiles from Cuba.*"

313

He couldn't help the momentous disappointment he had handed his daughters, but there was no way he could simply leave them at the horse show. He had bathed them with promises that he fully intended to keep, that there would be other opportunities, whether or not that might involve horses.

He moved quickly into the president's private office, saw Rusk, who stood briefly, a quick and enthusiastic handshake. Kennedy seemed weary, but beamed an energizing smile, and he looked up at Bobby, said, "Sit down, for God's sake. You always stand. It's time to take a breath ... well maybe. We're still waiting for confirmation, something in writing."

The phone rang on Kennedy's desk, and he snatched at the receiver, said, "Yes." He listened for a moment, then looked at Bobby again. "Fine. I'll tell him. He'll be there."

Kennedy hung up the phone, said to Bobby, "Well, don't get too comfortable. It seems Ambassador Dobrynin wishes to see you. He's asking if eleven o'clock will do, in your office. I agreed for you."

Bobby stood, glanced at his watch, twenty after ten.

"I'll be back, gentlemen."

Rusk laughed, more nervousness than humor.

"We'll be waiting, Mr. Attorney General."

Sunday, October 28, 1962, late morning
Department of Justice, Attorney General's Office

Dobrynin was smiling. Bobby could feel instinctively that it wasn't that typical *so nice to shake your hand but I have secrets* smile. It was open and toothy and it seemed as though Dobrynin was containing himself from giving Bobby a slap on the back.

"Mr. Attorney General, thank you for seeing me on such short notice. Premier Khrushchev personally extends his best wishes to your brother the president and to yourself."

"That's very nice, and well appreciated. Thank you."

Bobby forced himself to stay calm, waited for Dobrynin to say more. Dobrynin pulled a pad of paper from his valise, said, "If you will allow me, sir, I should like to read to you a message just received, directly from Premier Khrushchev."

"By all means, Mr. Ambassador."

"*Esteemed Mr. President.*

I express my satisfaction and gratitude for the sense of proportion and understanding you have shown of the responsibility borne by you at present for the preservation of peace throughout the world." He stopped, seemed ready to jump out of his skin. "With your permission, I will read the pertinent points. As we know, Premier Khrushchev does tend to wax philosophical and personal on occasion."

Bobby smiled, appreciated Dobrynin's frankness, motioned with his hand.

"Please continue."

"*In order to eliminate as rapidly as possible the conflict which endangers the cause of peace, to give an assurance to all people who crave peace, and to reassure the American people who, I am certain, also want peace, as do the people of the Soviet Union, the Soviet government, in addition to earlier instructions on the discontinuation of further work on weapons construction sites, has issued a new order to dismantle the weapons which you describe as offensive, and to crate and return them to the Soviet Union . . . I regard with respect and trust your statement of 27 October, 1962, that there will be no attack, no invasion of Cuba—not only by the United States but also by other nations of the Western Hemisphere, as you said in your message. Then the motives which induced us to render assistance of such a kind to Cuba disappear . . . Thus, in view of the assurances you have given and our instructions on dismantling, there is every condition for eliminating the present conflict."*

Dobrynin stopped, waited for a response, still the smile, fading a little, as though there might yet be some kind of complication. "I assure you, Mr. Attorney General, this message, in its entirety is right this moment being read over Moscow radio."

"I must emphasize, Mr. Ambassador, that one condition of this agreement is that you make no mention publicly of our intention to remove missiles from Turkey."

Dobrynin nodded, made a slight bow, another smile.

"Did you hear any such mention in the message? Premier Khrushchev is agreeing to your demands, if I may call them demands. We have our understanding, Mr. Attorney General."

Bobby absorbed the moment, fought to control himself, stood, moved out from behind his desk, extended a hand.

"Mr. Ambassador, this is wonderful news. You may be sure that the president will receive this in the spirit intended by Chairman Khrushchev. I believe this means that all of us . . . may once again enjoy a good night's rest."

October 28, 1962, early afternoon
The White House, Kennedy's private office

Bobby stood quietly, waited for Jack to complete his phone conversation.

"That's right, Ike. It's all public now. They agreed. I'll pull down the quarantine immediately." There was a silent pause. "That's right. It seems to be over or the hard part anyway. The UN will be brought in to take over from here and monitor things in Cuba, and more, on the high seas." Another pause. "Thanks, Ike."

Bobby was too nervous to sit, paced around Kennedy's office. The phone call ended and Bobby said, "Eisenhower?"

"Yep. I called Truman, too, let them both know."

"Good, good. Who else?"

Kennedy laughed.

"Easy, little brother. Word will spread just as it should. Excomm will be fully briefed this afternoon. The Joint Chiefs have been notified, and naturally, they aren't happy. They were so damn excited to go to war as soon as tomorrow, so to them, this feels like a big damn fizzle. Taylor passed that along to me, but he insisted he was dissenting from the others, that he was actually happy for a peaceful settlement. I suppose I believe him. I have no patience for that *shoot first, think about it later* mentality, but I can't change who they are."

"By God, Jack. This is . . . well, hell, I don't know what it is. I haven't relaxed in two weeks, I feel like my gut's got permanent knots."

"I know. Listen, I've got something I need to do. Jackie and the kids are down in Virginia, but that won't stop me from going alone. I think I need to go to church."

Bobby stopped moving, nodded, said, "Good idea. Damn good idea."

"What about you?"

"No, not right now. I've got something more important to do. I have to go to the horse show."

CHAPTER THIRTY-SEVEN

Pliyev

Monday, October 29, 1962
Soviet Army HQ, near Havana, Cuba

"Do you enjoy boxing, Captain?"

His aide seemed to fumble for words, surprised at the question.

"When I'm able to view a match, yes, I suppose so. My father was a great fan of boxing."

"Good for your father. In 1956, I was in Australia, commanding the guard to our boxing team for the Olympics that year. It was the first time, so I heard, that the Soviet Union could feel truly proud of our boxing skills, that we were certain to win a great many medals. We did too. Three gold."

Pliyev moved to the window, stared out, not sure if his aide was paying any attention.

"I especially enjoyed the middleweights. I was ringside and saw the match between one of our top fighters, Gennadi Schatkov, against some fellow from Chile. Schatkov was brilliant, dominated the fight, and won the gold medal. Afterward, I recall watching his face, full of victory, enormous joy. We had been told that our boxing team drew their inspiration from the Soviet flag, and perhaps that's true, though I'm not sure any mere flag could have produced the ecstasy I saw on that man's face. But oddly, I found myself watching the other fellow, the Chilean, who had failed to achieve the glory his own country expected of him. He was badly beaten, and for a long while after the match, he sat on the small stool in his corner with his head down, feeling the kind of pain no one outside the boxing ring can understand." He looked at his aide now, who stared at him with wide eyes. "Until now. I believe I know what the Chilean boxer felt, and not just the physical pain of being beaten with fists. His job . . . his duty was to achieve glory for his country. But it was denied him, as it has been denied me. Some will find fault with the job I have done here. Some will blame me because someone must be blamed, and after all, I am *here*."

He moved away from the window, sat slowly at his desk. His telephone was ringing, and he ignored it, his aide moving closer, Pliyev holding up a hand.

"Leave it be. If it's important, they will call back. These days, I suppose, everything is important. There are a great many beaten fighters in this place today."

The phone continued to ring, and Pliyev was increasingly annoyed, couldn't tune it out, pointed to it, the aide jumping in quickly to answer.

"General Pliyev's office. Yes. Yes." He put a hand over the receiver. "General Grechko wishes to have a moment with you. He is most insistent, sir."

Pliyev lowered his head. "Another blow to the body. Certainly, tell him I am available for the next few minutes."

"GENERAL PLIYEV, I was told . . . no, I was shoved hard to complete my antiaircraft installations. You berated me more than once for making slow progress, when Moscow demanded speed. Other commanders were given the same *advice*, from you and from Moscow. Finish the work, complete the job. Fine, we obeyed, we pushed our men hard, in miserable conditions. This place is a bug-infested hellhole. That is not a revelation to you, General. And work we did. General Statsenko, who commands the missile division, feels as bad about this as I do, and his people worked even harder than mine to get their missiles operational."

Grechko was shouting, and Pliyev let him go, knew that on this day, there was a great deal of shouting to go around. Grechko seemed to wear down, obviously surprised Pliyev had allowed him such indiscretions.

Pliyev said, "General, I do not dispute anything you say. But what would you have me do? Should I gather up all of my commanders here and sing a chorus of protest to Moscow? Should we ignore our orders and start a war, just because we are frustrated? I have worked all of my career to further the goals as they have been given me. I have followed my orders as explicitly as possible, because I understand that's what a good officer does. Well, General Grechko, we have new orders now, and they are very direct. We are to dismantle every missile launcher, every SAM site, we are to crate up every missile and transport them to the shipping terminals. There, they will be inspected by United Nations officials, and once on board the transport ships that will carry them back to the Soviet Union, they will be inspected again, at sea."

Grechko was visibly shaken now, said, "Do you approve of this?"

"General Grechko, that is an absurd question. My job is not to approve anything. It's to do what I am told. This is also your job. Your protests are noted. Your concern for the pride of the Soviet Union is noted. But you will follow your orders."

There was no fire in his words, his energy drained. Grechko eyed him, as though there was much left unsaid, but Pliyev ignored the hint, would not spew out his own feelings about what had taken place. After a short moment, Grechko said, "What of the Cubans? How are they responding to this outrage?"

Pliyev glanced at his watch.

"I am about to find out for myself. In ten minutes, Castro is due to grace me with his glorious presence. I am told he is . . . unhappy. General Grechko, please return to your post, and complete your new assignment."

CASTRO ARRIVED, ACCOMPANIED by General Aleksei Dementiyev, the officer charged with training Castro's forces to work closely alongside their Soviet counterparts. Now, Dementiyev's presence seemed more irony than particularly useful.

Castro was furious, no surprise to Pliyev. The interpreter strained to keep up, the words flowing from Castro in a molten torrent.

"I do not recognize this stupidity. I was not consulted, no permission was sought. Your country has abandoned us, left us to the wolves."

Pliyev waited for an opening, said, "My understanding is that the Americans have pledged not to invade your country."

Castro's eyes seemed to light up even brighter, the cigar clamped tightly in his teeth. He removed it now, waved it menacingly at Pliyev's face.

"Have you heard of Czechoslovakia? Abandoned to the Germans at the start of World War Two? The Allies sang a beautiful song together, oh no, there shall be no invasion by the Germans, *because Hitler has given his word*. So, now I am to swallow such nonsense? Especially since your wonderful Premier Khrushchev does not bother to communicate with me such decisions that directly affect the lives, and possibly the deaths, of my people? Well, be advised, General. I have issued my own plans for settling this crisis, for all the good it will do. I have instructed Chairman Khrushchev that this is the correct plan. The Americans shall remove their criminal blockade without delay. The Americans will stop supporting all harassments of my country by guerilla groups, and stop all raids against my country by these guerrillas. The Americans will end all illegal reconnaissance flights over Cuban airspace. And they will immediately withdraw from Guantánamo naval base. I was . . . ignored. Instead, your friend Khrushchev decided to surrender everything in sight." He pounded a fist on the table. "I curse him, General, as I curse you, and every one of my supposed allies here. You are dogs, obedient to the devil, forgetting who your true friends are. Khrushchev has abandoned us, tossed us aside, and for what reason? To bow down to the bullying Americans and their every absurd demand."

Pliyev kept his calm, felt his way into another slight opening.

"Perhaps you should be consulting with our ambassador, expressing your displeasure to him. As you must understand, I am under orders, and those orders are explicit. I am to remove all Soviet missiles from Cuba . . ."

"All of them? *All of them?*"

"Yes, sir. My orders are clear."

"Well, General, allow me to say that it is a fortunate thing your missiles are going away, because under my control, there would be a different result. I do not fear a fight, unlike your Khrushchev. Have you seen this?"

He produced a letter from his shirt pocket, stuffed the cigar back into his mouth, handed the letter to his interpreter.

"Read this aloud to the general."

The man was nervous, cleared his throat, obeyed.

"I would like to recommend to you now, at this moment of change in the crisis, not to be carried away by emotions. I would like to advise you in a friendly manner to show patience, firmness and even more firmness, so as to avoid additional provocations."

Castro spat to one side.

"He insults me even more, suggesting that I cannot control myself, nor can I control my military. I should like to remind you that it was not I who shot down the American spy plane. I did not provide such a *provocation* as your people did. Well, you may advise your Khrushchev that I shall order my military to shoot down American planes when I decide it is prudent. As for the United Nations inspectors said to be coming to trespass on our soil, be advised, that they had better wear battle armor."

PLIYEV WAS EXHAUSTED. He sat at his desk, his mind racing with Castro's bellicose claims, the raw abusiveness the Cuban leader had aimed at Premier Khrushchev. How wise is it, he thought, for any head of state to make such statements? This is a large stage, larger than I command, larger even than Moscow commands. Castro is angry, certainly, and perhaps much of what he claims is true. But he cannot stomp with heavy boots over carefully arranged agreements, no matter how he might not like them. Hell, *I* don't like them, but I cannot change what is happening.

He heard commotion outside, unusual, stood, went to the window. He peered out toward the main road, was surprised to see a vast crowd of people, moving slowly up the thoroughfare. They were chanting, signs held aloft, many of the people motioning toward his headquarters. The words were indistinct, but he saw the faces, could hear the raw anger in their voices. Good God, he thought. There are hundreds of them, maybe thousands. He thought of his guards, knew they could see this as well, would have come to alert already. Surely, they won't try to come in here. He heard the single word, *Khrushchev*, other words he didn't understand. Nothing I can do about that. But, clearly, this is why Castro shows his own temper. His people embrace that, mimic it, share his love of boisterous protest. How long will this last, he thought. How many days, and how long before the words turn to violence? What do we do then? Do we shoot them down? No, don't be ridiculous. That would create more problems for us all.

He backed away from the window, could still hear the chanting. Perhaps this is why it has to end. They cannot have any chance of using our missiles, of flying our bombers, flying our MiGs. And, Pliyov thought, I can honestly say, now that this is coming to an end . . . I'm really happy to leave this place.

CHAPTER THIRTY-EIGHT

Khrushchev

Tuesday, October 30, 1962
Moscow, the Kremlin

"I think that you and I, with our heavy responsibilities for the mainte-nance of peace, were aware that developments were reaching a point where events could have become unmanageable . . . Mr. Chairman, both of our countries have great unfinished tasks and I know that your people as well as those of the United States can ask for nothing better than to pursue them free from the fear of war . . ."

"Do we respond to President Kennedy today, Premier?"

Khrushchev put down the paper, looked at his aide.

"Not yet. There is no urgency. We have reached an under-standing. What remains is to carry it out. Is Marshal Malinovsky present?"

The aide made a short bow.

"I shall check with his office. I believe I saw the marshal a short time ago."

His aide moved out, the door closing, and Khrushchev scanned Kennedy's note again. He speaks of *controlling* nuclear weapons, he thought. As we have learned, there could be a time when there is no such thing.

There was a short rap on his office door, a familiar rhythm, and he called out, "Come in, Rodion."

Malinovsky entered, no smile, moved to a chair, sat without speaking.

Khrushchev said, "One would detect that you are in a foul temper, my friend. This should be a day for rejoicing."

Malinovsky looked at him.

"Rejoice what? The Soviet Union has been ultimately humiliated. And, as if that is not enough, Castro is refusing to allow UN inspectors onto Cuban soil. Thus, all inspections of our ships and their cargo will have to be done at sea, by the American navy. Now, I am hearing that you are being pressured to remove our IL-28 bombers from Cuban soil. Those planes were given to Castro as a gift. He is already growling about that, as he seems to growl about everything else."

"I agreed to remove all weapons from Cuba that the Americans defined as offensive. In the end, what use could the IL-28s be, if not offensive? They are long-range bombers that serve little use unless you plan to send them off to attack across distant borders. That sounds fairly offensive to me. The Americans have threatened to destroy them on the ground if we do not comply. Such harshness was unexpected, especially with an agreement on the missiles in place, but if I were in Kennedy's shoes, I would probably demand the same. Besides, the IL-28s are old and obsolete, and if he was thinking clearly, Castro would understand that he has no use for such a weapon, certainly not now. It is one more example of his need to hold on to anything that gives him power." He paused. "We should have recognized that part of Castro's character. It might have saved us some trouble."

"But the bombers . . . Kennedy never before mentioned them

specifically. If you now agree to remove them . . . well, Nikita, the Americans will crow like bantam roosters over that one."

Khrushchev tossed Kennedy's note aside.

"I do not believe there is crowing at all, Rodion, or if there is, it is kept tightly under wraps. Kennedy is no fool, no matter how I may have disregarded him in the past. He will not have his people, his military, parade their part in this negotiation as a great victory. They are doing nothing to jam our faces into humiliation. And for that reason, we will not take these events as a defeat. All of us, the Americans and the Soviets, have avoided a nuclear holocaust. There is victory aplenty in that."

"Nikita, with victory comes joy. There is no joy here."

Khrushchev was annoyed, but he knew to expect this.

"I will be blamed for our loss of prestige, for our loss of Cuba as a strategic military base. Castro is blaming me right now for every ill he can conjure up. I accepted Kennedy's demands, though even he would not label them as such. But the Americans did what they had to do to avoid an enormous threat to their country. Would we not do the same?"

Malinovsky seemed surprised.

"Nikita, there are still missiles in Turkey staring at us across the Black Sea. You have taken the word of the Americans that those will be removed . . . eventually. Some would say . . . that is the height of blind optimism. You are trusting Kennedy, that their secret pledge, the pledge they insist we never mention . . . that they will honor that. You must admit . . . it was a foolish gambit to accept those terms."

"I admit nothing of the kind. I accepted their pledge because I believe it to be genuine." He was angry now. "Rodion, no one benefits from threats of nuclear war. No one benefits from staring into the abyss. The Americans have a greater number of intercontinental ballistic missiles than we do, but throwing that into our faces would not benefit them in any way, because our missiles, though fewer in number, are just as capable of destroying every inch of the United States. What we avoided, what *I* avoided, Rodion, was losing control. No matter how much effort is made, once a war begins, no one truly has control. Look at the U-2 we shot down. A ridiculous mistake, a *lack of control*. Our field commanders reacted to a situation that seemed to be escalating. Many of those same field commanders were equipped with nuclear artillery shells. What if the Americans had made a foolish landing on the Cuban coast, and one of our officers, some nameless colonel, took it upon himself to respond with such weapons? If a thousand Americans had died as a result, there would have been a hard response, yes? There were opportunities for deadly accidents, Rodion. If even a single ground-to-ground missile had been fired, we would not be having this conversation, nor would you have had this pleasant opportunity to scold me for my failings. If I am to be condemned for this so-called failure, let me ask you this: Would you prefer seeing Marshal Kochov in charge? Would we prefer it if Kennedy was not president, and instead, we had to negotiate directly with the generals of their Joint Chiefs, perhaps General LeMay?"

Malinovsky stared down for a long moment.

"I understand all that you say. I understand, because you are my friend. But there are others, members of the Presidium, of the military, who see what you gave the Americans as a defeat. Your prestige . . . and possibly your power . . . is damaged."

Khrushchev sat back, could not be angry at his friend, could not be angry at the truth.

Wednesday, October 31, 1962
Gagra, Crimea, the Black Sea

He had left Moscow by plane, if only for a couple of days, an aching need to be away from scowling faces, from backroom cursing on his behalf. He walked now along the water with Nina, a long quiet stroll, the only sound the lapping of the surf on the rocky sand. He reached gently for her hand, still the quiet, and he turned to the water now, said, "You know, the scientists say the deepest waters here are anoxic. Nothing lives. It is why we occasionally find shipwrecks in such superb condition."

She stopped walking, stared at him, laughed.

"You have been in the center of one of the most dangerous crises the world has ever known, and you think of shipwrecks?"

He shrugged.

"It's why I come here. I can think about things that have nothing to do with governments or wars or Marshal Kochov. I do not concern myself here with legacies, whether Stalin's or my own."

She wasn't smiling now, took his hand again, said, "I am concerned about your legacy. Because I know it matters to you. Your greatest hope, always, has been to leave this nation in a more prosperous way than you inherited it. I have always thought you would succeed."

"Until now?"

She didn't respond, and he felt a thick blanket of gloom settling over them both.

"Have I failed so badly? The Chinese are positively ecstatic over this, condemning us for our Cuban folly. Already they are sidling up close to Castro to cozy his favor. They too might learn the foolishness of that one day. But I must wonder, Nina. Has Cuba been my great mistake?"

"It's not for me to say, Nikita."

"You don't have to say anything. The Kremlin is full of voices, all judging me. I cannot seem to make them understand that by agreeing to Kennedy's conditions, I most likely prevented a war, a war like this world has never seen. Why do they condemn me for that?"

They took a few more steps in silence, then she said, "Pride, my darling. To some of those people, it is better to die with your head held high, than to accept peace by walking away."

He sniffed.

"That's all well and good in the nineteenth century. A man dies from a bullet to his heart. His comrades fight on. Today, that bullet is a missile, and it destroys a city. How do you educate generals to understand that firing your best weapon at your enemy is no longer *sound strategy*? It is madness. And, it is suicide."

After a long pause, she said, "What will happen now, Nikita?"

"My hold on the Presidium will loosen. Some of the loud voices will grow louder still, and those who oppose my policies will be energized. And, in the end, if the voices become loud enough, they will remove me as Premier, as chairman of the Presidium."

"Surely they will not."

"Not right away. But those who seek opportunity will now believe they have one." He laughed. "Somehow, I do not believe this is what Kennedy was hoping for. It's a shame, really. He and I were just beginning to understand each other. Who knows, it's possible we could have become friends."

CHAPTER THIRTY-NINE

RFK

Thursday, November 1, 1962
Department of Justice, Attorney General's Office

"He said he preferred it this way. Said there's no reason for hiding anymore. Not sure what he meant, but he's waiting in the outer office."

Bobby sat back in his heavy chair, said, "Seriously? Well, he's the spy. But there's got to be more to this than what he's saying."

Siegenthaler laughed.

"Isn't that always the way with spies? I'll send him in."

Bobby waited, curious, hadn't seen Bolshakov in several days, before the meetings with Ambassador Dobrynin. Well, he thought, I wonder what new problem we've got.

Bolshakov was there now, as round as ever, but without the usual boisterous smile.

"Greetings, Georgi. You don't seem too happy to see me."

It was meant as a pleasantry, but Bolshakov responded with a deeper frown.

"It is apparent my usefulness to you is over. Before I take my leave, I just had to see you, to ask if there was something I had done, some error perhaps."

Bobby was puzzled.

"What are you talking about? I haven't had to see you through most of this Cuba mess because, as you know, I was dealing directly with Ambassador Dobrynin."

Bolshakov nodded, still the frown.

"He didn't know. You must believe that. He knew as little as I did. There were no lies."

Bobby felt a hint of clarity.

"You mean about missiles in Cuba? Once we verified the missiles being there, it didn't make sense that you would continue to lie about it. If you say you never knew in the first place, I'll believe you. I'll do the same for Dobrynin. That was a military decision made in Moscow, and it makes sense it was highly secret. Moscow surely knows that you and I talk, so it makes sense that they wouldn't tell you all the secrets. I don't hold a grudge about that. But why do you say your usefulness is past?"

Bolshakov stared at him for a long moment, searching him with his eyes.

"Did you not . . . as you say in the spy novels . . . blow my cover?"

"What the hell are you talking about?"

Bolshakov kept the seriousness, said, "Your newspaper columnist, Joseph Alsop. He mentioned my name, and my . . . um . . . position. It was assumed in Moscow . . . and assumed by *me* that you had given him the information. Moscow is not pleased, and they are recalling me. My usefulness has been compromised."

Bobby sat back in the chair, shook his head.

"Alsop is a friend to my family, and I respect his work. But I told him nothing. Obviously, he heard about you through other channels, and it sounded like a story worth telling."

"I must accept your explanation, Mr. Attorney General. I would just emphasize one more time . . . neither myself nor Ambassador Dobrynin lied to you about missiles in Cuba. We simply didn't know."

Bobby caught the sudden formality from Bolshakov, the distance already growing between them. Bolshakov made a short bow.

"I have enjoyed our acquaintance, although brief. I congratulate you on your success in defusing the Cuban crisis. Those are words I can never speak in Moscow."

"THEY'RE RECALLING HIM? That's not good, not for his future."

Bobby shook his head, pointed to a chair, Siegenthaler sitting.

Bobby said, "It's a damned shame. I don't know what kind of bug crawled up Alsop's ass, but I'll find out."

"Or maybe you won't. Sometimes it's best not to make a stink that can become public. Alsop has a lot of readers."

Bobby couldn't help the anger, but Alsop was a friend to his entire family. Revealing Bolshakov's name might have simply been a mistake, a clumsy error.

"You're right, I suppose. The only one hurt by Bolshakov's disappearance is Bolshakov. Still, I rather liked having a Soviet spy at my disposal."

"I would suggest, Bobby, that if the time comes, you now have the Soviet ambassador. And he has more clout."

Thursday, November 1, 1962
Hickory Hill, near McLean, Virginia

The Bolshakov news was depressing at best, no matter Siegenthaler's attempt to smooth it over. Bobby had responded by allowing himself a rare afternoon off, still felt as though he was riding a massive wave of stress over Cuba. Before leaving the city, he had visited the president at the White House, his brother dealing with the uncomfortable task of writing a personal letter to the widow of Major Rudolf Anderson, the pilot killed in his U-2. Bobby had driven across the Potomac engulfed by the single thought, that Major Anderson was the sole combat fatality of the entire crisis.

He walked now over his property, the expansive backyard, the great open patch where so many touch football games had been played and would be played again. His sudden appearance at home in the early afternoon had of course been a surprise, especially to his smallest children, but he couldn't entertain them, at least not now. Their energy and cheerfulness were welcomed, always, but Bobby felt the need for solitude. He moved past the horse paddocks, a glance at the animals looking back at him. He couldn't help a smile, thought of the horses, so blissfully unaware of all that had happened. And yet, you too would have been casualties. That was the point, after all. Nothing would survive, and if the war had come, and been what some foolishly called *limited*, what kind of life would the survivors have had?

He had thought about the UN, the fecklessness of U Thant, trying to solve a crisis that was beyond him, trying to please every part of the struggle, all the while being pressured by the nonaligned countries to find a peaceful solution at any cost. I don't recall that we gave that as much thought, as perhaps we should have. We begged for the support of the Latin countries, and they obliged us, which had to be a shocking blow to Khrushchev. But the African countries, the Middle East, Southern Asia . . . we ignored their concerns, believing our concerns were the greater danger. Perhaps if we had seen some of this through their eyes, it would not have gone so far. He scolded himself now. Don't be foolish. Khrushchev paid no attention to nonaligned nations either. This was a chess game between the big boys, except *checkmate* had an entirely different meaning. And Jack is right, there will be no gloating, no victory dance. We did not stand firm so that we would inflict damage on the Soviets. They would have found that completely unacceptable, and *unacceptable* would have meant war.

He looked toward the house, saw Ethel standing by the rear entrance, a piece of paper held high. She stood quietly, seemed to wait for him to decide what to do. All right, he thought. I'll come. I knew leaving the office after lunch was a bad idea. He called out to her, "Coming."

He hurried across the field, and she set the paper down on a table, moved back inside. She already knows what I have to do, he thought. For two weeks, I was part of something like the world has never seen. Jack relied on a cross-section of brilliant men to help him navigate this mess, those fellows plus his brother. I should tell him that perhaps the smartest thing he did was command someone to take the opposite sides. There could be no committee of yes-men. If the Joint Chiefs weren't always involved, their viewpoints had to be. I doubt there has ever been anything like the Excomm before. Hopefully, there will never be need for it again.

He reached the patio, picked up the paper, a message in Ethel's hand from Siegenthaler.

Martin Luther King requires a conference with you, immediately.

It suddenly came back to him, all that he had been avoiding, the great hole in his life the Excomm had filled. Now that's over, hopefully forever, and I'm back to being the attorney general.

The thoughts came in a flood, the responsibilities, tasks big and small, the demands on his time. I had quite forgotten about James Meredith, he thought. It seems he has survived his first few weeks at the University of Mississippi. Now, there will be more like him, more students who will push against the great white wall, what Teddy Roosevelt called the *lily-whites*. Change is coming in a galloping stampede, and it's my job to keep it from becoming too violent. I'm sure that's what Dr. King has on his mind. I know the FBI is compiling a file on King, as though any Civil Rights leader is a threat to our nation. What most people don't realize is that the greater danger is J. Edgar Hoover, keeping files on anyone he pleases. If he really wanted to be useful, he'd be keeping files on those idiots down south who think it's good sport burning crosses or those goons beating the crap out of someone just because they want to eat at a lunch counter. And of course, there's the Teamsters, that damned Jimmy Hoffa. He'd just as soon see me dead, and that's a threat I suppose I should take seriously.

He knew what he had to do, moved to the back door, opened it, leaned in, heard voices scattered throughout the house.

"Ethel?"

She responded from upstairs. "Yes?"

"I'm headed back to the city. I have work to do."

CHAPTER FORTY

Russo

Friday, November 2, 1962
Tallahassee, Florida

He had insisted they all come to the living room, the television news already making the announcement that the president was to make a brief speech. With word of a settlement of the Cuba crisis, Russo was like so many others, seeming to hang on any official word from the government, no matter how insignificant. But when Kennedy himself was talking, most Americans had learned that, these days, you took it seriously.

They sat on the sofa, Becky sitting on her mother's knee, Danny down to one end. As scheduled, the programming was interrupted, the announcer introducing the president.

"My Fellow Citizens,

I want to take this opportunity to report on the conclusions this government has reached on the basis of yesterday's photographs, which will be made available tomorrow. The Soviet missiles bases in Cuba are being dismantled and missiles and related equipment are

being crated and fixed installations at these sites are being destroyed.
The United States intends to follow closely the completion of this work
through a variety of means, including aerial surveillance until such
time as an equally satisfactory international means of verification can
be made . . ."

Russo kept his eyes on the television, was grateful the others did as well, grateful they were taking this seriously. Kennedy concluded his remarks . . . *"we will continue to keep the American people informed on this vital matter. Thank you."* Russo glanced at Danny, the boy looking back at him.

"Pretty cool, huh, Pop?"

"What's cool about it?"

"I mean, he told the Russians to get out of Cuba, and they did."

Through the eyes of a child, Russo thought.

"I'm sure it was more complicated than that, Dan-o. The Russians didn't just bow down to Kennedy without something pretty serious staring them in the face . . . staring us all in the face. You saw all those army trucks passing through here, heading south. I heard the Air Force bases all over Florida were packed full of aircraft and men. I think the Russians came to understand that Kennedy wasn't fooling around. I guess we'll never know just how close we came to a real war."

Beside him, Margaret said, "Do you think it was that serious? Did we almost go to war?"

Russo stood, turned off the television, paced slowly, faced her.

"I think it's a good thing we don't know just how close we came. That's when the president earns his pay. For the rest of us . . . I guess it's an act of faith, faith that good people are doing the right things, working hard to keep things from blowing up."

Saturday, November 3, 1962
Tallahassee, Florida

True to his word, Kennedy had released photographs, a clearly visible demonstration of the results of the showdown over Cuba. Russo had studied the photos as they came across the television screen, had marveled at the missiles lying in plain view on the decks of Russian freighters, missile launch sites reduced to rubble across Cuba.

He pushed the lawn mower over the uneven ground, a spray of grass clippings launched to one side. This had become Danny's job, the boy old enough the manage the mower, but today, Russo had let the boy off the hook. A week in the classroom had worn on him, his students as curious as he was as to just what was happening in Cuba. With the weekend, he welcomed the distraction, the mindless labor of mowing the lawn, the roar of the mower drowning out the chatter in his brain.

He swung the mower around, pushed back the other direction, could see his neighbor, Jerry, pushing a mower of his own. Russo tried to ignore the man, in no mood for any kind of neighborly chat, since, with Jerry, that always seemed to involve some form of politics. To his dismay, Jerry stopped mowing, made a beeline for Russo's yard. He obliged, shut down the mower, waited, Jerry coated with sweat and grass clippings.

"Hello, Professor. So, what do you think about your president now? Looks like he finally did something right."

Russo wiped his brow with a dirty hand, said, "What do you mean?"

"I mean, it looks like he told the damned Russians where to get off, and they ran off like mice. I knew it. That's all there is to it. Show those Commie bastards just how many missiles we've got, and they'll turn tail. Problem is, it ain't over. You can bet the Commies

339

are figuring out right now where else they'll hit us. Sneaky bastards. They're probably planting missiles all over Mexico or on a bunch of islands in the Pacific. We can't keep watch over everyplace, you know. I just hope Kennedy has the backbone to keep a sharp watch. If it was up to me, I'd have taken those people out all at once, no fooling around. Those convoys . . . the troops we brought down here . . . waste of manpower. All we needed was one good-sized hydrogen bomb, and Cuba would have been a sandbar. Then we could have dared the Commies to launch a missile at us, and when they did, we'd reduce that whole country to a dust pile. But nah. Kennedy doesn't have the guts. But you mark my words. The Commies ain't done yet. This was just chapter one."

"I really need to get back to my lawn. Good talking to you, Jerry."

He gave a hard pull on the cord, started the mower, Jerry still talking to himself. Russo backed the mower, then began the routine again. But the chatter in his head wouldn't leave him alone.

My God, he thought. Let's have a war, just to show the Russians who's boss? Let's obliterate mankind . . . damn him. Is this how people see things? Jerry can't be the only one. He's got his fallout shelter, so he's not afraid of a little thing like nuclear holocaust. How many idiots like him did Kennedy have to wrestle with in Washington? I'd like to believe there is no one like Jerry running things anywhere outside this neighborhood, certainly not anywhere we've got nuclear warheads. Maybe that's what terrifies me the most. It's not the Russians, though they might be scary enough. It's how to deal with the Russians, how to confront them, how to stand up face-to-face with them. It sure seems like Kennedy did that pretty well when it came to Cuba. Kennedy got his back up, said you can't have your damned missiles in Cuba, and instead of starting a war over it, Khrushchev pulled away. Thank God for sane men.

A car moved past slowly, a friendly wave, a familiar face, someone from the college. He spun the mower around again, his careful geometry, dodged a small tree, a breath of breeze blowing grass clippings over his bare legs. He saw Jerry again, back at his own mower, frowning purpose on the man's face. I never thought I'd know anyone who seems to lust for war. Ignore him. That's all you can do. Be grateful instead that your children can live what seems to be a normal life, without the constant reminder of the terror that hangs over us all.

Monday, November 5, 1962
Tallahassee, Florida

He waited in the driveway, had watched the bus coming up the street, depositing children at various stops. He knew the waiting wasn't necessary, that Danny was more than old enough to lead his little sister into the house. Whether or not he'd admit it to his son, he simply enjoyed watching them come home.

The bus pulled up in front of the house now, the squealing brakes, the large folding door swinging open. Like clockwork, both children were down, moving toward him up the driveway. Danny seemed slightly annoyed, a glance back toward his friends on the bus.

"You don't have to wait for us, Pop. It's okay."

"I know. It's just something I like to do. How about you, little Miss? You happy Daddy meets you at the bus?"

The girl grabbed his hand, waited for him to lead the way up to the house.

"I'm ready now, Daddy."

He laughed, led the way, kept pace with her short strides.

"So, anything exciting happen in school today?"

Danny didn't speak, an ominous sign, but Becky said, "I thought everything was okay now with the Russians. You said there wasn't going to be a war."

He stopped, looked down at her.

"That's right."

"Well, that's not what the principal said. Before we went to lunch, they made us do *duck and cover* again."

AFTERWORD

That this was the most dangerous crisis of the nuclear age does not tell us how dangerous it was.—McGeorge Bundy, Kennedy National Security Advisor

American history books are full of praise for presidents who win great wars. A word should also be said for those who prevent them.—Theodore Sorenson, Kennedy Senior Speechwriter

Do not put a loaded rifle on stage if no one is thinking of firing it.—Playwright Anton Chekhov

THE LEGACY OF JOHN F. KENNEDY

Following settlement of the Cuban Missile Crisis, Kennedy works tirelessly to prevent the same kind of clumsy interaction that he had suffered through with Khrushchev. To that end, a "hot line" telephone system is installed in June 1963, which allows either leader to contact the other directly without the typical delays in transmitting messages, which often requires four to six hours' time. It is one more step in normalization of the relationship between the American president and the Soviet leader.

In another gesture of the warming relationships between the

two superpowers, Kennedy and Khrushchev sign a partial nuclear test ban treaty, which prohibits nuclear testing above ground or under water. From this point on, all such tests are to be conducted below ground, thus alleviating fears of radiation pollution.

Kennedy also institutes a policy in Latin America, providing significant aid for stimulating growth in that region, as well as establishing more solid relationships between the OAS nations and the United States.

Kennedy's domestic agenda, known as the New Frontier, expands on many of the reforms first championed by Franklin D. Roosevelt. Unemployment and Social Security benefits are increased, a water pollution act is passed, the minimum wage is increased, and the most significant aid to farmers since 1938 is put into law.

Kennedy becomes the driving force behind the American space program, with a goal of *landing a man on the moon and returning him safely to Earth.* The goal is accomplished by 1969, six years after Kennedy's death.

Kennedy follows the lead of his predecessor, Dwight D. Eisenhower, emphasizing the vulnerability of foreign lands to potential Soviet domination. He pursues the policy of sending military advisors to the small nation of South Vietnam, believing that American strength there will fortify the Vietnamese into driving off a threat of Communist takeover. Though Kennedy will not send American combat forces into Vietnam, he expands the number of armed advisors from five hundred to more than ten thousand. Motivated by the need to confront the spread of Communism where it threatens most, he nonetheless opens the door for his successor, Lyndon B. Johnson, who radically expands the American role.

In June 1963, Kennedy signs into law the Equal Pay Act, to abolish disparity in salaries and wages between men and women.

Though the act is slow to move, it exists today as the law of the land, despite the slow progress in equalizing pay regardless of gender.

In an oft-forgotten capstone to the disastrous Bay of Pigs operation in 1961, after considerable negotiation with Fidel Castro, approximately eleven hundred prisoners from that operation are freed by the Cuban government, in exchange for a ransom of some fifty-three million dollars. While no doubt the decision to launch the operation was Kennedy's great mistake, he can at least claim that the final outcome has some measure of success. The return of the prisoners cements the bond between Miami's Cuban exile population and the president.

Perhaps no other part of Kennedy's legacy is as monumental to American society and culture as his Civil Rights agenda. A series of executive orders outlaw racial discrimination in federally funded housing and employment by federal contractors. On June 11, 1963, he gives a landmark speech, claiming that Civil Rights is a moral cause, proposing equal access to public schools, many other facilities, as well as protection of voting rights. This campaign drives forward after his life and leads directly to what will become the Civil Rights Act of 1964.

In November 1963, Kennedy is invited to speak at the Remembrance Day Celebration in Gettysburg, Pennsylvania, marking the one hundredth anniversary of Lincoln's Gettysburg Address. However, there is a conflict, a previously scheduled appearance in Dallas, Texas, what is to be a political hand-shaking event to smooth over disgruntlement among some Democratic officeholders there. To celebrate his visit, a motorcade is scheduled, which gathers a considerable crowd of onlookers as it winds through downtown Dallas. On November 22, 1963, Kennedy's motorcade passes through Dealey Plaza, beneath the windows of the Texas School Book Depository. On the sixth floor of that building, Lee Harvey Oswald waits for the motorcade to pass, and when the time is right, he fires three shots, one of which is a lethal shot into the president's skull. After feverish efforts to revive Kennedy at Parkland Hospital, he is, after a short time, pronounced dead. Kennedy is immediately succeeded in office by his vice president, Lyndon B. Johnson. Kennedy is the fourth U.S. president to die by assassination. He is forty-six.

If we cannot now end our differences, at least we can help make the world safe for diversity. For in the final analysis our most basic common link is the fact that we all inhabit this planet. We all breathe the same air. We all cherish our children's future. And we are all mortal.—John F. Kennedy

The Kennedy assassination killed more than a dynamic young president at the peak of his popularity. It also removed a leader who had stared down a Soviet challenge and begun, with his enhanced stature and reputation for toughness, to seek a new, more stable relationship with the Russians.—Journalist Max Frankel

ROBERT F. "BOBBY" KENNEDY

One of the youngest men ever to serve in a president's Cabinet, Bobby continues in the role of attorney general after his brother's assassination. He leaves the post late in 1964, to run for office as U.S. senator from New York, facing one of his principal nemeses, Kenneth Keating. Bobby wins the election and builds a stout reputation for his friendships and sympathy for the causes of many influential and important Civil Rights and worker's rights leaders. He is one of the voices strongly advocating for the Civil Rights Act.

He becomes devoutly antiwar, believing the Vietnam War, now under the leadership of President Johnson, is a disastrous mistake. His outspokenness results in a hard push for him to seek the office of president himself. When Johnson bows to antiwar sentiment and declines to seek a second term of office, Bobby is immediately deemed the frontrunner. The power of the Kennedy name virtually assures him of the Democratic nomination, and just as likely, the election. On June 5, 1968, after winning the important California primary, he is shot by Sirhan Sirhan, a Palestinian who disapproves of Bobby's support of Israel. Bobby dies a day later. He is forty-two.

Sensing the wave of antiwar sentiment that had propelled Bobby's candidacy, the eventual winner of the presidential race, Richard Nixon, begins a policy of reducing American troop numbers in Vietnam and eventually pulls the United States completely out of the war.

NIKITA KHRUSHCHEV

True to his own predictions, his power is substantially weakened by what many in the Soviet hierarchy consider his near-traitorous capitulation to the Americans during the missile crisis. However, his poor leadership in agricultural matters contributes even more to the growing dissatisfaction with his rule, as none of the loudly trumpeted plans he introduces amount to much improvement in the lives of Soviet citizens.

In October 1964, a conspiracy to oust him is led by Leonid Brezhnev. Upon returning to the Kremlin from an agricultural tour, Khrushchev is arrested by forces friendly to Brezhnev. He is asked not to offer resistance, for the good of the Soviet Union. Khrushchev, aging and unwell, agrees. Thus, the transfer of power is, by Soviet standards, relatively smooth.

Khrushchev is allowed a house, and his dacha, plus a comfortable pension of five hundred rubles per month. He begins work on his memoirs, a risky proposition, since he assumes that the KGB monitors his every move. Though the KGB ultimately confiscates the manuscripts, Khrushchev's son, Sergei, succeeds in smuggling a copy to a Western publisher. Thus, in 1970, is the memoir published under the title *Khrushchev Remembers* and is readily available to Western readers today. Upon its publication, the Soviet news mouthpiece *Izvestia* labels the book as a fraud.

Khrushchev dies of a heart attack in September 1971, at age seventy-seven, and is buried in a public cemetery. He is denied a state funeral.

> *I'm old and tired. Let them cope by themselves.*—Nikita Khrushchev

> *Khrushchev was at once a Stalinist and an anti-Stalinist, a Communist believer and a cynic, a publicizing poltroon and a crusty philanthropist, a trouble maker and a peace maker, a stimulating colleague and a domineering boor, a statesman and a politicker who was out of his intellectual depth.*—Historian Robert Service

> *There is no way to imagine the course of world events if Kennedy and Khrushchev had survived in office and been allowed to explore a less hostile relationship. The passions and suspicions produced by two decades of Cold War were not easily overcome. But the two governments fully absorbed the lesson that war between the superpowers had become unprofitable and that they were obliged to prevent peripheral issues from ever again creating a comparable risk of military clash.*—Journalist Max Frankel

JOSEPH RUSSO

The English professor continues teaching his subject, but never fails to expound on the experience he and his students shared during those two weeks in October. He begins to take a more active interest in politics, believing that the views of those like his neighbor are dangerously misplaced. He is thus devastated by news of the Kennedy assassination. The *Kennedy for President* bumper sticker remains on his car.

In summer 1964, he takes his family on a visit to the New York World's Fair and decides at the last minute to take a side trip to the battlefield at Gettysburg. Though he is well-read about the battle, he is caught off guard by the impact of walking the ground, and the storyteller in him becomes obsessed with putting that story to paper. But he is no historian, chooses instead to write the account as a novel. He spends seven years on the project, and once the story is completed, he is disappointed to find that none of the first fifteen publishers who see the book have any interest in publishing it. Finally, the book finds a small independent publisher, and in 1974, the novel is released. Surprisingly, the book becomes a monumental success, perhaps the most defining novel written on the Civil War.

Russo is active in the campaign of Lyndon Johnson for president in 1964, facing down the staunchly Republican community in which he lives. Vindicated somewhat by Johnson's overwhelming victory over Barry Goldwater, he is shocked by Johnson's expanded push into Vietnam.

He continues to teach by day, writing more stories by night. But, as was common for the time, he begins to suffer the effects of cigarette smoking, and dies in 1988, at age fifty-nine.

ABOUT THE AUTHOR

Stephanie Shaara

JEFF SHAARA is the award-winning *New York Times, USA Today, Wall Street Journal,* and *Publishers Weekly* bestselling author of many novels, including *The Old Lion,* as well as *Gods and Generals* and *The Last Full Measure*—two novels that complete the trilogy begun with his father's Pulitzer Prize–winning classic, *The Killer Angels.* Shaara was born in New Brunswick, New Jersey, grew up in Tallahassee, Florida, and lives in Gettysburg, Pennsylvania.